Praise for
Philip Luber's previous novel,
Deadly Convictions

"Can't miss . . . A terrific tale about the problems of the insanity defense in criminal trials . . . You won't be able to put down this page turner of a yarn with a message and a twist."
—LARRY KING, *USA Today*

"Sinister . . . [A] well-wrought tale of suspense on an issue of contemporary concern . . . Deftly plotted . . . [with a] stunning climax . . . Luber weaves these elements with the skill of a surgeon. . . . An excellent thriller that makes one hope Luber will keep on writing for years to come."
—*Philadelphia Daily News*

"This year's 'find of the year' . . . High-powered stuff . . . Its pages will whiz by like bullets."
—*The Syracuse Post-Standard*

"A riveting tale . . . particularly germane to our times."
—*Publishers Weekly*

FORGIVE US OUR SINS

Philip Luber

FAWCETT GOLD MEDAL • NEW YORK

A Fawcett Gold Medal Book
Published by Ballantine Books
Copyright © 1994 by Philip Luber

All rights reserved under International and Pan-American Copyright Conventions. Published in the United States of America by Ballantine Books, a division of Random House, Inc., New York, and simultaneously in Canada by Random House of Canada Limited, Toronto.

Grateful acknowledgment is made to the following for permission to reprint previously published material:

Jon Landau Management:
Excerpt from the lyrics of "Human Touch" music and lyrics by Bruce Springsteen. Copyright © 1992 Bruce Springsteen. Excerpt from the lyrics of "For You" music and lyrics by Bruce Springsteen. Copyright © 1973 CBS Inc.

Library of Congress Catalog Card Number: 93-91025

ISBN 0-449-14849-1

Manufactured in the United States of America

First Edition: May 1994

10 9 8 7 6 5 4 3 2

For Cindy and Holly,
with eternal and boundless love

CREDITS

Agent: *Alice Fried Martell, The Martell Agency*

Editor: *Susan Randol, Fawcett Books*

Story consultant: *David Greenleaf*

Technical assistance: *FBI Special Agent William McMullin*

Beacons in the darkest night: *Elaine More*
Lenny Gibson

With thanks for their encouragement and support:

Paul Benedict, Rick Casey, Michael Collins, Janice Davidowicz, Jane Doherty, Robert Dumond, Robert Fein, Carol Feldman, Joanne Forbes, Arlene Friedman, Mary Francis Gitto, Elaine Hill, Karen Katz, Fred Kelso, Arthur Posey, Gary Taylor, Carlton Watson

Special thanks to: *Margo Crisafulli*

The wise forgive but do not forget.
Two wrongs don't make a right, but they make a good
excuse.

THOMAS SZASZ

1: The Massacre

The president was at his oceanside retreat, still recovering from thyroid treatments, when they photographed him reading a copy of my book. Sales took off nicely after that.

The shopping mall massacre occurred three weeks later. Book sales skyrocketed.

If you look very, very closely, you can still see a bullet hole and a nickel-sized bloodstain. They're in a recess in the wall near the entrance to the Thom McAn shoe store.

An Austin sanitation department supervisor pointed them out to me months after the massacre. "They wanted us to get rid of every trace of what happened that day," he said. "Like out in San Diego, when they bulldozed the McDonald's where that psycho killed all those people back in '84. They weren't gonna bulldoze this whole shopping mall, though. So they settled for the next best thing. Putty in every bullet hole, sand it down and paint it. Mop up every stain, sandblast the ones they can't mop up.

"But it just didn't seem right to me," he continued. "One of the victims was a neighbor of mine." He fell silent for a moment and studied the back of his hand. "So I made sure we left that bullet hole, over there, and this patch of blood down here. I thought there should be something left, some reminder of what happened that day."

What happened that day: Karl Fenner was wearing Army fatigues when he burst through the west entrance of Austin's Highland Mall. It was noontime on the third Monday of February, 1992, and the mall was packed with people for its annual Presidents' Day sale.

Just inside the mall entrance, he bowled over two people. The first shopper was carrying several bags. The second shopper was carrying her infant daughter. Fenner carried a rifle: a .223 caliber Colt AR-15, loaded with a twenty-shot clip.

He raced up a stairway and moved to a position halfway down the upper level walkway, directly in front of Scarborough's department store. He leaned against the railing for support and took aim at the lower level doorway of Highland Music City. Three teenagers were on their way out of the store.

The first shot caught Rebecca Billingham a half inch below her right eye. The bullet's momentum jerked her head back and lifted her body off the ground. She fell backward into the store, arms outstretched, half of her face dissolved into pulp, blood pumping onto a display rack of blank audio cassettes.

Gloria Wells stood frozen as her friend lay dying. She covered her ears with her hands and screamed. Her cries were cut short by Fenner's second shot. The bullet pierced her left side near her armpit, splintered a rib, traveled a slightly downward trajectory, and punctured her heart.

Theresa Cummings dropped her Garth Brooks compact disk and bolted from the record store. She didn't get far. Fenner's third shot passed through her thigh and lodged in the front wall of the Thom McAn store. The next bullet penetrated deep into her belly, and another one splattered several grams of brain tissue across the lower level floor.

Fenner pivoted slightly and aimed once more at the entrance to the record store. Just then a young clerk from Scarborough's ran out to discover the source of all the commotion. He slipped on the walkway and bumped into Karl Fenner.

The killer spun around and faced the young man. "All he said was 'Devil,' " the clerk reported later. "His eyes looked crazy. Then I saw the rifle, and I smelled the cordite. I don't even remember what happened next."

What happened next: The clerk jammed the edge of his clipboard into the space between Fenner's nostrils and upper lip. Fenner's head rolled back slightly, and the clerk jabbed the clipboard into the killer's Adam's apple over and over again. The rifle discharged. The bullet grazed the clerk's arm, and the recoil pressed Fenner against the railing. The clerk swung wildly with his clipboard, catching Fenner flush on the forehead.

The killer teetered on the railing for a moment, then plunged head first to the lower level walkway. His dead body lay face up on the ground, his torso bent toward his feet at an impossible angle. The impact had caused him to bite completely through his lower lip, and his shattered teeth showed through the bloody gash like pebbles in a muddy stream.

"The man was a real creep," one of Karl Fenner's factory co-workers told a wire-service reporter. "He scared the hell out of all of us."

Fenner's next-door neighbor was more blunt. "I hated the son of a bitch. I'm glad he's dead."

Fenner was a Vietnam veteran with a psychiatric discharge who returned to Austin after his military service to lead an isolated, desultory existence. In the aftermath of the shopping mall massacre, no one could be found who had a kind word to say about him. He was a nuisance, he was a misfit, he was odd and frightening. He was a hating and hateful man. And now—to nobody's expressed regret—he was dead.

The police found Fenner's van parked outside the west entrance of the shopping mall. On the front seat was the morning newspaper, folded over to an advertisement for the Presidents' Day sale at Highland Music City.

Fenner had a one-room apartment near the airport. When the police searched it, they discovered a copy of my novel, *Soldier and Son*, on the window ledge.

Soldier and Son, my third book, was inspired by my

work years earlier as a psychiatrist at a Veterans Administration Hospital. It tells the story of an Army inductee from Austin who is sent to fight in Vietnam. After six months of search-and-destroy missions, he suffers a nervous breakdown and is returned home with a psychiatric discharge. But the war follows him, stuck inside his mind like a videotape on perpetual replay. He is depressed, he is anxious, he sees danger in every stranger's face. On page 275 of the book he dresses in Army fatigues and takes his .223 caliber Colt AR-15 rifle to an Austin shopping mall. He kills the owner of a record store and a customer, and he takes several persons hostage. He is mortally wounded in a hail of police bullets.

A three-week-old newspaper photo was attached with a paper clip to page 275 of Fenner's copy of my book. It was a picture of the president relaxing in Maine. He was sitting in front of a fire with his wife at his side, a cup of cocoa in his hand, and a copy of *Soldier and Son* propped open in front of him.

Among Fenner's belongings were some newly purchased compact disks, with various lyrics on the album inserts circled in red ink; pornographic magazines, with several graphic pictures defaced or torn; mail-order literature from a half-dozen TV evangelists; a dog-eared New Testament; and a photocopy of a letter he had written one month earlier. The letter began:

> *Luferac eb tsum ew, semit lla ta su hctaw yeht, uoy morf egassem terces a, od ot em tnaw uoy od tahw, won em llet, ereh spots kcub eht*

The unintelligible words continued for several paragraphs. Someone discovered that the message made better sense when it was rewritten from the end to the beginning. Thus decoded, the letter read:

January 15
The President
The White House
Washington (I cannot tell a lie), D.C.
Dear Sir:

Fire rules the human brain, a devil-fire brought forth upon this continent, conceived in liberty, and dedicated to the proposition that all men are sinners against the Lord,

Conceived, conception, copulation

Proposition, proposition, prostitution

Listen to the song, Lucifer's coat, play it backwards, the words "we fuck for Satan, we fuck for Satan, we fuck for Satan, we fuck for Satan" are plainly heard: a devil-message aimed at the heart of the little cunts and whores

I am armed, but dangerous only to the flesh merchants and devil songsters who aim at the cunt of the little hearts and whores, a soldier waiting for an order from his Commander-in-Chief

The buck stops here, tell me now, what do you want me to do, a secret message from you, they watch us at all times, we must be careful

Karl Fenner, A Christian Soldier

The phrase "Lucifer's coat" was apparently a reference to "Lucy's Fur Coat," a hit recording by a group called the Syntonics. Fenner had discerned a devil-worship message when he played the song backwards. Needless to say, audiophiles near and far listened for the message after Fenner's letter was released; and, needless to say, none found it.

In *Newsweek*, a renowned psychologist speculated thus: Fenner had sent the president a coded, psychotic dispatch—a warning about a Satanic message on the Syntonics recording, and a veiled offer to take up arms at the president's direction. Within days, Fenner saw something that he interpreted as a secret return communication: the news photo of the president reading *Soldier and Son*.

Fenner bought my book and read about a fellow Vietnam

veteran who, armed with a rifle just like his, launched an attack against a shopping mall record store in Austin. And then Fenner found an ad for a sale—*a Presidents' Day sale*—at the record store in an Austin mall. Featured prominently in the ad—and circled in red ink on the copy the police found in Fenner's van—was a photo of the Syntonics album.

Karl Fenner knew exactly what he had to do.

2: A Wave of Revulsion

A wave of revulsion passed through me when I heard about the massacre on the evening news. I recognized the link immediately, even though the story made no mention of *Soldier and Son*.

My nine-year-old daughter, Melissa, recognized it, too. "Isn't that like the man in your book, Daddy?" she asked.

"I don't know, sweetheart," I replied, but I knew instinctively that there was a direct connection. I considered calling a friend in Austin for more details about the killings, but I decided not to go in search of bad news.

That bad news caught up with me the following morning. My editor at Morgan Books called to tell me that the Austin police had learned about Karl Fenner's copy of my book and its apparent relationship to his murderous rampage. The media already had hold of the story.

"This is really something," Jeffrey Barrow said. "First the president gives your book a boost, and now this. You're a fortunate man, Harry."

"Then how come I don't feel fortunate?" The morning *Boston Globe* had printed yearbook pictures of Fenner's victims and a photo of the shopping mall carnage. I couldn't get the images out of my mind.

"I've heard from a half-dozen reporters already," my editor said. "They all want to talk to you. They know you're a psychiatrist. They want to know if you can explain why Fenner did what he did."

7

"And they want to know how it feels to be responsible for inspiring a mass murderer."

"Don't you think you're being a little extreme?"

"Try telling that to the dead girls."

"Calm down, Harry. The man was a lunatic. He would've exploded sooner or later, book or no book. Don't take it so personally."

I imagined Karl Fenner reading my book, making psychotic connections between his own life and that of my fictional protagonist. Then I thought about the horrible end Fenner's victims had met and the grief their loved ones surely were suffering. The last thing they needed was a media circus.

"I'm not giving any interviews," I said.

"Get a grip on yourself, Harry. You have to deal with it. This is big news, whether you like it or not."

"I don't care if it's big news. It's all so tragic. There's nothing I can say that would make any sense of what happened."

"Then say *that*," he replied. "Just make sure they spell your name and the book title correctly."

"For God's sake, Jeffrey."

Get a grip on yourself. Deal with it. My editor was right, of course. I'd given the same advice—though not so bluntly—to countless patients over the years. So I spoke with the reporters. And I continued doing the local Boston-area radio interviews and book-signings that Jeffrey Barrow had begun arranging after the president's photo appeared. I'm not proud of that; in fact, I feel like a charlatan when I look back on it.

My book made *The New York Times* bestseller list the first Sunday in April. The entry was wedged between the latest offerings from Danielle Steel and Stephen King. It read:

Soldier and Son, by Dr. Harold Kline (Morgan Books, $19.95). Dark psychological study of a tormented Vietnam veteran.

A week later I traveled to New York for an interview by Bryant Gumbel on the *Today* show. Another guest was already waiting in the green room at NBC when I arrived. Hunched over and motionless in his chair, he was so lost in thought that at first he didn't notice me. He had sunken cheeks and dark bags beneath his eyes. His expensive suit looked a size or more too large. He looked familiar and yet unfamiliar, like an acquaintance rendered unrecognizable by illness or misfortune.

We introduced ourselves, and I recognized his name immediately. He was a true-crime writer with several best-sellers to his credit. His latest book was about an Arizona priest who engineered the contract killing of his homosexual lover. I'd seen the writer's picture on book covers and advertisements, but the figure before me looked far more haggard than the one in those photos.

He recognized my name, too. "The psychiatrist, right? I haven't read your novel, but I did read your other books."

My previous books were nonfiction, both drawn from my work with trauma victims. The first consisted of case studies of Vietnam veterans; I'd examined hundreds during the earlier part of my career, when I worked at a Veterans Administration Hospital outside Boston. The second book focused on adult survivors of childhood sexual abuse.

He poured a cup of coffee. "My fourth one today," he said. "But who's counting? Actually, I hate the stuff, but I'm afraid I'll fall asleep in the middle of the interview if I don't tank up." He sipped from his cup. "You were smart to switch to fiction. When you write about real people, you have to deal with real problems."

He seemed to want to talk, and so I said, "What sorts of problems?"

His voice was soft and monotonic. He spoke haltingly, as if speaking required great effort and concentration. "I've been attacked by the Catholic Church *and* the gay community for my last book. . . . I've received death threats. . . . My family has been threatened. . . . My family doctor has me on Valium. . . . I've been an emotional basket case for the past month. I don't eat. I feel like sleeping all the time, and I don't feel much like doing anything else. . . . Some days it's even a struggle to get washed and dressed."

Some people think psychiatrists have powers bordering on the supernatural: a magical ability to discern inner thought from the sparest gesture, to reconstruct an entire life from a few words. Some of those people withdraw, wary of being found out. Others, like this man, act as if they're in a confessional booth.

"It happens every time I publish a book," he continued. "I wrote about some killings in Vermont, and the police chief sued me for libel. He said my book made him look incompetent. Hell, that SOB *was* incompetent. I was even sued by a confessed killer who said my portrayal of him caused him severe emotional distress. It's getting so I don't consider my work on a book complete until I've had to hire a lawyer." He sighed. "So, what do you think, Doctor? Am I paranoid?"

He wasn't paranoid; he was depressed. He had the classic symptoms of a major episode: the weight loss, sleeping disturbance, and loss of energy; the tone of despair in his voice. If he'd been my patient, I would've considered antidepressant medication instead of the tranquilizer his well-meaning general practitioner had prescribed. The Valium could have been making him feel worse.

"My doctor wants to send me to a psychiatrist. I told him, no way I'm going to see a shrink. No offense to you, Doctor. I'd just rather deal with it myself. I don't even take the Valium he gave me very often."

"Where do you live?"

"Baltimore."

"I know a good psychiatrist in Baltimore." I wrote a name and phone number on a piece of paper and gave it to him. "If you do decide to take your doctor's advice, you can call this person."

He gazed at the piece of paper, then folded it and placed it in his pocket.

He pressed his fingertips against his temples. "I get a headache just thinking about it," he said. "Maybe I should follow your example and write a novel next time." He leaned back in his chair and closed his eyes. "Are you working on another book?"

"Yes."

"What sort of story is it?"

I hesitated for a moment. "It's not a novel. I'm doing another book of case studies, along the same lines as my first two books. I'll be interviewing survivors of murder victims."

His eyes snapped wide open. "Survivors of murder victims?"

I nodded.

"No offense, Doctor," he said, "but *you* must be crazy."

Since Karl Fenner's rampage almost two months earlier, I'd pondered my own responsibility for what he'd done. I'd intentionally created one killer: the protagonist in my novel. Had I unintentionally created a second one as well?

Logic told me that eventually Fenner would have exploded into violence even without my book—that I was no more to blame for his actions than for the foreign trade deficit. But logic also told me this: that even if that were so, those particular teenage girls—the shopping mall victims— would still be alive were it not for my book. Whenever I heard, read, or thought about the murders, I felt wretched. And long after the final stories about them appeared, I still found myself thinking about Fenner's victims: Rebecca Billingham, Gloria Wells, and Theresa Cummings.

I knew how it felt to lose someone dear to me. My wife, Janet, had died five years earlier. It was the hardest blow I'd ever suffered; nothing else even came close. But Janet succumbed to an illness: We had an opportunity to say good-bye, and I had time to try preparing myself and our then-four-year-old daughter for life without her. Fenner's victims had been yanked from their families, violently and suddenly. I couldn't imagine anything worse than the pain those survivors were feeling.

I decided to base my next book on interviews with survivors of murder victims. I was planning to begin my interviews as soon as I returned to Massachusetts from New

York. It marked a return to the familiar territory I explored in my first two books: stories told by normal people having normal reactions to horribly abnormal events. And maybe it was a way for me to come to terms with my feelings about the shopping mall murders.

Several hours after my appearance on the *Today* program, I joined my editor, Jeffrey Barrow, and my agent, Phyllis Unger for a late lunch at Tavern on the Green.

Phyllis Unger was in her late thirties, a couple of years younger than me. Her petite appearance belied the cunning and tenacity that served her—and her clients—so well. She greeted me warmly, no doubt conscious that her ten percent share of my earnings would likely surpass $20,000 that year.

Jeffrey Barrow was editor-in-chief at Morgan Books. A few years older than me, he'd been my editor for all three of my books. He was tall and sturdy, a former star on an Ivy League basketball team. With his tailored suit, power tie, and meticulous manner, he looked every bit the successful businessman he was. Fifteen years earlier, he'd managed a chain of tabloid newspapers. When accountants and conglomerates began taking control over the book publishing industry, Morgan Books—traditional, staid, and failing— brought Jeffrey on board to revitalize the company. He was more interested in acquiring manuscripts than in the actual editing process, but he'd done well by Morgan Books, and he'd certainly done well by me.

Jeffrey was a Vietnam veteran; I think that's why he bought my first book for Morgan. And although he never once mentioned any of his own war experiences, his insights were invaluable as I prepared that book of interviews with veterans, and again as I worked on my novel.

The three of us talked first about *Soldier and Son*: publicity plans, foreign sales, film prospects. A few weeks earlier, I'd signed an agreement with Paramount for an option on the movie rights. Then the conversation turned to my work in progress. Phyllis said, "I'm glad you mentioned your next book on the *Today* show. It'll help build up interest."

"Which reminds me," Jeffrey said. "Someone called my secretary right after your interview this morning. He said he heard you talking about your next book, and he knew of a case you might be interested in." Jeffrey reached inside his leather carrying case and pulled out a large manila envelope. "He sent this to me by messenger."

He opened the envelope and dropped an eight-by-ten glossy photo in the middle of the table. It was a black-and-white interior shot of an empty church. Sharp beams of sunlight poured through a stained-glass figure of the Virgin Mary, coalescing on an alabaster-like object at the foot of the altar.

It was a naked body: headless. A surprisingly small pool of blood glistened beside it in the late-afternoon sun.

Phyllis averted her eyes from the photo. "Awful," she murmured. "Really awful."

"According to the information printed on the back of the picture, this is—was—a young priest," Jeffrey said. "Father Joseph Carroll was murdered last October in Philadelphia. They discovered his head underneath the altar. His killer was never found."

"God, Jeffrey," said Phyllis, "you're making me sick."

I studied the picture inch-by-inch. Every shape and shadow was in perfect alignment, like a time-exposure photograph by Ansel Adams. A tiny round object was wedged between the second and third digits of the corpse's left hand. "What's that in his fingers?" I asked.

"I don't know," Jeffrey replied as he eyed the picture. "I hadn't noticed it. Some sort of religious trinket, perhaps. Phyllis?" He pushed the photo toward her.

"Jeffrey! Please!" She turned her head away.

I looked at it again. "He's definitely holding something. Maybe a button he ripped from his assailant's clothing."

Jeffrey placed the photo back inside the envelope. A busboy replenished our bread supply and refilled our water glasses.

"The girls who were killed at the shopping mall," I said, trying to change the subject. "Their families have created a memorial scholarship fund. I sent a small contribution, anonymously. I'd like to send more, but I don't want it to get traced back to me."

"What would be wrong with that?" Phyllis asked. She believed any sort of publicity was good for book sales.

"It's just not the way I want to do it." I turned to Jeffrey. "I wonder if there would be a way of earmarking a portion of my royalties to go directly to the fund."

"I'll look into it," promised Jeffrey, and I knew he would. "I can't think of anything worse than having to bury your murdered child. There was a fellow who headed our subsidiary rights department for several years. Randall Tinkler. He retired about a year ago. He was never the same after his daughter was killed by a drunk driver about ten or fifteen years back. It was like the life went out of him forever. A damn shame."

Phyllis said, "I remember him. Outgoing to the point of obnoxiousness. I remember he used to refer to himself and everyone else by their initials."

"That's right," Jeffrey said. "I recall an argument you had with him because he kept calling you P. U."

"Funny," said Phyllis Unger, unamused. "Really funny."

"Did you ever meet him, Harry?" asked Jeffrey. "Big guy, about my size."

"The name sounds familiar," I replied.

"Have you heard from him since he retired?" Phyllis asked.

"He stops by the office once in a while," Jeffrey replied. "We keep him on the books as a consultant, invite him to meetings now and then. Mostly just to give him something to do. And to help him augment his retirement income a bit."

"Why, Jeffrey," she said with feigned surprise. "You *do* have a heart."

"Yes, well, please don't tell your colleagues. If word gets out, they'll try to bleed me dry when they negotiate contracts for their clients."

Our waiter arrived with the main course. I'd ordered the blackened swordfish. Jeffrey had the prime rib. Phyllis had the broiled coho salmon.

"I feel like throwing up," Phyllis said when she looked at her plate. The fish was seven inches long, filleted from neck to tail.

To make that cut, the chef had removed the salmon's head.

3: Have You Ever Wanted to Kill Someone?

Boston homicide detective Timothy Connolly remembered the case very well. "That gal took a long time to die, Doc. Her killer had a real healthy stomach, or no stomach at all."

I remembered the case, too. The details were splashed across the pages of the *Globe* and the *Herald* for several days in the summer of 1990. Beth Greenfield—twenty-six, attractive and popular, a promising young lawyer at a prestigious Boston firm—was brutally slain. A year and nine months later the murderer remained at large.

"Her body was discovered after dark by some kids heading home from a Red Sox game," Detective Connolly said. He pointed to a wall map of the Fenway area. "They were walking toward the Museum of Fine Arts, cutting through the park to get over to Huntington Avenue. The body was in plain sight, right here beside the pond."

Connolly looked like an aging linebacker: broad and muscular, with a hint of flab hanging over his belt. He had thick black hair and a ruddy complexion. Jaundice-colored nicotine stains suggested a long-standing addiction to cigarettes, which he was now trying to combat by popping pieces of hard candy into his mouth every few minutes.

I said, "According to the newspapers, Beth Greenfield was killed somewhere else."

Connolly nodded. "The medical examiner said she bled to death, but there wasn't any blood near the body. The

16

killer must've dumped her in the park after he was through with her. No blood in her apartment, either." He pointed at the map. "She lived on Queensberry Street, a block from where they found her."

Beth's father was Ellis Greenfield, Harvard law professor and former domestic policy advisor to Presidents Kennedy and Johnson. During Democratic administrations he was often mentioned as a possible nominee for the Supreme Court. His prominence made Beth Greenfield's murder a high-profile case.

A mutual acquaintance had provided me with an introduction to Ellis Greenfield and his wife. They agreed to be interviewed for my book. Our first meeting was scheduled for that very evening. The Greenfields hoped my book might generate publicity that would somehow result in breaking the case.

"That's not gonna happen, Doc," said Connolly. He slipped a hard candy into his mouth. "We only had one suspect, and we never had enough evidence to bring him to trial."

"Gerald Eckler."

Connolly grimaced. "Yeah. Gerald Eckler."

Beth Greenfield had traveled to New Haven one Friday twenty-one months earlier. On Sunday afternoon a friend saw her board the train for her return to Boston. That was the last time anyone who knew her saw her alive.

Her body was found the next night. She died from the cumulative effect of three dozen stab wounds. No single one was lethal, but the aggregate caused a fatal loss of blood. "The medical examiner said it took at least two hours to kill her," Connolly said. "And there were marks on her wrists and ankles that indicated she was tied down while it was happening. I think the killer enjoyed watching her suffer."

After several days of headlines, pictures, and stories, Boston police received their first and only break in the case. "We got a call from an elderly East Boston woman," Connolly said. "She said someone who looked like the victim got off the train Sunday evening at South Station. Said she was met by a man who was tall and completely bald, the sort of person who stands out in a crowd. And Ellis Greenfield said that sounded like Gerald Eckler."

Eckler was the ne'er-do-well son of a wealthy Newton contractor. His parents lived near the Greenfields, and he and Beth had dated on and off since high school. He'd beaten her on a number of occasions, but she never pressed charges. Eckler denied being with Beth the night she was murdered. The police found Beth's fingerprints and a few strands of her hair in Eckler's car, but they could have been deposited there on any of a number of occasions.

"We didn't find any blood in the car or in Eckler's Back Bay apartment. Hell, we never found blood anywhere, never did figure out where she was killed. All we had was that tentative ID of someone who looked like Eckler being seen with someone who looked like the victim. But our witness couldn't pick him out of a lineup. And I'll tell you something, Doc—even if she had, all by itself that wouldn't have been enough to bring Eckler to trial, much less convict him."

Connolly leaned back in his chair and propped his feet on the desk. "The case is still open, but it might as well be dead. We've taken it as far as it can go. When the DA decided not to prosecute, the Greenfields said they'd hire their own investigator to get evidence against Eckler. I don't think anything ever came of that. Eckler dropped out of sight a few months later. If his parents know where he is, they're not talking."

Connolly fumbled in his empty shirt pocket, looking for the cigarettes he was accustomed to carrying. Then he reached into his desk drawer and pulled out more candy.

"I don't know if you'll answer this question," I said, "but I'll ask it anyway. Do you think Gerald Eckler killed Beth Greenfield?"

Connolly began to nod. Then he stopped himself, grimaced, and tapped his fingers on the armrest of his chair. "You tell me, Doc." He gestured toward the case file lying on his desk. "What do *you* think?"

* * *

"Of course I think the bastard killed her!" yelled Ellis Greenfield, rising from his chair. "How can you even ask me that?"

Mildred Greenfield said, "Take it easy, dear. I'm sure Dr. Kline didn't mean to upset you."

"He killed her," Greenfield said, struggling to remain calm. "He knows it, I know it, he knows I know it, I know he knows I know it. We're both very knowledgeable."

He was a short man with a barrel-shaped chest, wide shoulders, and a deep, resonant voice. I once read that President Johnson used to call him Cannonball. As I watched him pace back and forth in his living room, I began to understand why.

"I just hope Gerald Eckler is still alive, wherever he disappeared to," Greenfield said.

"Why is that?"

"Because I'd hate to think the son of a bitch died without giving me the pleasure of knowing it." He sat down next to his wife. "Tell me, Dr. Kline, have you ever wanted to kill someone?"

I wanted to acknowledge his anguish, but I wound up unintentionally patronizing him. "I think we've all had fantasies like that at one time or another."

"Please, spare me the psychobabble crap. I'm not talking about childish fantasies of revenge over some minor insult or transgression. I mean real murder, complete and irrevocable. Plotting every move coldly and surely—when and where you'll do it, how he'll look as you watch the life leak out of him, how he'll sound as he begs you to stop. Or how you'll tighten your hands around his throat until his eyes bug out of his head, then relax your grip, then tighten it, relax it, over and over again, until he pleads with you to end his misery and kill him. That's what I'm talking about, Dr. Kline. Have you ever felt that much hatred for someone? So much hatred that you weren't sure you could keep it in check, or that you even wanted to?"

"No. I haven't. I'm sorry for your suffering."

We'd been talking in their spacious Newton home for ten or fifteen minutes when their doorbell rang. Mrs. Greenfield excused herself and walked to the front door. I heard her open it and say "Oh."

After a moment of awkward silence, another woman said, "Ellis told me you were meeting with that psychiatrist. He thought it made sense for me to be here, too."

Greenfield's mood brightened the moment the visitor walked into the living room. She was about thirty, tall and slender, dressed casually in jeans, running shoes, and a bulky sweater. Although it was only April, her skin was tan and there were sun-bleached streaks in the loosely curled auburn hair that hung below her shoulders.

Mrs. Greenfield said, "You didn't tell me Veronica was coming here, dear."

"Of course I did." He took the visitor's hand and brought her across the room to me.

"No, you didn't, dear," she said, with an icy edge creeping into her voice. But her husband wasn't listening.

Greenfield turned to me and said, "Dr. Kline, meet Veronica Pace. Veronica is a lawyer who's been handling certain matters related to my daughter's death. I thought it might be useful to have her sit in on this meeting."

I was surprised that Ellis Greenfield, himself a lawyer of national repute, had chosen such a young attorney to help manage his late daughter's affairs. We shook hands.

"Good," Greenfield said. "Let's go into the den, shall we? Dear, perhaps you can bring coffee for our visitors."

The sun was setting through the picture window in the den. On one wall were pictures of Ellis Greenfield standing with various luminaries he had known. Two walls were lined with pictures of the Greenfields' children and grandchildren. The largest photo was of Beth, stunningly beautiful in a modest swim suit, her red hair blowing in the breeze on Nantucket Sound. She had large green eyes. She was laughing as she cast a line into the water from the family sailboat.

For the next two hours, I learned about Beth's life and the powerful effect her death had on those who loved her. Her father did most of the talking; Mildred Greenfield provided an occasional detail. According to Greenfield, she'd been a model child, outstanding student, star athlete, and natural leader. "She never gave us a single day of heartache. She was terrific at everything she ever tried. She would have succeeded at any career she chose. I took it as a profound compliment when she decided to become a lawyer."

No one could be so flawless. I didn't know whether Greenfield was merely speaking with exaggerated fatherly pride, or whether Beth's death had somehow canonized her in his memory. I did know that he might never accept the loss until he was able to view her more objectively: It's hard to let go of something so perfect.

All the while Veronica Pace sat quietly, which I thought seemed odd for an attorney.

When he spoke about his daughter's life, Greenfield's excitement cast a glow over him; when he spoke about her death, his anger was palpable. But as the conversation wound down, both the ebullience and the bitterness faded. He sighed softly. He pushed his glasses onto his forehead and rubbed his eyelids. His body slumped as if all the air had gone out of it, and his chin rested on his chest.

Ellis Greenfield came from a long line of coal miners in western Pennsylvania. He was a wrestling champion at Penn State, a combat hero in Korea, and first in his class at Yale Law School. He'd enjoyed a distinguished career as a union lawyer, presidential advisor, and Harvard Law School professor. The man was accustomed to winning. Nothing could have prepared him for such a devastating loss.

I glanced at Veronica. She was looking at Greenfield, and I thought I saw a tear glisten in the corner of her eye.

Mildred Greenfield broke the silence. "Do you have any children, Dr. Kline?"

I nodded. "A daughter. She's nine."

"Love her, Dr. Kline. Love her often and well."

As I thought about Mildred Greenfield's words on my way home, I remembered something that happened when Melissa was four years old. We took her to Burlington Mall to see Santa Claus and the Christmas decorations. As we walked along the crowded concourse, Janet and I turned to look at a window display outside Filene's department store. Each of us thought the other had hold of our daughter's hand. When we turned away from the window a few seconds later, Melissa was gone.

We scanned the throng; we couldn't see her. We called her name; there was no response. "We've lost her!" Janet shrieked, horror spreading across her face.

"Easy. She couldn't have gone very far. You stay here and call her. I'll start looking."

I trotted past a few stores, then retraced my steps and moved the same distance in the other direction, scanning the crowd the entire time. I continued running back and forth, faster and faster, farther and farther, until I covered the length of the mall. Each time I passed Janet, we exchanged looks of terror.

A host of nightmarish questions plagued me as I ran. Who took her? Did we have a recent picture of her to give to the police? How much money would it take to circulate posters, place ads, hire a detective? Whose fault was this?

After several excruciating minutes, on my fourth or fifth run past Filene's, I found Janet clutching Melissa tightly, tears of relief pouring out of both of them.

"Is she okay?"

Janet smothered Melissa with kisses. "She's just fine. Aren't you, my little angel?"

"Good." And then I did something for which I've never really forgiven myself. I yelled at Melissa, howled at her, told her what a bad little girl she was for having scared us so. "Don't you ever, *ever* do that again!" And I grabbed the collar of her coat with both hands and shook her fiercely.

Melissa's eyes went wide with fear. Her body turned rigid for an instant. Then she pulled away, buried her face against Janet, and began to scream.

"Harry! No!" Janet wrapped her arms around Melissa and shielded her from me. "There, there, honey. Everything's alright now."

I heard someone say, in threatening tones, "Got a problem here, pal?" A loutish security guard was standing six inches from my face, his garlicky breath burning my nostrils.

"No problem," I mumbled, and I ushered Janet and Melissa toward the mall exit.

Inside our car, I tried to comfort Melissa. But every time I spoke to her or touched her, she cried harder and clung more tightly to her mother. Who could blame her?

It was one of our last family outings. A couple of weeks later Janet fell seriously ill. After a horrific and mercifully brief battle with pancreatic cancer, she died within the month.

Melissa and I still lived in the Concord home her mother and I bought shortly before she was born. Built around 1800, the former farmhouse sat on an acre near the North Bridge, where colonial Minutemen returned British fire for the first time. The barn had been converted into an apartment for our housekeeper, Mrs. Winnicot, who came to us shortly after we bought the house. Mrs. Winnicot, a widow, loved Melissa no less than she loved her own grandchildren. She embodied just the right mixture of tenderness and toughness to guide Melissa through the difficult adjustment to life without her mother.

Lost in thought, I missed my exit from Route 128 and had to circle back into Concord through Bedford. Mrs. Winnicot was in the kitchen when I arrived home. She handed me the day's mail. "Melissa is in bed. She wanted to stay up until you got home, but she was too sleepy."

"I'll look in on her in a few minutes. Thanks."

Mrs. Winnicot retired to her apartment. I poured a glass of water and opened a large envelope from the mail. Jeffrey Barrow's secretary had forwarded some letters that were sent to me in care of Morgan Books; she sent similar packets about once a week. My correspondents this time included a high school student from Duluth asking for writing tips, a stockbroker offering to share some "sure-fire" book ideas in return for a percentage of the profits, a psychologist from Tulane who enclosed articles she'd written about combat soldiers and post-traumatic stress disorder, and a

Vietnam veteran responding to my comments on the *Today* show.

My appearance on that program also figured in the thinking of another correspondent. The letter was typed on letterhead from an Austin investment banking firm.

Dear Dr. Kline:

I forced myself to watch your interview on the *Today* show this morning. It was not easy for me. My daughter, Rebecca, was one of the young girls slaughtered by Karl Fenner. I know she would be alive today had it not been for your book.

I tell myself that Fenner was a time-bomb, that even if he had not read your book, something eventually would have provoked him into violence. But that thought brings me limited comfort, for if something else had triggered him, he would have struck at a different time and place.

You have every right, I suppose, to say any damn thing you want, in any damn arena you choose, to milk another dollar or two from your book. But I have every right to object: to your exploitation of the tragedy you helped create, and to your furtherance of the pain my wife and I must endure. I think it has gone far enough.

Sincerely,
Edward Billingham

When I was on the *Today* show, I deflected questions about the shopping mall massacre, preferring to focus only on my book. Bryant Gumbel, my interviewer, didn't press the point. Apparently that hadn't been enough to prevent Billingham from feeling abused. His words cut to the bone, and I felt small and ashamed. Adding to the misery of anyone connected with that awful event was the last thing I wanted to do. I resolved not to do any more interviews.

The final letter bore a New York City postmark and no return address. It was printed in an erratic hand that tilted sharply to the right.

APRIL 13, 1992

I WATCHED YOU ON TV WITH BRYANT GUMBEL EARLIER TODAY. YOU MIGHT CALL IT "PROFESSIONAL INTEREST," SEEING AS HOW WE MET A NUMBER OF YEARS AGO IN THE COURSE OF YOUR WORK.

OTHER DOCTORS HAVE TRIED (AND FAILED) TO RELIEVE ME FROM MY GRIEF, BUT FOR ME THERE IS NO RESCUE.

BUT YOU KNOW HOW WE FEEL, THOSE OF US WHO UNFORTUNATELY MUST KILL INNOCENTS IN THE COURSE OF THE BATTLE. THE FIRST ONE ASKED ME WHY, AND I TOLD HIM, AND HE SAID IT WAS NOT FAIR, AND I AGREED. I SAID, "YOU PERISH FOR THE SIN OF RECKLESSNESS."

I WORKED QUICKLY IN ORDER TO MINIMIZE HIS SUFFERING. "CLOSE YOUR EYES," I SAID. "PRETEND YOU ARE DANCING."

ONE DOWN AND THREE TO GO. NEXT COMES THE SIN OF CARELESSNESS. ON APRIL 30 I WILL BE IN YOUR NECK OF THE WOODS FOR NUMBER TWO.

I WILL TELL YOU MORE AS I CONTINUE THE BATTLE. THEN YOU CAN BE MY OFFICIAL CHRONICLER.

YOURS,
ARTIE

It didn't take a psychiatrist to figure out that Artie was a troubled man. According to him, our paths had crossed once; he sounded like he might be one of the war veterans I'd examined earlier in my career, during my years at the Veterans Administration Hospital. Apparently he had some notion I might want to write about him and whatever private battle he was referring to.

I slid the pile of letters back into the envelope from Morgan Books—all of them except the one from Rebecca Billingham's father, which I buried in the bottom of the kitchen trash can. I didn't want to see it again.

I walked upstairs and looked in on Melissa as she slept. I tucked her blanket in where she'd kicked it loose. Her eyes fluttered open. She smiled and said, "Hi, Daddy. Are you staying home tomorrow?"

"No, sweetheart. I have to meet again with the people I talked to this evening, and then I'm going to talk to their children."

"How old are the children?"

"They're grown-up children."

"Oh." She glanced at the picture of Janet on her night table. "Were the people sad?"

"Yes, they were."

"Because someone in their family died," she said, more as a statement than a question.

"Yes." Melissa knew that I was writing a book about people who had died and the families they left behind. I'd refrained from telling her that the dead people were murder victims.

She thought for several seconds, then said, "I think this is a stupid book. I think you should write a happy book."

I leaned over and kissed her lightly on her forehead. "Someday, I promise. Good night, sweetheart."

"Good night, Daddy."

She smiled again, and she looked just like her mother. The left side of her mouth curled upward while the right side remained straight. Janet always called it a sideways-crooked smile.

"I love you, Melissa."

She closed her eyes and turned toward the wall. "I love you, too," she murmured without opening her eyes.

I looked at the picture of Janet. "Melissa, do you remember the time you almost got lost at the Burlington Mall?"

"Was that when we still had Mommy?"

"Yes, that was when we still had Mommy."

She thought for several seconds. "Uh-uh," she said, yawning. "I don't remember."

I shut her door and walked down the corridor to my bedroom.

After Janet died I couldn't bear being in our home. In the

space I'd shared with her for so long, everything suddenly seemed misshaped and out of kilter. I considered moving, but the mere mention of that possibility brought panic to Melissa's eyes. She needed the comfort of known surroundings to help her cope with her mother's death.

The nights then were especially difficult for me; I felt as though I were falling out of bed without Janet's body on the other half of the mattress to balance me. I wanted a change. So I refurnished and redecorated my bedroom, as if casting out the familiar would help me exorcise my grief. Instead the strangeness of the room made me feel even more forlorn. So I rearranged the new furniture to match the old setup, I returned some of Janet's belongings to the shelves, and over time I found a bearable balance between the new and the old.

My longing for Janet was always there, like a dull ache in the back of my mind. It felt stronger on some nights than on others. On this particular night, it was especially intense.

In my dreams, Ellis and Mildred Greenfield walked through a deserted shopping mall, crying out their daughter's name.

4: Who Might Want to Kill You?

Saturday morning broke, wet and gray. Northeasterly winds were sweeping a pocket of Canadian air into New England, and we were due for a weekend of cold and rainy April weather.

I drove to Newton to speak again with the Greenfields. Veronica Pace was there, pleasant and unobtrusive as she was the night before. I wondered how she fit into the picture.

It was almost noon when we finished. "I'll let you see the manuscript before I submit it to my publisher. If you're uncomfortable with anything, I'll take it out."

"What the hell," Greenfield replied. "Maybe someone with information about my daughter's death will read what you write and come forward. Not having any resolution makes it much worse."

Mildred Greenfield escorted me to the door. "You're going to see my children today, aren't you?"

"Yes. First Michael, then Laurel, and this evening I'll see Sylvia."

"Michael took Beth's death very hard. Ever since she died he keeps to himself. I'm worried about him. If you could talk to him, help him somehow . . . well, you know, I'd be very grateful."

"Can I tell him you're worried about him?"

She nodded.

"I'll see what I can do."

"I'd be happy to pay for your time."

"You don't need to do that."

I stood on the porch for a moment after the front door closed behind me. Sitting with the Greenfields, I'd grown more and more tense, in barely noticeable increments, until I felt like a tightly wound coilspring. I exhaled long and hard, then headed toward my car in the circular driveway.

Just as I was about to sit behind the wheel, the front door of the house opened again. Veronica Pace called after me. "I'm leaving, too," she said when she caught up with me. She held her raincoat over her head to shield herself from the drizzle.

We were practically touching as we stood in the small space between our two cars. She said, "You were very good with them."

"I felt like an intruder," I replied, shrugging off her compliment.

"Don't be so modest. You were really kind. I'm sure they appreciated it, Harry. May I call you Harry?"

"Sure."

It was an awkward moment: I wanted to linger, but I couldn't think of anything to say. She seemed to feel the same way.

I said, "Well, it was nice meeting you."

"Yes. Perhaps we'll see each other again."

She got into her car, I got into mine, and we drove down the long driveway.

Michael Greenfield owned a luxurious home in Cambridge's stateliest neighborhood, north and west of Harvard Square, just off Brattle Street. He answered the door in faded jeans, a full beard, and shoulder-length hair that was pulled back into a ponytail. He looked like a holdout from the late sixties, and I half-expected to see a waterpipe and a poster of Che Guevara in his living room.

I'd read about him a few months earlier. In the early eighties, while he was a graduate student at MIT, he developed an integrated business software program—database, graphics, spreadsheet, word processing, and electronic mail—that set a new industry standard. He formed a partnership with a young entrepreneur, and they made a modest fortune within two years. And on the first day their company went public, they became instant multimillionaires.

Around the time his sister was murdered, Michael's company was sold to a Japanese communications conglomerate. Since then he had generally kept to himself. Initially he rejected my request for an interview, then he agreed reluctantly. But it took only a few minutes of conversation for me to realize he wasn't ready to reveal any of his thoughts or feelings about Beth's life or death. I asked him if he wanted to postpone the interview until another time.

He sighed. "I didn't want to do this in the first place. It was my mother's idea. She wanted me to talk with you. Said it would be good for the family. I think she's wrong."

"She's worried about you."

"What makes you think that?"

"She told me so."

"Well, I can take care of myself."

"I'm sure you can. But something is obviously eating at you."

"Someone killed my sister and got away with it, and you wonder what's eating at me? You psychiatrists are all the same," he said with a dismissive gesture.

"Listen." I leaned closer to him and lowered my voice. "My wife died five years ago. She had a very lethal and fast-acting form of cancer. There was nothing I could've done to prevent it, but I still felt responsible. I told myself I should've noticed her symptoms earlier. After all, I'm a doctor. It wasn't rational—every cancer specialist I know told me that—but feelings aren't rational. Especially guilt, which is what I felt intensely, and what I think I recognize in you."

Michael walked to a window that overlooked a small flower garden. The rain on the window blurred the view, and the colors of the tulips and daffodils seemed to melt together as in an Impressionist rendering.

He stood with his back toward me and said, "You want to talk about guilt. Okay, let's talk about it. The day she died, Beth called me from New Haven. She told me what time her train was arriving in Boston that night. She said she really needed to talk to me about some problems she was having. She asked me to pick her up at South Station."

He turned to face me. "I was running myself ragged all that month dealing with the sale of my company. I hadn't slept in two days. I figured whatever was bothering her could wait a day, and I told her I couldn't meet her train. She asked again, I refused again, we started arguing, and finally I hung up."

He gazed out the window again. "Beth never made it home. She went straight from South Station with Gerry Eckler or whoever else killed her."

Michael continued staring out the window for several seconds, then walked over to my chair. "You and my therapist are the only people I've told. No one else knows. I'd like to keep it that way." He sat down. "Okay. Now tell me I shouldn't feel guilty."

"I can't tell you how you should or shouldn't feel."

"Gee, thanks," he said with undisguised sarcasm.

"I *can* tell you this: You didn't kill Beth. Maybe you're responsible for having a fight with her on the phone. You're *not* responsible for what happened afterward."

He took a deep breath and let it out slowly. "Yeah, well, like you said—feelings aren't rational."

Trauma victims often reason that if something bad happened to them, it must be because they are bad. I'd seen the phenomenon in rape victims and war veterans, and now I was seeing it in Michael Greenfield. But he was no more to blame for his sister's death than I was for that of my wife—or of Rebecca Billingham, Gloria Wells, and Theresa Cummings. I knew that; Michael probably knew it, too.

Knowing is one thing; believing is another.

I gave him my phone number in case he wanted to talk further, and then I left.

Laurel Greenfield lived alone in a ground-floor apartment in a Boston neighborhood wedged between Symphony Hall, Northeastern University, and the Museum of Fine Arts. She greeted me in the lobby as I was brushing the rain from my raincoat.

"Lousy weather, huh?" she said as she led me into her apartment. "Hope you didn't have to drive too far."

"No, just from your brother's house."

"Ah. And how is the Hermit of Cambridge these days?"

"He seems to be doing well."

"Right. And I'm Madonna."

She was twenty-three years old, five years younger than Beth would have been if she were still alive. Unlike Michael and her sister Sylvia—whom I was scheduled to meet that evening—Laurel hadn't settled into a stable career. She'd graduated from Northeastern almost two years earlier, a month before Beth died, and had worked since then in a series of go-nowhere jobs. "She's still 'finding herself,' " her father had told me. "Her self must be pretty damn well hidden."

She brought two cups of coffee from the kitchen and sat next to me on the sofa. She faced me, cross-legged with her back against the armrest, her legs almost touching mine. She was every bit as beautiful as the pictures I'd seen of Beth, with the same long red hair and the same piercing green eyes. She was built more fully than her sister; skin-tight jeans and a low-cut sleeveless T-shirt left no doubt about that. When she leaned forward to place her cup on the table, the rippling of supple flesh told me she wasn't wearing anything between her T-shirt and her skin.

She must have noticed me eyeing her, because she smiled and said, "Would you like to marry me?"

I was caught off guard. "Huh?"

"You're a doctor, right?"

"Yes."

"Jewish?"

I nodded.

"Well, do you want to marry me?"

"I, uh . . ."

"We could live together first, if you don't want to jump into things." She laughed out loud for several seconds, pleased at having taken command of the situation. "So," she continued, still smiling, "you're here to talk about the queen."

"Queen?"

"Queen Beth. Isn't that the picture Ellis and Mildred painted of her?"

"You call your parents by their first names?"

"I *refer* to them by their first names. Since I rarely see them, I seldom have occasion to call them by any name at all."

"You sound angry."

"And you sound like a psychiatrist."

I was losing control over the interview quickly. "Tell me about Beth," I said.

"Beth. Faster than a speeding bullet. More powerful than a locomotive. Able to leap tall buildings in a single bound. She could walk on water and raise the dead. A woman for all seasons."

"You sound jealous."

"And you still sound like a psychiatrist."

"Well . . . I *am* a psychiatrist."

She hesitated. "Well . . . I *am* jealous." She stopped smiling.

She'd grown up in her sister's shadow, and Beth was a tough act to follow. Sometimes failing to meet her family's expectations was Laurel's only way of getting noticed. She wore her cynicism like armor to protect her in relationships—relationships that were usually short, and always stormy.

She was a bruised romantic masquerading as a cynic, trying to fend off more hurt. Her bitterness when she talked about Beth seemed to spring from an unrequited desire to be close to her older sister, or to be more like her.

"Can you think of a time when you did feel close to Beth? When being with her didn't make you feel hurt or jealous?"

She thought for several moments. "About six or seven years ago, when I was in high school and Beth was a senior at Radcliffe. Old Ellis took quite a liking to one of his law students. It was always 'Veronica says this,' or 'Veronica does that.' He brought this person along on a family picnic one day and he fawned all over her. I'd never seen him pay that much attention to anyone other than Beth. And every time Beth looked at the two of them, she got this expression like she wanted to tear Veronica's eyes out. I actually felt a little sorry for my sister that day."

"Because you knew how she was feeling."

"It was what *I* always went through when *she* was around."

"What happened to the student?"

"Veronica? I assume she's a lawyer somewhere. I never saw her again."

Veronica Pace had been introduced to me as an attorney who was handling certain unspecified matters related to Beth's death. I wondered now what the exact nature of her involvement was.

Laurel continued. "You'd think it would go away, now that she's dead—the feeling that nothing I did mattered or made any difference to my parents as long as Beth was around. But it hasn't gone away at all." She sat silently for a minute.

"It's hard enough competing with someone who's alive," I said. "It's even harder trying to compete with someone who's become a myth."

She nodded, an acknowledgement that I'd understood her. She sighed, leaned back, and stretched her arms over her head. This pulled her T-shirt tightly across her chest, giving emphasis to her curves. I wasn't sure, but I thought she was doing it for my benefit—trying to make some sort of connection in her own way, a thank-you for having listened to her.

"About a year ago I invited my parents here for dinner, the first time I ever did that. I thought I should try to make a new beginning. But my father hardly said a word the whole time they were here. Later my mother told me my father was upset because I didn't have any pictures of Beth in the apartment. So she mailed me one. And I tore the damn thing into a hundred pieces." She looked away from me, sadness etched deeply on her face. "Real mature, huh?"

Then her expression brightened and she said, "Hey—I bet old Ellis would have a cow if he knew about *that*."

"Would you rather I not mention it in my book?"

She shrugged. "I don't care. Do what you want. They don't get to me anymore."

"Right," I replied. "And I'm Madonna."

It was still raining when I left Laurel's apartment at four-thirty. I'd promised Melissa I'd be home by six o'clock for our traditional Saturday night pizza. I had plenty of time, so I made a turn onto Hemenway Street at the end of Laurel's block, then circled the Fenway until I reached Park Drive. I pulled into a parking space and walked a block to the apartment building on Queensberry Street where Beth Greenfield had lived.

I hadn't planned on stopping there; I'm not sure why I did. I guess I wanted to see or touch some aspect of her world that wasn't filtered through the perceptions of those who mourned her.

The door connecting the foyer to the inside lobby was locked. I remembered reading the number of Beth's old apartment in the police file Detective Connolly showed me. There was no name on the bell for that apartment. I rang the bell; there was no answer. An elderly man opened the door from the inside as he prepared to leave the building, and I walked past him as if I belonged there.

Beth had lived on the second floor of the five-story building. There was an old, slow elevator, but I imagined she'd most often walked up the single flight of steps. So I ascended the stairs, remembering from years earlier how it felt to live alone in a box within a box, and wondering what it had been like for her.

On the second floor, I stood outside Beth's last residence. I knocked but there was no response. It was just as well. What would I have said if anyone had answered?

I returned outside, walked across Park Drive, and entered the park. I walked to the spot by the pond where Beth's corpse was discovered a year and nine months earlier. The two teenagers who found her were crying when the police arrived. Having seen police photos of the scene, I could understand why. It was obvious to anyone unfortunate enough to view the body that this was no ordinary killing. In most instances of multiple stab wounds, the placement of the punctures and cuts are random, inflicted hurriedly by killers who are enraged, frightened, or under the influence of drugs. But Beth's killer sliced with the precision of a surgeon, knowing exactly where and how to cut to prolong her agony.

I remembered those police photos. I hoped no one in Beth's family had been obliged to view them, and I said a silent prayer that they never would. I forced myself to imagine what it would be like to know that my own child had been so butchered, and I shuddered.

I thought: The monster who tortured and slaughtered Beth Greenfield could not have been a father. No one who ever watched a life unfold could do that to another father's child.

"Wait a minute, please," I said, interrupting Sylvia Ossler's narrative. "What was that you said about an abortion?"

I was sitting with the Greenfields' oldest daughter in her home in Belmont, a western suburb of Boston not far from my home in Concord. We were in the family room; her husband and two school-age children were scattered elsewhere in the cozy split-level house. I'd arrived at nightfall, after finishing the pizza dinner with my daughter.

"Didn't my mother tell you about the abortion?"

"No, she didn't."

"Oh." Sylvia hesitated for a few seconds. "I guess my father still doesn't know. That's why she didn't say anything. I probably shouldn't have said anything, either."

I reminded her of the agreement I'd made with her when I first requested an interview: She would have veto power over any part of my manuscript that was based on something she told me. I'd made the same agreement with everyone in the family.

She drummed her fingers on the armrest of her chair, considering whether to reveal what she was thinking.

"A month before she died, Beth asked me to go with her to talk to my mother. She told us she was pregnant. It was my mother who brought up the notion of getting an abortion, probably because she sensed that was what Beth wanted. I'm a nurse, so I helped Beth make the arrangements and I went with her to a clinic in Brookline."

I'd seen nothing in the police file to indicate that Beth had an abortion shortly before her death. A careful autopsy might have revealed that, but the primary focus of her autopsy had been to determine the precise number, location, and severity of her multiple stab wounds.

"Who else knows about this?"

"Just my mother and me, as far as I know."

"Did Beth say who the father was?"

Sylvia shook her head. "All she said was she had no intention of getting married to the father. Knowing what I know about Beth—and this is something my mother *doesn't* know—it's possible she wasn't even certain who the father was."

Eight years older than Beth, Sylvia had been her sister's confidante. For more than an hour she had been telling me about aspects of her sister's life that had remained hidden from the others in her family: an earlier pregnancy and miscarriage, her dalliance with cocaine, the series of stormy relationships with men who misused or abused her. "She reminded me of a line I heard in a Bruce Springsteen song," said Sylvia. " 'Her life was one long emergency.' "

We finished talking at nine-thirty. As I walked toward the door, I thought of one final question. "Do you know a woman named Veronica Pace?"

Sylvia frowned. "Who told you about her?"

"She was at your parents' house when I was interviewing them."

"You can't be serious."

I nodded. "Last night, and again this morning."

"I didn't realize she was back in the picture." That was all she would say on the matter.

I stepped outside. The sky was black and filled with rain,

and I was thankful that I had only a fifteen-minute ride back to Concord.

A host of questions ran through my mind as I walked down the block toward my car. Was there a relationship between the abortion and Beth's frantic call to her brother the day she was killed? Was Eckler the father, and did Beth's decision to abort the child enrage him to the point of murder? Was someone else the father, and did Eckler kill Beth out of jealousy? Was someone else the father *and* the killer? And how did Veronica Pace figure in any of this?

I realized I'd never make a good detective. It's a psychiatrist's job to raise questions, to broaden the range of possibilities in his patients' lives. A cop comes up with answers; he narrows possibilities until only the truth remains.

I wondered if it would help the police to know about Beth's abortion. I wondered if I had an ethical obligation to tell them. I decided to think about it in the morning.

My car was parked near a streetlight across the street. I could make out the shape of a car double-parked about thirty yards to my left. Its parking lights were on and its motor was idling. I hesitated for a second, then stepped into the road.

As I turned my eyes away from the double-parked car, I heard its motor rev, and then a loud squealing noise: the sound of a racing engine being jerked into gear. Startled, I felt my legs lock in place. The car bore down on me. With an instinctive defensiveness that flowed from some unknown place within me, I jabbed my briefcase forward like some primordial shield.

Suddenly the roadway was bathed in light as the driver flipped on his headlights. The rays blinded me. I thought of the summer sun, I remembered watching Melissa run along the shore at Crane Beach in Ipswich, and I knew I'd be dead in the next instant.

A split second before the car rushed through the space where I stood, the streetlight seemed to spring to life. It whizzed through the darkness and crashed into my groin. Its mass overpowered me, shoved me back onto the curb, then fell on top of me. And I realized it was a human form, the body of someone who'd hurled through the air to knock me to safety.

"Are you okay?" she said as she disentangled herself quickly and jumped to her feet.

It was Veronica Pace.

I gasped for air. "What are you doing here?"

"I'll explain later." She reached down and grabbed me with both hands, pulling me up. "Let's go, Harry," she said, stepping quickly into a Honda parked nearby. I stood woozily in place, the numbness in my groin giving way to sharp pain. "Now, damn it! I don't want to lose sight of him."

I collapsed into the passenger seat of her car. In one swift motion Veronica turned the ignition, hit the accelerator, and shifted into gear.

"He's driving a white-and-gray Oldsmobile," she said. Her hands were wrapped tightly around the wheel and her body was hunched forward. "He just turned at the corner up ahead."

I tried to speak, but at first could only manage a wheezing, crackling whoosh of air. "He must be drunk," I murmured.

"Drunk, hell. He aimed straight at you. He was waiting for you to leave Sylvia Ossler's house."

"How do you know that?"

"Because he's been following you all day. Ever since you left Ellis Greenfield's house." She turned at the corner. We drove past McLean Hospital and down the gently sloping hill toward Trapelo Road. "There he is. Two cars ahead. He doesn't realize we're following him."

I tossed my briefcase on the backseat. An open road map of Boston covered half the seat, and there were two empty Styrofoam cups, a bag from Burger King, binoculars, and a camera with a Telephoto lens.

"If you know he's been following me all day, then that means you . . . you were following me, too?"

"Let's just say I was following him following you."

The Oldsmobile turned onto Trapelo Road, heading west,

as did the station wagon immediately in front of us. Veronica followed suit.

I mentally reviewed the path I'd taken: from the Greenfields' in Newton, to Michael Greenfield's house in Cambridge, to Laurel's apartment and Beth's old apartment in Boston, back home for dinner, then on to the Osslers' place . . . *Home!*

"You mean he was at my *house*?"

"Uh-huh."

We crossed the town line into Waltham. The Oldsmobile was still two cars ahead of us, moving at forty-miles-per-hour past the small working-class homes on the well-lit, rain-slicked two-lane street.

"Do you know an Oliver Barclay from North Andover?" she asked.

"No. Why?"

She pointed toward the Oldsmobile we were trailing. "Because that's who that car is registered to. Think again. Are you sure you don't know him? How about anyone else named Barclay?"

She'd taken control so totally, it didn't occur to me at that moment to ask her how she knew the name of the car's owner. I thought for a moment. "Never heard of him or anyone else by that name."

"Well, maybe the car is stolen. Who else might want to kill you?"

I remembered the letter from the father of Rebecca Billingham, one of Karl Fenner's victims, then discarded the thought. "I don't know."

"One of your patients," she suggested, "or perhaps a former patient."

A cripple can grow to hate his crutch; a patient can grow to hate his therapist. But I couldn't think of anyone who seemed likely to follow me and hunt me down on the streets.

"When you were parked near Laurel's apartment I took pictures of him with my Telephoto lens. I don't know how much they'll show, though. He's had a Red Sox cap pulled way down to his eyes the whole time."

We coasted downhill to the intersection of Trapelo Road and Lexington Street. The crossroad was completely illuminated by the glow of service station signs and high-power streetlights.

As we all slowed down—the Oldsmobile, Veronica's Honda, and the station wagon in between—our westbound lane broadened into two lanes: one for left turns, the other for vehicles continuing ahead. Each lane was governed by its own traffic signal, and both lights were red. The Oldsmobile veered into the lane for left turns; the station wagon stayed in the westbound lane.

Veronica drove into the left-turn lane and said, "Duck down."

"Why?"

"Do as I say. We're coming up right behind him. He knows what you look like, remember?"

I ducked down. After a few seconds, I heard the impatient honking of a horn coming from behind us. "What the hell is going on?" I asked.

"The green arrow is giving us the go-ahead for a left turn, but now our friend has decided to go straight. He's inching to the right, waiting for the main signal to turn green, and he's blocking traffic in this lane, so the car behind us is honking. Our friend must think it's my horn, because now he's flipping me the finger."

Several seconds later she told me I could sit up. We were moving west again on Trapelo Road. "Where is he?"

"I let two cars get between us before I swung back into traffic. I don't think he saw me follow him across lanes."

The next traffic light was red. Just beyond the intersection were signs directing traffic to the northbound and southbound entrance ramps for Route 128. The Oldsmobile was second in line; we were fifth. We'd been driving for about eight minutes.

Suddenly the Oldsmobile pulled out of line. It swerved around the car ahead of it, accelerated, and burst past the red light.

"Damn!" said Veronica. "He's on to me." She wheeled to the left and pulled past the cars ahead of us. We zipped through the crossroad against the light. A driver coming through the intersection jammed on his brakes, his horn blaring as we sped through his path.

The rear end of her lightweight Honda shimmied toward the left. Veronica turned the steering wheel sharply and pulled us out of the skid. When we regained our bearings, the Oldsmobile was fifty yards out front, bypassing the northbound entrance to Route 128, crossing over the highway.

We followed him across the overpass. When he reached the southbound entrance ramp he floored his accelerator and shot past it into the darkness. Veronica followed, desperately trying to keep up with the Oldsmobile's more powerful engine.

Just beyond the overpass, the road narrowed. There were no streetlights. We crossed the town line into Lincoln, a heavily wooded enclave for the wealthy, and we passed from city to country in an instant. The road was deserted except for us and our target.

Rain continued to splatter on the windshield. We passed a string of huge colonial homes, set back far from the road, almost invisible in the blackness. The road entered a series of dips and bends, and I grabbed the door handle with one hand and pressed against the dashboard with my other. At every twist in the road, Veronica's headlight beams pierced the woods, and the shadows of trees upon other trees danced like shimmering ghosts.

On a highway he would've outdistanced us easily, but the twists and peaks in the narrow country road served as a brake on his speed. Veronica tracked him with the sure hand of a sharpshooter, leaning expertly into the curves and shifting gears in rapid succession.

Rounding a bend, her front wheels slogged through a wide pool of rainwater, sending a blinding stream across the windshield for several seconds. "You'll kill us! Let him go!"

"Shut up, Harry," she hissed, and she pumped her brakes to gain traction.

After racing almost three miles, we hit a straightaway

stretch and neared a crossroad. Seventy yards ahead of us, the Oldsmobile turned left. When Veronica reached the intersection, she shut her headlights and swung left. I yelled, "Are you nuts?"

The Oldsmobile's taillights shone ahead of us. "He's slowing down," Veronica said. "He can't see us without our lights on. He thinks he lost us." She hit the accelerator, honing in on the red lights. In a matter of seconds we were a few carlengths behind him.

Our quarry must have spotted us, because a moment later he turned his lights off, too, plunging the road into darkness.

"He's crazy," Veronica muttered.

She edged closer to him and flipped on her parking lights. The dim yellow bulbs reflected off the Oldsmobile's rear bumper; enough light for us to track him, but too little to illuminate the road. The fool was driving blind, and we were following in his path.

"*You're* the crazy one," I said. I leaned across her body and switched the bright lights on. She swung her elbow into my ribs. I collapsed against the door.

Ahead of us, the driver shot his right hand up, adjusting his rearview mirror to shunt the reflection of lights away from his eyes. And in the instant that he sat with one hand on the wheel and one on the mirror, unable to reach his own headlight switch—in that instant the road hooked sharply to the right.

He spun his wheel a second too late. The Oldsmobile banked hard off a tree on the left side of the road. It bucked and skidded sideways across the wet road, then crashed headfirst into a tree on the right side. The clatter of broken glass and crunching metal reverberated in the woods.

Veronica stopped directly behind the crumpled Oldsmobile. She bent over and grabbed something underneath her seat. In the reflection of her headlights bouncing off the other car, I saw the glint of a handgun.

"Stay here," she ordered. She opened her door and crouched behind it, then circled swiftly to the front of the Oldsmobile. She stood slightly bent on the balls of her feet, like an infielder poised between pitches. She clasped the handgun firmly in both hands and leveled it at the driver's head. She yelled something, waited a few seconds, then scurried zigzag to a position alongside the driver's door.

She peered through the broken glass, lowered her handgun, and stood up straight. She wiped the rain from her eyes with the back of her hand, then walked back to her car. "He's dead." She pulled a flashlight and a pair of thin gloves from her dashboard compartment. "Come look at him and tell me if you know him."

My legs were buckling underneath me as I walked to the Oldsmobile. Veronica aimed the flashlight beam through the broken window of the driver's door.

His body lady motionless against the steering wheel. Blood poured from a gaping hole in the center of his forehead, and a final reflexive nerve impulse twitched in his neck. I had to stifle the impulse to vomit.

"Take a close look when I pull off his Red Sox cap," Veronica said. She put on her gloves and reached through the shattered window. She removed his cap, revealing a head that was bloodied and completely bald. "Eckler," she whispered.

"What the . . . That's Gerald Eckler?" I leaned forward to grasp the door for support.

"Step back! Don't touch anything! You didn't touch anything, did you?"

I backed away from the car. "No."

"Good. No fingerprints."

She searched Eckler's pants pockets and removed his wallet. "No identification. Just money. Twenty, forty . . . a little over two hundred dollars." She replaced the money in his pants pocket. Then she pulled a piece of paper from his shirt pocket. She read it under the beam of her flashlight. "Hmm, that's interesting."

"What?"

She stuffed the paper into her own pocket. She looked around. There were no cars coming in either direction. She walked briskly back to her car. "Let's get out of here, Harry."

I stood where I was. "I think we should wait for the police."

"Let's go, damn it! Now!"

We jumped into her Honda. She turned the car around and began driving back in the opposite direction. I felt my pulse racing through a vein in my temple, and I wondered how much pressure it could take without bursting. A wave of nausea coursed through me. I opened my window and stuck my head into the cold rain. The chill overcame the nausea, and I closed the window and sank back into my seat.

I said, "It's against the law to leave the scene of an accident."

"I can live with it."

"Where are you going now?"

"Back to Belmont, so you can get your car at Sylvia Ossler's house."

"I don't feel like driving. Concord is the next town over from here. Take me home. I'll pick up my car tomorrow."

She shook her head. "No way. I don't want anyone at Sylvia's house to see you tomorrow and start wondering how you got home tonight. I don't want to get caught up in any police investigation of Eckler's death. Which means I don't want you getting caught up in it. As far as anyone else is concerned, we weren't here and we don't know anything about Eckler's accident."

"I said, take me home." I was surprised at how loudly my words came out.

"And I said, no way. Which word didn't you understand?"

Although she wanted to get away from the accident scene as quickly as possible, she drove within the speed limit in order not to draw anyone's attention. But her brisk manner betrayed her nervousness, as did her fidgeting with the windshield wipers and her biting down on her lower lip.

"We killed him," I said without expression.

"He killed himself. And he killed Beth Greenfield."

"You don't know that."

"He killed Beth Greenfield. And need I remind you, he also tried to murder you."

"I don't know. This is crazy. Maybe he wasn't dead yet. I could have tried to revive him. We could have called an ambulance."

"He was dead. If he wasn't, he was too far gone to save. And even if he could've been saved—so what?"

I didn't know what to say. In my work, I'd always found it best not to make judgments about the worthiness of people who needed my service. Veronica Pace apparently worked by another set of rules.

"Here," she said. "This is the paper I took from Eckler. Maybe this will knock some sense into you." She handed it to me.

I took her flashlight from the dashboard compartment and trained its beam on the rumpled paper. On it Eckler had written my home address.

"He probably wrote it when he followed you there," Veronica said, "just in case he had to return later to take care of you. Maybe that's where he was headed when he went off the road. He was certainly going in that direction. I heard you tell Mildred Greenfield that you have a nine-year-old girl there. So tell me, Harry, how much sympathy do you have for him now?"

Reading my address in the killer's scrawl filled me with fear, then rage. I thought of Melissa, tucked away in her bed, the picture of her mother watching over her. My arms began to shake. I remembered Ellis Greenfield's consuming hatred: *Tell me, Dr. Kline, have you ever wanted to kill someone?*

I hooked my left leg around Veronica's right leg and jammed hard on the brake pedal.

"Hey!" she yelled. "What are you doing?"

I kept my foot on the pedal until the car stopped. I grabbed her by the shoulders and pinned her against the door. "What the fuck is going on here?" I shouted. "Who the fuck *are* you?"

She stared at me coolly for several seconds, then bent her arms until her hands were on top of my wrists. Her grip felt like iron. She tore my hands off her as if they were pieces of paper. She pressed her thumbs sharply against the veins in my wrists; my hands turned numb and fell like dead weights into my lap.

Her voice was quiet and cold. "Never, *ever* try that again. If you do, I will hurt you."

I didn't doubt her for a second.

5: People Who Hurt People

Driving back to Belmont, Veronica pulled into the parking lot of a bar-and-grill. "I need a drink," she said. They were the first words either of us had spoken since our confrontation ten minutes earlier.

The room was half-full, with couples in their thirties and men in their forties. Soft rock played at medium volume through the sound system. The Red Sox game was showing on the television set behind the bar. We sat in a corner booth and ordered drinks: gin and tonic for Veronica, sparkling water for me.

I checked my watch; it was past ten o'clock. I found a pay phone and told Mrs. Winnicot that I'd be home later than planned.

When I returned to the booth, Veronica was leaning back against the padded bench with her eyes closed. She looked tired, though not as tired as I felt. She was tall, tan, and slender, and she looked like she could have been a model for women's athletic wear. Under normal circumstances I might have found her alluring. These were definitely not normal circumstances.

She opened her eyes when I sat down. She glanced at the Red Sox game and I rubbed the spots on my wrists where she had pressed her thumbs against my veins.

"Must be a road game," she said. "We've had too much rain today for them to be playing at Fenway Park." She noticed what I was doing to my wrists. "Do they still hurt?"

"You could say that."

"I'm really sorry. But I wanted to get out of there in a hurry, and I didn't have time to reason with you. Besides, *you* were hurting *me*."

"Yeah, well, I guess I shouldn't have grabbed you like that."

The waitress delivered our drinks. We sat silently for a few minutes.

Thinking about Gerald Eckler's lifeless form stretched over the steering wheel—his head split open and his brain matter splashed across the dashboard—made my stomach swirl. "I guess by now someone else has found him and called the police," I said.

"What's the nearest hospital to the crash site?"

"They'll probably bring him to Emerson Hospital in Concord, a mile or two from my house."

Veronica sipped her gin and tonic. "He'll be declared dead on arrival. The Lincoln police will discover that the car was stolen. They'll automatically notify the state police, the Massachusetts Department of Public Safety, and the Middlesex County district attorney's office. Then the state police will try to figure out the identity of the corpse. Through fingerprints, which might not work. Or through news reports that result in someone coming forward to make an ID."

"Are you sure it was Eckler?"

"I'm sure. If they haven't figured it out by the end of the weekend, I'll call Tim's office and leave an anonymous tip to put them on the right track."

"Who's Tim?"

"Tim Connolly," she said. "The Boston homicide detective you met yesterday."

"Hold it. Time out. Are you a cop? An off-duty detective, something like that?"

"What gives you that idea?"

"I'm not sure," I replied, mulling it over and putting the pieces together as I spoke. "The little description you just gave me of police procedure. The fact that you know Connolly. You drive like you've had special police training.

You have a gun, which you're obviously willing to use. That little maneuver you pulled to disable me when I grabbed you. A camera with a Telephoto lens. The very fact that you even noticed Eckler was following me. And how did you trace the license plate of Eckler's car?"

She didn't respond.

"And one more thing," I said. "I get the feeling you've been through things like this before. You're not nearly nervous enough for someone who's doing this for the first time."

Veronica stared at me for several seconds, as if she were debating whether to answer my questions. "What the hell," she said, and she reached into her purse. She pulled out a business card and pushed it across the table. Bold black letters were embossed over a faint blue federal seal. The card read:

VERONICA PACE
Special Agent
Federal Bureau of Investigation

"Terrific," I groaned, remembering how I'd grabbed her in the car. "I assaulted a federal agent. What does that mean—a *special* agent?"

"That's what we're all called. There's nothing special about being special."

"I don't get it. I thought you were a lawyer."

"That's exactly right. I *was* a lawyer."

She told me she graduated Harvard Law School. Ellis Greenfield was one of her professors. Most of her classmates took high-status or well-paying jobs after graduating: corporate counsel positions, clerkships for federal judges, associate positions at big-name firms like the one where Beth Greenfield had practiced. But Veronica went into the trenches: She became an assistant district attorney in Rhode Island's Bristol County. Within a few years, she was the prosecutor in charge of all homicide cases.

"I took that job because I had a mission when I decided

to study law," Veronica said. "I wanted to hurt people who hurt other people."

"From what I've seen, you should be very good at that."

"Thanks. I think."

Some people wind up in jobs by default or from necessity. But Veronica had chosen her profession, impelled by the desire to be an instrument of revenge. I wondered what manner of suffering—real or imagined—she herself had endured that made her so intent on going after people who made other people suffer.

"If you were on a mission, why did you leave that job?"

"You know that unsolved serial murder case in southeastern Massachusetts? All those drug-addicted prostitutes from New Bedford?"

"Uh-huh."

"Well, some of the leads pointed to Rhode Island suspects. My boss put me on a special interstate task force. The Boston field office of the FBI provided us with technical support, so I got to know the chief there pretty well, a man named Martin Baines. Then the New Bedford DA lost his bid for reelection, and the task force was disbanded a little while later. Martin recruited me for the FBI. I came over about six months ago."

"Is the FBI investigating Beth Greenfield's murder? Ellis Greenfield said you were a lawyer he hired to manage some of Beth's affairs. Was he lying?"

"Ellis didn't lie to you. I'm still a member of the bar, so I am a lawyer. And he didn't say I was managing her affairs. He said I was handling certain matters related to her death, and I am. Ellis asked me to review the case, see if I could find anything the police may have overlooked. Come up with some evidence that would enable the district attorney to get an indictment against Eckler. And Ellis never said he hired me. He didn't. Special Agents aren't permitted to do private investigations."

"So the FBI *is* investigating this case."

"No. I *am* doing this on my own, as a favor to Ellis. I haven't told my supervisor, though, because he wouldn't approve. So I can't afford to get caught up in any police investigation of Eckler's accident. I don't want to ruin things for myself at the Bureau. That's why I insisted we leave the accident scene before anyone saw us there. And that's why I took the paper he wrote your address on. I didn't want anyone to find it and come asking you questions. I didn't know if I could trust you to keep quiet about what you know."

She folded her hands on the table and leaned slightly toward me. "So. Can I?"

"Can you what?"

"Trust you not to say anything about any of this. Trailing Eckler, witnessing the crash, leaving the scene of a fatal car accident."

I thought for a moment. "I don't know," I replied.

"I see. Well. You'll do what you feel you have to do." She picked up her drink and smiled. "Hey—look how much information you got out of me without saying anything about yourself. I guess that's what you psychiatrists are good at, huh?"

"Sometimes."

"I thought you handled Ellis and his wife very nicely, but I told you that already. How did your interviews with their children go?"

"Well enough."

"Did any of them say anything about me?"

"What makes you think they would speak about you?"

"Answering a question with a question. I guess that's something else psychiatrists do." She sighed. "Poor, dear Ellis. I wonder how he'll react when he hears about Eckler's death."

"You and he must be very close."

She hesitated. "He's a great man. And he's a good man. No one should have to suffer the way he's suffered."

"I don't think his suffering will end anytime soon."

"Why?"

"He's holding onto a fantasy picture of Beth," I said. "No one is as perfect as he remembers her being. I've seen other people get stuck the way he has. You reinvent the past, you sanctify the person's memory, and then you dwell on it to insulate yourself against a miserable reality. Unless you begin to look at that past more realistically, the bad as well as the good, you keep yourself frozen. Maybe depressed, maybe bitter, but always frozen. Unable to move beyond the loss."

Veronica considered what I'd said for a few moments. Then she finished her gin and tonic and left enough money on the table to cover both our drinks.

It was a short drive from the bar-and-grill to my car in Belmont. As we rode there I said, "There's something that puzzles me. How did Gerald Eckler know about me? After dropping out of sight for so long, why did he materialize now?"

"Mildred Greenfield was friendly with Eckler's mother before the murder occurred. I think they still talk occasionally, without Ellis knowing about it. I figure Eckler was in contact with his mother all along, even after he supposedly disappeared. Mildred probably told Mrs. Eckler that someone was going to interview them and write about the murder, and she must've relayed the word to her son."

"And he was afraid I might stumble onto something that would incriminate him."

"That's my guess."

I pondered her explanation as she parked her Honda across the street from my car, down the block from Sylvia Ossler's house.

"I left the Greenfields a few minutes after you last night," she said. "You'd already driven halfway down the block when I pulled out of their driveway. I saw a white-and-gray car start up and follow you to the corner, where you both turned. I didn't think anything of it until this morning, when I saw the same car parked on the street when I arrived, and a man in a baseball cap waiting inside. You and I left there two hours later, and he was still waiting. When he began to follow you again, I figured I'd better tag along."

I looked outside. It seemed like hours since I'd been there, but only ninety minutes had passed since Veronica pushed me to safety from the path of Eckler's stolen car.

"Hey!" I'd been so caught up in the commotion of the chase and the accident that I hadn't had time to think about my close brush with death. "You saved my life!"

Veronica didn't say anything.

"I'm gonna have a hell of a time settling that debt."

"I'll tell you how you can repay me." She turned in her seat to face me. "Get in your car. Go home. Kiss your wife good-night, sleep well, and act like nothing happened tonight. Wake up tomorrow and convince yourself it was all a dream. And never say anything about this to anyone. Will you do that for me, Harry?"

We looked at each other for a very long time. The plaintiveness in her eyes gave her a vulnerability that I hadn't noticed before.

"I can't promise how soundly I'll sleep. And I can't kiss my wife good-night. I wish I could. She died five years ago. But I won't say anything."

I stepped outside before she could respond, crossed the street to my car, and drove home.

6: Dead Bodies Are Bad For Business

Sudden, bloody death: Never having witnessed it before, I was unprepared for its aftermath. I couldn't eat. I couldn't sleep. I was irritable, tense, and distracted. I went to a meeting in Lincoln; I circled through Lexington rather than cross the route of the fatal car chase. Melissa drowned her hamburger in ketchup one evening; I felt my stomach rise into my throat.

All the news outlets ran the story about Gerald Eckler's sudden reappearance and violent death. The police discovered that he'd been living in another state. The white-and-gray Oldsmobile was stolen from the parking garage at Logan Airport. Everyone wondered how it had come to pass that he'd flown to Boston, stolen a car, and traveled to and died in the suburban town of Lincoln. I was certain my involvement would be discovered and I'd be called upon by the police or the press to explain myself. But there really was no reason for anyone to connect me with Eckler's one-vehicle fatal accident on a wet, dark country road.

I honored my promise to Veronica Pace. I told no one what I knew.

Detective Timothy Connolly agreed to meet with me again to discuss the Greenfield murder case in the light of Eckler's death. He was still reaching reflexively for the pack of cigarettes he no longer carried, and turning instead to the jar of hard candy on his desk.

"Gerald Eckler's death doesn't close the book on Beth Greenfield's murder," Connolly said. "Technically, the case is still open, since no one was ever prosecuted."

"Do you mean it stays that way forever?"

"Unless we stumble onto something that conclusively ties Eckler to the murder, or someone else confesses."

"And neither one of those things is likely," I said.

"Nope. If there was sufficient evidence against him, we would've found it by now—unless maybe he admitted it to his parents or some other credible witness, and they come forward now that he's dead. As far as someone else confessing, that's not gonna happen, either, because—let's face it—Eckler was the one who did it."

"Ellis Greenfield certainly believes that. Maybe at least he can close his own book on the case now."

He stood and walked to the window of his tiny office. "Funny that Eckler would pick now to resurface." His back was toward me as he fiddled with the blinds. "That he'd fly into town, hot-wire a car at the airport, and crash it twenty-five miles away in Lincoln." He turned around, leaned against his windowsill, and gazed directly at me. "You live out that way, don't you, Doc?"

I could have said yes, since my house was a ten-minute drive from the crash site. On the other hand, I could have said no, since "out that way" leaves a lot of room for interpretation.

"I live in Concord," I said.

"Concord," he repeated. He mulled it over for a few seconds. "You wouldn't happen to have any ideas on the matter, would you?"

"No."

He stared at me for what seemed like half an eternity, then clapped his hands together and stood up. "Ah, what the hell. The son of a bitch is dead and who gives a shit, right?"

"Is that a rhetorical question?"

His phone rang. "Yeah, I guess. Hold on for a minute while I get this." He lifted the receiver off its hook. "Connolly. . . . Uh-huh . . . Uh-huh . . . That bad, huh?" He began to scribble notes. "Uh-huh . . . Okay. Be right over." He hung up and reached for his sport jacket. "Ever see a dead body before?"

"Before what?" I asked, still thinking he might be trying to trick me into revealing what I knew about Eckler's death.

He looked puzzled. "Before what? Before now."

I shrugged. "Cadavers in medical school."

"Ever see a homicide victim? Visit a murder scene?"

"No."

"A hooker was just found murdered at the Lafayette Hotel," he said. "If you think you've got the stomach for it, you can come along."

The Lafayette was a luxury hotel incongruously placed in the seamiest part of downtown Boston. Stores in the adjacent mall had often fallen victim to marauding gangs of preteen shoplifters. The thieves would descend on a particular store, and at a prearranged signal they would grab armfuls of merchandise and flee. The few who were caught suffered no penalty greater than a few hours of inconvenience at Boston Juvenile Court; their proceedings were continued without a finding and they were released into the custody of their parents.

On our way there, Connolly said, "Dead hookers—dead anybodies—are bad for business, especially at a place like the Lafayette. They'll try pretty hard to keep the press in the dark, but it never works. Wouldn't surprise me if a few reporters beat us there."

Connolly was right. A half-dozen police beat reporters and photographers were in the hotel lobby when we arrived. Most of them recognized the detective; he smiled grimly as the flashbulbs popped.

A uniformed police officer and a very distraught hotel manager were waiting for us in a deluxe suite on the twelfth floor. The officer addressed Connolly. "The doc is in there with the deceased," he said, gesturing toward the bathroom.

"He means the medical examiner," Connolly explained to me.

The officer must have realized that I was new to such scenes, because he kept his eyes on me as he said to Connolly, "It's pretty rough in there, Lieutenant."

I followed Connolly into the suite's spacious bathroom. The police officer and hotel manager came in after us.

The formaldehyde-filled cadavers we dissected in medical school always gave off a peculiarly sweet smell. Their faces were peaceful, almost beatific, and their torsos and limbs were laid out in peaceful repose. Not so the nude corpse stretched out on its back before us: Her arms and legs were splayed, each limb reaching awkwardly in a different direction. A rancid odor permeated the air. She was covered with blood from her shoulders up; an enormous quantity had flowed from her body and across the tile floor to the porcelain base of the toilet. Her eyes and mouth were wide open as if frozen in the middle of a scream.

A squat man knelt by the dead woman. It was April 30th, but he was wearing a wool suit, and he was sweating profusely.

Connolly said, "Dr. Harold Kline, this is Dr. Seymour Melville, our medical examiner. Doc, say hello to Dr. Kline."

The man looked up and scowled at me like an animal whose territory was being invaded.

I took a half-step backward. "Psychiatrist," I said. "Just visiting."

He nodded and turned back to the work at hand. He probed with his fingers at a wound below the corpse's chin. As I gazed at the area he was examining, I thought the woman looked like a figure in a Modigliani portrait, with an elongated neck that made her head appear about two inches farther from her shoulders than it should have been. But as I stared at the gaping wound in her neck, I realized that she'd been decapitated. Her head rested at a slight angle to her body.

A chill passed through me. I was completely repulsed by the gore, I felt like vomiting, and yet I couldn't take my eyes off of the medical examiner's fingers as they pressed against the bloody muscle-and-nerve pulp.

"So what do we have here, Doc?"

"Hispanic woman, twenty years old, if that much."

The uniformed officer said, "Her name was Maria Melendez. Been working this area for about a year. We've busted her three times. Two streetwalking charges, which were dismissed in court. One outstanding charge of possession of a Class B substance."

Connolly explained for my benefit. "Cocaine."

The patrolman continued. "She started out as one of the young and attractive ones, really went downhill fast. She was pretty hard near the end." He glanced at the hotel manager. "Not exactly a stranger to this place, either."

The hotel manager's face turned red. "Now, just a minute, Officer—"

Connolly cut the manager off. "Well, Doc," he said. "How long do you think she's been lying there?"

"Three, maybe four hours," replied the medical examiner.

"You figure out the cause of death yet?"

The manager gasped, the officer chuckled, and the medical examiner grunted and said, "Yeah. Shortage of breath." He stood and wiped the sweat from his forehead, inadvertently spreading a thin streak of coagulated blood above his eyebrows. "I'm finished."

Connolly walked around the corpse a few times, studying it from various angles. All the while he asked questions of the officer and the manager. An Elmore Winston had checked in the previous afternoon. He paid for the room in cash at the time of registration. He checked out at midmorning, and a chambermaid discovered the body while making up the room. The afternoon desk clerk hadn't arrived for work yet, and no one else had seen Elmore Winston—if that was really his name.

Connolly stopped in his tracks, peered down at the dead woman's right hand, then bent over to get a closer look. "Doc, you got tweezers in that bag?" The detective took the medical examiner's tweezers and slipped it between the second and third fingers of the corpse's left hand. "Well, well—look what we have here."

He plucked something from the rigid fingers and held the tweezers up to the overhead bulb. A penny glistened in the light. "Looks like the killer left a calling card," Connolly said.

I stared at the coin. "What do you suppose it means?" I asked.

He grinned. "Search me. You're the psychiatrist. What do *you* think it means?"

I didn't have a clue.

7: A Penny For Your Death

Melissa finished her pancakes, kissed me good-bye, and ran outside and down the driveway to wait for her school bus. Mrs. Winnicot stopped clearing the table as soon as my daughter was out of the room. She opened the cabinet underneath the sink and pulled out the *Boston Globe*.

"I thought you told me the paper hadn't been delivered yet," I said.

"I didn't want Melissa to see it before you did. There's something you should look at on the first page of the Metro-Region section."

On that page were an article about the decapitation murder of Maria Melendez the previous day and a news photo of Detective Timothy Connolly arriving at the Lafayette Hotel. I was pictured walking next to him; the caption referred to me as Connolly's "unidentified assistant."

"Are you involved in this case in some way?"

I shook my head. "I was visiting a police detective yesterday. I just happened to be with him when this picture was taken."

"I see." She untied her apron and draped it over the butcher block counter. "Can I speak frankly, Dr. Kline?"

We always called one another by our last names, in spite of our longstanding regard for one another. It was a matter of her New England sense of propriety. "Certainly," I said.

"You know how impressionable Melissa is. I don't think it's good for her to see you linked with all these murders.

The ones in Texas, and now this one. You ought to try to keep a lower profile."

Mrs. Winnicot was a staunch guardian of Melissa's welfare. An unspoken understanding between us allowed her to question or advise me on virtually any aspect of Melissa's upbringing. She never challenged me in front of my daughter, and she never tried to undercut me once a decision was made.

"One more thing," she said. "Melissa can't understand why you've decided to write a book about murder victims. I think it frightens her."

"How does she know about that?" I'd told Melissa that I was writing a book about the families of people who had passed away. I hadn't told her that the dead people had been murdered.

"You mentioned it yourself on the *Today* show a couple of weeks ago. Don't you remember?" She paused for several seconds, then said, "There. That's all I have to say. I won't mention it again. I'm going to do the laundry now."

Alone in the kitchen, I thought about my daughter and the sad times we endured after her mother died. And I remembered her telling me that she thought the book I was working on was "stupid." I guess I hadn't been listening closely enough when she said that. Like most kids, Melissa often used that word as an all-purpose adjective when she felt angry, sad, or frightened.

I read the *Boston Globe* article about the hotel murder. It was accurate as far as it went, but it made no mention of the penny that was found wedged between the dead prostitute's fingers. I wondered why that piece of information hadn't been released.

Twice now in a matter of days I'd observed physical trauma too gruesome for words. Just when I was beginning to shake off the effects of watching Gerald Eckler's life ooze away, now I had to contend with the previous day's sickening scene. Timothy Connolly had offered to send me a souvenir crime scene photo to commemorate the event. I declined the honor; the last thing I needed was another picture of a headless murder victim. . . .

Another picture!

The realization jolted me upright in my chair. I jumped up and darted out of the kitchen, down a long corridor, and into my office at the rear of the house. I opened my briefcase and pulled out the photograph of the decapitated priest from Philadelphia that had been sent to me in care of my editor. I'd noticed something unusual about the picture the moment Jeffrey Barrow first showed it to me, and I noticed it again now: Something was definitely wedged between the second and third digits of the corpse's curled left hand.

I stared at the photograph and wondered: Was I looking at an earlier piece of bloodletting from the same person whose handiwork I'd witnessed the day before?

I telephoned a former colleague who taught at the University of Pennsylvania. I told her I was doing research for a book and needed information from the Philadelphia newspapers. That afternoon, courtesy of my friend's research assistant, I received a fax transmission of several *Philadelphia Inquirer* stories about the unsolved murder of Father Joseph Carroll.

I read the articles carefully. Not one made mention of a penny or anything else that had been found in the dead priest's grasp.

"Captain John Riley, please."

"You got him."

There were several voices in the background on his end of the long-distance connection. I found myself shouting into the phone. "Captain, are you still in charge of the Father Joseph Carroll murder investigation?"

"Yep."

"I'd like to ask you something about the case."

"Are you white?"

"Yes." A strange question, I thought.

"Figures." He grunted. "Yeah, yeah. What do you want?"

"Can you tell me if the killer left anything in the priest's hand?"

Captain Riley placed his hand over his phone and said

something I couldn't make out to another person in the room with him. "I'm having a hard time hearing you. Give me your number. I'll call you back."

I gave him my name and my office phone number. Ten minutes later, the other push button on my phone—the one for my unlisted home number—lit up. It was Riley calling. He'd obviously been in contact with the telephone company and persuaded them to give him that number. He was someone to be taken seriously.

"What kind of a doctor are you?"

I hadn't identified myself as a doctor when I gave him my name.

"I'm a psychiatrist."

"Uh-huh. What makes you think the killer left something in the victim's hand?"

"I saw a photograph of the crime scene. It looked like the priest was grasping something with his left hand."

"What do you think it was?"

"A penny."

Riley paused for several seconds. "I think you'd better explain yourself, Dr. Kline."

"Explain myself?"

"First of all, we never released any pictures of the murder scene. Second, there's only two people who know about the penny. I'm one of them."

"Who's the other one?"

"Guess."

I hesitated. "The killer?"

"Bingo."

"Hey! If I were the killer, would I be foolish enough to give you my name and telephone number?"

"Probably not," he said, a bit less unfriendly. "Although they say confession is good for the soul. A priest would know that. And so would a psychiatrist."

It wasn't difficult to convince Riley that I had nothing to do with the killing of Father Joseph Carroll. I gave him a shorthand version of my résumé and dropped the names of a half-dozen respected Philadelphians who could vouch for me.

I told him about the murder of Maria Melendez one day earlier in downtown Boston. Riley agreed that it sounded like more work by the priest's unknown assailant.

"How did you get that picture, Dr. Kline?"

"I'm working on a book about murder victims. Someone who saw me talking about it in a television interview sent the picture to me. He evidently thought I might want to write about the priest's murder."

"Well, like I said—I never authorized the release of any pictures. Which makes me damn curious about the one you have and how you got it. Do you have a fax machine?"

"I do.'"

"Send the picture to me."

He gave me his fax number and I put the photograph through my machine. While the transmission proceeded, I asked Riley why he'd kept the penny in the priest's hand secret.

"Professional instinct," he replied. "I think the killer was sending some sort of message. I figured, keep it secret, he might think we didn't receive the message. Then he might try to get it across some other way. Maybe step out of the shadows and give us more clues. Besides, it helps weed out the confessional professionals."

"The who?"

"Confessional professionals. Over the years I've gotten calls from people confessing to everything from the Kennedy assassinations to the hole in the ozone layer. Anyone who confesses to killing Father Joseph Carroll, he better know about that penny."

The fax transmission to the Philadelphia police station took a little more than a minute. As soon as he saw the photograph, Riley said, "This isn't one of our pictures."

"What do you mean?"

"My guy took twenty-five pictures. This isn't one of them. Someone else took this picture. And when we got to the scene, there was lots more blood than there is in this picture. So this picture was taken by someone who was there before we were."

Neither one of us spoke for several seconds. "In other words," I said, "it has to be the killer himself."

"Yep. And it sounds like he really wants a part in your next book."

It was late in the afternoon when I reached Veronica Pace at the Boston office of the FBI.

"Well, well," she said when she heard my voice over the telephone. "You save a guy's life, and he takes almost two weeks to call you back."

"I need to see you."

"*Now* we're getting somewhere."

"I'm serious. It's important."

She dropped the flirtatious tone. "What's wrong, Harry?"

She'd been busy all day and hadn't read the morning *Globe*. I told her about Maria Melendez's murder. "And that's not all. Last October a priest was murdered in Philadelphia. They don't know who did it, but I think it was the same person who murdered that woman yesterday."

"Why?"

"They were both decapitated, and the killer left a penny in both victims' hands."

"A penny?"

"A penny."

"That's unusual. How did you find out about the priest?"

"I have a picture of the corpse."

"You have a *what*?"

"A picture. Taken by the killer. He sent it to me himself. He saw me on the *Today* show talking about the book I'm working on, and he sent it to my editor to give to me."

A few seconds of silence elapsed. "I think I'd better see that picture."

"I can fax it to you."

"No. I want to see the original. Where is it?"

"Right here on my desk."

"Leave it where it is. Don't touch it again. Is it alright if I come to your house?" I began reciting directions. "I know the way already. I tailed Gerald Eckler there when he was following you, remember?"

An hour later she drove up the long gravel driveway leading from Monument Street to my house. When I saw her Honda, images of Veronica from the last time I saw her—knocking me down in the street, driving wildly down the wet roads, slinking like a cat toward Eckler's car with her gun in hand—passed through my mind, all condensed into one instant. I went outside to meet her.

"Nice place," she said as she stepped out of her car. She carried a leather portfolio. She wore a lightweight knee-length skirt and a blouse with an earth-tone floral print befitting the first day of May. She'd been driving with her window down; her long curls were swept into a thick mass behind her.

We entered the house through my office entrance. As we walked I told her about my conversation with John Riley of the Philadelphia police. "I have some newspaper articles you can read about that case. A friend faxed them to me a few hours ago. I called Timothy Connolly right after I spoke with Captain Riley. It's his day off, so I left a message, said it was urgent. Then I called you."

We stepped into my office. Veronica asked for a glass of water, and I went to the kitchen to get it. When I returned, she was standing near my desk.

"Is this where you see your patients?"

I nodded.

She looked around the room. There were four comfortable chairs: one behind my desk, three facing it. In the corner was a children's play area.

"No couch?"

"I'm not a psychoanalyst. They're the ones with couches."

Books lined the entire wall—volumes on psychodynamic theory, post-traumatic stress disorder and psychopharmacology, and the three books I'd authored: *Battle Dreams: Vietnam Veterans Relive the War; Invisible Scars: Adult Survivors of Childhood Sexual Abuse;* and *Soldier and Son.*

She lifted *Soldier and Son* from the shelf. "So this is the book that's been getting all the publicity," she said. She glanced at the blurb on the cover. "Sounds interesting."

"You can borrow it, if you like."

"Thanks, but I can never find enough time to read." She placed the novel back in its place beside my other books.

Veronica leaned over my desk and examined the picture of the priest without picking it up. "There's something almost ritualistic about this scene," she said. "The way his limbs are positioned so symmetrically. Is that how yesterday's victim looked?"

"No. Her arms and legs stuck out at crazy angles. Like a pile of trash that someone dumped there."

"Maybe he was in more of a hurry yesterday. Or maybe he's become more mentally disorganized during the past six months. But I guess that's your area of expertise."

She opened her portfolio and drew out tweezers and a Ziploc food storage bag. She plucked the photograph off of the desk without laying a hand on it, then slid it into the bag. She placed the bag and the newspaper articles in her portfolio.

"Now I need to take a set of your fingerprints," she said. "It'll make less of a mess if we do it near a sink. Your kitchen, perhaps."

I led her through the long corridor that connected my office to the rest of the house. As we walked she said, "An agent from our New York office will get prints from your editor. Any prints on the photograph that didn't come from him or you may belong to the murderer. Then we'll use a laser scanner to feed those prints into our computer in Washington, see if they match up with any other prints in the files. It's a fairly new system, though, so chances are he's not in it—unless he's been fingerprinted in the past few years by us or some other federal agency, or in one of the states that has computerized records. Otherwise, his prints won't be much use unless we have a specific suspect to match them against."

We sat at the kitchen table. Veronica opened her portfolio and pulled out an ink pad and a piece of paper divided into twelve boxes, ten small and two large. She grasped my left hand with both of her hands and rolled the entire surface of my thumb across the ink pad and then across one of the small compartments on the paper. She repeated this with all of the fingers on that hand. Then she pressed my palm against the ink pad and took a print of the entire hand in one of the large boxes on the paper.

As Veronica began to work on my right hand, Melissa and Mrs. Winnicot came inside. They'd been gardening together on the far side of our property. When I saw my daughter, without thinking I tried to pull my hand away from Veronica's grasp. But Veronica's grip was strong, and she kept hold of my hand.

I made introductions all around, then tried to think of an explanation for the scene my daughter was witnessing. Before I could speak, Melissa marched up to Veronica and asked, "Why are you doing that to my daddy? He didn't do anything wrong."

I could tell she was frightened. I said, "Of course not, sweetheart. She knows I didn't do anything wrong."

Mrs. Winnicot looked on with an expression of confusion mixed with disapproval.

"Then why is she making your fingerprints, like they do on TV when they arrest somebody?" She turned to Veronica and said, "Are you with the police?"

"I work for the FBI. Have you ever heard of that?"

"Sure. They catch spies and things. Are you a G-man?"

"Well, I guess I'm a G-woman."

"I didn't think girls could do that."

"Neither did J. Edgar Hoover."

"Jay who?"

"Nobody important."

"Daddy, why is she making your fingerprints?"

"Well, uh . . . remember when I worked at the hospital for soldiers?"

"Uh-huh."

"Well, they keep fingerprints of everybody who used to work there. They lost mine, so they sent this lady here to get new ones."

Melissa considered that for a moment, then asked, "Why does the hospital keep copies of everybody's fingerprints?"

I sighed. "I don't know, sweetheart. I never asked."

Melissa frowned. "Sounds stupid to me."

Veronica laughed out loud. "You're right, Melissa. That does sound stupid." She closed the ink pad. "Your daddy can wash up now."

Mrs. Winnicot took Melissa's hand. "And you have to wash up, too, young lady. Let's go upstairs." She ushered Melissa out of the room.

Veronica packed her portfolio. "That's two fresh corpses you've seen in thirteen days," she said. "You're not going to make a habit out of this, are you?"

"I hope not. I went into psychiatry because it was the only branch of medicine where I wouldn't have to deal with blood."

She laughed. "This is a very strange book you're working on, Harry."

"I know. And I'm rapidly losing my appetite for it."

We stepped outside and walked toward her car.

"I think your housekeeper disapproves of me."

"It's me she doesn't approve of. She thinks Melissa is getting exposed to too many things a young girl shouldn't have to deal with."

"I like your daughter. She has spirit. Didn't hesitate to challenge me when she thought I posed some danger to you."

"I'm the only parent she has. She's very protective of me."

"Is that why you tried to pull your hand away from me when she came in?"

"I guess so."

"You're sure there wasn't anything more to it?"

"Like what?"

"I don't know. I just thought . . . you seemed suddenly uneasy with me." She tossed her portfolio through the open window of her car. "That last time we were together—I had the feeling you might call me afterward."

"Well, it would've been pretty hard to top our first date for excitement," I joked.

She shrugged her shoulders and opened her car door.

"I thought about calling," I said as she started to get into her car. She stopped and listened. "But it's not something I generally do, what with Melissa and everything."

"She won't let you see other women?"

"It's just . . . I guess I don't know how to go about that sort of thing anymore. It's been a long time."

"You've heard the expression 'like riding a bicycle,' I assume."

"Yeah, well, I was never a very good rider in the first place."

She sat behind the wheel and scribbled a Watertown telephone number onto a piece of scrap paper. "My home phone and my beeper number," she said as she pressed the paper into my palm. "Just in case." She turned her key in the ignition. "I'll return the photograph and the newspaper articles as soon as I can."

"No hurry. Just mail them when you're done with them."

"I'll bring them back myself."

"You don't have to go to that much trouble."

"God, you really are a lousy bicycle rider, aren't you?" She slipped her car into gear. "I'll bring them back myself, Harry. Count on it."

8: Ashes to Ashes

Ellis Greenfield called me early the next morning. I hadn't spoken with him since my visits to his house two weeks earlier.

"How is your book coming?"

"Slowly," I replied. The truth was, I hadn't written a single word. Every time I tried, I thought about dead bodies.

"Are you busy today?" he asked. "I have something important to do and I'd like some company. Someone who knows how to keep a secret. I also have a favor to ask of you."

I didn't have any plans. It was Saturday. Melissa was spending the weekend with her grandparents. My former in-laws and I weren't exactly crazy about each other, but they loved Melissa dearly, and she them. The relationship enabled all of them to keep Janet's memory alive. It helped Melissa feel connected to her past, and allowed Janet's parents to feel that their own daughter's spirit lived on in their grandchild.

"What sort of favor?"

"I'd rather ask you in person," he replied. "If you give me directions to your place, I'll pick you up. Bring along something to protect yourself against the wind and the sun. And Dramamine, if you tend to get seasick."

"Where are we going?"

"To put my daughter to rest."

He picked me up a half hour later. From Concord we

headed east on Route 2, through Lexington and Arlington and into Cambridge. Greenfield drove his late-model sedan along Fresh Pond Parkway, past the entrance for Memorial Drive, and onto Storrow Drive heading into Boston. I didn't know exactly what his plan was, but I knew from his quiet manner that it would be an occasion of purpose and solemnity.

When he turned onto Park Drive, I thought he might be headed to Laurel's apartment. I was surprised when he parked near the Queensbury Street apartment where Beth had lived, and flabbergasted when he let us into the building with a key. We walked up the same flight of stairs I used when I slipped into the building two weeks earlier. On the second floor, we stood outside the door to his daughter's last residence, just as I did previously.

"This is where Beth lived," he said. He slid his key into the lock and swung the door open. A foyer opened on various sides into a bedroom, living room, and kitchen. The apartment was empty except for two chairs in the kitchen and a bare mattress in the bedroom. There were blinds, but no curtains; telephone jacks, but no telephones. There were no rugs, clocks, or pictures—nothing to personalize the empty space in any way.

"I don't understand," I said. "It looks like no one lives here."

"After Beth died, almost two years ago, Mildred and I couldn't bear to go through her belongings. So we left this place as it was for a couple of months, just kept paying the monthly rent. Her lease was up for renewal that September. I told Mildred that I'd get rid of Beth's furniture and clothing, but I couldn't do it. I couldn't bear to clear everything out, knowing that the apartment would go to a stranger and there'd be no trace left of Beth. I renewed the lease that September, and again last September. Mildred doesn't know."

He walked slowly through the entire apartment, stopping now and again as if he were listening to the trace of a sound that only he could hear. He raised the living room blinds, dispersing the dust that had accumulated there; the specks drifted slowly through the air, reflecting the sunlight like hundreds of miniature planets.

"With Gerald Eckler dead and buried," he continued, "it finally seemed fitting to put things here to rest. Last weekend I paid movers to take everything out, told them they could do whatever they wanted with her things. I don't know why they left the chairs and mattress."

He opened the kitchen cupboards, checked to make certain they were empty, then closed them.

"During the past couple of years I came here once in a while, emptied the junk mail from the mailbox, picked up the utility bills, sometimes just sat here and thought. I brought Veronica here once." He paused, perhaps to see how I would respond to that. When I said nothing, he continued. "Except for her, you're the only one I've told."

He walked into the bedroom, reached up to the shelf in the closet, and pulled down an oak box about the size of a brick. "When we dispersed Beth's ashes, I secretly kept some of them. I wasn't ready to let them go, any more than I was ready to let this apartment go. Everything was too unresolved. But this is my last visit here. And today is the day I scatter these ashes."

Janet once told me—long before we had any reason to seriously contemplate her dying—that she wanted to be cremated. But preserving her ashes seemed too ghoulish, and scattering them seemed too final. So we didn't cremate her, and we buried her in Sleepy Hollow Cemetery, a mile from our house. Knowing she was there helped sometimes.

We left the apartment. Greenfield got back onto Storrow Drive, still heading east. We picked up the Central Artery and drove south. Then we traveled down Route 3 toward Cape Cod, winding up at a dock in Wood's Hole. An hour and three-quarters after leaving Beth's apartment, Ellis Greenfield and I were sitting in the sun on the top deck of a ferry bound for Nantucket.

"The island was Beth's favorite place. When we enter Nantucket Harbor, I'll scatter her ashes from the deck. We can stay on the boat and take the next trip back."

We sat silently for most of the two-hour ride. When the

island appeared on the horizon, he asked, "How old are you, Harry?"

"Forty-one."

"Are your parents still living?"

"In a condo outside Miami."

"In good health, I hope."

"Very good," I said, smiling. "They'll probably outlive me."

He winced. "I hope not, for their sake." He shielded his eyes from the sun and gazed at the island in the distance. "I have a theory that each of us can identify the exact moment when he appreciated—truly appreciated in his heart, not just his head—his own mortality. One morning a few weeks before my twenty-seventh birthday, I felt a dull pain in my side. It persisted for a few days, then faded. I'm not worried about it, I told myself, but I would be if I were older. After all, once you reach a certain age you have to carefully weigh the seriousness of each new symptom. Then it struck me—I had just reached that certain age. Otherwise I wouldn't even have thought about it. And I realized that I'd never again be safe from the reality of my own mortality."

I remembered my own moment of truth. My father was exactly twenty-four and a half when I was born. Thus on his forty-ninth birthday, I was exactly twenty-four and a half. Until that day, I'd always been less than half his age. From that day on, I'd always be closer to his age than to my own birth. I'd never catch up to him—not as long as he was alive—but I'd be gaining on him all the time, like an asymptote edging closer and closer to a curve as they stretch toward infinity.

"Beth was twenty-six when she died. Sometimes I wonder if she'd had that experience yet, if she knew—really knew—how limited life is." Ellis Greenfield rubbed his eyes, then scratched at one of the liver spots on the back of his hand. "You have to realize how limited life is before you can understand how precious it is."

The ferry drew closer to the island, then turned to the

east and followed the coast toward its docking point in the town of Nantucket.

"I told you I wanted to ask a favor of you. I want you to tell me everything you remember about Gerald Eckler's death."

I'd honored my promise to Veronica not to tell anyone that she and I witnessed that event. "I only know what I saw in the news," I said.

"I know what time you left Sylvia's house in Belmont. Eckler died no more than a half hour later—and just about a fifteen-minute ride from Sylvia's house. Besides, you visit with the police, with me and my wife, then with our children, you ask all kinds of questions about Beth's murder, and then her killer shows up for the first time in months— dead. Pretty big coincidence, don't you think?" He paused. "Anyway, Veronica told me."

"She told you?"

He nodded. "She told me she was there. She said you were with her. She told me why she left the scene before the police arrived. And she said she thought she could trust you not to tell anyone. Obviously, she was right." He paused. "But since I already know you were there, please— tell me what you saw."

I described everything: Veronica's rescue of me, the reckless chase through Lincoln, the fatal crash, and the death scene. Greenfield closed his eyes while I spoke, as if he were trying to visualize the tableau and commit it to memory.

"How many seconds did he lose control of his car before he came to a stop?"

"Five seconds, maximum."

"Long enough to feel terrified of dying?"

"I suppose so."

"You said you saw his neck twitch. Do you think he knew what was happening at that moment? Did he know he was dying?"

"I'm not sure he was capable of knowing anything at that point."

"Do you think he suffered?"

"I don't know. Probably."

"I hope so. God forgive me, I hope so."

When we reached the lip of the harbor, the other passengers on the top deck walked to the rail closest to the dock. Greenfield and I walked toward the other side. The open horizon stretched out before us. "Wait here for a minute, Harry, please."

Greenfield walked alone ten yards farther along the rail. He pulled the oak box out of his jacket pocket and stared out at the Atlantic. I saw his lips move, but I couldn't hear what he said. He opened the box, held it over the rail, and turned it upside down. A small clump of grayish-white ashes was scattered immediately by the strong sea breeze.

I was standing downwind. A few flakes brushed against my cheeks, and my whole face felt cold. I remembered the photograph in the Greenfields' den: Beth standing on the deck of a sailboat, her red hair blowing in the same Nantucket breeze, her beauty frozen for eternity by the lens of the camera.

9: A Very Fresh Kill

Our chilly spell finally broke early in May. That week Melissa and I tended the garden; we went for a long walk in the woods by Walden Pond; we rode our bikes into Lexington and back, tracing the path the British took between that town and ours more than two hundred years ago.

On a Friday night we went to Fenway Park and watched Roger Clemens pitch a three-hit shutout over Baltimore. A friend with season tickets offered me his box seats for the game, but Melissa preferred the excitement of the right field bleachers: beach balls being batted around in the stands, security guards ejecting rowdy drunks, contests between patrons to see who could curse loudest, longest, and most creatively.

The next morning—the day before Mother's Day—we walked to Sleepy Hollow Cemetery and placed flowers on Janet's grave. When we went there five years earlier, on the first Mother's Day after Janet's death, there were dozens of other people making similar pilgrimages. "Let's come early the next time," my then-four-year-old daughter said that day. "Mommy needs quiet to hear us from down in the ground." We'd been coming a day early ever since.

She didn't speak of Janet in the present tense anymore. The years spent without her mother now outnumbered the years spent with her. But sometimes I would hear Melissa stir in the middle of the night, and in the morning I would find her sleeping with her picture of Janet cradled in her arms.

I ran my fingers over the chiseled letters of Janet's name, and a dozen scenes from our shared years passed through my mind.

We left Janet's grave and walked toward the far end of the cemetery, up a steep incline to the section known as Authors Ridge. There lay Louisa May Alcott, along with Emerson, Thoreau, and Hawthorne.

"Maybe they'll bury you here, Daddy."

"No, I'll be buried down there, next to your mother."

"Even if you get married again?"

"I'm not getting married again."

"Will I be buried with you and Mommy?"

"No, sweetheart. When it's time for you to be buried—a long, long, long time from now—you'll be buried with your husband."

"But if you don't get married, I won't either. I'll stay with you so you won't be lonely."

"I won't be lonely. I'll always carry you in my heart, no matter where you are."

"Do you still carry Mommy in your heart?"

A collage of scenes from my life with Janet passed before my mind's eye in an instant. "Yes, I do."

"I do, too." She rolled her hand into a fist and held it up for me to see. "My heart is only this big, but it has room inside to carry both of you. I think you can still love someone after they're not alive anymore."

There were moments when my daughter seemed like some alien being, possessed of intelligence and sensibilities far beyond her chronological age or genetic heritage. In those moments I felt not just boundless love, but humility and awe as well.

We left the cemetery and walked along Monument Street toward North Bridge and our home. When we approached our driveway, Melissa ran ahead and pulled the mail from our roadside box. In singsong cadence, she called out, "I have the mail, you can't catch me. I have the mail, you can't catch me." Then she ran toward the house.

I let her gain some ground on me, then took off after her. She ran clockwise around the house toward the back door. I went around the other way and caught her near the path between the main house and Mrs. Winnicot's apartment. I swooped her into my arms and we both laughed long and hard. She handed me the mail and skipped off to play. As I watched her go, I thought: I will never, ever let anything bad happen to you again.

I dropped the mail on the kitchen table. Amidst the bills and circulars was a very large envelope from Morgan Books. Inside were several unopened pieces of correspondence that had been forwarded by my editor's secretary. The largest of those envelopes was marked "Do Not Fold" and was reinforced on the inside by cardboard. It had a New York City postmark and no return address, and my name was printed in sharply tilted characters that I'd seen once before. I opened the envelope and a one-page letter dropped out; I reached inside and pulled out two pieces of thin cardboard sandwiched around an eight-by-ten glossy black-and-white photograph.

Maria Melendez looked just as I remembered. Her naked body lay faceup on the cold, hard tile of the bathroom floor, her limbs and severed head bent at awkward angles to her body. There was something out of place, though—some subtle difference between the scene I'd witnessed and the one captured on the sheet in front of me—but my sudden nausea and trembling hands kept me from examining the picture long enough to discern what that difference was.

I picked up the letter and read:

MAY 2, 1992

TWO DOWN AND TWO TO GO. I TOLD YOU I WOULD BE IN YOUR "NECK" OF THE WOODS ON APRIL 30. HAVE THEY FIGURED OUT HER TRUE NAME YET?

THE SECOND TIME FOR ANYTHING IS USU-ALLY EASIER THAN THE FIRST. SO IT WAS HERE. PERHAPS WOMEN ARE ALWAYS EASIER THAN

MEN: NO ADAM'S APPLE. I WILL FIND OUT SOON ENOUGH.

IT WAS ALSO EASIER CONVINCING HER TO DISROBE. AFTER ALL, THAT WAS PART OF HER JOB DESCRIPTION. PRIESTS ARE EXPECTED TO REMAIN COVERED AT ALL TIMES.

I ASSUME THEY CHECKED HER FOR SIGNS OF ENTRY, FORCED OR OTHERWISE. THERE WERE NONE, I ASSURE YOU. I WAS THERE FOR BUSINESS, NOT PLEASURE. I TAKE NO PLEASURE IN KILLING, ONLY IN MAKING MY VICTIMS SUFFER. I UNDERSTAND MY FIRST VICTIM DIED: GOD IS GOOD, GOD IS GREAT. THE BATTLE GOES WELL.

YOU KNOW HOW WE FEEL, THOSE OF US WHO UNFORTUNATELY MUST KILL INNOCENTS IN THE COURSE OF THE BATTLE. THE SECOND ONE ASKED ME WHY, AND I TOLD HER, AND SHE SAID IT WAS NOT FAIR, AND I AGREED. I SAID, "YOU PERISH FOR THE SIN OF CARELESSNESS."

I WORKED QUICKLY IN ORDER TO MINIMIZE HER SUFFERING. "CLOSE YOUR EYES," I SAID. "PRETEND YOU ARE DANCING."

I SAW YOUR PICTURE IN THE PAPER THE NEXT MORNING. WHEN I SELECTED YOU AS MY OFFICIAL CHRONICLER, I HAD NO IDEA YOU WOULD BE ON THE CASE SO QUICKLY. "UNIDENTIFIED ASSISTANT," THE PAPER SAID. IT WAS WISE NOT TO REVEAL YOUR NAME: YOU ALWAYS HAVE MORE OPTIONS WHEN THEY DO NOT KNOW WHO YOU ARE OR WHAT YOUR MOTIVES ARE.

TWO DOWN AND TWO TO GO. ON MAY 20, IN A PLACE DEDICATED TO HEALING, SO CLOSE I CAN ALMOST SMELL THE ANTISEPTIC FROM HERE, I WILL AVENGE THE SIN OF INCOMPETENCE.

THE FINAL DANCE COMES SOON AFTER THAT,

RETRIBUTION FOR THE WORST SIN OF ALL: DIS-
HONESTY. WE WILL HAVE TO MOVE QUICKLY,
YOU AND I.

                                        YOURS,
                                        ARTIE

I cast my eyes over the photograph once more, and I realized how it differed from the scene I remembered. By the
time I arrived at the murder site, a heavy flow of thick,
half-dried blood had spread over the woman's face and
across the floor. But in the picture, there was only a small
puddle by the side of her head.

The picture had been taken before anyone else arrived on
the scene.

I was looking at a very fresh kill.

10: Making Other Plans

The early morning sun reflected off the Charles River as I drove east across Cambridge on Memorial Drive. Sunday morning joggers and strollers were making their way along the path by the water. As I passed Harvard I noticed a young couple walking arm in arm. They paused for a moment and kissed, then laughed and continued walking, each folded in the other's partial embrace.

A dozen years earlier Janet and I walked that very path, planning our upcoming wedding and our future with one another. I imagined the couple that passed before me making those same plans: how they would marry, have a family, and grow happy and old together. I doubted they were planning for one of them to die at age thirty-two, leaving the other behind with a child to raise: lost, alone, and damaged beyond words.

"This isn't what we planned," I said one evening as Janet lay wasting away in a bed on the cancer ward at Mass General Hospital. "This isn't the life we planned at all."

She smiled wanly. "Life is what happens while you're busy making other plans."

I drove on, past the Central Square turnoff and MIT, across the Longfellow Bridge and into Boston. The city streets were nearly deserted. I found a parking space directly across the street from the JFK Federal Office Building in Government Center.

Veronica Pace met me in the reception area on the ninth

floor of the nondescript high-rise. "Happy Mother's Day," she said, then winced. "I'm sorry. A dumb joke. I wasn't thinking."

Janet and I celebrated our first Mother's Day when Melissa was still in utero. Our then-unnamed daughter was thrashing like a wildcat that morning, churning through amniotic fluid, sending a series of ripples across Janet's swollen belly. The more she tumbled, the harder we laughed; the more we laughed, the harder she tumbled. We were already a family, and we would stay that way forever. That was the plan.

Veronica escorted me to a small, Spartan office that overlooked the Suffolk County courthouse. "Did you bring the letters?" she asked.

I removed a folder from my briefcase and emptied its contents onto her desk: two envelopes with New York City postmarks, each one containing a letter from the killer who placed pennies in the hands of his beheaded victims. One also contained the picture of Maria Melendez, the dead woman at the Lafayette Hotel.

Veronica used tweezers to unfold the letters, careful not to disturb any fingerprints or to add any of her own. She placed the letters side by side. She read one in its entirety, then the other. Then she took five empty Ziploc bags from her desk drawer, one for each letter, one for each envelope, and one for the snapshot of the killer's latest victim. She left the letters unfolded when she placed them in the bags so that they could be read through the clear plastic. She also had the photograph of the priest that I'd given her nine days earlier.

After a brief stop at a Xerox machine, we rode the elevator two flights up. When the elevator doors opened on the eleventh floor, I saw a muscular man sitting behind a desk in the corridor with his arms folded across his chest. The butt of a pistol stuck out from a holster inside his suit jacket. He glanced at Veronica, then studied me from head to toe.

"We're here to see the boss," Veronica said.

"I know. He stepped out for a minute. He said you should wait in his office."

At the end of the hallway was a corner office with a nameplate that identified the occupant as Martin Baines, Special Agent in Charge. One large window opened onto City Hall plaza; the other overlooked Faneuil Hall and Quincy Market. The walls were lined with various diplomas, certificates, and photographs.

One particular picture caught my eye: An elderly J. Edgar Hoover stood behind a desk, his gnarled and beady visage glaring directly at the camera. He seemed to tower over the two taller men flanking him, an optical illusion brought on by the power of his presence. On his left was the late John Mitchell, Attorney General under Nixon and eventual Watergate felon. On Hoover's right was a thin young man with closely cropped hair and a pencil-thin mustache.

"Those were the good old days," a voice behind me said.

When I turned, the third man in the photograph was standing beside Veronica. The mustache was gone, and there were a few splashes of gray in his hair, but otherwise Martin Baines looked just as he had twenty years earlier. He was taller than me, and his height was accentuated by his wiry build and erect bearing.

Baines was dressed casually. His sleeves were rolled neatly and evenly just below his elbows. We shook hands when Veronica introduced us, and I noticed several small patches of scar tissue on his right forearm. They were circular, each one about a quarter-inch in diameter, and they were neatly arranged in a semicircle a few inches above his wrist. I'd seen something like that once before: A Special Forces veteran I interviewed at the VA hospital had a similar arrangement of scars where a Viet Cong interrogator had burned him methodically with a lit cigarette.

Baines saw me take notice of the scars and nodded briefly as if acknowledging a shared secret. Then he pointed at the photograph that had caught my attention. "Mr. Mitchell was the head of the Justice Department at that time, so he was the Director's boss," he said. "Officially, that is. But no one could keep Mr. Hoover from doing something he wanted to do."

"So I've heard. Not a very reassuring thought."

He sighed. "Well, different methods for different times. Back then my mustache made me quite the radical within the Bureau. And now," he said, gesturing toward Veronica, "we even have women." He laughed.

Veronica said, "I'm sorry to drag you into the office on a Sunday."

Baines dismissed her apology with a wave of his hand. "I should be thanking you. I was supposed to spend the whole day with my wife's mother." He directed us to a conference table at one end of his office. "Veronica has told me about your correspondent, Harry. Let's take a look at his letters."

Veronica gave him copies of the killer's letters. She placed the photographs in the middle of the table.

"By the way, Harry," said Baines, "why did you bring all of this to Veronica?"

I shrugged my shoulders. "Two murders, two different states. It seemed like something I should notify the FBI about."

"I understand that. But why Veronica?"

As I fumbled for a response, Veronica spoke. "We have a mutual acquaintance."

"Who?"

"Ellis Greenfield."

"The lawyer?"

She nodded. "He was one of my professors at Harvard."

"How do you know him, Harry?"

"I, uh, I've done some work for him. And his family."

"I see," Baines said.

"It's confidential, of course," I said after a few seconds of awkward silence.

"Confidential," he repeated. "Of course."

That seemed to satisfy him for the moment, or at least I hoped it would. For Veronica's sake, I didn't want him to guess about her unsanctioned involvement in the investigation into Beth Greenfield's murder.

Martin Baines unfolded a pair of reading glasses and placed them midway up the bridge of his nose. He perused the letters without a sound. His impassive expression gave nothing away. Were we sitting at a poker table, Baines could have held either a straight flush or total garbage without tipping his hand.

"Let me see if I understand this," he said. "This fellow kills his first victim in Philadelphia last October 12th. Then on April 13th a messenger hand-delivers a photo of the corpse to your editor, Jeffrey Barrow. Are you certain of that?"

"Yes. I remember the date because I was interviewed on television that morning, and then I—"

"Wait a minute—you don't understand. I'm not asking if you're certain of the date. I'm asking if you're certain the picture was delivered to him, that he didn't already have it in his possession or get it in some other way."

"How else would he get it?" It took a few seconds for what he was implying to sink in. "Jesus. Are you trying to say you think it might belong to Jeffrey? That he was the photographer?"

"Relax. I'm not trying to say anything. I'm just asking questions right now. How do you know a messenger delivered it to his office that day?"

The question had never occurred to me; I was beginning to mull it over when Veronica said, "We checked with Jeffrey Barrow's secretary. She couldn't remember whether she saw it delivered or whether she found it on her desk after her coffee break that morning."

"Did she get an invoice?" Baines asked.

"If she did, she didn't hold onto it."

"Any fingerprints?"

"On the picture itself, we just found Harry's and Jeffrey Barrow's. On the envelope, it was Harry, Barrow, and Barrow's secretary."

"You'd think the messenger would've left a print on the envelope," Baines said.

"Unless he didn't want to," Veronica replied.

"Maybe he was wearing gloves," I suggested.

Baines said, "In the middle of April? Possible, not probable."

"Bicycle gloves," I said. "A lot of messengers get around by bike in New York."

"Perhaps." Martin Baines aligned his copies of the letters side by side and adjusted his reading glasses. "You say you got the first letter in the mail a few days after you got the first photo. Let's have another look at it."

He read the letter aloud, very slowly. His tone was flat and neutral, in marked contrast to the bizarre content of the words he recited.

" 'I watched you on TV with Bryant Gumbel earlier today. You might call it "professional interest," seeing as how we met a number of years ago in the course of your work.

" 'Other doctors have tried (and failed) to relieve me from my grief, but for me there is no rescue.

" 'But you know how we feel, those of us who unfortunately must kill innocents in the course of the battle. The first one asked me why, and I told him, and he said it was not fair, and I agreed. I said, "You perish for the sin of recklessness."

" 'I worked quickly in order to minimize his suffering. "Close your eyes," I said. "Pretend you are dancing."

" 'One down and three to go. Next comes the sin of carelessness. On April 30 I will be in your neck of the woods for number two.

" 'I will tell you more as I continue the battle. Then you can be my official chronicler.

" 'Yours, Artie.' "

I thought back to the night when I read that letter for the first time. I'd just returned home from my initial meeting with Ellis and Mildred Greenfield. The packet of letters awaiting me contained the angry note from Edward Billingham, the father of one of Karl Fenner's victims. I felt so ashamed after I read Billingham's letter that I barely paid attention to the one from the man who called himself Artie; I dismissed it as the harmless ranting of a war-torn emotional invalid. I made no connection between that letter and the photograph of the priest I'd gotten earlier in the week. And I certainly didn't identify the writer as a killer. Listening to Baines read that letter now, I wondered how I'd missed that.

Baines must have realized what I was thinking, because he said, "Hindsight can be a lousy thing, Harry." I didn't know what to say. Veronica shuffled her feet on the floor. "So the killer strikes again in Boston on April 30th. You recognize the similarities between the two murders, and you give this picture to Veronica." He pointed at the snapshot of Father Joseph Carroll's corpse. "Then yesterday you received another letter and the picture of Maria Melendez's corpse."

Baines read from the second letter.

" 'Two down and two to go. I told you I would be in your "neck" of the woods on April 30. Have they figured out her true name yet?' "

I'd read both letters countless times since the previous afternoon, so I wasn't expecting any surprises when Baines began his recitation. But his reading was chilling: Crisp, calm, and devoid of histrionics, his voice was like a crystal-clear glass that framed the killer's words, letting them pass through without distortion.

" 'The second one asked me why, and I told her, and she said it was not fair, and I agreed. I said, "You perish for the sin of carelessness." ' "

He paused for a moment.

" 'On May 20, in a place dedicated to healing, so close I can almost smell the antiseptic from here, I will avenge the sin of incompetence.

" 'The final dance comes soon after that, retribution for the worst sin of all: dishonesty. We will have to move quickly, you and I.

" 'Yours, Artie.' "

Martin Baines leaned back in his chair. Deep in thought, he placed the fingertips of one hand against those of the other, forming the shape of a steeple, and touched them to his face. " 'Two down and two to go.' I don't see any reason to doubt that the writer is who he says he is—the person who committed both of these murders. So I take him at his word when he tells us he's planning two more."

"May 20th is a week from Wednesday," Veronica said. "That doesn't give us much time."

"I know." He paused. "We either have to identify Artie quickly, or we have to discover who he intends to kill next so we can intercede. Uncover some connection between the two people he's already killed, and then figure out who else is linked to them. It's a long shot."

I asked, "Does this mean the FBI is taking over this case?"

"We don't work that way. Boston Homicide has the Melendez case, Philadelphia has the Carroll murder. Officially, all we can do is advise or provide technical assistance—if they want us to."

Veronica said, "I already spoke with Tim Connolly. He'll be grateful for any help we can give him. He hasn't even been able to locate the dead woman's family yet. And he can't find any reports of a missing person by the name of Maria Melendez. That line in the second letter—'Have they figured out her true name yet?'—makes me think that Maria Melendez was an alias, and that the killer knew that."

She continued. "Philadelphia isn't quite so happy to have our help. I talked to John Riley, the detective in charge of that case. He wasn't very forthcoming. He's from the old school. Doesn't like anyone interfering on his turf. He hasn't even filed a VICAP report."

Baines explained for my benefit. "VICAP stands for Violent Criminal Apprehension Program. The Bureau runs it out of its training academy in Quantico. They collect police reports on unusual murders, help the local departments develop psychological profiles of persons who might be involved in certain crimes, those sorts of things."

"You said you can only advise Riley if he wants your help."

"Officially, yes." He glanced at the picture of J. Edgar Hoover and nodded. "Unofficially, we can do any damn thing we please. No one can stop us from looking into the case on our own. Veronica, talk to Riley again, and tell him he'll be looking at an obstruction of justice charge if he doesn't suddenly become more cooperative."

"It would never stand up in court," she replied.

"I realize that. And so will he, probably. But he'll also realize we can give him one hell of a publicity headache if we let the press know how uncooperative he's being. Make the threat, Veronica. He'll get his ass in gear."

Martin Baines was clearly accustomed to getting his way, and he was willing to bend rules if he had to. It was better to have him fighting with you than fighting against you.

Baines continued. "From the postmarks, and the fact that the first picture was hand-delivered to Morgan Books, our best bet is that he lives in New York City. He says his next killing will happen in a place dedicated to healing, so close to where he is that he can smell the antiseptic. That sounds like a hospital."

"There are a lot of hospitals in New York," I noted.

Veronica said, "We can give copies of the envelopes to our New York office and see if they can identify the postal station where the letters were canceled. That might help us get a fix on his location, narrow down the hospital list."

Baines pointed at the letters. "Harry, what do you think of this fellow?"

I told them I thought Artie's letters were quite unusual. On one hand, his abilities to plan and organize his behavior seemed intact. On the other hand, there were signs of substantial mental confusion. "For example," I said, "he says he's killing innocent people in the course of battle. But how can they be innocent if they're being punished for these sins he says they've committed? Something is obviously wrong with his thinking there."

"Go on."

"He says he tries to minimize his victims' suffering. But in almost the same breath, he says he takes pleasure in making his victims suffer. That doesn't make sense, either."

"Anything else?"

"Here in the second letter, where he says, 'I understand my first victim died.' He cut the man's head off, and here he is acting as though he learned after the fact that his vic-

tim died. Which implies the belief that his victim might
have survived the killing, even though he was beheaded.
That's a good sign of just how disturbed this man is. And
dangerous."

"What do you think is wrong with him?"

"Well, the psychotic thinking, the lapses in logic and reality testing—all of that could indicate schizophrenia. Or he
could be undergoing a severe depression, so bad that it im-
pairs his contact with reality. I'm thinking of that line
where he says doctors have tried to relieve him from his
grief, but that there's no rescue for him. But someone with
that sort of depression wouldn't be planning his moves
months in advance. Or he could have a rare type of seizure
disorder, one that causes personality changes even when the
person is between seizure episodes."

Veronica jotted a few notes on a pad of legal paper. Martin Baines sat quietly, considering my words with the same
impassivity with which he'd read the killer's letters.

"Finally," I said, "there's the distinct possibility that everything I just said is a bunch of crap. There's no way you
can diagnose someone solely from his writings. He could
be making this up, trying to look sick, when all the while
he may have the clearest, sanest reasons in the world for
killing these people."

Baines took his reading glasses off. "He wants you to be
his official chronicler. What do you make of that?"

I shrugged. "He thinks he's on a mission, maybe a divine
one. He's dispensing an odd sort of justice and he thinks
it's important for the world to know about. I guess he wants
someone to write about it, and he picked me because he's
familiar with the work I do and the things I write about."

"Another satisfied reader," Veronica said. "Maybe you
can get him to write an endorsement for the cover of your
next book."

I tried to ignore her jibe. "It's almost as if he wants me
to provide him with some sort of immortality for what he's
done."

" 'Men seek immortality through their deeds,' " Baines
said, " 'and women, through their loves.' "

"Who said that?" asked Veronica.

"I don't remember."

I added, "Trite as it sounds, maybe part of him wants to be caught. You know, 'Stop me before I kill again.' Maybe that part of him hopes his letters will result in his arrest."

Baines smiled for the first time. "You've been watching too many police dramas."

Veronica placed the tip of her pen against her lips and thought for a moment. "He says he met you during the course of your work. He remembers you, Harry. The question is—do you remember him?"

"No."

"Veronica tells me you used to work at a Veterans Administration hospital. Do you suppose that's where he met you?"

"That's my guess. I was at the Bedford VA for about six years. That line about killing innocents in battle—I figure he must be a combat veteran who was at the hospital during my tenure there. But I have no idea who."

"Have you worked anywhere else?" Baines asked.

"Not really. Just my residency at McLean Hospital in Belmont. Since I left the VA, I've done some consulting and some supervising and teaching. But mostly I write and see patients in my home office."

Baines nodded. "I agree the best bet is a patient from the VA. But I wouldn't rule anything out at this point, Harry— McLean, a former patient in your private practice. Someone who knows you—or feels like he knows you—is involved in something pretty horrible. And like it or not, now you're involved, too. I assume you've tried to remember if you ever treated someone named Artie."

I nodded. "Or Elmore Winston."

"Elmore Winston?"

Veronica explained. "That's the name the killer used when he registered at the Lafayette Hotel. I'm sure it's not his real identity. Only a fool would use his own name to take a hotel room he plans to use for murder."

I said, "I don't think this man is a fool."

Martin Baines leaned back in his chair and gazed out his picture window. "No," he said. "Neither do I."

After dinner that evening Melissa and I walked into the center of town for ice cream at Brigham's. It was a Sunday tradition in our home, going back to the days when Melissa was too young to make the trip without being carried. Continuing that tradition after Janet died was painful, but ending it would have been even more difficult.

We walked past the centuries-old homes that lined Monument Street. Some of them had been passed from generation to generation since before the Revolution. One house even displayed a small hole that was made by an errant musket ball during the 1775 skirmish at North Bridge between the Minutemen and the British; the hole was covered by a plate of glass, preserved for generations to come.

Melissa and I ordered double-scoop cones of vanilla fudge at Brigham's. As we headed toward the door with our ice cream, two friends entered the shop with their toddler daughter. Phil was a few years older than me, Cindy my age or a little younger. They had struggled for many years to conceive a child, finally succeeding at an age when most parents are preparing to send their children out to raise families of their own. Watching Phil and Cindy walk hand-in-hand with little Holly, I longed for that earlier, sweeter time in my own life, when Janet, Melissa, and I made that same walk.

We stopped to say hello. Holly smiled at Melissa, grabbed her leg, and uttered a two-syllable approximation of her name. Melissa reached down to stroke the little girl's hair.

Cindy said, "She really likes you, Melissa."

Just then Holly released Melissa's leg, turned around, and burrowed her face into her mother's skirt. "Mommy."

"Holly and I are treating Cindy to a Mother's Day chocolate sundae," Phil said.

There were a few seconds of awkward silence, which Melissa broke by asking how their dog was. She and I watched him when Phil and Cindy were at the hospital giving birth to Holly. Melissa enjoyed taking care of him, and afterwards I offered to get a dog or a cat or any other pet she wanted. But she refused. "Pets die," she said.

Our friends headed toward the ice cream fountain and Melissa and I walked outside. We retraced our steps up Main Street, past the flagpole and the grassy ellipse in the center of town, and back to Monument Street. After a few minutes I said, "Do you remember meeting Veronica Pace?"

She shrugged her shoulders, which could have meant "No," or "I want to hear more before I say anything," or "I don't want to hear any more about it."

"You met her a little over a week ago," I continued. "She was with me in the kitchen."

"The FBI lady," she said, more a statement than a question.

"That's right, the FBI lady. Well, she wants me to help her with something important. There's a very sick man who's been hurting people, but nobody knows who he is. The FBI has some clues, and Veronica thinks I may be able to help them figure out who he is."

"Because you're a psychiatrist."

"Right. So I may have to go on a trip with her for a few days to help her look for more clues."

"Where?"

"Philadelphia and New York. Maybe some other places, too."

"Can I come?"

I could count on one hand the number of times my daughter and I had slept under separate roofs since Janet died five years earlier. "I don't want you to miss any school," I said.

Melissa stopped in her tracks and asked, "Is she your girlfriend?"

"Is she my . . . No, no, that's not what this is about." I thought I saw a hint of relief flash across my daughter's face. "She needs my help, that's all."

We continued walking toward our home. After several moments, she said, "I don't think I like her, Daddy."

Before I could think of a reply, a Toyota station wagon passed by and pulled to the side of the road just ahead of us. Cindy stepped out of the front passenger seat. "Melissa, Holly has a present for you." She opened the rear door and lifted her daughter out of her car seat. The little girl handed Melissa a tiny picture of her mother and herself, one of those one-inch square photos that come as part of a department store portrait package.

"Thank you, Holly." Melissa put the photograph in her pocket. "I'll keep it in my bedroom, right next to the picture of my mother."

Cindy kneeled, placing herself at Melissa's eye level. She reached out for my daughter's hand. "Melissa, you can come visit us anytime you'd like. If you want to play with Holly, or take our dog for a walk, or just to keep me company—anytime you want to, you can call me. Even if you just want to talk on the phone when you feel lonely, that's okay. I get lonely, too, sometimes."

Cindy leaned forward and kissed Melissa on the forehead. Melissa lunged toward her and held onto her tightly for several seconds.

"It's okay, baby, it's okay." Melissa released the woman and stepped back. A tear trickled down one side of my daughter's face. "You're a good girl, Melissa, you really are."

Our friends got back into their car and drove away.

Melissa and I resumed our walk home. I reached for her hand, but she pulled hers away and stuck it in her pocket.

"Do you want to talk about it?" I asked.

"No!"

A minute or two later Melissa grabbed my hand and squeezed it. "I'm sorry, Daddy."

"You didn't do anything wrong, sweetheart."

We walked the rest of the way home in silence.

11: You Owe Me

"Mr. Barrow's office. How may I help you?"

"Hello, Gwen. It's Harry Kline."

"Sweetie, how are you?"

This call was Veronica's idea. She sat behind her desk and listened on an extension phone while I spoke with my editor's secretary.

"Gwen, you'll be getting a visit today from a New York FBI agent. One of the letters you forwarded to me contained an anonymous murder confession. I notified the FBI, and they think the letter is for real. They've asked my permission to intercept all the mail that gets sent to me in care of Morgan Books."

After a brief silence, Gwen said, "Oh. So you're the one."

"The one what?"

"An FBI agent came here a few days ago and requested fingerprints from me. He said one of our authors—he wouldn't tell me which one—received a death threat in a letter that I forwarded. Funny, but he didn't say anything about a murder confession. Anyway, he said there were fingerprints on the envelope and he wanted to see which ones were mine and which ones belonged to the person who wrote the letter. And then he asked me not to tell anyone about it, even Jeffrey." She paused. "To tell you the truth, it was all rather embarrassing. I was glad Jeffrey was out of the office."

I said, "They didn't take his prints?" Veronica glared at me. She ran a finger from one side of her neck to the other, signaling me to cut the conversation.

"No. He was away all last week. Anyway, why would they? I'm the one who handles the letters and sends them to you. His fingerprints wouldn't be on them. So tell me about it—what murder did he admit to? And why did he confess to you?"

Veronica again made the cutting motion across her neck.

"They asked me not to talk about this with anyone," I replied. "They were pretty insistent on that."

"So—you didn't really receive a murder threat?"

"No. The agent you saw must've been confused. No death threat."

"Well, that's good. Jeffrey would hate to lose a cash cow."

"You never know, Gwen—it could be good for sales. Jeffrey might appreciate that."

"Just the same, you take care of yourself, sweetie."

I placed the phone in its cradle and wheeled around to face Veronica. "What the hell is going on? Why was Gwen told I received a death threat? How did you get Jeffrey's fingerprints?"

She stood and picked up her purse and leather portfolio. "We're running late. We can talk about this on our way to the courthouse."

I grabbed her wrist as she headed toward the door. "I want to talk about it now."

Slowly she lowered her eyes and stared at my hand on her wrist. I remembered how easily she disabled my grip that night in her car after Gerald Eckler's fatal crash. Her voice was calm and cold now as she said, "I told you, we can talk about it on our way."

I released my grip and followed her out the door. We took an elevator to the lobby and exited the building, heading for the nearby Suffolk County courthouse. Detective Timothy Connolly was waiting there. He'd called Veronica an hour earlier, before I arrived in her office, to tell her that Maria Melendez's pimp was due to appear in court.

Connolly planned on asking him some questions, and he'd invited Veronica to join him.

As we crossed Tremont Street, I repeated, "How did you get Jeffrey's fingerprints?"

"Army records."

"Why? Why not just ask him, like you did with Gwen?"

"The less anyone knows, the better. There isn't much time to work with, and I don't want any distractions—like your editor going to the press with this story to generate a little more publicity for your books. If I could've found a less direct way to get the secretary's prints, too, I would have. And if I had a way to intercept any more letters from Artie without involving the secretary, I would."

"Why did your man in New York make up that story about me receiving a death threat?"

"He probably just made up an excuse to get the secretary's cooperation, one that wouldn't make mention of the picture so that it wouldn't be obvious we were talking about you. Like I said, the less anyone knows about this, the more I like it."

"Well, I'm not happy about lying to her. I don't see the reason for it. The more that occurs, the less I like it."

We walked a half block up Somerset Street until we came to the courthouse, then circled around toward the main entrance. I said, "There's something else you're not telling me."

"And just what would that be?"

"You and your boss suspect Jeffrey, don't you?"

"I haven't ruled anyone out."

"Damn it, Veronica. Answer me!"

She stopped in her tracks and turned to face me. "How much do you know about Jeffrey Barrow?"

I tried to remember things I'd read and learned about him over the years. "He used to manage a chain of tabloid newspapers. Morgan Books brought him in to pump life into the company. He's been a roaring success as far as that goes."

"And how would you describe him?"

I thought about it for a moment. "Intelligent. Strong-willed."

"Arrogant?"

"Sometimes."

"Ruthless?"

"Perhaps. Depends on who you talk to. So what?"

"I told you I got his fingerprints from his Army records. Would you like to know what else I found there?"

"What?"

"Saigon, 1967. A teenage girl was hacked to death with a machete. Jeffrey Barrow and two of his pals were suspected of the killing."

"Suspected."

"Right."

"Were any charges brought against him?"

"No."

"No court-martial, no dishonorable discharge?"

"Not on him. Not on any of them. After all, she was *only* a South Vietnamese whore. No big deal, right?"

"Anything else in his Army record?"

She sighed. "No."

"How about after the Army, since I'm sure you've already begun checking him out. Any major bloodlettings associated with him?"

"Only of a corporate nature."

"Embezzlement, perhaps, or larceny? Tax evasion? Maybe some unpaid parking tickets?"

"I don't find this very funny, Harry."

"Neither do I."

We stood in front of the courthouse, a few yards from the main doorway. The work week was just beginning, and dozens of people went streaming past us.

"Let's get something straight," I said. "You want my help to track him down—Artie, or Elmore Winston, or whatever his name is. And you're calling the shots. But I don't want any more surprises. I want to know what's going on. And if you want me to tell lies, you'd better give me a good reason first. Now—who else do you have on your list of suspects?"

A trace of a smile began to curl her lips. "I've pretty much crossed you off," she said.

"Well, that's just great. And to what do I owe that?"

"Oh, I don't know. Maybe it was how sick to your stomach you got when you saw Eckler's corpse, or how considerate you were of Ellis Greenfield and his wife." Her grin broadened. "Or maybe it's because last October 12th, the day Joseph Carroll was murdered in Philadelphia, you were in San Francisco giving a speech at the annual meeting of the California Psychiatric Society."

"How do you know that?"

"When I came to your house, I looked in your appointment book while you were out of your office getting me a glass of water. I saw you'd been scheduled to speak at that meeting."

"How do you know I actually went there?"

"Airline records, credit card receipts." She shrugged her shoulders. "These things aren't hard to discover, once you know what you're looking for. You flew out on Delta, stayed at the Mark Hopkins Hotel. As best as I can tell, you ate, drank, and slept alone."

The thought of someone rummaging uninvited through my private appointment book—through my life—infuriated me. "What else have you discovered about me?"

She laughed. "Nothing relevant to this case."

I was dumbfounded. All I could think to say was, "How goddamn thorough of you." I turned and began to walk away from her.

"Harry—wait." Veronica ran after me and spun me around by my arm. "I'm sorry, I really am. But just remember—in nine days, your friend Artie is going to kill someone else. I don't want you to hate me, but even if you do, I still need you to help me. Please." She paused. "Besides, you owe me."

She was right about that, of course. It's not every day that someone saves your life.

"No more surprises?" I said.

"No. I swear, no more surprises." She held out her hand. "Truce?"

I hesitated for several seconds, then shook her hand. "Truce," I said.

We walked into the courthouse and passed through a metal detector. Only three of the building's eight elevators were in working order; we took one of them to the fourth floor.

The interior of the courthouse was as dreary and oppressive as that of any building I'd ever visited. The corridors were narrow and dimly lit, with walls that hadn't been painted or even washed in years. A quarter of the fluorescent lights were dead; others flickered with an intensity that could trigger a seizure. Glancing into some of the offices, I saw grime-layered windows that turned the sunny spring morning into a gray and gloomy day.

The fourth floor hallways were packed with at least a hundred people waiting to file into the courtrooms. A dense haze of cigarette smoke hung in the air, like fog from a warm-weather inversion that might not lift for hours. Clerks and court officers shuffled through the hallway like automated windup toys.

There were a dozen young women—girls, actually—congregating in groups of three or four. They were pale and weathered, and they were dressed in tightly clinging low-cut Spandex outfits.

"Defendants," Veronica said when she saw me noticing them. "Streetwalking cases. Some will get dismissed today for insufficient evidence or lack of prosecution. A few will get continued to another date, when they'll probably be dismissed as well. A few others might get fined, and one or two will be continued without a finding on the condition that they enter a drug treatment program, which they most likely won't follow through with. That's what this is all about—turning tricks to get money for drugs, usually cocaine. It's the drugs you see on their faces."

We entered a large courtroom. Several clerks, court officers, and attorneys were waiting for the judge to appear. A few dozen people—defendants, witnesses, and miscellaneous visitors—sat on rows of benches in the spectators' gallery.

Detective Timothy Connolly was standing against the wall near the front of the room. Connolly was expecting Veronica, but he was surprised to see me. "Hey, Doc—what are you doing here?"

Veronica explained. "Harry brought me some evidence about the Melendez case over the weekend. A letter from the killer. Two letters, actually."

She pulled copies of the letters from her portfolio and handed them to Connolly. As he read them he began to mutter "Holy shit" over and over.

"And there's this, too." Veronica gave him a copy of the photograph of Maria Melendez. "It came with the second letter."

Connolly studied the picture for several seconds. He shook his head, then folded the letters and placed them in the pocket of his sport jacket. He gestured toward a steel door a few feet away; court officers stood on either side of it. "Miguel Gomes is in the lockup pen. We've been looking for him all week, everywhere except the most obvious place. Turns out he's been in Nashua Street Jail the past two weeks awaiting trial for distributing cocaine. Which knocks him out as Maria Melendez's killer, since he was in custody when the murder took place."

Connolly led us to a small interview room near the lockup cell. Bars divided the room into two sections. He instructed a court officer to bring Miguel Gomes in. A minute later a short, wiry Hispanic man ambled into the room, on the other side of the bars. "Hey, man, you ain't my lawyer," he said to Connolly. His Puerto Rican accent made *lawyer* sound like *liar*.

"No shit, Sherlock."

Gomes paced slowly back and forth across the room. Connolly matched him step for step on the other side of the bars.

"Hard staying out of trouble, huh, Miguel?"

"It's a bullshit charge, man." *Boolsheet.* "They got nothing on me. I'll be outa here in an hour."

"Maybe yes, maybe no. Depends on how cooperative you are."

Gomes wriggled his nose and sniffed the air. "You must be a cop. Your friends there don't smell so good, either. What the fuck do you want, man?"

"One of your, uh, employees ran into some trouble last Thursday. Maria Melendez."

A flicker of anxiety showed on the prisoner's face for just an instant.

Connolly continued. "I guess you could call it an on-the-job accident."

"Hey, man, maybe she can file for Workman's Compensation."

"She's dead, asshole. But you know that already, don't you?"

Gomes hesitated. "Could be. So? What do you want from me?"

The two of them continued pacing. "For starters, I want you to tell me everything you know about her. You see, I have a little problem here. You help me with my problem, I help you with yours."

"What problem?"

"We're not sure Maria Melendez was really Maria Melendez."

Gomes looked perplexed. "What do you mean?"

"I checked her arrest records. Each time she was picked up, she gave a different social security number. None of them check out. I figure it's probably not even her real name. And we can't find anybody who knows for sure who she was or where she came from. Thought you might be able to clear this up for us."

Gomes shrugged. "I don't know nothing about it, man. She ain't my sister." *Seester.*

"Yeah, well, she's somebody's *seester*, Miguel. Somebody's daughter. Maybe even somebody's mama. And we haven't even been able to find a family to notify."

Gomes stopped pacing. Neither of them spoke for several seconds. "Her family don't know yet?"

"Uh-uh. No one to claim the body. The city had to bury her, and there was no one even at the burial to mourn her.

One person sent flowers and a short poem, but he didn't sign his name. Was that you?"

"Hey, man—do I look like someone who sends poems to people?" Gomes shook his head and sat on one of the small benches in the cell. "Damn," he muttered. "Look, man. I don't know who told you I know anything. I known her just a few months. Girls like her, I don't ask them their life story, you know? We did some business together, I found a place for her to stay, helped her make some connections. That's all. I can't help you, man."

"Who can?"

Gomes paused. "Check with that white dude. You know, that Jewish guy. The dentist."

"Barney Cohen?"

"Yeah, that's his name. Barney Cohen. Maria was one of his girls before she came to me. So—you gonna help me here, or what?"

"Depends. First I talk to Barney Cohen, see if what you say is true."

Gomes began to stand. "Hey, you son of a—"

"That's okay, Miguel. No need to get up. We can find the door. It's been a real pleasure meeting you."

"Hey, fuck you, man!"

"Likewise, I'm sure."

Connolly led Veronica and me out of the chamber and back into the main corridor of the fourth floor. "Barney Cohen is a dentist. He was busted last year for running a prostitution ring out of his townhouse on Commonwealth Avenue."

Connolly made a phone call and learned that five months earlier Barney Cohen pled guilty to one count of attempted bribery of a police officer. He was still serving his five-year sentence, and he was being held at a pre-release center on Park Drive. Connolly made arrangements to go there directly from the court to interview the man. He asked Veronica to go with him so they could continue talking about the case. "You, too, Doc, if you're interested."

Connolly's unmarked police car was parked in flagrant violation of a half-dozen city ordinances: in a no-parking zone, halfway onto the sidewalk, blocking access to the nearest fire hydrant. Veronica sat in the front passenger seat of the box-shaped Plymouth, I sat behind her, and Connolly drove toward the entrance to Storrow Drive, behind North Station.

"Cohen ran a high-class operation," he explained. "Professional clientele, computerized records, all major credit cards accepted. Had his dental practice in the same building, like a full-service shop—we drill you, then you do some drilling of your own. He received a reduced sentence in return for taking a couple of vice detectives down with him, guys who ignored what he was doing in return for the usual sorts of payoffs and favors."

We headed west on Storrow Drive, with the Charles River on one side of us and the rear facades of Back Bay townhouses on the other.

"Any idea who sent the flowers to Maria Melendez's grave?" Veronica asked.

"No. The florist couldn't remember the transaction."

"You told Gomes there was a poem with the flowers," I said.

"I wrote it down," he replied as he fumbled through his pockets. "Yeah, here it is." Veronica read it, then passed it to me.

> *You were slowly dying*
> *You gave a final call*
> *But there was nothing I could do*
> *To keep you from that fall*

"Sounds like at least one person cared about her," I said.

Connolly reached into his sport jacket pocket for his copies of the letters the killer had sent to me. He held them against the steering wheel and reread them as he drove. Cars whizzed by us in the passing lane as Connolly drove and read at the same time. "Don't worry, folks. I do this all the time. Hey—at least this guy has a sense of humor."

"What do you mean?" I asked.

"In the second letter, where he says he told you he'd be

in your neck of the woods on April 30th, he has the word 'neck' in quotation marks. Like he's making a pun, referring to the way he murders his victims. He must think he's pretty clever."

He returned the letters to his pocket and thought about what he'd read. "Do you know where the letters were mailed from?"

"New York," Veronica said.

"Okay. So nine days from now, a week from Wednesday, he's gonna kill someone in New York, and then a fourth and final victim sometime after that. And one of them—at least one—will probably be a woman, judging from his remark about Adam's apples. You get the feeling that he already has his victims picked out. I wonder what the priest did that would qualify as recklessness. If it was a rabbi, doing circumcisions and stuff like that, I could understand."

"I can think of lots of ways a prostitute could be careless," I said.

"Not from personal experience, I hope," Connolly replied.

For perhaps the five hundredth time since realizing that one person killed both Joseph Carroll and Maria Melendez, I tried to think of some hypothetical link between them. "What if Joseph Carroll and Maria Melendez are only connected in the killer's mind?" I asked. "What if their sins are imagined, or the product of psychotic thinking, or just general sins that have nothing to do with the killer at all?"

"In that case," Connolly replied, "good luck figuring it out in nine days."

He pulled off of Storrow Drive at the exit ramp for Park Drive. "Maria Melendez was killed on Thursday, the week before last," he said. "The Friday *Globe* carried a picture of you and me, Doc. Artie refers to that picture in his letter, which was mailed from New York on Saturday. I wonder— did he return to New York right after the murder and then see the picture in an out-of-town edition of the *Globe*, or did he stay over in Boston until Friday and see it locally?"

Veronica said, "You can check the hotels to see if

Elmore Winston registered anywhere in the city the night after the murder."

"Already did that. No go. Of course, he'd have to be an idiot to use the same name if he did stay another night. No information from Amtrak or Logan Airport, either, on someone named Elmore Winston."

"Maybe you can check the hotel registrations for Friday night—the night *after* the murder—for anyone named Artie or Arthur who listed a New York address."

He sighed. "It'll be a pain in the ass, but we can try. Most of the hotels just keep the first initials in their computers, so it would mean hand-checking the desk copies for first names."

"Check last names, too," she suggested.

"Last names?"

"It's a long shot, but Arthur could be his last name."

I hadn't thought of that.

Veronica asked, "Did you get a description of the man who checked into the hotel room Maria Melendez was murdered in?"

"He was white."

"That's all?"

"A real observant desk clerk. Wouldn't know where his ass is if it wasn't stapled to him."

The Plymouth followed the curves of Park Drive, past the Fens on our left and the turnoff for Boylston Street and Fenway Park on our right. A few blocks later Connolly parked and we walked toward the entrance of a five-story apartment building at the corner of Park Drive and Jersey Street. As we walked Connolly said, "The prisoners in pre-release centers are allowed out to go to work, see counselors, attend Alcoholics Anonymous meetings, things like that. After a while they can get passes to go on visits to see their families, sometimes overnight. The Department of Correction transfers prisoners here when they're within a year of getting out."

"I thought you said Barney Cohen had only served five months of a five-year sentence."

"Welcome to the wonderful world of Massachusetts justice, Doc. He's eligible for parole in one more month. His regular patients who go more than six months between checkups won't even realize the good Dr. Cohen has been away."

A plaque on the building at the corner read: DEPARTMENT OF CORRECTION, PARK DRIVE PRE-RELEASE CENTER. There was nothing else to distinguish the exterior of the building from the others on the block. But inside, on the first floor, what once were apartments had been gutted and turned into a large kitchen and dining room, a living room, and a small den.

A plainclothes corrections officer monitored activity in the common areas via video screens in the main corridor. When Connolly introduced himself, the officer said, "I held Cohen back from work after you called. Looked kinda nervous when I told him the police wanted to talk with him."

"Where does he work?"

"He's a dentist at a public health clinic at Tufts Medical School. I'll go get him. You can wait in the den. I'll make sure no one else comes in while you're talking to him."

As we entered the den, Connolly said, "The clinic Cohen works at is a five-minute walk from the Lafayette Hotel."

A minute or two later Barney Cohen was escorted into the room by the corrections officer. He was in his early fifties, a plump man of average height with thinning gray hair combed across a wide bald spot. The officer left him with us and closed the door.

Cohen clenched and unclenched his hands several times and looked nervously from Connolly to Veronica, then to me. Connolly told him who we all were.

Cohen cleared his throat and leaned back in an overstuffed chair. "I've been expecting someone from your department, Detective. I presume you've come to talk with me about Maria Melendez."

12: You Were Slowly Dying

She arrived at Barney Cohen's home fifteen months earlier in the company of a Boston police detective. She was carrying one medium-sized suitcase, she had less than two hundred dollars to her name, and her lightweight jacket offered little protection against the frigid February morning.

"This is Maria Melendez," the detective said. "She's been living in the Greyhound terminal for the last couple of days. I thought you might be able to help her."

After the detective left, Cohen brought her into the kitchen and brewed a pot of coffee. Her hand shook as she reached for the cup he held out to her. "Christ, it's so cold in Massachusetts."

"Your first trip north?"

She nodded.

"How long will you stay?"

"I don't know."

Cohen regarded her red-brown complexion and her lightweight clothing, and surmised that this young woman with the Hispanic surname came from Texas or California or some point in between.

"How old are you?"

"I'll be eighteen in a few months."

Maria Melendez sipped her coffee, and her shivering became less pronounced.

"Do your parents know where you are?"

She shook her head.

"They must be worried about you."

"They must be celebrating. If they've even noticed I'm gone."

"Perhaps you don't give them enough credit."

"Perhaps you don't know what you're talking about." She paused. "I'm sorry."

"That's alright." He carried his empty cup to the sink. "Have you had breakfast?"

"Uh-uh."

"What can I get you?"

"I don't know. Anything is good compared to the food at the bus station. That cop who found me—why did he bring me here?"

"He's one of my patients. He knows I have some space to rent, and you obviously need a place to stay."

Barney Cohen broke an egg into a small bowl, scrambled it, and tossed it into a frying pan. As he did that, he explained the layout of the house to her. He lived on the first floor. He rented out eight rooms on the three upper stories. His dental office was in the basement, with a separate entrance for his patients.

"I rent to young people like yourself—well, a bit older than you, usually. It's safe here, and I try to select a nice group of people. I guess the detective thought you could use something like that."

"Well, if you want my opinion, he just wanted to screw me."

Cohen was taken aback by her bluntness. He knew she was right about the detective, but he said nothing. The detective was well aware of Cohen's illegal enterprise, but he didn't interfere, and once before he'd even delivered another young woman to Cohen for potential employment. Cohen reciprocated with various considerations, financial and otherwise. It was a business arrangement, pure and simple. It began as a not-so-subtle act of extortion by the detective, but things were evenly balanced now: Both of them knew that if Cohen were ever to take a fall, the detective would go with him.

She asked him how much he charged for rent. He told her, then he placed the scrambled egg in front of her. She ate it without speaking, then pushed the plate away and stood. "Thanks for breakfast. I think I better find a shelter or something until I get a job and make some money."

"If you'd like, you can stay as a guest for a few days, look for work, figure out what you want to do next."

"And what do you get out of it?"

"Who says I have to get something out of it?"

"Because everyone always does. That's how things work."

" 'There are more things in heaven and earth, Horatio, than are dreamt of in your philosophy.' "

"Huh?"

He smiled. "Nothing, nothing. Just a little something from *Hamlet*."

He escorted her upstairs. He dropped her suitcase onto the bed, then left to gather some bedding from a linen closet in the hall. When he returned the bathroom door was closed and the shower was running. Cohen reached into the suitcase for her wallet. It contained a hundred and eighty dollars, no charge cards. Her driver's license bore a San Antonio address. She was a few months shy of her eighteenth birthday, just as she'd told him, but her name wasn't Maria Melendez. The face on the license photograph belonged to a Mary Mendez.

Cohen returned to the first floor. He entered his den, switched on the television, and stretched out on the rug directly in front of it. He scanned the closed-circuit channels that enabled him to monitor activities in the eight upstairs bedrooms. Each room had a mirror that was bolted permanently into place. Behind each mirror, ensconced in a recess in the wall, was a video camera with a built-in microphone. Only Cohen knew the cameras were there.

He flipped through the eight channels. One of the young women was alone, fast asleep. Two had company: their last clients from the previous night. Clients paid a hefty premium for those end-of-the-night time slots, and the women were allowed total discretion in choosing whether and with whom to fill them. Cohen detected movement underneath the sheets in one of those rooms; he watched for a moment—less for prurient purposes, more to keep track of business—and then continued scanning. Four of the young women had already departed their rooms for their day jobs or classes.

He turned to the final closed-circuit channel. He saw Maria Melendez walk out of her bathroom, naked except for a small towel draped over one shoulder. He knew immediately that she would have high-demand potential if she stayed. Her body was taut and ripe, and the Hispanic cast of her skin would make her popular with clients from the western suburbs who wanted a taste of color, but who weren't bold enough to couple with the black woman in one of the second-story rooms.

He was just about to turn the television off when he noticed Maria kneel beside the bed. She leaned her elbows on the mattress and clasped her hands beneath her chin. She closed her eyes and stayed motionless for several seconds, as if in prayer. Tears began to flow down her cheeks, but she didn't move for several minutes. Then she stood and walked to the mirror. Unknowingly, she was staring directly into the camera at close range. Her face filled Barney Cohen's television screen. He switched the set off, unwilling to gaze any longer at the unbearable sadness etched in her eyes.

"She was only with me for a few months," Cohen told us. "It didn't take long for her to become more trouble than I could afford."

Veronica said, "That's a little harsh, don't you think? Considering what you did to her."

"What I did to her?"

"Turned her into a whore. Which, need I remind you, is what eventually got her killed."

"Turned her into a . . ." Cohen glared at Veronica. "Let me tell you, it didn't take a certified genius to figure out what was going on at my place. Maria knew what she was getting into from the beginning. I didn't force her to do anything she wasn't already prepared to do."

"You took advantage of a runaway teenager in a weak position."

"Listen, miss. That very first day Maria came to me, I offered to buy her a plane ticket back home, but she refused."

"You can't prove that," said Veronica.

"Of course not." He addressed Connolly. "I'll tell you what I can prove, though. After she refused the plane ticket, I made her let her parents know she was safe. I told her she couldn't stay in my home unless she called them first. She spoke with her mother. I monitored the call on my speakerphone to make sure she wasn't talking to the weather recording. Check my phone records, February of last year. You'll see a call to San Antonio. That should give you what you're looking for."

"And what do you think I'm looking for?" asked Connolly.

"The news stories say you haven't been able to locate her family. I assume you've wondered if you even have her correct name. Now you've got your answers. Her real name was Mary Mendez, and my phone records should lead you straight to her mother."

"She was murdered over a week ago," said Connolly. "Why didn't you come forward on your own?"

Cohen sighed. "Because when the parole board hears about your visit, they won't even consider my release until they investigate the situation. It's a reflex on their part. 'The police came to talk with him'—hell, you even brought the FBI—'so let's hold him back until we figure out exactly what it's all about.' I was due to see the parole board next month. There's no telling how long this is going to set me back now."

Connolly asked, "How come you only kept her for a few months?"

"Condoms and cocaine," replied Cohen. "Too little of one, too much of the other. I ran a safe place. That was one of the rules—no matter how much extra a client offers on the side, you're not allowed to go without a condom. The camera gave her away."

"What about the cocaine?"

"She couldn't stay away from it. She brought the problem with her from Texas, and she couldn't shake it."

"So you just kicked her out," said Veronica.

Cohen sighed, exasperated by Veronica's hostile approach. "No, I didn't. First I paid for her to enter a four-week hospital program for cocaine addicts. When she started getting high again less than a week after her discharge, I gave her two options—return to the hospital program, or leave my house. She made the choice, not me." He took a deep breath. "I never wanted her to go."

I spoke for the first time. "You just didn't want to help her ignore her drug habit."

"Precisely. By the way, what kind of doctor are you?"

"Psychiatrist."

He addressed Connolly. "You brought a psychiatrist to examine me?"

"He's not here to examine you. He's helping us get a handle on the perpetrator."

"So you have a suspect?"

Connolly hesitated. "I can't say anything about that."

"I see."

"Do you have any ideas about who may have killed her?"

He shrugged. "Turning tricks on the street, trouble was bound to come sooner or later. Especially with the drugs mixed in."

Veronica asked, "Do you know anyone in Philadelphia?"

Cohen appeared confused by the sudden switch in topics. "A cousin. Distant."

"Ever visit him?"

"Years ago."

"Are you sure you weren't there last October, around Columbus Day?"

"Quite sure. What are you getting at?"

Connolly interrupted. "Do you recall where you were last Columbus Day weekend?"

Cohen pondered for a moment. "No. I had already been arrested, and I was out on bail until my trial date. One of the bail conditions was that I stay in Massachusetts, but I don't remember anything in particular about that weekend."

Cohen appeared ill at ease. Was he merely perplexed by the turn the questions had taken, or did he have something to hide?

Veronica leaned forward and peered intently at the man. "You've been working at a medical center recently."

Cohen nodded. "Everyone at pre-release is expected to work."

"How far is the medical center from the Lafayette Hotel?"

His face turned red and he grabbed the arms of his chair. "Listen, miss—my times in and out of this place are carefully recorded. So are my times in and out of New England Medical Center. Check them out to your heart's content. Match them against the time Maria was killed. Let me know what you learn. Meanwhile, if you want to pursue this line of questioning, we can terminate the interview until my lawyer is present." He addressed Connolly. "Who's in charge here, anyway?"

In the awkward silence that followed, I stared at Barney Cohen and wondered how he'd come to this point in his life. He was an educated and obviously intelligent man. He was successful in the profession for which he'd studied and trained. Why had he jeopardized his career by running such a questionable and high-risk venture? Was it greed? Loneliness? Some secret self-loathing that only years of therapy might illuminate?

In my profession, I've discovered you can learn a lot about a person by asking him to describe someone else. I said, "Tell me what you remember about Mary Mendez."

"I always thought of her as Maria Melendez. That was the name she chose, and that was the name I always used. I think she was trying to make a break from her past. She didn't want to have anything to do with her family."

"What was she like?"

He smiled softly at the memory. "Sometimes she seemed incredibly naive. Other times, I thought she was jaded beyond her years."

"Did you talk with her at all after she left you?"

"Once, several months later. She called and asked me to help her get back into the drug rehab program. I made all the arrangements, but when I called her back at the number she'd given me, she said she'd changed her mind." His voice grew quiet. "I knew I couldn't help her any more after that. That was the last time I spoke to her."

I recalled the poem and flowers that someone sent anonymously to the young woman's burial site. I recited, " 'You were slowly dying. You gave a final call. But there was nothing I could do to keep you from that fall.' You sent those flowers to her graveside, didn't you?"

He looked at me sorrowfully for several moments. Finally, he nodded. "Not long after that last phone call, I received a call from a private detective her family had hired to find her. I don't know how he traced Maria to me."

"What did you tell him?"

"I gave him the last phone number I had for Maria. I figured it couldn't do any harm. Maybe her mother could talk some sense into her."

Connolly spoke up. "When did that detective call you?"

"I'm not sure. Sometime last year, before my trial."

"What was his name?"

"I don't remember." He closed his eyes for a few seconds and tried to dredge the name from his memory. "Winslow, I believe. Or Winter. Something like that."

Connolly, Veronica, and I looked at one another, three minds with the same thought. Connolly said, "How about Winston? Could that be it?"

"Perhaps." He thought for a moment. "Winston. That sounds right. Why? Do you know him?"

Veronica said, "Do you remember anything about him? His voice—an accent, how old he sounded, anything striking about his choice of words?"

"I really can't say. It was one phone call, months ago. Why are you so interested in this man?"

Connolly grimaced and rubbed the bottom of his jaw. "We think Maria Melendez may have been murdered by someone from her past, someone who went out of his way to find her. Someone who knew her real name was Mary Mendez. And when the killer checked into the Lafayette Hotel he registered as Elmore Winston."

His face grew pale. "I don't . . . I don't understand."

"You stupid bastard," hissed Veronica. "You talked to the killer. If you hadn't told him where he could find her, she would still be alive."

Driving back to Veronica's office, Connolly made eye contact with me in his rearview mirror and said, "Nice job back there, Doc. You got some good information out of him."

"Thanks. Do you think he knows anything about the murders?"

"Nah, not really. We'll check him out, see if he can account for his time when Maria Melendez was being killed. But it's unlikely he had anything to do with either murder. How would he have mailed the letters from New York, or—better yet—delivered that picture to your editor, when he's been serving his sentence in Massachusetts that whole time? And how would he be able to get to New York next week for the third murder without eloping from the pre-release center, which would really screw up his chances for parole?"

We reached the end of Storrow Drive and Connolly headed for Government Center.

"When did Cohen begin serving his sentence?" Veronica asked.

"December," replied Connolly.

"Five months ago," she said. "So the man who calls himself Winston called Cohen at least five months before Maria Melendez was murdered. Either he took a long time to track her down, or he stalked her for some time before killing her."

Connolly navigated his car through the complex maze of turns underneath the Central Artery and around Boston Garden. He double-parked alongside the federal office building that housed the FBI field office. "It shouldn't be difficult for me to get the number of the Mendez family from Cohen's telephone records."

Veronica said, "Alright. I'll give you a call later today, or tomorrow from San Antonio. I'll fly down there in the morning to see what I can learn about Maria Melendez, or Mary Mendez, or whatever name she went by when she was living there. You might as well hold off notifying her parents about the murder. It might be better if I tell them in person."

"You think you can be tactful about it?"

"I know how to do my job, Timothy. Sometimes I wonder about your department, though."

"What do you mean?"

"How long was Barney Cohen running his little enterprise?"

"Almost three years."

"What took you guys so long to bust him?"

"Veronica, you were a prosecutor, so you should know— sometimes the hardest thing to prove in the eyes of the law is the thing everybody knows."

"Especially if your own people are on the take," she said, then opened her door and stepped out.

As I started to follow suit, Connolly turned to me and said, "She's all yours, Doc. Good luck."

Veronica and I rode the elevator back to the ninth floor. As we walked toward her office she said, "I'll have my secretary arrange two tickets for San Antonio. We should try to catch a morning flight tomorrow."

" 'We?' "

She paused. "Come on, Harry. You're part of this investigation now, whether you like it or not. And you don't expect me to tell Maria Melendez's family the bad news all by myself, do you? Besides, I hate to keep reminding you of this, but . . ."

"I know, I know—I owe you. How much mileage do you plan to get out of that one?"

She smiled. "As much as I can."

13: Everyone Needs Pity

After lunch, Veronica and I drove separately to Concord. She parked at my house and we rode together in my car to the Veterans Administration Hospital I used to work at in nearby Bedford.

The hospital is in a wooded area, and the grounds resemble a low-rent version of a university campus. The buildings are much like the patients: clean and well tended on a day-to-day basis, but decaying and in desperate need of repair.

I began working there shortly after completing my residency training at McLean Hospital, a posh psychiatric facility set atop a rolling hill outside Boston. McLean has a long tradition of treating the rich and famous—catering to them, some might say. I could have remained on the staff after my residency, but I was weary of dealing with the patients and families who believed their names, wealth, or position made them more worthy than the rest of humanity. So I went to the Bedford VA, where people grappled with problems far weightier than that of trying to figure out the family time-sharing arrangements at summer estates in Bar Harbor and Martha's Vineyard.

As we pulled into the visitors' parking lot, I spied a small group of wheelchair-bound patients congregating under a shade tree fifty yards away. I recognized one of them, a chronic kidney patient who had somehow hung on for the five years since I'd worked there. Two fleshy stubs

hung over the front of his chair, tragic reminders of his encounter with a Viet Cong land mine near Hamburger Hill.

Veronica and I entered the administration building and
proceeded to the Hospital Director's office. The secretary
wasn't at her desk. "I hope he got the message I needed to
see him," I said.

A voice boomed from the inner office. "I sure as hell
did, you old son of a gun."

Suddenly the gargantuan form of Dr. Monte Backus appeared in the doorway to the inner office. He bounded toward me, thrust his large, meaty hands outward, and pulled
me hard against him. He was more than six and a half feet
tall, and my face was pressed against his upper chest.

It was known amongst my former VA colleagues as the
Backus Bearhug: his typical greeting to anyone he hadn't
seen for more than a week. Ostensibly a gesture of com-
radeship, it was really his way of reminding others of his
power and their subordination.

Standing there in his office, I felt for a moment as
though I might suffocate inside the Bearhug. Then he
pushed me away and held onto my shoulders, shaking me
as he spoke. "Let me look at you, Harry. How the fuck are
you?"

He towered above me. Faint ethyl alcohol fumes from
his liquid lunch burned my nostrils as I stood trapped in his
grasp. "I'm well, Monte. And you?"

"Never better, never better." He released me and
pounded his palms against his massive thighs. "Strong as a
horse." He laughed and slapped me on the back. Then he
noticed Veronica for the first time. "And who might this
lovely lady be?"

I introduced them to one another. Backus took a small
step toward Veronica and begin to extend his hand for what
no doubt would prove to be a vigorous handshake. She
edged backward and glared at him. *Touch me and die*, her
eyes seemed to say. Then she produced a small billfold,
opened the flap, and flashed her FBI badge and identification just like they do in the movies.

Backus turned toward me again, grabbed me by my

shoulder, and directed us into his office. Veronica and I sat on a worn sofa. Backus settled his oversized form into a chair opposite us.

"How's Melinda?" he asked.

I ignored his mistake. "She's doing well. Finishing up the third grade now. I'm very proud of her."

"Good, good." He sighed, the obligatory small talk over. "My secretary said you have something urgent to discuss with me. And you've brought an FBI agent with you." He smiled broadly and looked at Veronica. "Am I in some sort of trouble?"

"I wouldn't know," she answered. She clearly didn't appreciate his overbearing manner. Monte Backus didn't make a very good first impression—or second, third, or fourth impression, for that matter.

After a short, awkward silence, Backus began to chuckle. "Very good, Ms. Pace. I like a woman who knows how to banter."

Veronica and I hadn't spent much time together, but I knew her well enough to tell that she wasn't bantering. She said, "Dr. Kline received some unusual letters from someone who was a patient at this hospital when he worked here. The FBI is investigating the situation. We need access to the names of all the patients who were here between 1981 and 1987."

"Sounds like you want to identify him pretty badly," Backus said, obviously fishing for more information.

Veronica nodded slightly.

He looked at me, no doubt hoping that I'd supply more information than Veronica had. When I failed to add anything, Backus furrowed his brow. "I'm sure you realize that what you're asking for is confidential information. What do you plan on doing with it?"

"The letter writer lives in another state," Veronica answered. "He signed the letters with his first name. We'll search your lists for anyone with the first name he's using, then try to identify which ones might be living in his area."

"You said the letters were unusual. What did you mean?"

"I really can't reveal any information about our investigation."

"And yet you want me to reveal this hospital's confidential information. Well, I'll need more to go on before I can even think about giving you what you want."

Veronica considered that for a moment. "I can tell you that the letter writer has killed two people so far."

Backus rubbed his chin and sighed. "I don't know. I just don't know." It would take more to satisfy him than Veronica had provided. He wanted to know the details of the letters. More than that, he wanted the pleasure of wheedling something out of her that she said she didn't want to give.

She paused. "We know he selects his victims carefully. He stalked one for several months. We know he's out for revenge, that he kills specific people who he believes have wronged him in some way. And we know he plans to kill at least two more people."

"Who?"

"We don't know."

"Who are the two people he's killed so far?"

"I can't tell you, specifically." Veronica hesitated for several seconds. "I can tell you that both of them were hospital administrators."

As Backus digested those last words, Veronica sat calmly, her facial expression impassive and inscrutable. He began to laugh nervously, wanting to believe that she was joking, but the confusion on his face told me that he couldn't tell whether she was joking, lying, or revealing a frightening truth.

Backus said, "I suppose you could get a court order for the records you want."

"I suppose I could. But I'm trying to save time. That's why I came directly to you." She smiled for the first time. "I'd like your help."

She'd given him an opening—a way to give in while making it look like it was his decision. "What the hell." He smiled broadly. "Us federal folks need to help each other out, don't we? I'll see what I can do, Ms. Pace." Backus said it would take several hours to gather the information, and he agreed to fax it to her office the next day.

"Give my regards to Melinda," he said as Veronica and I stood to leave. "And you should bring her up some weekend. Go to the beach, have some lobster, maybe do a little sailing."

He and his wife had a weekend home near the ocean on Cape Ann. "Sure," I said. "When?"

"Anytime, you old son of a gun. Anytime. Just give us a call."

"Sure."

"Splendid."

It was the sort of invitation I'd expect from someone like Monte Backus: one that puts the onus on the prospective guest to make all the arrangements. I knew he didn't really want Melissa and me to visit, and he knew I'd never take him up on his unheartfelt overture.

As Veronica and I walked toward the parking lot she asked, "Does he have any redeeming social qualities?"

"Scientists are still investigating."

"That could take a long time."

"No rush. It's a civil service position. He'll be here forever. Unless they find him buck naked with a child, a patient, or a small animal, his job is secure until he dies or retires."

"Whichever comes first."

"Right—whichever comes first. Very good, Ms. Pace. I like a woman who knows how to banter."

An energetic young man in tattered jeans ran up to us. He reached out to shake my hand and said, "Charlie Peck, write-in candidate for President. I need your vote. 'No more Styrofoam.' " He darted off toward the wheelchair patients under the shade tree and began glad-handing them.

"He's probably a patient on the psychiatric ward I used to direct. Catchy campaign slogan, but I don't think the major candidates have much to worry about."

"You never know," replied Veronica. "They say it's the year of the outsider. If he adds Astroturf and radio call-in shows to his list, he might get my vote."

We got into the car and headed back toward my house. As we crossed the hospital grounds, we passed a man who'd been admitted to my psychiatric ward at least a dozen times during my six years there. I knew him to be almost exactly my age, but he seemed to age twice as quickly. Less than a year after quarterbacking South Boston High School to the conference championship, he became a paralytic victim of the heaviest fighting Vietnam had seen since the Tet Offensive. His hospital admissions all came on the heels of suicide attempts. I was sorry to see him back at the hospital now, but pleased to see him still alive.

As I drove past my former patient, I recited to Veronica. " 'The time you won your town the race, we chaired you through the marketplace. Man and boy stood cheering by, and home we brought you shoulder-high.' "

"What was that?"

"The first stanza from a poem. 'To An Athlete Dying Young,' by A. E. Housman."

"What brought that on?"

I sighed. "Nothing in particular." The former football hero faded from sight in my sideview mirror. "Just thinking about someone I know."

I drove through the center of Bedford, past the trailer park and defense contractors that ringed the north side of Hanscomb Air Force Base, and on toward the Concord town line.

"Why were you so reluctant to tell Backus anything about the letters?"

"I really wasn't," she replied. "I just pretended to be. I had him pegged as the sort of person who hates giving people what they want. I decided to hold back at first, then make it look like I was giving in to him, so he'd be more likely to give me what I wanted. Sometimes you can get what you want by offering less than you're prepared to give."

"Run that one by me again."

"I said, sometimes you can get what you want by offering less than you're prepared to give." She laughed. "Should I write it down for you?"

It had been an eye-opening day: In the morning, Veronica admitted to invading my privacy and keeping her actions secret from me. Then, in the span of a few hours, I watched her badger Barney Cohen, insult Timothy Connolly, and manipulate Monte Backus. She would threaten or lie, promise or plead—or do whatever else was necessary—to get what she wanted. This would take some getting used to.

I checked my watch. "I told my daughter I'd pick her up after school. Is it okay if I stop there first? Then I'll drive home so you can get your car."

"Sure."

The driveway entrance to the Alcott School was at the end of a side road off of Walden Street, behind Emerson Playground. Sometimes it seemed as though everything in Concord was named for one of the town's famous nineteenth-century Transcendentalists. Melissa and I even swam and played tennis at the Thoreau Club. They cut down several prime acres of trees to make room for the pools and courts, then named it after the grandfather of American environmental awareness.

Melissa was sitting on the grass in front of the school. Her face was buried in a book as I drove up, so she didn't notice me until I called out to her. She smiled, clutched the book in both arms, then ran around the car to the passenger side. She opened the front door and was about to hop onto the seat next to mine when she noticed it was already occupied.

"Oh," she said, stopping suddenly with one leg poised awkwardly in midair.

"Melissa, you remember Ms. Pace, don't you?"

Just then the book slipped from my daughter's grasp and fell to the ground. Veronica bent over to retrieve it, but Melissa shouted "No!" and grabbed the book herself.

"Melissa! Where are you manners? Apologize to Ms. Pace."

"I'm sorry, Ms. Pace," she said in the deadpan cadence children use when they don't really mean the words they've been forced to say. She opened the rear door and slunk

down onto the backseat. She wrapped her sweater around
the book; if it hadn't been so out of character, I would have
sworn she was trying to hide what she was reading.

"That's alright, Melissa. And please—call me Veronica."

I put the car in gear and headed home. As we drove, I
asked Melissa about her day at school, but with her mono-
syllabic responses she eventually achieved her goal of shut-
ting off further conversation. I glanced in the rearview
mirror; I saw my daughter scowl at Veronica from behind,
no doubt regarding her as an interloper of undetermined
threat.

After several minutes Melissa said, "Do you really work
for the FBI?"

Veronica turned around to face my daughter. "Yes, I really do."

"Do you know how to use a gun?"

"Uh-huh."

"Do you own one?"

Veronica hesitated, then nodded.

"Do you have it with you?"

"No."

I pulled off of Monument Street and up the gravel driveway to the side of our house. As I turned off the ignition,
Melissa asked, "Did you ever shoot anyone?"

"I'm sorry," Veronica replied. "I'd rather not talk anymore about guns right now."

Melissa opened the rear door without saying another
word and ran into the house. I escorted Veronica to her car.

"I think your daughter dislikes me."

"She's a moody child. She doesn't get along very well
with strangers. Don't take it personally."

"I've heard that children with only one parent get very
nervous when someone else starts sniffing around that parent."

"Sniffing around—is that what you're doing?"

She shrugged. "That's my job." She opened her car door
and sat behind the wheel. "I feel bad for Melissa."

"She doesn't need anyone's pity," I said. It was a reflex

reaction, designed to spare me from thinking about how sad my daughter's life often seemed to others, herself, and me.

"Everyone needs pity, Harry."

"Well, *I* don't need anyone to explain my daughter to me."

She paused. "Of course not. I'm sorry."

Embarrassed at having snapped at her, I tried to change the topic. "Well, *did* you ever use a gun on anyone?"

She waited several seconds before answering. "Aim it at anyone? Yes. Shoot anyone? No. Unfortunately. I wish I had."

I waited for her to elaborate on her curious response, but she didn't. All she said before starting her car and driving away was, "I'll see you at the airport tomorrow morning."

The kitchen was quiet when I entered. Melissa was upstairs changing into her playclothes, and Mrs. Winnicot was doing the weekly grocery shopping.

Everyone needs pity. I thought about the people who were deserving of it: the erstwhile soldiers at the VA; athletes dying young; Maria Melendez, Father Joseph Carroll, and their families. Even Artie—or Elmore Winston, or whatever my tormented pen pal really called himself—seemed pitiable in his madness. If they merited pity, then surely Melissa did, too.

I walked upstairs to Melissa's room to ask her if there was anything she wanted to talk about. She was in her bathroom; the door to her bedroom was open. From the doorway I could see the book she'd been reading as she waited for me after school. It was from the school library, and I craned my neck to see the title.

It read: *This is Your FBI.*

14: I Have No Daughter

It was only May 12th, but San Antonio was already summertime-hot. Men in cowboy hats and boots strolled through the airport baggage claim area, as if a Hollywood casting director had populated the scene with indigenous-looking movie extras. A travel poster on the wall read: "The sun has riz, the sun has set, and we ain't out of Texas yet." The first suitcase to come down the baggage chute bore a sticker: "If they want to take my gun, they'll have to pry it from my cold, stiff, dead fingers." Most of the airport employees were Mexican-American. All in all, I felt as if I had arrived in another country.

A middle-aged man in a neatly pressed lightweight suit approached as we were waiting for our luggage. He was lean and muscular, and he looked like he could run circles around men half his age. He scanned the crowd as he walked toward us, and I knew he must be the local FBI agent who had been sent to meet our plane. His hair hung partway over his ears and down to his collar, no doubt skirting the edge of what was acceptable under departmental regulations. "Excuse me, ma'am," he drawled. "You're Veronica, right? Veronica Pace?"

She said nothing to confirm or deny his supposition. "Who are you?"

"Billy Ray Dalton, San Antonio field office, at your service." He grabbed my hand and pumped it vigorously.

"You must be Harry. Welcome to Texas. Y'all have a good flight?"

I said, "How did you know we were the ones you were looking for?"

He turned toward the rest of the passengers in the baggage claim area and made a sweeping gesture with his hand. "You're the only man and woman waiting together for your bags. With married couples, even couples that aren't married, the woman stands back while the man pulls the bags from the carousel. But men and women traveling together on business always wait for their own bags, if you see what I'm saying." He grinned sheepishly.

Veronica nodded, acknowledging his show of deductive reasoning. She held out her hand; he accepted it reluctantly, unsure of how hard or how long to shake hands with a woman.

We gathered our bags. Our escort insisted on carrying Veronica's suitcase.

"Thanks, Dalton," she said.

"Please—it's Billy Ray, or just plain Billy if you like. You Yankees always call people by their last names. Down here, the only folks who do that are divorce lawyers and undertakers."

His car was parked near the terminal entrance. Veronica took the front passenger seat, I sat behind her, and Billy Ray Dalton drove away from the airport and onto U.S. Route 281. He drove ten miles per hour faster than the other drivers on the road. He zipped from lane to lane, looking for openings in the traffic like a fullback picking his way through a defensive line.

Small protrusions were embedded in the asphalt between lanes, and each time Billy Ray switched lanes there was a short burst of staccato clicks and a small vibration as the tires hit the bumps.

"What do you call those things?" Veronica asked.

He shrugged. "I call 'em road pimples. Got reflectors in 'em, too, for nighttime driving. So you get three kinds of warning every time you go across them—sight, sound, and touch, if you see what I'm saying. Your first visit to Texas?"

"Yes," she replied.

"You, too, Harry?"

"I was here once before," I said. "Austin, actually— doing research for a book."

"You wrote a book about Texas?"

"No. A novel, set in Texas."

"A fiction novel?"

Veronica rolled her eyes.

"Exactly," I said. "A fiction novel. Good guess, Billy Ray."

He drove on, ignoring the speed limit. "How long've you been with the Bureau, Harry?"

"Harry's not with the Bureau. He's a psychiatrist. He's consulting with me on the case I'm working on."

"What kind of case?"

Veronica said, "A teenage girl from this area was murdered in Boston a couple of weeks ago. Her parents don't know yet. We're here to tell them about their daughter's death and see if they have any information that can help us track down her killer."

"You flew all the way to Texas for that? Someone here could've handled it for you."

"It's an unusual situation." She summarized the case for him: the two killings to date, the promise of two to come. "I'm far enough into the case that I wanted to come here myself to question the girl's parents. There is something you can help with, though."

"You name it."

"The man who killed her has used the name Elmore Winston. Can you check the local records—you know, voters' registrations, telephone listings—for someone with that name?"

"Sure. I'll start on it while you're registering at the hotel."

The Hilton Palacio del Rio was situated on the Riverwalk, a two-mile paved path along the San Antonio River in the middle of the downtown area. The walkway was neatly landscaped and lined with shops and restaurants, set a full story below street level like a sunken treasure. Billy Ray dropped us off at the hotel entrance, and we made plans to rendezvous an hour later.

"Palacio del Rio," I said as we waited our turn at the front desk. "River palace."

"You speak Spanish?" asked Veronica.

"*Un poco,*" I replied. "A little bit."

"Good. It may come in handy when we speak to Maria Melendez's parents."

"Mary Mendez," I corrected her.

"Right. Mary Mendez."

There was some momentary confusion as we checked in. Only one room had been reserved for us, which Veronica attributed to a mistake on the part of either her secretary or someone in the San Antonio field office. I rectified the situation, then we proceeded to our rooms to unpack. I called home and gave Mrs. Winnicot the phone number of the hotel.

I looked out my window at the Riverwalk below. The water was no more than fifty feet across, bounded by paved sidewalks. It looked more like a man-made canal than a river. A sightseeing barge with a dozen passengers passed by, its pilot taking care to avoid colliding with a teenage couple in a rented two-seat paddleboat. Underneath my window the girl in the paddleboat reached impulsively for her companion, pulling him toward her and kissing him long and hard. I wondered if they'd always remember that moment: holding one another tightly, time freezing in a tableau that would remain etched in their memories forever.

My phone rang. "I just called Boston," Veronica said. "Tim Connolly came through. He checked into Barney Cohen's phone bill and came up with the location of Mary Mendez's family. The phone is listed under the name Jorge Mendez. Must be Mary's father. We'll get Dalton to drive us there. You know, I've been thinking of questions to ask them that might shed light on the murders, and I haven't even considered how to tell them that their daughter is dead. Help me on this, will you?"

After I hung up, I stripped off my shirt and lay across the bed, contemplating the task ahead. I remembered a winter morning more than five years earlier, returning home shortly before dawn from the hospital room where Janet had just died in my arms.

Mrs. Winnicot was in her quarters and Janet's parents were in the guest room, all of them still asleep. I walked upstairs to Melissa's room and sat on the chair next to her bed, waiting quietly for her to stir, silently reviewing one last time the little speech I'd been practicing for several days.

Melissa awoke and sat up in bed. I tried to say the lines I'd rehearsed—about Janet's suffering, and God loving Janet too much to see her suffer any longer, and Janet going to live with God where together they would watch over us forever and ever. But I couldn't get a single word out.

"Mommy's dead, isn't she?"

"Yes, sweetheart. Mommy's dead."

I thought she might cry; I thought she might scream; I thought she might yell at me or strike out at me, the messenger bearing the worst news of all. If she had, I might have known instinctively how to comfort or calm her. But instead she walked slowly to her window seat and gazed out her picture window at the field beside our house. For several minutes she sat there, motionless: no tears, no wailing, no reaching out to me in anger or pain. I tried to hug her, but she pulled away. I tried to get her to talk, but she kept her thoughts buried inside. She turned a blank stare to the snow outside.

She remained in her room until Janet's funeral two days later, and then for a week beyond that. Whenever I looked in on her she was sitting on her window seat, staring out at the snow-covered field. She asked for nothing, said hardly anything. I couldn't reach her in the secret place to which she'd retreated. Even now, five years later, there were times when she just seemed to shut down, withdraw to that same hidden spot inside herself, almost oblivious to the world around her. It would come on without warning, then leave just as suddenly minutes later. It used to scare me; now it just made me very, very sad.

I met Veronica in the lobby at the appointed time. Billy Ray Dalton joined us a few minutes later. "No Elmore Winston in San Antonio, as best as I can tell so far," he said. "We'll keep working at it, check out the surrounding towns."

Veronica showed him a slip of paper with the Mendez family's address and asked him to take us there. He read the street number out loud and said, "I think I know where this is. It's in a Meskin neighborhood, just a few miles from here."

Meskin no doubt meant Mexican. I didn't know if the expression was meant to be derogatory. But I figured that someone who wouldn't take the trouble to pronounce a nationality correctly wouldn't make much effort to know or appreciate its people.

He consulted his street map after we returned to his car. Then we got on the highway and headed south. The Tower of the Americas rose high above HemisFair Plaza to our left, and the sun was beginning its descent toward the distant rolling hills off to our right. It was almost four o'clock, but Billy Ray wasn't hampered by the late afternoon traffic. He weaved in and out of lanes effortlessly, apparently confident that others would make way for him.

After ten minutes we left the highway and entered a residential neighborhood. The small stucco houses all had the same basic one-story design, laid out in small plots on streets named after major cities of the Southwest. The homes were in various states of upkeep, trim lawns alternating with patches that were overgrown with weeds. One front yard had a porcelain bathtub neatly placed at its center with a flagpole standing inside, flanked by two plastic pink flamingos.

We turned onto the block Mary Mendez had called home. Several brown-skinned youngsters were playing dodge ball near the corner. They parted in the middle when they saw Billy Ray's car heading toward them. Some waved; one of the older children raised his middle finger.

Billy Ray returned the boy's salute. "Gee, ain't America great."

I thought, *This used to be their country, Billy Ray*. But I said nothing.

He pulled alongside the curb and parked. "That's the house, across the street."

The Mendez house was lined along the front with rose bushes. An Arizona ash tree was off to one side. Bark mulch was laid around the base of the tree in a perfect circle, and in a rectangle underneath the rose bushes. A child's beat-up tricycle was lying on its side near the ash tree. A huge live oak tree stood behind the house, shade against the Texas heat. A large built-in fan expelled air from one side of the attic, no doubt sucking a breeze into the windows and through the house.

"You wait here, Billy Ray," Veronica said. "No sense overwhelming them with three people."

He eyed me and frowned. "You want *him* to go with you instead of *me*?"

"Harry knows the case. Don't get bent out of shape. I'll call for you if we need help."

"Yeah. You do that."

"Here. Read this and see what you come up with." She handed him photocopies of Artie's letters, and some of her notes on the case.

Veronica and I set out toward the Mendez home. We cut an odd appearance on that hot afternoon in that working-class Chicano neighborhood: two Anglos, conspicuous intruders, strolling across the street in business dress.

Behind a screen door, the front door of the house was wide open. A television set played nearby, and the sound of running water came from further inside. A small, stocky boy watched us through the screen door as we approached. He looked like he was between two and three years old, and he was sucking on a pacifier. He stood silently behind the screen door in shorts and a sleeveless undershirt.

"Is your mother or father home?" asked Veronica.

He continued watching wordlessly.

"Tu madre, tu padre—estan en casa?" I said, translating Veronica's question into Spanish.

He stayed there another minute, staring at us as he mouthed the pacifier he should have outgrown long ago, then walked away from the door. Someone turned down the television volume, and a moment later a wide-bodied Chicano man about my age was standing there. Like the boy, he stared at us without speaking, waiting for us to make the first move.

Veronica broke the silence. "Jorge Mendez?"

He nodded slightly.

"Mary Mendez's father?"

He glared at Veronica with narrowed eyes and tightly drawn lips. *"No tengo hija,"* he hissed. *"Mi hija esta muerta."* He walked away, slamming the paneled door shut behind him.

"What did he say?"

" 'I have no daughter. My daughter is dead.' "

Veronica furrowed her brow. "How did he find out?"

"I have no idea."

The paneled door cracked a few inches, then slowly opened. A short, slight woman in an apron stood before us. "Yes? May I help you?"

"Mrs. Mendez?" asked Veronica.

"Si, señorita."

"Mrs. Mendez, we'd like to talk with you about your daughter, Mary."

"Do you know where my Mary is?" Her eyes widened, and she rubbed her hands against her apron nervously, over and over.

Veronica looked at me, silently entreating me to move the conversation forward.

"Ma'am, your daughter has been living in Boston. I'm afraid . . . I'm afraid there's been a terrible accident."

Hearing myself say that, I felt like a bad actor in a low-budget B-movie. I was also dimly aware of the television set being turned off, and Jorge Mendez looming in the shadows behind his wife. She was wiping her hands on her apron furiously now.

The woman opened the screen door and stood next to us. "Mary! Where is she! What's wrong with my Mary?"

Jorge Mendez stepped outside and grabbed my arm, his hand a giant and unyielding pincer. "*¿Quien es usted?*" he demanded, then repeated himself in English. "Who are you?"

"I'm a doctor."

Still grasping my arm, he gestured toward Veronica. "And you?"

"I'm with the FBI."

Mary Mendez's mother began to shake uncontrollably. Looking at Veronica, she said, "*¿Policia?*"

No translation was needed. "Yes," said Veronica. "Police."

"*Dios mio.*" She moved close to me and whispered, "Tell me. Is Mary dead?"

I hesitated. "I'm so sorry. Your daughter died about two weeks ago."

"How?"

I glanced at Veronica; her eyes were trained on Jorge Mendez, who was looking at his wife.

"She was murdered. We don't know why."

The woman turned toward her husband. They stared at each other for a moment, a torrent of private meaning passing between them without words. Then she raised both hands above her head and brought them down hard against his chest, pummeling him again and again. "*¡Tu hiceste esto! ¡Tu hiceste esto a ella!*" You did this! You did this to her!

He tried to fend off her blows, letting go of my arm in the process. "Anna, no!" he shouted. He grabbed both of her wrists with one hand and slapped her with the other.

Anna Mendez kicked wildly and pushed her husband with all her strength. He stumbled against Veronica, and he and Veronica tumbled to the ground.

The woman began to swoon; I reached out to steady her. She held onto my arm and doubled over, spasming and making horrible retching sounds from deep within her.

Then she pulled away from me and walked toward the street.

Just as Veronica and Jorge Mendez were getting to their feet, the woman emitted an ear-shattering scream. It was unlike any sound I'd ever heard—the bray of a horrendously wounded creature. And as she screamed she picked up speed, trotting and then running toward the street.

I took off after her. Across the street, Billy Ray Dalton was stepping out of his car, no doubt impelled into action by the woman's screaming. He began to run toward us.

Anna Mendez dashed several yards down the block and into the middle of the street, then just stood there. She tried to scream again, but the sound wouldn't come. A pickup truck rounded the corner and headed for the spot where she stood.

Billy Ray and I reached the woman at the same instant. We pulled her out of the vehicle's path. The driver slammed on his brakes, swerving toward the opposite curb. The truck sideswiped a parked car and came to a halt. The driver got out and inspected the damage. He raised his hands, gesturing wildly and screaming Spanish insults at the three of us.

We led her back to her house. Jorge Mendez opened the screen door and we all stepped into the living room. Haltingly, he reached out to hold his wife—the uncertain, awkward gesture of someone not given to tenderness. She glared at him, keeping him at bay without a word. He stepped back and muttered something underneath his breath.

Anna Mendez collapsed on a frayed sofa and buried her face against a pillow, muffling her sobs. *"Mi niña, mi niña,"* she said, over and over. *"¿Que hicieran a ti?"* My baby, my baby. What have they done to you?

Billy Ray Dalton knew exactly what to do. As he explained afterward, he instinctively treated the situation like a domestic violence call. "Rule number one," he said later. "Protect any children present. Move them away from the scene if you can. Rule number two, separate the man and woman. Put them in different rooms. Better yet, take the man outside while your partner talks to the woman."

Billy Ray called for a next-door neighbor to take care of the boy. Then he told Jorge Mendez he needed to ask him some questions, and the two of them walked outside together.

Anna lay crying on the sofa, oblivious to what was happening around her. Veronica sat next to her and did her best to comfort the woman, but there was precious little soothing a stranger could offer. She handed tissues to the woman, but neither one of us knew what to say to her.

After a few minutes, Anna's sobs relented. She looked at Veronica, then at me, and asked, "Where is Willie? Where is my little boy?"

"Your neighbor is watching your son," I answered. "He'll be fine."

She dabbed at her tearstained cheek with a tissue. "He's not my son," she said. "He's my grandson. He's Mary's son."

15: People Die For No Reason

They had Mary after five years of marriage, after the doctors said it would take a miracle for Anna ever to bear a child: precious water in a barren desert.

Anna never lost sight of that miracle; maybe that's why she had such a hard time acknowledging the girl's failings. School was always difficult for Mary. And good friends came hard, and bad friends came easy. The older she grew, the worse it got.

Anna accepted all of Mary's excuses without question and even supplied a few of her own, making matters worse. Jorge tried to rein Mary in with restrictions, but this, too, just made matters worse.

One evening soon after Mary's sixteenth birthday, they found her locked in an embrace with a boy; her blouse was unbuttoned, her bra was unfastened, and her hands were buried deep inside the boy's unbuckled pants. Jorge chased the boy out of the house, then he called his daughter a whore, slapped her hard across the face, and locked her in her room.

The next morning Jorge tacked a list of rules to his daughter's bedroom door.

Things you must do to avoid punishment:
1. Do not make us hear anymore from your school.
2. If anyone calls you on the phone, you will tell me who it was and what you talked about.

3. *You will tell me where you are at every time, and you will be home when you are told to be home.*
4. *You will not go anywhere without my permission.*
5. *Do not argue with me. My decision is final and you will be happy to follow it.*
6. *If you are unhappy, go into another room and cry. Do not return with sniffles or tears in your eyes. Return with a smile.*
7. *Answer all questions. Do not make me ask you a second or third time.*
8. *No friends in the house when we are not home, and none in the house when we are home without permission first.*

Soon afterward, Mary brought them more heartache: She was pregnant. Abortion was never even discussed as an option by any of them. But Anna prayed the Lord would cause a merciful end to the pregnancy, even as she begged forgiveness for contemplating such a wish.

Little Willie was born before Mary turned seventeen. Mary was too much of a child herself to handle him, so Anna and Jorge became surrogate parents by default. Mary played the part of the rebellious and reluctant older sister.

When the child was less than a year old, Mary was suspended from high school after she and a friend were found with vials of crack cocaine. Jorge exploded when he heard the news. Harsh words turned to physical blows: He hit her. She hit him back. Anna tried to separate them and caught the worst of it from both ends. Then the girl and her mother fell into each other's arms, crying. Jorge said, "To hell with both of you," then stormed out of the house. He returned hours later in a drunken haze.

In the middle of the night, as Jorge slept stuporously, Anna was awakened by noises coming from the room Mary and Willie shared. When she stepped into the dimly lit hallway, she found Mary standing at the top of the stairway with a suitcase in her hand. Their eyes met. Neither one spoke for several seconds.

"Where will you go?" Anna whispered.

"I don't know," came the hushed response.

"When will you come back?"

"I don't know."

In the few seconds that passed as they stood there, an array of images flashed through Anna's mind: the joyful pain of Mary's birth, a kiss on a skinned knee, first Holy Communion.

"Don't try to stop me," her daughter said, and then Anna did something she would regret forever: nothing.

Mary walked downstairs and opened the front door. Anna whispered, "I love you," but she never knew whether or not the girl heard her.

Mary telephoned a week later. She wouldn't say where she was. Anna pleaded with her to come home. Just as Anna sensed her daughter's resolve weakening, Jorge stumbled into the room holding a can of beer.

"Is that the whore?" he said, with slurred speech loud enough to carry over the phone line. "Tell her to come back for her little bastard."

There was a catch in the girl's throat, and then the words, "Good-bye, Mama," the last words Anna would ever hear Mary speak.

There was a clicking noise, then a dial tone, and then her precious daughter was lost to her forever.

Everyone's pain is private and unknowable. I once made the mistake of telling a patient I knew exactly how he was feeling. "That's bull," my patient replied. "At best, you might know exactly how *you* feel." And so I tried to imagine Anna's sorrow, but I knew I really couldn't.

"It's been more than a year now. We don't talk about it much. Sometimes I blame Jorge, but not as bad as I know he blames himself. Sometimes I blame Mary. Most of the time I just blame myself."

Anna Mendez spoke softly, her sobs having dissolved into a stream of silent tears as she told her story. Veronica supplied her with a steady flow of tissues.

"You never heard from her again?" asked Veronica.

"No. She called her friend Felicita a couple of months

later, and Felicita told me Mary was okay. I never found out where she went, not until you came here today. How could this happen, *señorita*? Who could do this to my baby?"

"I don't know. I wish I did. Do you have any ideas?"

The woman shook her head.

"Has anyone called you, looking for Mary, since she left?"

"Just a couple of her friends, early on."

"Does she know anyone named Artie, or Arthur?"

She shrugged. "I don't know. Not that I remember."

"How about Elmore Winston? Does that name mean anything to you?"

"No. Why?"

"We think someone using that name may have been the last person to see her alive, but we don't know where to find him."

"Do you think he killed my daughter?"

"Yes."

Anna Mendez tore a damp tissue into tiny shreds as she sat on her sofa. "What was Mary doing in Boston? How did she die?"

Veronica didn't know what to say; she looked to me for help.

I paused. "She was found in a hotel. We don't know exactly where she'd been living or what she was doing." It was a lie, but a lie I could live with.

"Did anyone here know where she'd gone?" asked Veronica. "What about that friend you mentioned?"

"Felicita said Mary didn't tell her where she was when she called."

"Have you talked to her since then?"

"No. Felicita is the one who gave Mary the drugs that got her kicked out of school. I don't have anything to say to her."

"How can I get in touch with her?"

"She lives near the high school." Anna walked into her kitchen and returned a moment later with a telephone directory. She thumbed through its pages. "Here. This is it. The family's name is Sanchez."

Veronica copied the address and phone number. "Did your daughter ever visit Philadelphia?"

"She's never been outside of Texas before now."

"Have you ever heard of a man named Joseph Carroll?"

Anna paused to think, then began to shake her head. "I don't recognize that name. Who is he?"

"He was a priest in Philadelphia. He was murdered last October. We don't know who killed him, but we believe it was the same person who killed Mary."

Anna pondered that, and tried again to place the priest's name. "I'm very sorry. I don't know him."

"No, I didn't think so. And you and your husband didn't hire a detective to look for her, did you?"

"No."

Jorge Mendez walked into the house with Billy Ray Dalton close behind. Billy Ray made a small wave of his hand to Veronica, a gesture to let her know that things were under control. Jorge's eyes were red and the smell of beer emanated from him. I wondered if Billy Ray had ever gone drinking with a "Meskin" before.

Jorge sat on the sofa next to his wife, touched her hand awkwardly, and whispered something into her ear in Spanish. Her whole body shuddered very slightly for an instant, then she leaned against him and quietly cried on his shoulder.

Veronica began to ask Jorge the same questions she'd put to Anna. "He already asked me," Jorge said, pointing to Billy Ray.

Billy Ray was a quick study; with only a few minutes to glance over the materials Veronica handed him when we left him sitting in the car, he'd grasped enough about the case to make the proper inquiries of Jorge Mendez. Veronica nodded at Billy Ray, acknowledging his thoroughness.

Veronica asked the Mendezes if they had any recent snapshots of their daughter. Anna walked over to a bookcase and pulled a photograph album from the shelf. She gave the album to Veronica, who pulled a picture from the book. "May I borrow this?"

"Please, *señorita*, if anything should happen to it . . ."

Veronica touched the woman's arm. "Don't worry. I'll make copies and return it to you in a few days."

Jorge spoke. "Will it help you find the person who did this?"

"I hope so."

We returned to Billy Ray's car and Veronica handed him Felicita Sanchez's address. He consulted his street map, then started his car and pulled away from the curb. "Well, you folks sure know how to show a guy a good time," he said. He began to laugh. "He's not such a bad guy, Jorge Mendez. He's worked hard to make something of himself."

"You mean, he's pulled himself up by his own bootstraps?" I asked.

"Right." My sarcasm was lost on Billy Ray. "He's done a lot of different things over the years. Ambulance driver, security guard, short-order cook. He got a landscaping job about ten years ago and now he has his own company. He's done well by his family, if you see what I'm saying."

"You mean, he's a credit to his people, if you see what I'm saying."

"Right. So why are we going to see this girl?"

Veronica explained. "Mary Mendez lived with a man named Barney Cohen for a few months when she first came to Boston. Months before Mary was murdered, someone called Cohen looking for her. Said he was hired by the family to find her, which was a lie. Cohen gave the caller information about her whereabouts. I think the caller was the same man who killed her."

"So the question," said Billy Ray, "is how the killer traced her to Barney Cohen."

"Exactly. If her parents didn't tell him, maybe her friend Felicita did."

The Sanchez house was across the street from the local high school. It was bigger than the Mendez house, but not as well tended. Veronica knocked hard at the front door and a portly middle-aged Chicano woman answered. Veronica displayed her badge. "We're here to question Felicita Sanchez."

The woman's eyes opened wide and her hands flitted nervously by her sides. She left us standing there, and a minute later we heard her arguing with someone in a distant part of the house.

After a few moments of silence, a teenage girl appeared. It was late afternoon, but she looked as though she'd just gotten out of bed. Her face bore red ridges where she'd been lying, and her long, straight hair was all awry. She wore a rumpled knee-length T-shirt with the name of a rock group I'd never heard of. She stretched and yawned. "Yeah?"

"Felicita Sanchez?" asked Veronica.

"Who wants to know?"

She displayed her badge again. "FBI."

The girl quickly scanned our faces. She was nervous, but she tried to hide it. "Uh-huh." She yawned again and opened the screen door. She shuffled into the living room and we followed her. She sat down on the floor with her legs folded in front of her, her head bowed, and her eyes half-closed. She waited for one of us to begin the conversation.

Billy Ray said, "We want to ask you about Mary Mendez."

"Uh-huh."

"She left home about fifteen months ago."

"Really," replied the girl, without a trace of emotion in her voice.

"Listen. Don't jerk us around, Felicita. We know you talked to her since then."

Veronica kneeled beside her and spoke quietly. "We're not here to cause you any problems. We need your help. We know you were Mary's good friend."

The girl raised her head and opened her eyes slowly, as if awakening to an awareness that something was terribly amiss. "Is she in trouble?"

Veronica hesitated. "We think she's in danger. We need

to find her so we can protect her. Someone wants to kill her."

The girl's body tensed for a split second, then she bowed her head again and resumed her semisomnolent pose. "She called me a couple of times to find out how her little boy was doing. I never talk to her parents, so I just made stuff up when she called."

"Do you know where Mary is?" asked Veronica.

"Boston."

"Do you have her address?"

She shook her head.

"A phone number?"

"I lost it."

Billy Ray interrupted, unable to contain his exasperation. "Damn it, you little shit. This is no game."

"Nice talk, mister. You kiss your mother with that mouth?"

"Listen, goddamn you—"

She pulled herself to a half-standing position. "Hey, I don't need this. I got stuff to do. What's your problem?"

Veronica said, "There's no problem, Felicita. You're being very helpful. Stay, please."

The girl remained in her crouch for a few seconds, then sat down again.

"Now, this is very important," Veronica said. "Has anyone else called you or visited you to ask about Mary?"

She sat silently, head bowed, for a long time.

Veronica put her hand on the girl's shoulder. "Felicita?"

A single tear began to slither down the girl's cheek. "You're too late, aren't you? She's already dead."

Veronica sighed. "Yes."

"In Boston?"

"Yes, in Boston."

The girl buried her face in her hands. "He gave me money."

"Who gave you money?"

"The man who was looking for Mary. Two hundred dollars."

"What did you tell him?"

"I gave him the phone number of some dentist who owned the house Mary was living in."

"What did this man look like?"

"I don't know."

"Jesus Christ, girl!" barked Billy Ray.

"I don't know!" she repeated with a whine. "I never met him. He called me on the phone, then he sent me the money, then he called again and I gave him the phone number."

"Was it a check?" asked Veronica, no doubt planning to trace the transaction.

"No. Cash."

"What else? Close your eyes and think, Felicita. What else do you remember?"

She closed her eyes, then opened them a few seconds later. "I don't know. I don't remember."

"How about his voice? Did he have any kind of accent? Did he sound like he came from around here, or someplace else?"

She thought for a moment. "I don't know."

"What was his name?"

"His name?" The girl bit her lip and pondered. "Kent, I think. Or maybe Salem. I remember it sounded like a cigarette."

"Could it be Winston?"

"Huh. Yeah. Winston. I bet that's it." She smiled, pleased with herself, but the smile quickly dissolved into a look of terror. "Oh, God—is he the one?"

In a Tex-Mex outdoor restaurant on the Riverwalk, Billy Ray Dalton watched the evening sun through the bottom of his second empty beer mug. Veronica had matched him beer for beer, while I stayed with sparkling water.

Billy Ray put the mug down and said, "So the killer comes to San Antonio looking for Mary Mendez. She's gone, but somehow he learns that Felicita Sanchez is her friend."

Veronica swished a shrimp through the green sauce on

her plate and took a bite. "Tasty. What did you say this is called?"

"Camarones al cilantro," I replied. "Shrimp grilled in a sauce of garlic butter and coriander."

"Very nice. Want some?" She reached toward me and placed the rest of the piece in my mouth.

Billy Ray watched her do that with intense interest, then continued. "So Felicita sells him Cohen's phone number, and Cohen gives him another phone number, and eventually the killer catches up with her. But he's not ready yet. For some reason he has to wait until . . . what was that date?"

"April 30th," I said.

". . . April 30th. So he keeps track of her whereabouts, or maybe he hires a private detective to do that, until he's ready to strike."

Our waiter walked by. Billy Ray ordered two more Coronas—one for him and one for Veronica—and I asked for a refill on our supply of tostada chips and salsa.

"When did you say he's going to kill his next victim?"

"May 20th, a week from tomorrow," I said.

"It doesn't give you much time. And you still don't have any handle on motive. No way of predicting who he'll go for next. Or why he sticks pennies in their hands after cutting their heads off."

I used the edge of my fork to slice a piece of my beef enchilada. "Well, so far he's killed a holy man and a sinner. Maybe there's some kind of symbolic religious connection."

"The way I see it," he replied, "the next victim might be a proctologist."

"Why a proctologist?"

Billy Ray smiled. "He's killed a priest and a prostitute. Both start with the letters *P-R*. Maybe he's working his way through a dictionary of occupations."

Veronica laughed. She threw her head back and shook her long brown hair. The beer was beginning to kick in.

Encouraged by her laughter, Billy Ray continued. "It reminds me of an old joke about Abraham Lincoln. Did you know he was so tall they couldn't fit him in his coffin when he died?"

Veronica leaned forward, one arm touching his, the other touching mine. "No. Do tell."

"So they had to cut his head off. And you know what they did with it?"

"No," she said.

"Harry?"

"Let me guess," I said, amazed by his boorishness. "They stuck it on a penny."

He glared at me for a moment, then forced a smile. "Very good, Harry."

Veronica looked confused for a few seconds, then broke into laughter and tossed her hair back again.

"Y'all don't have the death penalty up in Massachusetts, do you?"

"We used to," I replied. "We may get it back. The new governor is a former prosecutor. And a Republican."

"So if we're lucky," Veronica said, "it won't be long."

I've never cared much, one way or the other, about capital punishment. But Veronica's advocacy didn't surprise me. *I had a mission when I decided to study law. I wanted to hurt people who hurt other people.*

Billy Ray said, "You won't need the death penalty if Jorge Mendez gets his way. He's angry enough to do the job himself when you identify his daughter's killer."

I thought about Ellis Greenfield and the rage that had driven him for nearly two years. "I think I'd feel the same way."

"Not me," said Billy Ray. "I'd want the son of a bitch alive so I could make him suffer forever."

"Do you have kids?" I asked.

"A boy and a girl. They're in Houston with my ex-wife."

"Wouldn't you have thoughts about killing the man who murdered your child?"

"Maybe. More likely, I'd have thoughts about killing *his* child so he could know what it's like. An eye for an eye, if you see what I'm saying. That would be worse than death. And that would be justice."

"You're a sick man, Billy Ray."

He laughed. "Thanks, Harry. I guess you're the expert on that."

"Boys, boys—this is much too serious for me." Veronica quaffed beer number three.

"So, Veronica—can I give you a little moonlit tour of the city? You too, Harry, of course."

"No, thanks," I said.

"Me, neither. Harry and I already have plans."

That was news to me.

"Oh," he said. "Are you two, uh, you know . . ."

Veronica patted my hand. "Harry is carrying my baby." She laughed again, and Billy Ray forced himself to join in. "Besides, we have to get up early for a flight to Philadelphia. We're going to see what we can learn about Father Joseph Carroll, Artie's first victim."

Billy Ray ate a few more chips and drained mug number three. "Well, that's it for me. I guess I'm the odd man out. Y'all behave, and don't do anything I wouldn't do." He offered to drive us to the airport in the morning, then tossed two twenty-dollar bills on the table. "My treat, folks."

After he left, Veronica smiled and asked, "Is he?"

"Is he what?"

She leaned close to me, and her breath was warm against my neck. Her breast brushed against my hand, but she made no effort to pull back. "Is he the odd man out?"

I pulled my hand away. "I think he's very odd. Don't you?"

"Nice evasion, Harry. Am I embarrassing you?"

"What do you think?"

"What do you think I think? Or do you think I think at all?"

"I think you've had too a little too much beer."

"I think you think I drink." She stood up, a bit shakily. "Come with me. There's something I want to see. The map in my room said it's a couple of blocks that-a-way, pardner." She made a broad, sweeping gesture with her thumb, then began to laugh again.

A few yards down the path, Veronica stumbled and almost took a header into the river. I grabbed her arm to steady her. She hooked her hand inside the crook of my elbow, escort style, and we continued along the walkway. A few minutes later she pulled free and ran to a nearby wrought-iron stairway leading from the Riverwalk up to the street. I followed behind.

"This way," she said at the top of the stairs. She grabbed my hand and pulled me along. We turned left at the corner and she stopped in her tracks. "There it is."

The Alamo stood before us. The Lone Star flag flew above that symbol of the state's battle for independence from Mexico. Battered and worn, it was smaller than I'd imagined. Tucked amid buildings two centuries younger, like a dowager at a debutante ball, the ancient mission had undeniable character and majesty.

"I want to touch it," Veronica said. She let go of my hand and walked to the nearest wall. She closed her eyes, ran her hand slowly over the pock-marked adobe facade, and began to recite. " 'To the people of Texas and all Americans in the world. The enemy has demanded a surrender, otherwise the troops are to be put to the torch. I have answered the demand with a cannon shot, and our flag still waves proudly from the walls. I shall never surrender or retreat. I am determined to sustain myself as long as possible and die like a soldier who never forgets what is due to his own honor and that of his country.' "

"What was that?"

She opened her eyes. "A passage from a letter the commanding officer wrote, about a month before the Mexicans stormed the mission. I memorized it when I was a girl, along with the Gettysburg Address and Patrick Henry's 'Give me liberty or give me death' speech." She turned to face me. "I wanted to believe people die for a reason."

"I had a teacher who used to say that if you didn't have something worth dying for, you couldn't have something worth living for."

"Do you believe that?"

"I think so."

"What would you die for?"

"My daughter. Any father would."

"Not any father."

"Any good father."

"How do you know you'd die for her?"

"I just know."

"You'd do it gladly?"

"Not gladly, but without thinking twice."

She sighed. "Well, it's certainly a nice thought." We turned and walked slowly toward the stairwell leading back to the Riverwalk. "But those speeches I memorized, that stuff about dying for a reason—it's all a bunch of crap. People usually die for no good reason at all."

I thought about Janet's death and the countless times I'd searched for some meaning in it. "I can't accept what you're saying."

"No good reason at all, Harry. And sometimes it gets very ugly. You think Mary Mendez died for a reason? When her little boy is old enough to understand what happened, what sense will he make of it? Will he accept that? How will he get over it?"

"People get over things. I once treated a young girl who had witnessed her own mother's murder, and—"

She covered her ears with her hands. "Enough!" She ran the remaining distance to the stairwell, then down to the river level. I ran after, catching up to her several yards down the path where she'd stopped to watch a couple in a paddleboat. She'd been crying; a tiny smudge of out-of-place eye makeup made her look vulnerable and alone.

"Are you alright?"

Veronica turned toward me and smiled softly. "You're sweet." She looped her arm inside mine and we headed back to our hotel. She held tightly to me, and her body rubbed up and down against mine as we walked. I'd experienced few such moments since Janet died, and the pleasure never equalled the sadness those moments brought.

In the year following Janet's death, I had vivid dreams about her. The content was always mundane: everyday scenes from average days. It felt so normal that I almost thought it was real. But I always knew it was a dream, and that she'd be gone if I awoke. So I'd try to fend off awakening, as if a sheer act of will could prolong the fantasy.

"It didn't work," I said.

"What didn't work?"

"Oh, nothing. I was just thinking to myself."

"Well, I for one am tired of thinking."

Veronica stopped and turned to face me. She wrapped her arms around my waist and pressed her mouth to mine. Her lips were soft and moist, and as they parted slightly I felt the tip of her tongue dart against mine. A wave of trepidation hit me like an electric shock, and I snapped away quickly.

"I'm sorry," she said. "Is it me?"

I shook my head. "It's me. I've never been able to handle this sort of thing. Not since my wife died."

"How many years?"

"Five."

She stepped back and said, "You're a fine one to talk about people getting over things, Harry Kline."

Back in my hotel room, I reached for the phone to call Melissa. Then I remembered it was an hour later in Concord; she was probably already asleep. So I lay on the bed, clicking aimlessly through the television channels, and thinking about what had just happened.

My relationship with Janet hadn't ended with her passing. It not only endured, it continued to change, colored by the unfolding events in my life and the reactions I imagined she would have if she were still with me. If she were watching, what would she think about everything that had happened today?

The new Bruce Springsteen video was playing on MTV. Standing against a dark and somber background, stripped to his waist and pounding on his electric guitar, he sang:

> *That feeling of safety you prize*
> *It comes with a hard, hard price*
> *You can't shut off the risk and the pain*
> *Without losing the love that remains*
> *We're all riders on this train*

16: Priests

Billy Ray Dalton parked his car in a restricted zone outside the terminal and walked with us to the baggage check-in area. When he thought Veronica wasn't watching, he flashed a conspiratorial grin at me. Then she excused herself for a few minutes, and Billy Ray cast a salacious glance at her form as she walked away. "Nice," he said, then smirked. "But I guess you know that already, huh?"

"Listen. Let's get something straight. Veronica and I aren't lovers. We aren't even good friends. I met her very recently and I'm helping her with this case. That's all there is to it."

"But last night, when I offered to show her the city, she said—"

"I know what she said. She was bullshitting you."

"Why would she do that?"

"Well, gosh and golly, Billy Ray, that is a puzzle, isn't it?"

"Hell, that's a fine how-do-you-do," he replied, with a furrowed brow and puzzled look. He grunted. "It's just as well you're not involved. She'd be hard to tame."

"That's very enlightened of you. You should get an award."

"You think so?"

Veronica returned while Billy Ray was trying to figure out if I was being sarcastic. We said our good-byes, and he called after us as we headed toward our boarding gate,

"Don't be strangers, y'all hear? Let me know how this case turns out."

"A good investigator," Veronica said. We took seats in the crowded waiting area. "Neanderthal, Cro-Magnon at best, but a good investigator. Riley's not bad, either."

"Riley?"

"John Riley, the Philadelphia detective you spoke to on the phone. He finally sent his report to my office in Boston, and they faxed it to me yesterday." She tapped her leather portfolio. "It was waiting for me when we returned to the hotel. You can read it on the plane. Anyway, Riley may be stubborn, and he may not want anyone helping or interfering, but he knows his job. It made for interesting bedtime reading." She smiled. "Besides, I had to do something to pass the time."

I didn't know what to say to that.

"Look, Harry—I'm sorry if I was out of line last night. I just misread your signals, that's all."

"I didn't realize I was sending any signals."

"Apparently you weren't. Forget it. It's no big deal. Besides, we have work to do. I guess we don't want to do anything to get matters confused, do we?"

Her tone of voice suggested that she was open to argument on the point. There was a moment of uncomfortable silence, broken by a voice on the loudspeaker that announced the boarding of our flight. We waited in line to pass through the gate. "What did you do last night?" Veronica asked.

"Not much. Watched some TV. Thought about Jorge Mendez."

"What about him?"

"Your child rejects you like that, and then she's murdered before you have a chance to work things out with her." We passed through the tunnel leading from the terminal to the plane. "He'll take that burden to his grave."

I offered Veronica the window seat, but she preferred the aisle. She handed me the packet of papers from Detective Captain John Riley of the Philadelphia Police Department. I glanced through them: a summary of the forensic evidence, police interviews with people at or near the church where the killing occurred, follow-up interviews with friends and family of the dead priest. None of it yielded any leads for the police, and none of it held my interest.

But I was struck by the official photographs of the murder scene. I'd studied my own picture of that scene long and hard—the picture the killer had snapped and sent to me. Looking at the police photos was like viewing alternate takes of a familiar movie scene: They were virtually identical to the version I remembered, but the small differences were magnified by my familiarity with the original. A different angle here, more background there, and in all of them more blood: They had been snapped later than my version, after additional fluid had seeped from Father Joseph's lifeless form. I knew it was my imagination, but even the photos felt cold.

The last shot was a closeup of the corpse's right hand. A penny was clearly visible, wedged between two fingers. It was heads up, and the detail on the picture was fine enough to reveal the coin's date.

I pointed at the penny. "Do you think this date means anything?"

She glanced at the picture. "1976. The Bicentennial, fireworks, a lot of boring speeches."

"No—I mean, do you think it might have some special significance to the killer?"

She considered it. "I hadn't thought of that. What was the date on the penny you saw in Mary Mendez's hand?"

"I didn't get that close a look."

"I'll make a note to ask Tim Connolly."

As she jotted a reminder in her notebook, I thought back to that much-ballyhooed Fourth of July. I was still in medical school. Janet and I had just begun dating. A friend loaned me a small pleasure craft he kept docked in Maine, and Janet and I sailed deep into Penobscot Bay. Night fell, a quarter-moon shone on the water, and we were completely sealed off from whatever was happening anywhere else in the universe. There were no words, no sense of time, no sense of place. It could have been a thousand years ago, or next week, or now. It was a memory I'd come back to a million times, especially since Janet's passing.

Veronica was saying something, but I hadn't been listening.

"I said, what was she like?"

"Who?"

"Your wife. That's who you were thinking about, isn't it?"

I gazed out the window. The plane was darting in and out of a series of light clouds. I had no idea where we were. And I didn't know how to answer her question.

"Do you remember what you said about Ellis Greenfield?" she asked. "You said he was frozen, caught up in a reinvented fantasy of the past. That he wouldn't be able to move on until he began to think more realistically about the past, the bad as well as the good."

I continued looking out the window.

"I'm out of line again, aren't I?" she said.

"Maybe. I don't know."

We landed in a light but steady rain. It was almost noon.

John Riley was supposed to send an officer to escort us, but no one showed up at either the gate or the baggage claim area. We waited for a half hour. The longer we waited, the angrier Veronica got. "That son of a bitch did this on purpose."

We hailed a cab outside the terminal. As the driver pulled away from the curb, Veronica gave him the address of Riley's station house. The driver pulled back to the curb and put the cab in neutral. "That's North Philadelphia. Spade City. I don't drive there, and you gotta be nuts for going there yourself."

I said, "That's against the law, isn't it?"

"So call a cop. I don't drive there."

Veronica shoved her badge in front of his flabby, unshaven face. "Yes, you do. Or I'll fix it so you can't even drive out of your garage."

He looked intently at her for a moment, then glanced at me, trying to determine whether to take her seriously. "Believe her," I said. He muttered something and began driving.

Forty minutes later we came into North Philadelphia. We passed a major intersection; the street sign informed us we were at the corner of Germantown and Lehigh Avenues, but it was bent and bowed and I couldn't tell which street was which. The area was teeming with people, all of them black. The streets were littered with refuse. The heads were missing from half of the parking meters, and the rest were mostly bashed and broken. Every storefront had a retracted metal security grate along its entire length; when dropped down at the end of the day the gates wouldn't prevent windows from being smashed, but they would probably keep looters out.

A few stores and several houses were boarded up and abandoned. "Plywood is a thriving industry here," said our driver. An elderly man rummaged through an overflowing trash barrel, picking out beer bottles and cans. "A local entrepreneur," the driver remarked. "Frank Rizzo had the right idea."

"Who's he?" I asked.

"Former mayor. God rest his soul."

I gathered this Rizzo had had something to say about the area that appealed to our driver, but I decided not to ask what that was all about.

We reached our destination: a drab, block-long brick building, three stories high. Veronica paid the fare on the meter but didn't tip the driver.

"That's just great," he said. "You realize there won't be any fares for me in this part of town, and I'll have to waste a half hour of my time driving to an area where I'll get some business."

"Sorry."

"Yeah, I bet you are." He pulled away from the curb, shouting something unintelligible at us as he drove away.

The station house interior reeked of stale cigarette smoke and a dozen unidentifiable odors. A uniformed officer sat behind a desk in a screened-in cubicle, hunched over the sports page. Veronica told him who we were looking for.

"Second floor," he said without looking up. We headed for a nearby stairwell. "Hey, hold it! You can't just—"

I hesitated for a second, but Veronica kept going and I followed. Near the top of the stairs was a door bearing Captain John Riley's name. Veronica barged in. I trailed behind. A group of men were laughing at something, but they stopped abruptly and stared at the two of us. In the center of the group, sitting with his feet propped up on his desk, was a heavyset black man about sixty years old. An inch-wide semicircular swath of white hair surrounded his otherwise bald head.

"Riley," said Veronica.

He nodded and said, "Who the hell are you?"

She ignored his question. "You were supposed to send someone to meet us."

Riley glanced at me. "Oh, right." Someone else in the room chuckled.

The officer from the downstairs cubicle stumbled into the room. "Sorry, Captain," he said, panting. "I tried to stop them. You want me to take them somewhere?"

"No, Dixon. These people are my guests. Roll out the red carpet. Strike up the band."

"Huh?"

"Never mind, Dixon. Leave us be. The rest of you, too. Leave us be for now." The room emptied out in seconds. John Riley removed his feet from his desk. "Pace, isn't it? Verona Pace."

"Veronica," she corrected him.

"And you're Dr. Kline. The one who got me involved in this thing. Well, sit down, sit down, the two of you. I have things to do, so let's get going. Did you get my report?"

Veronica nodded.

"So why are you here? You think I missed something?"

"I didn't say that."

"You didn't have to. Joseph Carroll. Joseph Carroll. I'm so goddamn sick and tired of hearing about Father Joseph Carroll." He slapped his meaty palm against his desktop. "Let me tell you something."

He reached into his desk and pulled out a file. He looked

inside and began reciting from it. "Charlotte Washington. Dead from a gunshot wound to her head. Sitting in her kitchen over a bowl of soup when a stray bullet from a drive-by shooting took her down. Marcus Reese. Punched to death outside his junior high, probably by another student. Probably for not handing over his lunch money. Or for not having enough to hand over. Or for no particular reason at all. Vera Rainey. Stomach ripped out with a jagged piece of glass. Left to die inside her convenience store two blocks from here. All of these cases are still open, just like the Carroll case. Guess what these three victims have in common, besides being dead. How are they different from Joseph Carroll?"

I spoke for the first time. "He was white. These other people were all black."

"Good guess. How did you know?"

"When we spoke on the phone the week before last, you asked me if I was white."

He smiled, and he actually looked embarrassed for a moment. "You are, aren't you?"

"So it seems."

"That's what makes the Carroll case different. A black person is murdered in this precinct, that's 'dog bites man.' "

"And what you have with Joseph Carroll," I said, "is 'man bites dog'?"

"You got it. And white folks in this city have a hard time with that. The Commissioner's office spent more energy on this case than any other one I know of."

"And still you came up dry," said Veronica.

"Yeah." He sighed. "Funny, isn't it? I think we stand a better chance of finding the people who killed Charlotte Washington, Marcus Reese, and Vera Rainey. But they don't count, do they? The FBI isn't interested in them."

Veronica stood in front of Riley's desk and glared down at him. "Listen, you smug bastard. The same man who killed Joseph Carroll killed a dope-snorting Hispanic hooker. He's got two more victims lined up, and I don't know if they're white, black, brown, purple, or chartreuse.

Frankly, I don't care. What I care about is stopping him. And that's all you should care about."

He stood and faced her. "You read my report."

"I read your report."

"And what does our fabulous FBI have to say? Was there something lacking? Some lead we didn't follow? A clue we didn't notice?"

"No," said Veronica. "You were very thorough. Of course, it would've been nice if you had filed a VICAP report."

"Aagh, red tape crap." He snickered and made a dismissive gesture with his hand. They both sat down. "You sure the two cases are related?"

"Yes."

"Let me hear."

Veronica went through everything we knew about Mary Mendez and her death. She showed Riley copies of Artie's letters, and I answered a few questions about my work with mentally ill veterans at the Bedford VA.

"So you're looking for someone named Arthur. Or someone named Elmore Winston. But you don't know if those are real names. And you don't have any suspects."

"Right." She didn't mention her suspicions about my editor, Jeffrey Barrow.

"And you want to figure out if the first two victims are related in some way, so you can figure out who's next. But the next murder is scheduled for next Wednesday, a week from today."

"Yes."

He was quiet for a moment, and then he began to laugh uproariously. "Child, I hope you got no promotion riding on this. Because you got no chance of catching him by then with what you have so far. And what the hell is chartreuse?" He laughed again, and this time Veronica began to smile in spite of herself. The edge was off of the conversation for the moment. "I bet you have a picture of her."

Veronica showed him the photograph she'd borrowed from Anna Mendez. "This was taken about a year and a half ago, a couple of months before she ran away from home. Her mother says it's a good likeness."

"Is it, Doctor?" Riley passed them to me.

"I guess so." I studied it for the first time. Mary Mendez was sitting in the yard behind her house with her baby on her lap. Her innocent smile gave no hint of the troubles she endured or the horrible end awaiting her. She was very pretty, childlike yet alluring, just as Barney Cohen had described her. It was hard to connect this vibrant image with the bloody, lifeless form I'd seen on a bathroom floor at the Lafayette Hotel.

Riley said, "You see pictures like this on milk cartons, you don't stop to think about them as people. Do you have children, Doctor?"

"Yes."

He looked at Veronica. "You?"

She shook her head.

"My boy's in Seattle. Out of this cesspool." He sighed. "The church where Joseph Carroll was murdered is near here. We can Xerox some copies of this picture, take them there, see if anyone recognizes the girl. Not likely, if you ask me."

There was a small fenced-in lot behind the building that held a dozen cruisers and a few unmarked cars. Riley led us to his Ford sedan and we placed our bags in the trunk. "You want to take the short route, or the scenic route?"

"There's a scenic route?" Veronica said.

"Nope."

We drove a few blocks, and Riley pointed to a dilapidated brick building. "Baker Bowl used to stand here. The Phillies played there when I was a kid. Shibe Park was a half mile west of here. That's where the Athletics played. I never came here then. The whole area was white in those days. So were the teams. The Athletics moved to Kansas City, then to Oakland. The Phillies play in South Philly in one of those concrete stadiums that all look alike. I never go there, either. I hate Astroturf. Well, here we are—Our Lady of Sorrow. What a name, huh?"

The church was on the corner of a narrow residential

street. It was lined by a small patch of well-tended grass, the only such patch on the entire block. Heavy mesh screens surrounded two small stained glass windows. The glass had been removed from the message board in front of the building. The board contained a passage from Second Chronicles:

AND WHEN HE WAS IN AFFLICTION
HE BESOUGHT THE LORD HIS GOD
AND HUMBLED HIMSELF GREATLY
BEFORE THE GOD OF HIS FATHERS

"I get it," said Riley. "The hooker stops here on her way to Boston. Gives her confession to Joseph Carroll. Tells him something that someone else doesn't want anyone to know. So that someone else kills both of them." His sarcastic tone made it clear that he thought the scenario he described was ridiculous.

"I doubt Mary Mendez was ever here," I replied.

"Unlikely," said Veronica.

The church secretary showed us into a chamber beside the chapel. An elderly, frail black man in a short sleeve shirt and priest's collar was sitting behind a large oak desk. He was writing on a pad of paper when we entered. He wore a hearing aid in each ear, the old type with wires running to a control box in his shirt pocket. His thick glasses weighed heavily on him. His writing hand moved slowly and laboriously across the page. He was small and pencil-thin, and he looked like he might give up the ghost at any moment. He continued writing for several seconds, oblivious to our presence, until the secretary gently tapped his shoulder.

"Father Steven?" she said.

Startled, he dropped his pen and reached reflexively for the hearing aid volume control. "Yes? Yes?" He saw us standing in the doorway. "Ah—Captain Riley, isn't it?"

"John, Father. Call me John."

"Ah, yes, of course. Well, do come in, John." He began to struggle to his feet.

"Please don't get up." Riley walked closer to the priest and Veronica and I followed a few steps behind. "Father, I brought some people to meet you. Veronica Pace. FBI. Dr. Harold Kline. Psychiatrist."

The old man reached his gaunt arm across the desk to shake my hand. His fingers were warm and soft, and as he grasped my hand he removed his glasses and stared directly at me. His eyes remained locked on mine for several seconds, as if taking measure of something within me.

I broke contact first and turned away, embarrassed, wondering what he had divined. He nodded briefly at Veronica, put his glasses back on, and leaned back in his chair. "John, I presume you've come to talk some more about Father Joseph."

"Yes, Father."

"Our dear Father Joseph." He shook his head slightly from side to side. "What a sad, sad day for the people who loved him." The priest closed his eyes for a moment and sighed. "Has there been—what is it you people would say—a break in the case?"

"A small break, maybe. Ms. Pace is investigating a murder in Boston. She believes that murder is related to this one."

"And what do you believe, John?"

Riley shrugged. "Maybe. Or maybe it's just another murder."

"There's always another murder, isn't there? It's the misery of the world that keeps both you and me in business, isn't it, John?"

"Unfortunately."

"Yes. Unfortunately." Father Steven looked at me again. "And may I ask what your involvement is, Dr. Kline?"

"It's a long, unhappy story, sir."

"I listen to long, unhappy stories every day. I imagine that's something we have in common. What would you like to tell me?"

For the next several minutes I told Father Steven everything I could think of about the two murders. I told him about the letters, the pictures, my own presence at the scene of Mary Mendez's murder. And then, drawn in by his accepting silence, I told him more: I talked about the book I'd begun work on, and how that work grew out of my guilt over the actions of a crazed killer who may have been spurred into murder by something else I'd written. I told him about my firsthand acquaintance with suffering and death, in my work and in my own life. I talked about Janet, and I talked about Melissa, and I probably would have talked on and on about every sadness I'd ever known if I hadn't forced myself to stop.

Father Steven asked if he could see Artie's letters. Veronica handed copies to him. After he read them he turned to me and said, "I see. This matter has become part of your life. The killer has selected you, and you have selected him in return."

I pondered that for a moment. I had no reply.

"Do you really feel some responsibility for what that other murderer did in Texas?"

"For the fact that he murdered? No. For the fact that he killed those particular people at that particular place and time? I think so."

"That must be a weight on you." He pointed at Artie's letters. "This man has a weight on him, too. Some terrible guilt, or some unsquelched grief. It won't let go of him, and it drives him to do terrible things." He paused. "Are you certain that Artie is a man?"

I glanced at Veronica, who said, "We're certain, Father. Why do you ask?"

"Oh, just something that occurred to me as the doctor was speaking. The name Artie reminded me of Artemis. The goddess of the hunt. It would fit, wouldn't it? From what you say, your murderer selects his victims, tracks them, then strikes them down. I don't suppose you've ever killed anyone, have you, Doctor?"

I shook my head.

"And you, Ms. Pace?"

"No."

He turned toward Riley, and the detective averted his eyes. Father Steven didn't ask anything of him. Instead he said, "I killed a man once. Yes, I see your surprise, John. I was a chaplain in the Korean War, and certain circumstances arose. That is my particular weight. Are you a Catholic, John?"

"Sometimes."

"Yes. Well, perhaps one day we can talk about that."

Veronica spoke. "The killer writes about punishing people for certain sins. Recklessness, carelessness, incompetence, and dishonesty. It almost sounds as if there's a religious element to his plan. Does it strike a chord with you, Father? Do you see anything that could help us identify him, or help us identify his next two victims?"

The old priest perused the letters once more. "The theme of retribution does have an Old Testament feel to it. Other than that, nothing comes to mind immediately. These sins he refers to aren't part of any text or liturgy I know of. If you leave these copies with me, I'll be happy to continue thinking about your question."

"Thank you. I know Captain Riley has already asked you this, but do you have any idea who might want to hurt Joseph Carroll?"

"No. Joseph was a truly remarkable young man. I've heard many people say they are color-blind when it comes to the issue of race. In my experience, the very statement shows that the person thinks in terms of color. Joseph never made such a statement, and yet I've never met anyone who was more able to separate normal human prejudices from the way he viewed people. He was only here for a short time, but he was very much loved by the congregation. And by me."

I said, "A very psychotic man once told me it's better to be feared than loved. When you're feared, you will be sought after. When you're loved, you may end up with a knife in your back."

" 'Hold thy friends closely,' " said Father Steven, " 'and thine enemies even more closely.' A very sobering thought." He placed his copies of the letters in his desk drawer.

Veronica produced the photocopies of the snapshot of

Mary Mendez and handed one to Father Steven. "Do you recognize this young woman?"

He looked at it and said, "She's very attractive. Is this the young woman who was murdered by the man who killed Father Joseph?"

"It is."

"Her family must be devastated." He regarded the photo once more. "I don't believe I've ever seen her before."

"I'd like to leave these copies with you. Perhaps you can ask other people here if they recognize her."

Our conversation ended, and Father Steven called for his secretary to escort us out. He asked us what our next step was. Veronica said we were going to interview Katherine Carroll, Joseph's mother.

"I'm surprised she agreed to meet with you. I understand she is quite reclusive since Joseph's death."

"She hasn't agreed," Veronica replied. "She didn't return my calls. I left a message saying that I would visit her today, but I don't know what she'll do when I arrive."

"There is an old saying," the priest said. "Perhaps you've heard it. 'When your parents die, you lose your past. When your spouse dies, you lose your present. When your child dies, you lose your future.' My heart goes out to her. Joseph's father died earlier this year, a few months after the murder. I imagine you know that already."

Veronica nodded.

"I've never spoken to Katherine Carroll, but I'm certain she must be a remarkable woman, knowing how Joseph turned out. Because his father was . . ." He searched for the right word. "Unpleasant. He was not of this faith, of course, and I believe the fact that his son became a priest made things difficult between them."

As we were leaving, Father Steven said, "You're trying to discover what relationship exists between this man and his victims. You might also want to figure out what his relationship is with you, Doctor."

"We're waiting for a list of all the patients I may have come into contact with at the hospital where I worked."

"I'm referring to the relationship he has with you in his

mind. What impression does he think his letters are creating? What does he think you're going to do? What does he think you think of him? He's confessing to you, Dr. Kline. You've become his priest."

Back in the car, Riley said, "He was a little prick."

"How the hell can you say that about him?" I said.

"Huh? Oh—I don't mean Father Steven. I mean Mansfield Carroll, Joseph's father. He had a reputation for being a prick. I met him. He lived up to his reputation." He began to drive. "He inherited a toilet paper company. It fit him very well. You know anything about him?"

"No," Veronica and I said at the same time.

"Old-line Philadelphia WASP. Family money. He took the company he inherited and turned it into an international conglomerate. He was a big industrial polluter. Killed rivers and lakes for a living. Then once a year he had this big party for kids with cancer, and everyone called him a great humanitarian."

Riley continued. "He and Joseph's mother, Katherine, got divorced when the boy was still a baby. Really nasty—lots of press, lots of sensational stories. 'The Toilet Paper King.' "

"I think I remember that," I said. "Back when I was in college. They accused each other of doing things that sounded anatomically impossible. New and creative uses for certain exotic fruits and vegetables."

"That's the one," said Riley. "She wound up with the family mansion and a huge annuity. He married a model he had waiting in the wings. When he died a few months ago, he left half to his second wife, half to Joseph. Mansfield didn't change his will after Joseph was killed. And Joseph's will left everything to his mother, Katherine. So when Mansfield Carroll rammed his Ferrari into a tree it looked like the wife would have to go fifty-fifty with the ex-wife. The wife wanted it all. She threatened to sue Katherine. And here's the interesting part. Katherine Carroll didn't even hold out for a settlement. Said she didn't need the money. Didn't want the money. Good luck and God bless to the second Mrs. Mansfield Carroll."

"What's she like?" Veronica asked.

"Hard to say. Only met her once, when I went to inform her of the murder. Her lawyers were good at keeping her shielded the rest of the time."

The sky was clearing in the west and we headed in that direction, toward the string of wealthy suburban towns known as the Main Line. The squalor gradually abated the farther we moved from our point of origin, but even the middle-class neighborhoods of Philadelphia looked dirty and in disrepair.

"The city doesn't even have money to mow median strips," Riley said. "If Mansfield Carroll was still alive, he and a couple of his WASP buddies could probably buy the whole thing. If they were crazy enough to want it."

Sunlight broke through the clouds as we entered Gladwyne, a pretty town with streams, rolling hills, and lush greenery. "Some merchants in downtown Philadelphia got together recently," Riley said. "Started a private company to keep the streets and sidewalks clean. Good idea, great for business—fix things up, try to lure shoppers back. But then the city's sanitation workers' union filed suit. And the civil liberties folks protested when the businessmen tried to relocate the homeless people in the area. It's a goddamn shame, all of it." He looked at one of the Main Line mansions and shook his head. "The people who live out here have no idea."

Katherine Carroll's twenty-acre property was surrounded by a wrought-iron fence. We couldn't see the mansion from the road. Two men in dark suits sat in a security booth by the closed gate at the entrance to the estate. One stepped outside when Riley pulled his Ford to the gate. There was a bulge underneath his suit jacket. I assumed he was carrying a pistol. "Can I help you people?"

Riley began to open his car door. The man leaned his body against it and the door wouldn't budge. "No need to get out, sir. Can I help you?"

"We're here to see Mrs. Carroll," Riley replied.

"Do you have an appointment?"

"She knows we want to speak with her," Veronica said.

"I'm sure she does. Do you have an appointment?"

When none of us spoke up, the man asked us to produce identification. Veronica and Riley displayed their badges. I showed him my driver's license and a business card. The man returned to the security booth and picked up a phone. We couldn't hear what he was saying. The second guard stepped out of the booth to watch us as the first man talked. He started to whistle show tunes. The first man completed his call and hung the phone up. The second guard continued whistling. When the phone inside the booth rang, the first man picked it up, received his instructions, and walked back to the car. "Would you please step out of the car, sir?"

Riley hesitated, then moved to open his door.

"Not you, sir." The guard looked at me. "Would *you* please step out?"

"Why him?" asked Riley.

"Mrs. Carroll says she'll speak with the doctor."

"How about us?" Veronica said.

A tight, unfriendly smile curled his lips. "Mrs. Carroll says she'll speak with the doctor."

"What the hell is going on?" I whispered to Veronica.

She shrugged her shoulders.

Riley turned to me and said, "She's with the FBI. I'm black. You're a psychiatrist. You're probably the only one someone like Katherine Carroll has any experience with."

Veronica handed me the picture of Mary Mendez. I already had copies of Artie's letters and the pictures he'd sent to me, although I didn't envision showing them to Katherine Carroll.

I got out of the car. The first guard said, "My colleague will accompany you to the residence." He turned to Veronica and Riley. "The two of you can wait here if you like."

The second guard stepped behind the booth, and a moment later he drove a Volvo sedan into view. I opened the passenger door and stepped inside. He resumed his whistling as we drove onto the estate.

The property consisted of manicured lawns and well-tended trees and shrubbery that obviously were selected and placed with care. The meandering path was just big enough

for two cars going in opposite directions to pass one another. After a minute the stone mansion came into view. It
sat atop a small hill. To its left were a swimming pool and
a clay tennis court. "We put a bubble over them for use in
the winter," the guard said. He made a sweeping gesture
with his hand. "This'll make a nice country club after she
dies."

"I can tell you feel very close to Mrs. Carroll," I said.

He stopped his whistling. "Huh?"

"Nothing. It wasn't important."

He pulled into a cobblestone area in front of the mansion
that was big enough for at least a dozen vehicles. As soon
as I stepped out of the car, the front door of the residence
swung open. An elderly dark-skinned woman with a West
Indies accent told me that Mrs. Carroll was waiting for me
in the library. The woman escorted me across a spacious
tile foyer. The foyer rose to the four-story height of the
building, and sunlight poured through a skylight that ran its
entire length and width.

The library was two stories high and at least fifty feet
square. Dark bookcases, all of them full, surrounded the
room on three sides. On the fourth were large picture windows that framed the green hills and vegetation. Standing
by one of the windows was a slender middle-aged woman
in a vibrant blue sundress. Her blond hair was streaked with
gray, and it was pulled behind her head and held tightly by
an elastic the color of her dress. A small gold crucifix dangled around her neck. Her skin was tan and her eyes were
bright green, and her voice had a soft, gentle rasp in it as
she spoke.

"Good afternoon, Dr. Kline. It's a pleasure to meet you."
She held out her hand to shake mine. "When the woman
from the FBI left a message to say she wanted to talk with
me, she didn't mention that she was coming with you. I
watched your interview on the *Today* show a few weeks
ago. Have you come to interview me for your book?"

17: Curare

After a few minutes of small talk, Katherine Carroll said, "I still have difficulty speaking about Joseph's death." She paused. "I've written about it. I thought it would be good therapy for me. Perhaps you'd like to read what I wrote."

"Of course."

She walked to an antique rolltop desk and pulled out several pages of expensive stationery.

She handed the pages to me, and I glanced at her handwritten paragraphs. "This is written in the present tense," I said.

She smiled. "That's how it felt when I wrote it. It still feels that way."

I read the pages.

You always believed that hell existed.

You were right.

You always assumed you'd have to die to get in.

You were wrong.

When Mansfield, your ex-husband, shows up at your door for the first time in years—when he comes in the company of your priest and an obese black police detective from the city—when that happens, you know it is not a social call. It takes no special genius to realize that something is terribly, terribly wrong.

You invite them into the sitting room. Ever the proper hostess, you ask if they prefer tea or coffee. Your ex-husband and the priest decline. The detective asks for black coffee, no sugar.

Mansfield sits silently in the corner of the room, averting his eyes. The priest rambles for a few minutes about eternity and God's plan. It is the black detective who finally cuts through the euphemisms: dispassionate, neither cruel nor kind. It is obvious he had been through this before.

I regret to inform you that your son is dead. He was murdered earlier today. His body was discovered in the church.

How could this happen?

The detective ignores the cosmological aspect of your question; he focuses on the concrete. He was stabbed, that is how it happened. Stabbed: This, too, turns out to be a euphemism.

It is good that you are sitting, because your own body quickly turns rigid. If you were standing you would certainly topple over, unable to fine-tune your movements to the kinesthetic feedback from the changing vagaries of your own center of gravity. You remember a passage from your college biology textbook, something about experiments in which animals are injected with a chemical that causes motor paralysis without deadening the senses or dulling consciousness. Researchers use the chemical when they want to monitor physiological responses to trauma; unable to yank itself away from the pain-inducing electrodes, the animal suffers in helpless, miserable silence.

Curare. That's what the chemical is called, you remember: Curare. South American Indians used it to poison arrowheads. The animal feels the pain, is excruciatingly aware of all that is happening, but is powerless to move. He looks dead. He is not.

Joseph Cotton looked dead in an old episode from the Alfred Hitchcock television series. He played a character who became paralyzed in a car accident. Awake and aware, he was unable to communicate the fact that he was alive to the people who found him, pronounced him dead, and placed his shrouded form in the morgue. When they came to prepare him for burial, a single tear alerted the mortician to the life that still coursed through him.

Perhaps your son, also named Joseph, still lives, too. Take me to him, take me to him, let me pull back the sheet that cloaks his body. He is crying, he is crying, can't anyone see his tears?

As the detective continues, he reveals the nature of the dismemberment of your son's body, and you realize that Joseph will never cry or laugh, ever again. His face, his beautiful, angelic face: How could anyone do something so monstrous?

Somehow you make it through the night, through the next few days, through the wake and the funeral service. People come and people go, talking of things both small and important. Some are helpful, some are hurtful, and none of it really matters at all.

Afterwards, some of your best friends make special efforts to avoid you, as if death were a contagion you might breathe upon them. Their silence hurts even more than the unintendedly hurtful things some others say: God must have needed him badly to take him so young; time heals all wounds; just think about your happy times together.

Your ex-sister-in-law tells you that you should be grateful for the twenty-four years you had with your son. She is from the New England branch of Mansfield's family, chilly as the snow. Her tone of voice suggests that you must be selfish to want more. But the Carrolls have always thought you greedy. They could not imagine any other motive for a poor Catholic girl marrying into their family and diverting some of their precious wealth. Of course, this spoke volumes, indirectly, about their feelings toward Mansfield: They could not believe anyone would want to marry him for love.

A curious thing happens over the next few months: You and your ex-husband grow close. You are haunted by the memories of Joseph that will not fade—memories you will not let die, because they are the last hold you have on your son. And Mansfield is haunted by the absence of memory, by the guilt and the emptiness he feels for not having known his son better. And now the two of you are drawn to one another, reaching out across the chasm formed by years of anger, lies, and broken promises.

One winter night a sudden snowstorm keeps him from returning to his home and his wife. The two of you lie on top of your bedspread, fully dressed, and hold each other close through the night. In the morning, he tells you that he is to blame for Joseph's death. It is the life I have led, he says, the horrible things I have done. My son has been punished for the sins of his father, and I am beyond redemption.

A few days later Mansfield runs his foreign sportscar into a bridge abutment and he, too, is gone. Your doctor prescribes Xanax, a little something to take the edge off your anxiety, just a temporary salve. But you like it, not for how it makes you feel, but for how it keeps you from feeling. You take a little more than you should, more often than you should, for longer than you should, and before you know it you wonder how you ever got along without it.

In February, four months after you lost Joseph and one month after Mansfield dies, an old friend invites you to a ladies' luncheon. It is time to rejoin the living. You know most of the people there casually. Some you haven't seen since Joseph's funeral, most since before that. Midway through the lobster bisque, one of the other guests begins complaining about the problems her college-age son is causing—something about his insistence on majoring in fine arts instead of following a pre-law or pre-med course of study. You cannot bear this. You see yourself jump to your feet, you watch your hands grabbing your water glass and flinging its contents in the woman's face, you hear yourself shouting: At least you still have your son!

The small talk continues all around you, people seemingly oblivious to the turmoil churning inside of you. At first you think they are ignoring your angry little paroxysm. But you look down and realize that you are still seated. Your filled water glass is in front of you. Your imagination is running wild. How long has this been happening? No one has even mentioned Joseph's death the whole afternoon. Perhaps you have imagined everything: his murder, your sorrow, the pain and emptiness of the past several months.

On the way home your chauffeur drives along Montgomery Avenue. You notice a young man on the sidewalk and your heart jumps. He is wearing the same winter coat you gave him on his last birthday, just before he entered the priesthood. Hunched over against the wind, he has that same gangly stride as he lopes along, the same shock of brown hair hanging over his coat collar, the same long arms dangling at his side. You command your driver to pull over. By the time you swing your door open, you have lost sight of him. You step outside. Is that him down the block, turning into a store? You run in that direction, but you cannot find him. There he is, on the corner, waiting for the bus. When you get there, he has vanished. There, near the post office. There, outside the food market. There, walking up the steps to the library. Back and forth you run, always a moment too late. Your driver finally catches up to you, grabs you forcibly by your arm, and leads you back to the car.

Warm water in your tub speeds your circulation. Ice cubes pressed against your wrist numb the nerves. You remember a song one of Joseph's friends sang at the funeral:

> I couldn't believe what they said when they told me
>   you died
> I never did know you that well but I broke down and
>   cried
> Just another star in the sky
> Just another sail in the wind blowing by
> And in only the blink of an eye
> We will be sailing home

The blade cuts. The blood spurts. You are floating naked in the warm Mediterranean near Monaco. You are so very, very tired. The skies grow dark, the tide carries you out to sea, and you are helpless against the current. Make it quick, you think. Make it quick.

The sailboat skims toward you. It is bathed in a soft light that seems to come from its core. It moves along the top of the ocean, lightly kissing the crests of the small waves, on the water but not in it. From its helm the young, gangly priest with the shock of brown hair smiles as he slowly bears down on you. He holds out his hand and a luminescent lifeline flies from his fingers, entwining itself around you, spinning itself into a golden robe as it lifts you above the swirling sea.

Bless me, Joseph, for I have sinned.

"I must have changed my mind," Katherine Carroll said. She reached for her cup of tea and I noticed the telltale latticed etching of scar tissue on her wrist. "I don't remember changing it, not really, but apparently I managed to wrap a towel around the cut and called for my housekeeper. I guess I lost my courage to finish the job."

"Some people would say you stopped because you had the courage to go on."

"Perhaps. That would be a nice thought, wouldn't it? Anyway, I spent a week in Lankenau Hospital. They took care of the incision and they detoxed me from the Xanax." She shrugged. "Some things heal, some things don't."

"Do you have a good doctor?"

"You mean a therapist? I see a psychiatrist in Bryn Mawr twice a week. She wants me to try an antidepressant, but I don't want to look at another pill as long as I live. So we talk. And we talk. She's a good listener, like you." She placed her teacup in its saucer. "I hope I haven't inconvenienced Ms. Pace and Captain Riley too badly. Her message said she wanted to talk with me about my son's death, and I really didn't feel like subjecting myself to that."

"And yet you've spoken with me."

"Yes, well, you psychiatrists certainly know how to make

the rest of us talk, don't you?" She smiled. "When you came in a little while ago, you said there had been a second murder."

"A teenage girl in Boston, two weeks ago tomorrow. And we believe he intends to kill two other people very soon."

"Do you have any idea who he is?"

"We have some leads. But no suspects."

"You've been spending too much time with your FBI friend. You're beginning to sound like a police detective." She smiled again. "Before you know it, you'll be saying things like, 'Just the facts, ma'am, just the facts.' "

I told her about the second killing and its similarity to her son's murder. It was the first she'd heard about the penny that the killer had left in Joseph's hand; Riley really had kept that information secret, just as he told me when I first spoke with him on the phone. I showed her Mary Mendez's picture and tried to think of all the questions Veronica would ask if she were in the room. Katherine Carroll had no insight into any connection that might exist between her son and Mary Mendez, and she had no idea who the killer might be.

She handed the picture back and looked at me for several seconds. "There's more, isn't there?"

I returned the picture to its envelope. "More?"

"That's a large envelope for one small snapshot. There's something you're not showing me, something you haven't told me about because you think it might upset me."

I hesitated. I didn't plan on showing her the killer's letters or the pictures he'd sent, so I hadn't seen any point in mentioning them.

She sighed. "Well, I'll trust your judgment on that." She walked across the room and took a checkbook from the top drawer of her desk. "Do they need money?"

"Who?"

"The parents of the girl who was murdered."

I paused. "I don't know."

"I know what you're thinking, Dr. Kline. You're thinking that compared to me, just about everyone needs money.

Don't be embarrassed. You're probably right." She wrote a check and handed it to me. "Will you see to it that they receive this money?"

The check was for five thousand dollars, and it had my name on it. "Why did you make it out to me?"

"I don't want to make myself known to them. I'm not looking for any credit, and I don't have any reason to enter into a dialogue with them."

It would probably do all of you some good, I thought, but I said nothing. I placed the check in the envelope that held the snapshot of Mary Mendez and the killer's letters and pictures.

She returned to her chair. Just then an aging terrier walked slowly from the foyer into the library, his nails clicking and clacking on the hardwood slats. He flopped on the floor beside Katherine Carroll, panting from the effort. "My son's dog," she said. "Elmo, say hello to Dr. Kline." The dog just nuzzled his head against her leg.

"How old?"

"Fourteen. I bought him for Joseph on his tenth birthday. He developed multiple myeloma a year ago and I've spent several thousand dollars keeping him alive. But I'm very fortunate. Most people would have had to euthanize a pet under those circumstances." She reached down and gently rubbed the dog's neck. "I'll miss him so very much when he goes."

I remembered what Melissa said when I offered to buy a dog for her: Pets die. I once had a patient who stoically endured the death of his wife, holding back the tears like a concrete dam. But when his dog died a year later the dam broke and he sank into utter despair.

"He stayed behind after Joseph left home. But Joseph always visited at least once a week. Sometimes Elmo sits by the window now and pines. He never did that before. I see it and it breaks my heart, because obviously there's no way I can explain any of this to him. I can't even explain it to myself." She looked out the window. "It's turned into a pleasant afternoon, both the weather and the company. May I walk you back down the drive?"

We walked toward the front gate, past a line of ash trees and carefully sculpted shrubbery. Off to the right was a small duck pond and a gazebo. "This must seem like living in heaven," I said.

"Heaven," she repeated. "I do still believe in heaven. I can't believe that the uniqueness of a beloved human being is lost forever. Tell me, Dr. Kline, how long does it take for things to return to normal after something like this?"

I thought about Janet and the hole she left in my life. I remembered how I froze the night before when Veronica reached out for me. I sighed and said, "I'm the wrong one to ask."

"Oh?" She studied my face, and her look of inquisitiveness gave way to one of sad understanding. "Oh."

Further down the path and off to the left I saw a row of stone slabs. "You have a cemetery on your property?"

"An old Carroll family burial ground. It's really quite lovely. Come see."

We took a detour down a narrow walkway and through a gap in an old stone fence. The cemetery held about thirty graves. Some of the tombstones went back before the Revolution. Off to the right stood the newest and largest marker. Its fluted and beveled design set it apart from the others. It read:

MANSFIELD AMORY CARROLL
October 12, 1935–February 15, 1992

"It's a bit ornate, don't you think?" she said. "His widow selected it. A woman whose taste is, well, idiosyncratic. At least it doesn't say 'Here lies the Toilet Paper King.' She has access here whenever she wants it. I've left instructions at the gate to let her in without calling me. She's never come, though. And now that tennis and golf are upon us, I don't expect her until fall at the earliest." She paused. "You'll have to excuse me. Such ugliness is unbecoming, I know."

I glanced around at the other tombstones. "I don't see your son's grave."

"It's in Villanova, on the grounds of his seminary. I wanted Joseph to be buried closer to God."

John Riley's car came into view as we rounded a bend on the main driveway. "Your friends are probably very upset," Katherine Carroll said. "Please apologize to them for me. I think I'll leave you now."

"It was very nice meeting you, Mrs. Carroll."

"Katherine."

"And I'm Harry."

"Harry," she repeated. "Do you have a pen?" I handed her a pen and piece of paper, and she wrote down her name and a telephone number. "It's my private line. If you or your FBI friend need to ask any more questions, you can call me there. I hope you're wrong about this man killing two more people."

"I promise you we'll try to find him."

She shrugged. "I hope this doesn't sound cold, but it doesn't matter very much to me. Mansfield was obsessed with finding Joseph's killer. He even offered a half-million dollar reward for the killer's identity. And you always read about the survivors of murder victims going to the killers' trials, hanging on until the end to make sure that justice is done. That isn't me. My son is dead. That's all I know."

18: Nothing in Common, Something in Common

The sun was setting behind us as we headed back into Philadelphia. Riley had agreed to drive us to the train station. Veronica and I were headed for New York to try our luck at identifying and locating Artie.

Riley was quick to conclude that I'd wasted everyone's time speaking with Katherine Carroll. "But we had fun waiting for you," he said, with obvious sarcasm. "Two of the most interesting and useful hours in my entire life."

"He's right," I said to Veronica. "All I learned was what we already assumed. Katherine Carroll doesn't know who Artie is. She's never heard of Elmore Winston or the Mendez family. She's never been anywhere near San Antonio, doesn't think Joseph ever was, and she has no reason to think that her son had anything at all to do with Mary Mendez. There's no way there could be any relationship between the two victims."

"There's a relationship," Veronica said. "Something is motivating him. We just don't see it yet. Some common thread exists, even if it's only in his mind."

Riley turned onto a multilane highway that skirted a river. "Schuylkill Expressway," he said. "Christmas Eve, about ten years ago. Guy driving in this direction opens fire on the other cars. Three people killed. Psychiatrist testifies that the guy is crazy. The jury lets the guy off. Not guilty by reason of insanity. Guy gets sent to a psychiatric hospital, gets out six months later, and then guess what?"

The question was directed at me. "I have no idea."

"He shoots the psychiatrist."

"Thanks for sharing that with me."

"Don't mention it, Doctor."

On our left, perched on a hill overlooking the river, was a columned building that could have passed for a Greek temple. "That place looks familiar," I said.

"The Philadelphia Art Museum," replied Riley. "Sylvester Stallone ran up the steps in *Rocky*."

"Which *Rocky*?"

"All of them, I think."

Riley pulled off the expressway at the exit for 30th Street and said, "That half-million dollar reward Katherine Carroll told you about. It's real. Mansfield Carroll's executor controls it. All you have to do is identify the killer. The will says nothing about coming up with enough evidence to arrest or convict him. Just identify him to the satisfaction of the executor, and it's all yours. She can't accept it, because she's FBI. And I can't take it, either. It's all yours, Doctor." He laughed. "Easy as pie."

"I wouldn't feel right taking it."

"And I wouldn't feel right cheating on my wife if Whitney Houston invited me to bed. But sometimes we have to make sacrifices."

Riley pulled alongside the curb next to the train station. He opened his trunk and we took out our bags. "Hope you enjoyed your stay," he said as he squeezed his large form back behind the steering wheel. "Look at it this way. Your unsolved murders have two things in common. First thing is, the victims have nothing in common. Second thing is, they're both unsolved." He laughed and drove away.

Inside we purchased tickets for the next train to New York and grabbed some cholesterol and saturated fatty acids at Burger King. It was after six o'clock. I located a pay phone and called home.

"Melissa had one of her episodes this afternoon," said

Mrs. Winnicott. "She stared out the window for about two minutes, just a blank expression on her face. I couldn't get through to her, as usual, and then it was over as quickly as it started."

The first episode occurred the day Janet died. They came infrequently now, and they never lasted long. Early on I'd taken Melissa to a neurologist to make certain she didn't have a subtle seizure disorder. She didn't. It was just a psychological retreat, one that would come on without warning and disappear just as suddenly.

Melissa came to the phone. "I got yelled at in school, Daddy. I forgot my bathing suit again." Her class had swimming lessons at an indoor pool about twice a month. Melissa was forever leaving her bathing suit at home. It was beyond the point of coincidence. "I'm sorry, Daddy."

"I'm sorry you had a bad day, sweetheart."

"Are you coming home tonight?"

"No, not tonight. We should be back by the weekend." I wished I had said *I* instead of *we*.

"The *weekend*? But Daddy, it's only Wednesday."

"I know, sweetheart. Friday night, I promise."

"That's just great," she said, obviously bitter.

"I'll see you soon, sweetheart. Let me talk again to Mrs.—" But all I heard was a dial tone.

I walked back to the long wooden seat where Veronica was waiting.

"Something wrong?"

"My daughter is angry with me. I've never been away from her for so long since Janet died."

"She misses you."

"Yes."

"And you miss her."

"Of course."

Veronica leaned back against the hard bench. "You're lucky to have her. That's something I'll never experience."

"You never know. You're what, about thirty?"

She nodded.

"You still have plenty of time," I said.

She shook her head. "It's a question of biology, not timing. I won't bore you with the medical details."

A young Hispanic woman walked by with an infant in her arms and a toddler in tow. Veronica stared at them intently. The woman noticed us and smiled. I returned the smile; Veronica lowered her eyes.

"Half of the children I see I want to kidnap and make my own," Veronica said. "The other half I want to throttle, because I know I'll never have one and it makes me angry."

When I was a boy we used to play stickball in the street. We sliced white rubber balls—we called them pimpleballs—in half. Those half-balls were incapable of breaking anything or hurting anyone. But whenever one landed anywhere near the house at the corner, the woman living there would immediately rap against the window, scowl, and shake a finger at us. Once or twice she even called the police. I complained about her to my mother. I hate her, I said, because she hates my friends and me. She doesn't hate you, said my mother. What she hates is not having a child of her own.

"You seemed alright with Melissa," I said. "You didn't act like you wanted to throttle her."

"I liked your daughter. But I do believe she wanted to throttle me."

We boarded the train and found seats. Veronica pulled out a notepad and reviewed what she'd written in Riley's car when I described my conversation with Katherine Carroll. "What was she like?"

"Pleasant. Sad. Almost noble in her pain, like Jackie Kennedy after the assassination."

"I've seen pictures of that. But I was too young to remember it."

I looked out the window. The sky to our left had a faint glow where the sun had set. The train whizzed past the city streets; children were playing in them, grabbing onto the last moments of daylight. Several minutes passed. "What are you thinking about?" Veronica asked.

"Waylon Jennings."

"The country singer?"

I nodded.

"Why?"

"Buddy Holly and some other performers were on a tour in Minnesota or Wisconsin, someplace like that, in the middle of winter in 1959. Most of the people were traveling by bus, but it was cold and uncomfortable, so Buddy Holly hired a small plane one night to take him and a few others to the next town on the tour. Waylon Jennings was supposed to go with him, but at the last minute he gave his seat to Richie Valens, because Richie had a cold and needed a rest."

"And the plane crashed."

"Right," I said. "And Buddy Holly and Richie Valens were killed. So I was just wondering—how would I feel if I were Waylon Jennings? I go out of my way to help someone, and they die as a result. Was I supposed to live, and was this God's way of keeping me safe? Or did I unwittingly foil some master plan God had regarding who should live and who should die? Or maybe it's like you said last night—people just die, for no good reason at all. Hell, when you look at everything that's happened to the country since Kennedy was killed, it's hard to make a case that some divine purpose was served."

"How old was she?"

"Who? Jackie Kennedy?"

"No. Katherine Carroll."

"She looked a little bit older than me."

"Was she pretty?"

"Yes. Very."

"You liked her. I can hear it in your voice."

"Yes, I did. I just hope I didn't upset her too much, bringing up such awful memories."

"I'm sure she thinks about it all the time, whether or not anyone brings it up. I've seen how you talk to people about painful things. That's your job, Harry. You and I both rummage through other people's lives. I guess that's something we have in common."

"Whenever anyone asks me how I got interested in psychiatry, I think about something that happened when I was a kid. The telephone circuits in my neighborhood got crossed one day and I could hear other people's conversations over our line. A woman talking to her friend about cake recipes. A man dialing one auto parts store after another, looking for a carburetor for his '47 Chevy, getting more irritated with each call. Two young girls calling all the drugstores in the neighborhood, asking them if they had Prince Albert in a can. It was pretty boring stuff, actually. But I was fascinated."

"Just as I thought. If voyeurism was an Olympic event, all you psychiatrists would be going to Barcelona this summer. What a strange way to make a living."

I didn't spend very much of my time practicing psychiatry anymore, just one morning a week seeing three or four patients in my home office. When Janet died, I received a million dollar life insurance payment. Between that, Janet's trust fund, and the money I now earned from writing, I really didn't need to practice my profession at all. But I didn't want to abandon it completely.

I had Janet's father to thank, indirectly, for that life insurance payment. He never liked me; I never liked him. He was an avaricious bastard with the heart of a swindler and nary a concern for anyone other than himself. When Janet and I married, her father obtained a million-dollar policy on me, and he purchased an annuity that would cover the premium for thirty years. He thought it was a wonderful gift, a guarantee that his daughter and his then-unborn grandchildren would have a nest egg if I should die. But I recognized the gesture for what it was: at best, a subtly stated belief that I would be incapable of planning for my own family's welfare; at worst, an unconscious expression of his wish that I would drop dead at the earliest convenient moment.

Janet resented the implication that my life was somehow more valuable than hers. She insisted that we purchase a million-dollar policy on her. It was ironic: Were it not for her father's purchase of the policy on me, we never would have bought the policy on Janet that later became so important.

It was dark now. I gazed out the window at lights from the cars we passed. And I remembered something that happened early in my marriage. Janet and I were getting into our car. She had driven the car last. For the five thousandth time she'd forgotten to push the driver's seat back to give me enough room to get in. And for the five thousandth time I rammed my knee against the steering wheel. I muttered, I cursed, then I glared at her and said, "I've asked you over and over to push the goddamn seat back when you get out of the car, and you obviously don't give a shit. But do yourself a favor. Push it back and make yourself a millionaire."

"How would that make me a millionaire?"

"Because I'll have a heart attack from the shock, and you'll collect on your father's fucking million-dollar insurance policy."

It was a very unpleasant memory, one I'd never recalled in the years since Janet's death. I'd tried to dwell only on the good times, but this recollection had snuck up without warning. Funny, but I still felt angry about it so many years later.

"You're thinking about her, aren't you?" Veronica asked.

I didn't know if she meant Janet, Melissa, or Katherine Carroll. I just said "yes," and left it at that.

19: You Never Come Back From Hell

Early Thursday morning, Angela Paradisi led us into a conference room in the FBI offices in Lower Manhattan. "I've been assigned as your liaison here," she said to Veronica. "Your supervisor, Martin Baines, briefed me about the case you're working on." She hesitated for a moment, then said, "I think you should know, I've never actually worked on a murder investigation before."

"How long have you been with the Bureau?"

"Just a few months."

When she'd met us minutes earlier in the reception area, I assumed she was someone's young secretary. She could have passed for seventeen and had the well-scrubbed look of a high school cheerleader. Whatever were the minimum FBI requirements for height and age, I was certain Angela Paradisi had barely squeaked by. Her hair, long and blond, was bunched up and tied behind her. With high cheekbones, bright green eyes, and a face unmarred by lines or blemishes, she looked like a perfectly formed figure that had been chiseled from marble by a master sculptor.

She excused herself after bringing us to the conference room. As soon as Angela was out of earshot, Veronica said, "They should have given me someone more experienced. And you can put your eyes back in your head now, Harry."

"Sorry."

"Why is it men always think women don't notice them staring at other women? It must be genetic."

Angela returned with a stack of papers and sat across the conference table from us. "Harry, I've been checking with your editor's secretary every day to see if they get any mail for you." She passed a half-dozen letters to me; all of them had been opened. "I don't think there's anything noteworthy here."

I glanced at the letters. They were all from readers commenting on *Soldier and Son*.

"Veronica, Mr. Baines said they checked out hotel registrations in Boston for the night after the Mary Mendez murder. They didn't come up with anything. No one used the name Elmore Winston at any hotel in the area the night after. And no one registered either night named Arthur, first name or last, who came from New York." She turned toward me. "The VA hospital sent Mr. Baines a list of everyone named Arthur, first name or last, who was a patient there when you were on staff. I have a copy."

She gave us a computer printout list of four or five dozen patients. It included names; social security numbers; and birth, admission, and discharge dates. A column entitled "service code" contained three-letter abbreviations denoting the inpatient units to which they had been admitted.

"Someone placed asterisks next to three of these names," Veronica noted.

"I did that," Angela replied. "I had the local social security office run the numbers of all the patients on the list. According to their records, those three have New York addresses."

I studied the three names and the information next to them. Morton Arthur was admitted to the surgery unit for a month shortly after I began working at the hospital. "Never heard of him," I said. Arthur Mendoza was an internal medicine patient for two weeks midway through my six-year tenure. "Don't remember this one, either."

"What about the last one?" asked Angela. "The service code says 'PSY.' Does that stand for the psychiatric unit?"

"It does." According to the printout, Arthur Chillingsworth was admitted two times during my years at the VA; each stay lasted between one and two weeks. "The name doesn't ring a bell. You have to remember, I saw hundreds of patients there over the years. And I didn't meet every patient who came in." I looked at the name for several seconds, but I couldn't come up with anything.

Veronica asked, "How about the postmarks on the letters the killer sent to Harry? Any luck figuring out what part of the city the letters came from?"

"The first letter went through the automated postmarking procedure at the center that handles mail for all of Manhattan. It could have come from anywhere in the city." She produced the large envelope that had contained Artie's second letter and the photo of Mary Mendez. "But this envelope required extra stamps, so the killer apparently took it to his local post office, just to make sure he had enough postage. The clerk canceled it by hand with his own postmark stamp. I was able to trace it to a post office on the Upper East Side. Madison Avenue near East 88th Street."

"What kind of neighborhood is that?" asked Veronica.

"Classy. Expensive shops. Town houses and luxury apartments."

Veronica considered this, then said, "Know anyone who lives in that area, Harry?"

I spoke reluctantly. "Jeffrey Barrow."

"Your editor?" asked Angela.

I nodded.

Veronica brushed a curl from her forehead. "You don't say. That's very interesting." She turned back to Angela. "We think the killer plans to take his next victim at a hospital in his neighborhood. Where does that leave us?"

Angela was prepared for that question, no doubt from her briefing by Martin Baines. "There are three possibilities." She passed three packets of information to Veronica. "Lenox Hill Hospital is less than a mile south of the post office where the killer mailed the second letter. Mount Sinai is about the same distance north. Then there's Metropolitan Hospital, farther out to the north and east. As you can see from the maps in front of you, all three are very big."

"Trying to patrol those areas is probably hopeless," Veronica said. She pointed at the computer printout list of VA patients. "What else do you have on the three men you've marked with asterisks?"

"All of them receive VA disability payments. None of them pay city payroll taxes. So I assume none of them work."

"Do you have their addresses?"

"Morton Arthur is in the East Village. Arthur Mendoza is in Gramercy Park. And would either of you like to guess where Arthur Chillingsworth lives?" Angela smiled broadly and answered her own question. "Upper East Side. Fifth Avenue. In ten minutes he can walk to either Mount Sinai Hospital or Lenox Hill. Like he said in his second letter, 'a place dedicated to healing, so close I can almost smell the antiseptic from here.' "

Veronica nodded. "Good work."

Angela was beaming. "Thank you very much."

"I think I'll pay a visit to these gentlemen."

"Where are we going first?" I asked.

"You can't come with me, Harry. Suppose one of these men really is the killer. Right now he has no idea how close we are to finding him. But he remembers you, even if you don't remember him. The minute you walk into sight he'll know what's going on. And we can't prove a damn thing yet, so unless he's suddenly struck by an impulse to confess and surrender, he'll be even more careful to keep us from stopping his plan."

She was right. The slight benefit my presence might offer was outweighed by the concern she'd just described.

"I'll come," Angela said. "That is, if you want me to."

Veronica looked at the woman without responding.

"I promise not to get in the way," Angela continued. "I'll do whatever you say, including nothing at all, if that's what you want."

Veronica sighed. "Alright, Angela, let's go. Harry, I'll catch up with you later at the hotel."

"Here's Lenox Hill Hospital, pal."

"I don't want to get out," I said. "Drive around it so I can get a good look at the whole thing."

My cabby shrugged his shoulders and pulled back into the stream of traffic.

The hospital consisted of several mismatched interconnected buildings. It occupied a square block bounded by Park and Lexington Avenues and East 76th and 77th Streets. "I've never been here, but this place looks very familiar."

"Maybe you seen pictures. They brought John Lennon here after he was shot."

"Could be. It's funny how the death of someone famous seems to redefine everything associated with it."

"Huh?"

"Nothing. Just thinking."

"Uh-huh."

Metropolitan Hospital spanned the two-block area between First and Second Avenues, and East 97th and 99th Streets. And Mount Sinai stretched for three blocks, East 98th through 101st Streets, bounded by Fifth Avenue on the east and Madison Avenue on the west. Veronica was right: It would require a midsize battalion to patrol all three hospitals.

"It's hopeless," I mumbled.

"Huh?"

"Nothing. Just thinking again."

"Uh-huh. You thinking of having a procedure done, pal?"

"Excuse me?"

"I mean, you have any other hospitals you want me to show you?"

"No, not today."

I asked him to take me to an address on Fifth Avenue near 52nd Street. He looked surprised when I finally disembarked there. "Good luck, pal," he said. "Hope you find what you're looking for."

Morgan Books occupied two stories in the building. I took the elevator directly to Jeffrey Barrow's floor, bypassing the general reception area on the floor below. What did I expect to accomplish by surprising him? What was I looking for? A sudden confession, blurted out in the confusion of the moment?

Jeffrey's secretary wasn't at her desk. I approached my editor's office. He was standing in the open doorway, shaking hands with a visitor who appeared to be leaving. When Jeffrey saw me, his face registered surprise for a moment. "Harry—what brings you here?"

"Visiting a friend in the city. I thought I'd stop in before I leave."

He glanced at the other man, then said, "Harry Kline, you remember Randall Tinkler, don't you?"

The man turned to face me. He was tall and powerfully built, like Jeffrey, but older. His grip was strong as he shook my hand. "It's good to see you again, Harry." His voice was high-pitched, like a choirboy's—different from what his size portended.

He looked familiar, but I had no idea who he was. Jeffrey rescued me from my embarrassment. "Randall was in charge of subsidiary rights until he retired last year. He's the one who got Knight-Ridder to buy serialization rights to your first book."

"Of course," I replied.

"Jeffrey told me about the book you're working on. I'll look forward to it." He gazed at the floor for a few seconds, then looked intently at me. "I lost my only child in an accident many years ago, Harry. It's something that stays with you forever."

"It must be like going to hell and back."

"You never come back from hell," he said. "Not completely. Part of you remains there forever, and part of it stays with you."

The two of them shook hands once again, lingering in the grasp, and Jeffrey patted his visitor on the shoulder. "Let me know if you need anything, Randall. If there's anything I can do."

"You've been a good friend, J.B.," the man said, and then he walked down the corridor and out of view.

"You mentioned him to me before," I said as I settled into a soft chair in Jeffrey's office. "When we had lunch after my interview on the *Today* show. You told me how everything fell apart for him after his daughter's death."

"That's right."

"He looks awful."

"I think he's dying. He didn't come right out and say it, but I know he's been pretty sick, and this felt like a 'good-bye forever' visit." He sighed, then sat down.

We engaged in some small talk about *Soldier and Son*: sales figures, Paramount's progress on developing a script for the movie. Then he asked me how my new book was coming along.

"Pretty slowly. It's a difficult project." I didn't tell him I'd been spending all my time lately running around the country with a maverick FBI agent in search of a serial killer—and how Jeffrey himself figured in my companion's suspicions.

"Will you meet your deadline?"

"I hope so."

He grimaced. "Well, deadlines can be flexible, I suppose. Just remember you're sitting on half of a $90,000 advance."

There was a harshness in his voice and a coldness in his eyes that I was unaccustomed to. I had a momentary fantasy of Jeffrey grabbing his letter opener and slitting my throat with it. We'd worked together for years, and I considered him a friend, yet how well did I really know him? I knew he lived near Central Park, but I'd never visited his home. I knew he was married, but I'd never met his wife. I knew he had children of college or near-college age, but I didn't know their names, or even how many he had. And even though he'd been intimately involved with my three books—two of which had Vietnam themes—I didn't know the first thing about his wartime experiences.

He slapped the top of his desk. "What the hell," he said. "I have faith in you. You've always come through for us before."

"Well, three down, one to go." It was the line I expected Artie to begin his next letter with, after the third murder. I studied Jeffrey's face, but I couldn't read anything in his reaction.

"Three what?"

"Three books down, one to go."

"Of course."

"I'm just having a hard time getting untracked. Call it the sin of incompetence." I drew the sentence out, emphasizing those words that figured so prominently in Artie's correspondence. Again I looked for something in his reaction, some telltale flicker of recognition, anger, or fear. I saw nothing.

"Incompetent? Don't be so hard on yourself, Harry. Everyone has dry spells. Anything I can do to help?"

I paused for a moment. "Tell me—when you were in Vietnam, did you kill anyone?"

"How will that help you?" He looked confused. "I was a soldier, Harry. Decorated. But I don't like talking about it."

"Did you kill any civilians?"

"No, damn it, of course not." He regained his composure. "Sorry, I just don't see how this . . ." He drummed his fingertips on his desk and turned his swivel chair toward the window.

"Did you witness any civilians getting killed?"

After several seconds, he replied, "One. A prostitute. A soldier in my company sliced her pretty badly, and she bled to death. There was another soldier there, too. I'd like to say I tried to stop it, but it happened too fast for me to do anything."

"What happened to the soldier who killed the girl?"

He sighed. "Nothing. There were no witnesses."

"But you . . . the other soldier . . . you just said . . ."

Slowly he wheeled around to face me. "There were no witnesses."

"I see."

"It was a rotten, stinking shitheap of a war. I guess they all are."

"I guess so."

"Why are you asking me these questions, Harry?"

"I'm not sure. Why are you answering them?"

"I have no idea. I don't think I want to answer any more." He looked at me for a few seconds, then smiled. "You're always full of surprises, Harry." He checked his watch. "I really need to leave. I'm taking an agent to lunch at La Grenouille. We ate there together once, didn't we?"

I nodded. "You treated me to a twenty-dollar tuna sandwich."

"You need to make reservations several days ahead of time, even for lunch. I don't dare be late." He stood and deftly escorted me to his office door. "Give me a call when you get back to Boston. We'll talk some more about the book."

I crossed Fifth Avenue and stood across 52nd Street from the entrance to La Grenouille. Jeffrey finally arrived a half hour later. He'd been telling the truth when he said he was due there for lunch, but he'd ushered me out of his office well before he needed to leave. Why did he rush to get rid of me? Was it merely his discomfort at the personal turn the conversation had taken? Or had my indirect references to Artie's letters made him wary of me? "Hell, maybe he just had to use the john."

"Excuse me?" said a well-dressed passerby.

"Oh, nothing. Just talking to myself."

"I see," he said, sneering. "We do get a lot of that, even in this neighborhood." He hurried away.

I remembered the wintertime push in Manhattan several years earlier to persuade mentally ill street dwellers to seek shelter. It almost turned into a pitched battle: civil libertarians on one side, and on the other an unlikely alliance of do-gooders and people whose sensibilities were offended by having to look at the homeless. I was unable to decide which side I came down on, until Janet said, "After we're gone, if Melissa ever becomes that ill, I hope someone cares enough to make her come in from the cold."

I headed west on 52nd Street, back across Fifth Avenue. Midway down the next block I came upon the Museum of Television and Radio. I entered, selected a tape from the archives, and sat at a viewing console with headphones. There I watched Walter Cronkite struggle to hide his tears as he announced that President Kennedy had been pronounced dead. It was the first real intrusion of death into my young life, and even now the loss seemed so large and so personal.

The clerk at the desk when I checked out was younger than the events chronicled in the tape I'd been watching. She noted my viewing material and said, "A lot of people in your generation ask for that one."

"What's popular here with people your age?"

She smiled. "The 'Who Shot J.R.?' episode of *Dallas*."

I shrugged. "Same story, different cast."

The irony was lost on her. "November 21st, 1980. It was seen by more people than any single episode of a regularly scheduled series, before or since. You want to know who shot J.R.? It's a good trivia question for parties."

"The man on the grassy knoll," I said.

"Excuse me?"

"Nothing. Just a poor joke. What was the old record holder, before that *Dallas* episode?"

"The final episode of *The Fugitive*. August 29, 1967. After four years on the run, Richard Kimble finds the one-armed man who killed his wife and clears his own name. It grabbed a seventy-two percent share of the TV audience."

"I remember that one. Great show, wasn't it?"

The clerk shrugged. "Search me. I was still in diapers."

I took a cab back to the Vista International Hotel. Images and thoughts of widely disparate events flowed in and out of one another as I sank deeply into the frayed upholstery of the taxi's backseat. In the fall of 1963, Richard Kimble—played by David Janssen—is wrongly convicted and sentenced to death for the murder of his wife. Two months later the president is gunned down, a seminal event in the life of a generation, and two days after that his presumed assassin is murdered before a national television audience. For seventeen years it remains TV's most famous shooting, until J. R. Ewing, played by Mary Martin's son, is shot by his young sister-in-law, played by Bing Crosby's daughter. Meanwhile, Bing and Elvis die within weeks of one another, sandwiched around my marriage to the only woman I ever loved. Then she dies, as do Joseph Carroll,

Mary Mendez, and the three innocent victims of Karl
Fenner's shopping mall rampage. And six days hence a
man named Artie would kill again. He saw me as his
chronicler, someone who would understand his actions and
explain them to the world. But I didn't understand a damn
thing, couldn't explain a bit of it, and I was as helpless to
save his next victim as I was to undo any of the other
deaths—from Kennedy, to Fenner's victims, to my beloved
wife.

Back in my room, I fell into a fitful afternoon sleep that
was punctuated by dreams about television, murder, and my
one-armed editor threatening to frame me for my wife's
death. I heard her calling my name and awoke in a cold-
sweat start.

Veronica was standing by the side of my bed, gently
shaking my arm. "Harry? Harry, wake up. Hey—take it
easy. It's just me."

"What the . . . How did you get in here?"

She pointed at the connecting doorway between our adjoining rooms. It was wide open. "You left your side unlocked," she said.

"I don't think so."

She shrugged. "Well, it's unlocked now."

"What do you want?"

She took three shallow breaths and walked uneasily to a
chair. She sat down and looked at me without speaking for
several seconds. Tiny perspiration beads dotted her forehead and upper lip. She ran her hands along the folds of her
skirt.

"Well? What is it?" I asked.

"I don't know how you could forget someone like him,
Harry. I thought he was going to kill me."

"What are you talking about? Who was going to kill
you?"

"I'm talking about your friend," Veronica said, her voice
quavering. "I think I just met Artie."

20: Suspects

Angela Paradisi had been so grateful for the chance to accompany Veronica that she ran her mouth nonstop all the way down the elevator and across Federal Plaza. By the time they reached the taxi stand, Veronica had heard more about the young woman's life than she had any need to know: her short-lived attempt to become a nun after high school, the infirm mother she resided with and cared for, and the lack of any romantic relationship in her life. This spate of self-revelation bothered Veronica; a good agent would show more discretion in the company of a stranger.

In the minute it took them to walk from the federal office building to the curb, at least a half-dozen men stared in obvious fashion at Veronica's young companion. Two of them slowed down considerably to give themselves a longer look, and one stopped dead in his tracks. Angela didn't appear to notice. This, too, bothered Veronica; a good agent would be more aware of the effect she was having on others.

They took a cab to the East Village. Morton Arthur lived on East Ninth Street near Tompkins Square Park. There was an Indian restaurant at the corner of the block, and an upscale frozen yogurt emporium on the opposite side of the street. The neighborhood was alive with a multicultural mixture of color and sound.

Morton Arthur had a second-story walkup apartment in a building that was old but well tended. He buzzed Veronica and Angela in without asking them to identify themselves over the intercom. They found his door ajar. Veronica knocked, and a voice from a back room yelled, "Come on in. I'll be ready in a minute."

The living room was bright and airy, with off-white walls and wide windows. A dozen flowering plants spilled over the lips of pots and boxes all around the room. The soft-sculpture sofa and chairs clung close to the floor. An ashtray on an end table contained the stubs of five or six joints of marijuana. Next to it was a ceramic trivet bearing the phrase "Practice Random Acts of Kindness and Senseless Beauty." There was a faint smell of sandalwood incense in the air.

To the left was a small kitchen; to the right, a corridor leading to a bedroom. Both areas were separated from the living room by strings of beads that stretched from the ceiling to the floor.

Morton Arthur was running water in his kitchen sink. He was about five-eight, thin but well proportioned. He wore tight faded jeans and no shirt, socks, or shoes. He picked up a hand towel and dried his face as he walked through the bead curtain into the living room. A healed surgical incision ran across his flat, muscled stomach; a jagged, mottled scar stretched around the side of his torso.

"A beautiful day, isn't it?" He pulled the towel away from his face and caught sight of his visitors for the first time. "Oh, gosh. Excuse me. I was expecting someone else."

Veronica said, "Are you Morton Arthur?"

Angela was staring at the man's chest, blushing. He noticed and suddenly seemed self-conscious about his seminakedness. He grabbed a T-shirt from the side of a chair and quickly slipped it on. "I am," he replied to Veronica's question. "Have we met before?"

Veronica introduced herself and her companion. "We're with the FBI," she said, and she noticed him glance for an instant at the joint remnants in his ashtray. "We won't take much of your time." She stared directly at the ashtray, then waved her hand at it and shook her head slightly as if to say she couldn't care less about what she saw there.

"Sit down, please," he said. "The FBI, huh? Far out."

Veronica said, "The Veterans Administration has reported several problems with benefits checks to people living in this zip code."

"Problems?"

"Delayed deliveries, lost deliveries, forged endorsements. Things like that. Have you had any problems with your checks?"

He shrugged his shoulders and said, "None that I'm aware of. The government takes good care of me, all things considered. But I have to tell you, I'm not always the charming guy you see now. Some days I have very bad pain. I wake up feeling like I put my shoes on backward the night before, and I hate everything and everyone I see. Days like that, my check could show up late or missing and I might not notice for a week."

The computer printout from the VA listed him as being forty-three, a veteran from the Vietnam era. His breezy, chipper manner made him seem younger, while the lines across his face and the scars on his body created an aged, wizened impression.

Morton Arthur turned to Angela Paradisi and said, "A beautiful name. Angel of paradise. Why are you here, really?"

"We *are* with the FBI," Angela protested. "Really."

"But why are you here?" His tone was more inquisitive than accusatory. He turned to Veronica. "I'd expect the Postal Service to investigate the problem you've described, or maybe the Treasury Department. Please, tell me—is one of my friends in some sort of trouble?"

Just then someone rang his doorbell. He stood and buzzed the visitor in. A few minutes later a short, stubby teenager appeared in the doorway. He was a Downs Syndrome boy, and a moment later two other Downs Syndrome boys followed him into the apartment. The first boy said "Hi, Uncle Mort," and the two of them embraced.

"Ladies, this is my nephew, Paul, and his friends, Ricky

and Chuck. It's Paul's birthday, and the Yankees are playing an afternoon game. Isn't that great?" He reached out and tousled Paul's hair. "Boys, say hello to Veronica and Angela, two friends of mine."

"Are you coming with us?" Paul asked.

Veronica smiled. "No, we just came by to say hello to your uncle. We're leaving now. Happy Birthday, Paul." She looked at Angela and gestured toward the door.

"Wait, please," the man said. "You haven't answered my question. Is one of my friends in trouble?"

"I don't think there's any trouble here," Veronica replied.

"But I don't understand . . ." He thought for a moment, and then his eyes lit up. "Maybe I'm not supposed to understand. That's it, isn't it? This is some kind of test, but I have no idea what I have to do to pass." He smiled. "If it's about that ambassadorship the president promised me, could you tell him I'm afraid I'll have to turn it down?"

"I know he'll be very disappointed. Thank you for your time, Mr. Arthur."

Back on the sidewalk, Angela said, "I don't think he's the one."

"Why not?"

The younger woman hesitated for a moment, then explained. "Because the person who wrote those letters seems preoccupied with his own suffering, whatever that suffering might be. But this fellow downplayed his problems. He seemed much more concerned about others' welfare. I liked the way he hugged his nephew, the way he seemed to look out for him. And when he learned who we are, his first thought was that a friend might be in trouble. No defensiveness, no indication that he had any reason to worry for himself. And he was sensitive enough to realize I felt embarrassed when he walked in without a shirt, and he did something about it right away. He just seemed like a nice guy." She paused. "How did I do?"

Veronica said, "I agree with you."

"Wow—really?"

"I agree that he seemed like a nice person. And he didn't

do or say anything to make me suspicious of him. But nice people can kill, and killers can seem nice."

They took a cab to Second Avenue near 23rd Street. The VA computer list put Arthur Mendoza at seventy years of age, a veteran from the World War II era. From an actuarial point of view, Veronica knew, Mendoza's age made him an unlikely suspect. But Angela said something that caught Veronica's interest. "Two blocks from here is a Veterans Administration Hospital."

There was no response when they rang Mendoza's door-bell. An elderly man sat on the front stoop, an unfiltered cigarette dangling from his mouth. His bony fingers were yellowed from several years' worth of nicotine. Veronica told him who they were looking for.

"Left about a half hour ago, miss."

"Any idea when he might return?"

"Dunno. You can ask him yourself, though. When he ain't here, he's at Zemo's Tavern down on the corner. Don't like to go too far. He don't walk too well no more. Neither does his dog."

"The sign on the door says 'no pets.' "

"They made an exception for Arthur, seeing as how it's a Seeing Eye dog. Blind as a bat, like the expression goes. Since Iwo Jima." The old man eyed the two women. "Pity. This is one time I'm sure he'd enjoy looking at the people talking to him."

They walked to the corner. There were three patrons and one dog at the bar in Zemo's. The dog lay by the feet of a frail old man who wore wraparound glasses with black plastic lenses. As Veronica and Angela approached the bar, they heard the bartender address the blind man by name. He was Arthur Mendoza.

Veronica gestured toward the door. "Really no reason to bother the poor old guy," she said after they reached the sidewalk. "Let's move on. Two down, one to go."

"That sounds like something Artie would say."

Veronica shuddered. "You're right."

They grabbed a late lunch on the run from a fast food

joint next to Zemo's, then they hailed a cab for the Upper East Side. Veronica leaned against her window and watched the street activity as their driver negotiated the dips and potholes at breakneck speed. "I wonder what Harry is doing to pass the time."

"Are you and he ... umm ... Never mind, it's none of my business."

Veronica laughed. "We don't have that sort of interest in each other."

"Oh." Angela hesitated for a moment, then continued. "I think I could, you know, have that sort of interest."

"My, that was certainly quick."

"Yes," replied Angela, clearly embarrassed.

"Believe me, you're wasting your time even thinking about it." She noticed Angela's hurt expression and said, "Nothing against you. It's just that he's completely hung up on his wife." Veronica saw no need to mention that Janet was dead.

Angela sighed very softly and turned to gaze out her window.

Their final subject was Arthur Chillingsworth, age forty-four, another Vietnam-era veteran. He lived in a twenty-story Park Avenue condominium building. Veronica counted twenty mailboxes in the lobby, one for each resident, and she presumed that each unit comprised an entire story of the building. Chillingsworth apparently was a very wealthy man. Veronica said, "How much disability does he receive from the VA?"

"About twelve hundred each month."

"Tax free?"

"I think that's how it works," Angela replied.

"Looking at this place, I don't think he needs the money."

The lobby was spacious and pristine. Thick carpets stretched across the expanse. Large abstract pastels graced the walls. A uniformed security guard stood when the two women entered. He was about Veronica's age, lean and well muscled. "May I help you, ladies?"

"We're here to see Mr. Chillingsworth," replied Veronica.

"Is he expecting you?"

Veronica evaded the question. "My name is Veronica Pace. This is Ms. Paradisi."

"I see." He briefly scanned both of them from head to toe—not the leering look of a sidewalk ogler, but a quick survey by someone expert at assessing others' intentions from minimal data. He reminded Veronica of a Secret Service agent she knew; she wondered if he were carrying a concealed pistol. He dialed Chillingsworth's number on the house telephone.

As he dialed, Angela lightly touched Veronica's arm to get her attention, then nodded in the direction of a video camera mounted unobtrusively in the frame of the pastel painting behind the security guard's desk. No doubt whoever answered the security guard's call would be viewing the two visitors at the same time.

The guard announced the women's names into the phone. Then he said to Veronica, "Mr. Chill would like you both to turn around very slowly, one at a time, three hundred and sixty degrees." The guard cocked his head slightly toward the video camera behind him. The women did as they were instructed, first Veronica, then Angela. The guard listened to the voice on the phone for a moment, then held the handset in Angela's direction. Veronica intercepted it and pressed her ear to the receiver.

The voice on the other end was low and raspy. "I wanted to talk to the other one."

"Ms. Paradisi is my assistant. I can answer your questions."

"Who are you?" the voice demanded.

"We're from the FBI."

"What do you want?"

"We'd like to speak with you about your VA benefits."

The man on the other end breathed two or three times, his mouth very close to his phone. "Let me speak with the guard again."

Veronica handed the phone back to the security guard. He listened to the voice, then said, "Mr. Chill will see one of you." He pointed toward Angela.

"Tell him that's unacceptable," Veronica said loudly enough for the voice on the phone to hear.

The security guard listened to the phone, then pointed at Veronica. "He says he'll see you instead."

"That's also unacceptable. He can either speak with both of us, or he can respond to a federal attorney's subpoena."

Angela looked at her wide-eyed, no doubt wondering just how often and how far Veronica was willing to bend the truth to get what she wanted.

"Yes, sir," the security guard said into the phone. "Very well, sir." He hung up and said, "He'll see you both." He escorted the women across the lobby and inserted a key into a plate on the wall near the elevator door. Quietly, as if to avoid being overheard, the guard said, "I believe you've made him angry. That's unfortunate."

"You called him Mr. Chill," said Veronica. "Why?"

He sighed and shook his head. "His full name is Arthur Maxwell Chillingsworth. He calls himself Max Chill."

"Max Chill?"

The guard nodded. "He's quite insistent about that. He says he's had his name legally changed, but I see all his mail, and I know that isn't true."

The elevator door opened and the two women passed through. "Why are you telling me this?" Veronica asked.

The guard shrugged. "Professional courtesy, I guess." He began to smile just as the door shut between him and the women.

Inside the elevator another camera was mounted above the door. There were no buttons for the various floors, just one for the lobby and a slot for a key. Either the security guard or Arthur Chillingsworth was controlling their ascent.

The door opened on the nineteenth floor. They stepped off the elevator and it shut quickly behind them. They were standing at the end of a corridor that ran the length of the floor. Immediately across the corridor was an open doorway leading into a high-ceiling living room.

"Hello?" Veronica called out. "Mr. Chillingsworth?"

There was no reply. They waited for several seconds; the only sounds were the distant street noises coming through open windows.

They stepped across the hall into the living room. The air was rank with the foul smell of ammonia. Two emaciated cats slept next to a box of stale kitty litter. Scum adhered to the sides of their water bowl. The fireplace was piled high with trash. Empty beer and vodka bottles were strewn about the room.

A shoulder-high bookcase ran the length of the wall to Veronica's left. The books were arranged in alphabetical order by author. She scanned the shelves and midway down the wall found two books that caught her eye: *Soldier and Son* by Dr. Harold Kline and, by the same author, an earlier nonfiction book entitled *Battle Dreams: Vietnam Veterans Relive the War*. The two books were worn; they'd been read. Veronica picked up *Battle Dreams*. On the title page, in a handwriting familiar to her, she found an inscription:

> To Max Chill—
> > Welcome home
> > > —Harry Kline
> > > September 16, 1989

"Drop it right now!"

Angela gasped. Veronica turned and saw their host: a massive round-shouldered hulk who had materialized behind them without the slightest sound. He looked as if he hadn't shaved or bathed for several days. Even from a dozen feet away, Veronica could tell that he reeked of alcohol. His dirty hair was pulled into a ponytail. A diamond stud earring adorned one ear. He wore a black jumpsuit, its sleeves rolled up to reveal his fleshy arms. His body had the sagging look of a once well-toned unit that had atrophied from neglect.

The man took one step toward them; both women reflexively took a step backward. Veronica realized that he was blocking the route to the elevator. Even if he weren't standing in the way, they would still need his elevator key to retreat.

Arthur Chillingsworth's voice was harsh and gravelly. His speech was slurred and his eyes were bleary. "What's this all about? You—the blond one with the big chest. Why are you here?"

Veronica stepped sideways toward Angela, standing between her and Chillingsworth. "I told you why we came. We want to talk to you about your benefits checks."

The man continued staring at Angela and shook his forefinger at her. "What is this? I talk to you, and words come back at me from the other one's mouth. Are you some kind of goddamn ventriloquist?" He turned abruptly to face Veronica. "Do you think I'm stupid? You think Max Chill doesn't know what's going on here?"

He advanced toward Veronica purposefully, backing her into a corner. She cursed her own stupidity for having let him get the advantage. And she regretted having brought the woefully underexperienced Angela along, for now she had to worry about the younger woman's safety as well as her own.

He stuck his face inches from Veronica's. His nostrils flared and one eye twitched. "Who sent you? Was it Dr. Carswell? Which one of you has my Klonopin?"

Angela's voice, faint and tremulous, came from behind him. "I have it," she said. "It's in my briefcase. I left it in the hallway by the elevator."

Chillingsworth wheeled around and moved toward Angela. "There's nothing in the hallway," he hissed. "You're trying to trick me."

Veronica followed a step behind him, taking care this time to keep her back toward the center of the room. "Listen to me," she said. She thought for a moment, then said, "You don't want to hurt anybody, Artie."

The man stopped suddenly. His body stiffened. Still facing Angela, he said, "What did you call me?"

"I called you Artie," replied Veronica. "Hasn't anyone ever called you that before?"

"Nobody calls me that!" he said, and then emitted a low, subhuman growl. He pivoted toward Veronica. In his hand was a small kitchen knife, its four-inch blade gleaming as he wiggled it in small circles. He must have had it concealed inside a pocket in his jumpsuit.

Veronica and Chillingsworth both moved counterclockwise for a few seconds, like boxers circling each other in the ring waiting to land the first blow. First he stopped, then she did, and then he stood with his legs spread and coiled, ready to fling himself across the narrow space between them in the next instant.

Suddenly there was a loud thud. Chillingsworth's eyes bulged in their sockets. His body lurched forward. Veronica jumped to one side as the man's huge form crashed to the floor next to her. He rolled onto his back and grabbed at his crotch. His mouth opened wide in a silent scream.

Angela stood on his other side clutching a heavy fireplace andiron in both hands. She flung it across the room. "The next time I'll cut them off and stuff one in each ear! Now, where's your fucking elevator key?" She leaned hard and long on the f in fucking, spitting it out as if it were a foul-tasting liquid she'd been forced to ingest against her will.

Chillingsworth gasped for air. His lips formed the words, "My pocket," but no sound came out.

Angela searched his pockets until she found the key. Suddenly Chillingsworth flung his arm out and latched onto her wrist with a vise-like grip. Before Veronica could step in to help, Angela lifted her right foot off the floor, then thrust the ball of her foot against his side, just below his rib cage. He emitted a soft gurgling sound and released his grip on her.

The two women rushed to the elevator. Angela inserted the key; a few seconds later the door opened and she pressed the button to return to the lobby. As the door shut behind them, Angela threw the key into Chillingsworth's hallway.

"Thanks," Veronica said. "That was quite a move you made with the fireplace iron."

Angela was out of breath. "By the time I was thirteen, I was already in a support bra. I learned early how to deal with creeps like him."

"I hear some men really like that understated approach."

Angela smiled. Her breath was still racing. Her face was flushed. She reached behind her neck and undid the tie on her hair. Loose blond curls cascaded down past her shoulders. "Do you like me?" she asked.

"You can play on my team anytime."

The young woman leaned forward and placed her lips against Veronica's. Her touch was soft and quick, the kiss over almost before Veronica knew what was happening. As the elevator door opened onto the lobby, Angela said, "I told you I could have that sort of interest."

"Angela must have been a big hit at the nunnery," I said after Veronica finished telling me about the day's events.

"I don't think that's funny."

"Sorry. Just a little homophobic humor."

"Very little." We were seated on two mismatched chairs in my hotel room. Veronica sipped a gin and tonic she'd poured from the prestocked mini-bar. "What's Klonopin?" she asked.

"An antianxiety medication."

"A tranquilizer?"

"Something like that. It's like a long-lasting Valium. It can be pretty addictive. It's easily abused, and it's prescribed inappropriately by some doctors. I try to stay away from it in my practice."

"So what does it tell us about Arthur Chillingsworth?"

"I don't know. Most likely, that some doctor thinks he needs calming down, rightly or wrongly."

"Rightly, if you ask me. Are you sure nothing about him rings a bell with you?" She described his appearance once more.

"Nothing."

"And the inscription in your first book?"

"It's dated about a month after the book was published. I did some book-signings in New York that fall. Maybe Chillingsworth came to one and mentioned that he was a Vietnam vet himself. That would account for the 'Welcome home' message. I can call Jeffrey to see if he kept track of the dates, to see if the date in Chillingsworth's copy matches the date of one of the book-signings. Or you can wait until I get home tomorrow and I'll check my 1989 appointment book. Anyway, it probably doesn't matter. Like I said, I don't remember him."

"But something else on your schedule for that day might jog your memory. A party you might have met him at, or something like that."

"Maybe."

"Well, let's wait until you check your appointment book. No sense raising your editor's suspicions by calling him to ask him about something that happened nearly three years ago."

"Suspicions? Damn it, don't tell me you still think he might be the one we're looking for. I know Jeffrey. He's not a killer."

"What about the girl he and his buddies killed in Vietnam?"

"He didn't do it. He told me so himself."

She narrowed her eyes and focused them on me. "You never told me that."

"He never spoke about it until today. I visited him a few hours ago."

"And it just happened to come up in conversation?"

"Of course not. I knew about it already from you, so I just asked the right questions until he told me about it. He was a witness to the murder. He would have stopped it if he had the chance. But he didn't do it."

"And you believe him."

"Yes."

"My, aren't you the clever detective." She put her drink down hard on the windowsill and walked back toward her adjoining room. When she reached the doorway, she whirled around and glared at me. "I don't tell you how to prescribe Klonopin. Don't tell me how to do my job. And don't try to do it for me."

21: Can It Be That Easy To Forget Someone?

We took an early shuttle back to Boston on Friday morning and went directly to the FBI office in Government Center.

Martin Baines gazed out his window at Faneuil Hall while we filled him in on our trip. "You two have had a busy week," he said after we finished. He looked at Veronica. "Sounds like this Arthur Chillingsworth may be the one you're after."

Veronica said, "Angela Paradisi will try to dig up more information on him. And the others, too—just in case. We already have all three under surveillance. If one of them makes his move next Wednesday, we should be able to stop him from killing anyone."

"With enough evidence to hold onto him?"

"I don't know."

"When are you going back to New York?"

"After the weekend."

"You, too, Harry?"

"Yes," I replied.

Baines took a sip of coffee. "I wonder who Artie's going after—a patient at one of the hospitals, or someone who works there?"

"Unlikely it would be a patient," I said.

"Why?"

"These days, insurance companies force hospitals to discharge people pretty quickly. The killer has had May 20th in mind for some time. If he knew that far in advance that the person would be there on that date, that person probably works there."

Baines said, "And we have no idea who that person is. If one of your suspects is the killer, and if he goes through with his plan to strike on Wednesday, you can stop him. But if the murderer is someone else, you're pretty much waiting for him to kill again, hoping you'll learn enough from murder number three to go after him."

"Yes," Veronica said.

"Not much of a game plan," Baines replied.

"I know."

"Melissa isn't back from school yet," Mrs. Winnicot said when I arrived home. "She'll be relieved to see you. She wasn't sure you'd make it home today."

"I told her I'd be here before the weekend."

"I know. But she was uncertain, just the same."

I went into my office and looked up September 16th in my 1989 appointment book. On that day I'd been at a book-signing at the B. Dalton store near Jeffrey Barrow's office. I had no idea how many people I might have signed books for that day, but apparently Arthur Chillingsworth was one of them.

I began to thumb through my mail and telephone messages. I heard the clatter of my daughter's shoes racing along the corridor from the kitchen to my office. She ran to my side, threw her arms around me, and clung to me very, very tightly.

"Daddy! What did you bring me?"

"Sweetheart, I was so busy . . ."

"Oh," she replied. "Well, I'm glad you came back. I was afraid you'd forget the school play on Monday."

"No, I didn't forget."

"Good," she said, hugging me again.

"But, honey—I can't come. I have to go back to New York."

She looked up at me without speaking for a few seconds, then said, "Are you going with *her*?"

I knew she meant Veronica. "Yes. Let me—don't pull away like that, honey—let me explain."

"I don't care!" she yelled.

"Veronica is trying to catch a very dangerous man. A murderer. If I don't help, then some other child may lose a parent. You wouldn't want that to happen, would you?"

It was a cheap shot, but I didn't know what else to say. Melissa stood there with a puzzled expression, trying to balance her own needs against what I'd just revealed. "I understand," she said, her voice suddenly very quiet.

"I'm glad."

"I understand you'd rather be with her."

She turned to leave. I reached out for her hand, but she yanked it from my grasp and headed for the door. "Honey, wait." I started to follow her. She suddenly bolted from the room and hurried to the kitchen, then flung open the back door and dashed outside. I heard her footsteps as she ran down the gravel driveway.

Melissa had never run from me like that before. I checked the impulse to chase after her. I figured she needed a few minutes of privacy more than she needed my reassurances. But a half hour passed, then an hour, and she was still gone. I called all of the neighbors, but no one had seen her. I decided to drive around the neighborhood to search for her. Before I could leave the phone rang.

"Did you check your appointment book?" asked Veronica.

I told her what I'd found.

"I struck out, too," she said. "Remember the close-up of Joseph Carroll's corpse? The one that showed the 1976 on the penny in his hand? Well, I called Tim Connolly to find out what the date was on the penny in Mary Mendez's hand, looking for some common element."

"And?"

"They can't find the coin. Can you believe that? A simple thing like preserving a piece of evidence, and they screw it up."

"I don't think it matters. I think we're just grasping at straws."

"Well, we've got some suspects," she said. "And we have a few possible sites where the next murder might occur. So the week wasn't a total loss." She laughed. "I got to see the Alamo for the first time, and I even had FBI agents of both genders make passes at me. And tomorrow I get to play tennis with my father at his place in Wellesley. Hey—you play tennis, don't you? Would you like to come with me?"

"I don't think so. I want to spend time with Melissa. She got really upset when I told her I was leaving again. She ran out of the house over an hour ago. I have no idea where she went. I was just getting ready to look for her when you called."

"We can bring her with us. My father has horses. I'll give her a riding lesson. She'll have fun."

"I don't think she'll want to come."

"I'll make a deal with you. If I tell you where to find Melissa, will you come tomorrow?"

"How do you know where she is?"

"Just a guess. When we drove to your house on Monday, I saw a cemetery about a mile from your house. Is that where your wife is buried?"

"Yes."

"Then that's where you should look for your daughter."

"She's never gone there without me."

"Maybe, maybe not. Fathers don't always know everything about their daughters. Look for her at your wife's grave. If you find her there, then you owe me—again."

The late afternoon sun cut through the leaves of the maple trees, throwing patches of light on the ground where Janet was buried. Melissa was sitting on the grass by the headstone, her back toward me as I approached. I sat next to her without saying anything. She stared straight ahead. If she was surprised by my presence, she didn't let on.

After a minute or two she said, "I don't remember what she looked like."

"Of course you do, sweetheart. You have her picture by

your bed, and then there's your photo album and our videos—"

"That's just it. Somebody at school asked me what my mother looked like, and all I could remember was the pictures and the videos. I can't remember anything except them."

She turned to face me. Her eyes were red from crying. "Oh, Daddy—can it be that easy to forget someone?"

I pulled her against me and held her in my arms.

22: The Spirit of a Murder Victim

Veronica cruised west on Route 16, through Newton Lower Falls and into Wellesley. "I'm glad you decided to come, Melissa," she said.

My daughter grunted from the backseat. I hadn't given her any choice in the matter. Veronica wouldn't take no for an answer from me, and Mrs. Winnicot had the weekend off. Melissa had to come, like it or not.

"Have you ever gone horseback riding before?"

"Uh-uh."

"Well, my father has a very nice horse I think you'll like."

"I don't want to."

"He's very gentle, Melissa. He won't hurt you."

"I don't *want* to ride some stupid old *horse*!"

"Melissa!"

"It's alright, Harry. Don't worry, Melissa. You won't have to do anything you don't want to do." Veronica turned around and smiled at my daughter, but Melissa just stared out her window.

Donald Pace's estate backed up on the Charles River, not far from the mansion reserved for the president of Wellesley College. The Georgian home had a square main body, with latter-day additions spreading out from its sides like bookends. A tennis court, horse barn, and riding corral dotted the heavily wooded property.

"Impressive," I said as we pulled up the long driveway. "You grew up here?"

"We moved here when I was eleven. My father's law firm made a fortune that year. They represented corporations bidding for business in China after Nixon opened relations there."

Donald Pace bounded down the front steps as we pulled alongside the house. He was of medium height, tanned and trim, with a full head of closely cropped gray hair. He wore a red and gold Nike warmup suit and carried a wide-head tennis racquet. When we stepped from the car, he embraced his daughter. "Ronnie, it's great to see you." He looked at Melissa and me. "These must be the guests you told me about."

Veronica made introductions all around. Just then a woman my age or a little younger stepped outside. She looked vaguely Eurasian. Her warmup outfit matched Donald's, and she was equally tanned and trim.

"Shana," said Donald, "Ronnie brought along a tennis partner for you." He introduced me to his wife, and then she and Veronica engaged in a perfunctory embrace. The woman spoke with an exotic but hard-to-place accent.

Donald and Shana led the way into the house. When they were out of earshot, I turned to Veronica and said, "Ronnie?"

"He wanted a boy."

"Don't you have any brothers?" Melissa asked.

"No brothers, no sisters. There's only me."

Melissa pondered this information, no doubt comparing Veronica's situation to her own.

After some small talk and soft drinks, we proceeded to the tennis court. Melissa sat in the shade and listened with earphones to her portable CD player. On one side of the court, Veronica and her father teamed up as if by some unspoken prior arrangement. Shana and I took the other side. After a few minutes of volleying, Veronica announced that it was time to play a best-of-three-sets match.

Donald spun his racquet. I called "up," but the racquet landed with the Prince logo facing down, so they had the first serve. Veronica moved to the right-hand corner of the baseline. Shana dropped back to the corresponding position on our side of the net, prepared to receive Veronica's serve. As she walked past me, she spoke softly, for my ears only. "The little exercise you are about to see is aimed at me, not you. I endure it because she has to try to conquer me before she can be nice to me. I understand this, and so you need not worry about my feelings."

Veronica's first serve left her racquet like a cannon shot. It smacked down against the clay surface to Shana's left, then skipped away out of reach. It was almost a service ace, but it landed an inch wide of the center line. Her second serve was almost as strong. Shana managed to reach the ball, but she had to stretch so far that her racquet head was open and the ball lofted up in a weak lob directly above the net on Donald's half of the court. Donald readied himself to smack it in my direction. But Veronica rushed forward and smashed it to a spot three inches in front of Shana, handcuffing her. "Fifteen-love," Veronica said.

For the next forty-five minutes, the same theme was played out again and again. Donald Pace and I were fairly well matched in spite of our fifteen-year age difference. What he surrendered in power, he almost made up for in quickness and positioning. But while Shana was a more-than-adequate player, she was outmatched by Veronica's strength and conditioning. And Veronica took every advantage of the differential, straining to aim shots at Shana that could have been directed more easily toward me.

They won the first set, six games to four. Shana and I eked out a win in the second set, thanks to some strong backhand play on her part and several unforced errors by Donald. But the third set was all theirs. It was mercifully brief, a shutout, and it ended on a cross-court forehand smash by Veronica. We all advanced to the net, and Veronica smiled and gave Shana a peck on the cheek. Shana cast a knowing glance at me. Then all five of us sat down to more soft drinks that had been placed on a nearby table midmatch by Donald's housekeeper.

The women retired from the group momentarily to do

whatever it is women do when they retire from groups momentarily. Melissa returned to her CD player and her spot in the shade. Donald asked me what I did for a living, then spoke knowledgeably about a controversy regarding a new antipsychotic medication with potentially lethal side effects.

He motioned toward my daughter and said, "Cute kid. Have any others?"

"No."

"Divorced?"

"Widowed."

"Oh." He furrowed his brow. "I guess Ronnie has told you about her mother. Such a terrible loss. Very hard on Ronnie. Rachel was only thirty when she died. I was thirty-four. You?"

"I was thirty-five."

"Changes everything, doesn't it?"

I nodded.

"I was a wreck for a long time. Then one day, a year or so after Rachel died, I was looking for something in the refrigerator and I found it right away. I thought to myself, 'It sure is great to be able to see inside this refrigerator again.' You see, Rachel used to make three or four portions of everything she cooked or baked. Then she'd fill the refrigerator with Tupperware containers and plastic bags, and I could never find a damn thing."

He sipped his Diet Coke and continued. "For a year after she died, I couldn't focus on any of the negative aspects of our relationship. Then gradually things fell into a more balanced perspective, and things began to get better for me. The next year Ronnie and I moved out here, and that helped, too—being in a new place where we could make new memories."

The women walked outside, engaged in conversation. Shana rested a hand on Veronica's shoulder. Veronica pulled back reflexively for an instant, then relaxed under the older woman's grip.

"I married Shana a few years later. Hard for Ronnie to accept, but the best thing that could have happened to me. I love Shana as much as I loved Rachel. The one doesn't diminish the other." He looked at me. "Ever think of getting married again?"

"Maybe they'll bury you here, Daddy."

"No, I'll be buried down there, next to your mother."

"Even if you get married again?"

"I'm not getting married again."

"I don't think that's likely," I said.

"I see." Veronica and Shana were walking toward us. "How long have you and Ronnie been seeing each other?"

I chuckled. "You're assuming facts not in evidence."

"Come again?"

"Isn't that something you lawyers sometimes say during trials?"

He shrugged. "I'm not a litigator. I haven't been inside a courtroom for years. But these are the facts *I* see in evidence. She brought you here to meet me. She isn't afraid to beat you in tennis, let you see her strong side. And she wants your daughter to like her. I can see it in Ronnie's tentative approach to Melissa, just like I still see it in Shana's approach to Ronnie."

The five of us moved to a sundeck at the back of the house. The housekeeper brought a hamburger for Melissa, Cajun chicken breast sandwiches for the rest of us. We looked out over the river as we ate. Three or four canoes passed by during the meal and we exchanged waves with the people in them. Birds and crickets sounded all around us. Now and again one of the horses could be heard neighing in the barn. It was all a far cry from the events of the previous week. I was glad for the respite.

I considered what Donald said about his wife and his daughter, and I watched the two women interact. I did a little addition and subtraction in my head and figured that Veronica was no older than fifteen when Donald married Shana. I noticed that she neither addressed Shana by name nor as her mother. She couldn't decide how to relate to the woman. After all these years, Veronica was still trying to accommodate herself to her father's second wife. And so I knew that she was still trying to come to terms with her own mother's death.

I remembered what Veronica said as we walked near the Alamo: *People usually die for no good reason. When Mary Mendez's little boy is old enough to understand what happened, what sense will he make of it? Will he accept that? How will he get over it?*

I wondered why Veronica hadn't mentioned her mother's death to me. True, it's not the sort of thing that necessarily comes up in conversation with people you don't know all that well. But it would have been natural for her to say something to me, knowing about the loss Melissa and I had suffered.

I thought about Melissa's struggle. I glanced at her and imagined her twenty years older, still torn inside by her grief. The thought of my daughter carrying her unhappiness into adulthood made me very sad.

After lunch Veronica gave us a tour of the house and grounds. Melissa maintained her disinterested attitude. We rejoined Donald and Shana, exchanged some parting pleasantries, and were on our way back to Concord.

We'd driven on the major roads to get to Wellesley; I showed Veronica an alternate route back to my home, through Wayland and Lincoln. Melissa plugged her earphones in and ignored us.

"Your father thought we were dating."

"Fathers!" she said with mock exasperation. "What do they know?"

From the corner of my eye I saw Melissa smile. She wasn't really ignoring us.

"Well, I liked him," I said. "I liked both of them."

"I was in puberty when my father married her. Shana was barely out of it. It's hard to think of someone only ten years older than you as your parent."

"She's your stepmother?" Melissa asked, joining the conversation.

"Yes."

"Where does your real mother live?"

Veronica paused. "My mother died a long time ago."

"Oh," said Melissa. "How old were you when she died?"

"Nine."

"That's how old I am."

"I know. My mother died when I was your age."

"Oh." Melissa took the information in for a minute, then asked, "Was she sick for a long time?"

"No. It was very sudden."

"Was she in an accident?"

"Something like that," she said.

"Oh." It was the first time all day Melissa had directed more than five words in a row to Veronica. "Do you still remember what she looked like?"

"Yes. Sometimes I forget, but it always comes back to me."

We rode in silence for several minutes. We turned off Route 117 onto Bedford Street in Lincoln. A short while later we crossed the intersection with Trapelo Road.

"This looks familiar," Veronica said.

"You drove into this intersection once before, coming from the right on Trapelo Road."

"Did I?"

"That night after I interviewed Sylvia Ossler, the Greenfields' daughter." I knew Melissa was probably listening to us, her earphones notwithstanding, so I didn't want to make direct mention of our race in pursuit of Gerald Eckler.

"Well, I'll be damned," Veronica said.

We reached my house ten minutes later. Veronica pulled to a stop alongside the garage and left her motor running. "Thanks for coming, both of you."

Melissa said, "Do you want to eat pizza with us for dinner? We have it every Saturday."

"That sounds nice, but I have some things I need to do."

Melissa got out of the car and walked to the field next to our house. She sat down on an old stone bench and stared at the woods on the other side of the field.

"I'll meet you at the airport, Harry. Monday morning, the eight o'clock shuttle." She looked through her windshield at my daughter.

I reached over and turned her ignition key into the off position. "Tell me about your mother."

"What do you want to know?"

"How did she die?"

She looked down at her hands and stayed silent for a while. "A burglar murdered her."

"Oh, no."

"My father was on a business trip. One night I heard a loud noise coming from my parents' bedroom, like something being thrown against the wall. It woke me up. I tried to get back to sleep, but a minute later I heard it again. I went in my parents' room. A man in a ski mask was beating my mother. He kept punching her and punching her in the face. She saw me and tried to say something. I think she was trying to tell me to run. But I just stood there and screamed. That's when he realized I was in the room. He stopped for just a few seconds. Then he smashed her head against the wall and she crumpled to the floor. Her skull was broken. Massive brain hemorrhaging. I knew right then that she was dead."

She stopped speaking. I reached out and touched her hand. It was ice cold. "I'm so very, very sorry," I said. The words sounded pitifully inadequate.

Veronica turned away and continued. "He started to walk toward me. My father's gun was on the bed. I guess she'd reached for it when the man came in her room, then lost it in the struggle. I picked it up and pointed it at him. He backed out of the room very slowly. I kept the gun aimed at him the whole time. I tried to pull the trigger—God, I tried. But I was so scared. I just froze. Even after he ran down the steps and out of the house, I just stood there with the gun in my hands, still pointing it at the doorway. I couldn't move. I couldn't talk. All of a sudden I started firing the gun, three times, maybe four times, until there were no more bullets. A neighbor called the police. I was still standing there with the gun when they arrived. It seemed like forever before I could even tell them what had happened."

She looked directly at me. "I've gone over that scene nearly every day of my life. Not only what he did to her, but my own actions. If I'd gone into her room when I heard the first noise, I might have been able to help her."

"Or you might have been killed along with her. You were just a child. You couldn't have saved her."

She sighed. "They never caught him. A few years later, when I was in junior high, I read a Greek tragedy where the spirit of a murder victim was condemned to wander in limbo until the person who killed him was brought to justice. I can't tell you how much that has haunted me."

I wanted to hurt people who hurt other people. That's what Veronica told me had motivated her decision to study law and become a prosecutor. I understood that a little better now.

"The other day, you told Melissa you had aimed your gun, but that you hadn't shot anyone. And then you said 'unfortunately.' "

"I still feel that way. I always have. I always will."

I looked out at Melissa. "I know what she's gone through because of what happened to her mother. I can't imagine what you had to go through."

"That's right. No offense, but you can't imagine. And I can't describe. And you say you know what your daughter has gone through, but you don't and you can't." She looked at Melissa, then at me, and then at Melissa once again. "But I can."

She got out of the car. She walked over to my daughter and sat next to her. The two of them stayed there and watched as a flock of Canada geese circled and landed at the far side of the field.

23: Ye Have Sinned a Great Sin

"First of all, Arthur Mendoza really is blind," said Angela Paradisi. "The records from the local VA hospital are clear about that. He lost his sight in the South Pacific during World War II. He's been on a total disability status ever since."

It was Monday morning, May 18th—two days away from Artie's next scheduled killing. We were seated again in the conference room in the FBI office in Lower Manhattan. Angela was reviewing what she'd learned about the three men she and Veronica had interviewed the previous Thursday.

"Morton Arthur, the first one we saw—he's a genuine war hero."

She looked at her notes. "Graduated NYU *summa cum laude*. Turned down a medical school deferment to enlist. Did two tours of duty in Vietnam. Was involved in some sort of secret operation, I couldn't get any details. He wound up highly decorated and completely paralyzed. Spent two years solid in the VA hospital, made a miraculous recovery. Has full disability payments, is rumored to have some other sort of stipend from either Army Intelligence or the CIA. Supports his sister and her mentally retarded son. Won a Mayor's Humanitarian award two years ago for rescuing three children from a burning apartment building." She glanced up at Veronica. "I *told* you I liked him."

"How did you get access to their hospital records?" I asked.

"The hospital's chief of security is a former agent. I explained the situation to him. He connected me with a sympathetic hospital administrator."

Veronica said, "What about Arthur Chillingsworth?"

"Chillingsworth receives full disability payments, too. But he's never been treated at the local VA, so I don't know the specifics of his situation. I did call your former boss, Harry, to ask for information about Chillingsworth's two admissions to your old hospital."

"Monte Backus?"

She nodded. "Very ingratiating. Entirely unhelpful."

"Sounds like Monte."

"I checked with the police, did some other asking around. Chillingsworth's family owns a chain of discount appliance stores down south. He lives off a very substantial trust fund. He was arrested twice in the eighties. First for aggravated rape, then for assault and battery with a dangerous weapon. Each time the charge was dismissed."

Veronica said, "I'm sure he can afford a very good lawyer."

"I'm sure he can," Angela agreed. "And he'll need one if he shows up at Mount Sinai the day after tomorrow. We'll know the minute he leaves his building. Besides the front entrance on Park Avenue, there's a service entrance around the corner. We've been watching both entrances since Thursday evening, a couple of hours after you and I visited him. He hasn't left the building."

"How do you know he was there when your surveillance started?" asked Veronica.

"I called him. I recognized his voice when he answered, then I hung up." Angela smiled. "His telephone number is unlisted. But when we were walking around his apartment, I saw his phone and made a mental note of the number."

"My, my," said Veronica. "You're full of surprises, aren't you?"

Angela blushed and averted her eyes. "I need to talk to you, Veronica. I have to explain something. Maybe later, when you have a few minutes free."

* * *

I said, "When she talked about having a few minutes free, I think she meant 'when Harry isn't here.' "

"Obviously. She's probably worried I might do something to jeopardize her job. Heterosexuality is the Bureau's official sexual orientation. Old J. Edgar was something of a fanatic about that."

"Didn't he live with another man for most of his adult life?"

She nodded. "One of his top assistants."

"I'm sure it was because they had many work-related matters to discuss."

"No doubt. Anyway, Angela doesn't have anything to worry about from me."

We hailed a cab for the Upper East Side. Veronica wanted to see the three hospitals firsthand. Angela had departed for Jeffrey Barrow's office to see if I'd received any noteworthy mail at Morgan Books.

Veronica and I surveyed each hospital for about half an hour. Afterward we stopped for lunch at a sandwich shop on Second Avenue, near Metropolitan Hospital. Veronica said, "Patrolling any one of these hospitals thoroughly would be difficult. It would require dozens of people. Imagine trying to get the manpower and nail down the logistics for three hospitals at once."

Just then her beeper went off. Veronica found a pay phone and called Angela at the FBI office. When she returned to our table she said, "Angela wants us to come back now. She says you got a very interesting letter in the mail."

MAY 15, 1992

"YE HAVE SINNED A GREAT SIN; AND NOW I WILL GO UP UNTO THE LORD, PERADVENTURE I SHALL MAKE ATONEMENT FOR YOUR SIN."

AND THE LORD SAID: WHEN I NURSE A GRUDGE, IT'S AS GOOD AS GOLD.

YOURS,
ARTIE

"The first line sounds like something from the Bible," I said.

"Any ideas?" asked Veronica.

"I'm Jewish, so I don't know much about the New Testament. Hell, I don't know much about the Old Testament, either. But going up to the Lord to atone for the sins of others—it sounds like the crucifixion. So I'll guess it was something Christ said at the Last Supper."

Veronica studied the photocopy of the letter that had arrived that day, addressed to me, at Morgan Books. The original was being checked—no doubt fruitlessly—for fingerprints. She said, "We have the King James version on a CD-ROM disk in my office in Boston. I'll call and ask my secretary to cross-reference the words 'peradventure' and 'atonement,' and we'll see if we can find the source of the quote."

Angela Paradisi smiled. "That won't be necessary."

"You have a copy of the disk here?"

She tapped her forehead with her index finger. "I have a copy of the Bible in here. I know the source of the quote." She opened her portfolio and brought out a Bible. "Exodus, chapter thirty-two, verse thirty. That's Old Testament, Harry. I think it'll help if I read the line that comes immediately after the one Artie quoted." She turned to a passage that she had set off with a bookmark. " 'And Moses returned to the Lord, and said, Oh, this people have sinned a great sin, and have made them a god of gold.' "

"I remember now," I said. "When Moses brought the Ten Commandments down to the people, he saw that they'd been worshipping a gold calf. He flung the tablets to the ground and smashed them."

"I saw the version with Charlton Heston," Veronica chimed in. "I wonder why he's writing to you now?"

"It's dated and postmarked last Friday," Angela said. "Maybe something happened last week to stir him up."

"Like a visit from two FBI agents," Veronica suggested.

"What about the rest of the letter?" I said. " 'When I nurse a grudge, it's as good as gold.' "

Angela replied, "Well, that was pretty much the stance

God took when Moses came back up the mountain to beg forgiveness for his people. God said, 'Whosoever hath sinned against me, him I will blot out of my book.' He had Moses take the sinners to a prearranged place, and then the Lord smote them."

Veronica said, "Maybe we can get an indictment against Moses and God for conspiracy to smite. What's the statute of limitations on that?"

Angela cast a disapproving glance in Veronica's direction. She continued. "Artie probably wrote 'good as gold' as a clue—maybe on an unconscious level, as you psychiatrists like to say."

"A clue to what?" I asked.

"He's telling you that his desire for vengeance is undeterrable. And he's also telling you where that vengeance will occur."

"What do you mean?"

"The mountain where Moses spoke to God. Where the people grew tired of waiting for him and made a god of gold." She closed the Bible and folded her hands over it. "Mount Sinai."

24: Bloody Wednesday

Dr. David Isaacs, the president of Mount Sinai Hospital, closed his eyes and dropped his chin against his chest. He was a small man approaching retirement age, and he was nearly swallowed up by his oversized leather chair.

He pressed his fingertips against his temples and rubbed vigorously. "Such a headache I have, you wouldn't believe." He looked at Veronica and me and said, "And you two aren't helping matters. How certain are you that one of my people is in jeopardy?"

"We're treating this matter very seriously," said Veronica. "We believe the man who made this threat has killed at least two other people."

"I'd like our security director to hear this, if you don't mind."

"Of course."

He spoke to his secretary through an intercom and asked her to page the man. He rubbed his temples again. "What's your role in this matter, Dr. Kline?"

Veronica answered for me. "Dr. Kline is consulting with the FBI on this case."

"Psychiatrist?" asked Dr. Isaacs, looking at me.

"Yes," Veronica replied.

"We have an excellent psychiatry department here." He sighed. "As if that should matter to you right now. You'll have to excuse me. I spoke at one of our fund-raising breakfasts this morning. I'm still in my salesman mode."

The hospital security director arrived and Dr. Isaacs made introductions all around. Amos Saunders was a middle-aged man with a two-way radio strapped to his belt. He moved a half-step back and studied Veronica's face when he learned she was a Special Agent.

Veronica gave the man the same bare bones outline of the case that she'd just given Dr. Isaacs. Someone was planning to murder a staff member at Mount Sinai that Wednesday. We didn't know who he was or who his intended victim was, but we had every reason to believe the threat was very real.

"Amos, I want you to do whatever Miss Pace asks you to do. I want to protect our people. I want to give the FBI our fullest cooperation. And I want an aspirin for this terrible headache I have. Does anybody have some?" He rummaged through his desk but came up empty.

"We have a few suspects," Veronica said. "We're monitoring their movements. If one of them comes anywhere near Mount Sinai on Wednesday, we'll close in on him."

"But what if the killer isn't one of these suspects you're following?" Saunders asked.

In that case, we're screwed. That's how Veronica answered me when I asked that same question a few hours earlier.

"In that case," she told Saunders. "we need to cover the hospital well enough to catch him in the act, without making our presence so intrusive that we scare him away. If we scare him off, he may wait until he feels safer carrying out his plan. Wednesday is our best chance to stop him."

Dr. Isaacs said, "I hope you'll be the one calling the police department, Miss Pace. If we call to ask for coverage from them, they'll bill us."

"Really?" I asked.

"Welcome to the nineties, Dr. Kline." The old man sighed and rubbed his temples once again.

"You didn't tell them very much about the case," I said.

"What good would it do to tell them more? It would just cause panic."

"Is that why you kept answering for me?"

"I was afraid you would tell them more than I wanted them to know."

"Thanks for the vote of confidence."

She shrugged. We crossed Fifth Avenue and headed into Central Park. Dozens of late afternoon joggers were making their way along the track that ran around the reservoir.

"Who's the third suspect you have under surveillance?"

"Excuse me?"

"You told Saunders that you have a few suspects."

"A couple."

"Not a couple. A few. I know about Morton Arthur. I know about Arthur Chillingsworth. Who else? And don't tell me it's the blind guy from World War II." When she didn't respond, I said, "It's Jeffrey, isn't it? You just can't let that go."

"What do you want me to do? I can't just un-suspect him because he's your friend."

"If Jeffrey Barrow is Artie, I'll . . . I'll . . ."

"You'll what? Make it good, Harry. I just love it when you try to tell me how to do my job."

"Yeah, sure."

She was right, but I didn't like it.

Veronica spent all day Tuesday coordinating a police and FBI coverage plan. She was pessimistic about the chances for success. "If Artie isn't one of my suspects," she said, "the best we can hope for is to catch him after he's done something to make himself known."

"You mean, after he tries to murder someone."

She nodded. "Let's just hope his victim runs fast and screams long and loud."

We both tried to get a few hours of sleep on Tuesday afternoon. My alarm went off at ten o'clock that night. Wednesday, May 20th, would begin in two hours.

At ten-thirty we entered the security office in the Annenberg Building at Mount Sinai. Veronica, Amos Saunders, and a city detective named Hector Nunez discussed their plans. About a hundred plainsclothes police officers and FBI agents were deployed around the institution, to be relieved by others at noon if we were still playing the waiting game. The officers and agents were all connected by two-way radio to Saunders's security office. Detective Nunez would coordinate activities out of that office.

Staff were informed that the extra security was being implemented to protect an Arab potentate who had just donated millions of dollars and who would be touring the institution sometime that day.

And so the wait began.

Veronica, with me in tow, spent several hours making the rounds among the various buildings. By noon we'd visited every ward twice and seen all other areas of the hospital complex at least once. We'd observed a fistfight between two orderlies, a dramatic attempt to revive a case of cardiac arrest, and a well-known organized crime figure surrounded by a phalanx of bodyguards as he went to visit a patient on the Guggenheim Pavilion's deluxe private unit.

The Guggenheim was the newest and nicest of the buildings. It had two atriums that were landscaped with trees and bathed in natural light. Each patient room opened onto a view of Central Park or one of the atriums. The private unit had accommodations that put most deluxe hotels to shame. We were sitting in one of the Guggenheim atriums when Veronica said, "I can't believe how easy it is to walk around in hospitals without anyone asking you what business you have being there."

"I guess they figure no one is going to come here unless they have a good reason to. It's not the sort of place people come to just for kicks."

After lunch we wandered through a gallery of oil portraits of distinguished physicians from Mount Sinai's past. Many had identified diseases or clinical phenomena that now bore their names. Veronica leaned forward to read the scientific name for Moschcowitz Disease. "Thrombotic thrombocytopenic purpura. What in the world is that?"

"A disease that strikes mostly women. It usually kills you within three months. You don't want to know the details. No one knows what causes it. At least they didn't when I was in medical school."

"What a way to go down in history," Veronica said, "getting your name attached to something like that."

"It's better to have a disease named after you because you discovered it than to do it the way Lou Gehrig did."

"What do you mean?"

"He died from Lou Gehrig's Disease."

"That's quite a coincidence."

The afternoon was more of the same: aimless wandering, waiting for an unknown person to find an unknown victim in an unknown location. "I hate hospitals," Veronica said.

"Most people do, unless you're there to have a baby."

"Were you there when Melissa was born?"

I nodded. Images from that day zipped through my mind. Just then Veronica and I entered a ward populated by cancer patients, many of whom would likely never leave the hospital again. Now memories from the days preceding Janet's death came to me, warring with the images of Melissa's birth for my attention. I wanted to dwell on one and forget the other, but they bounced around inside my mind, inextricably entwined.

By early evening we were well into our second shift of agents and police officers, and I was dead on my feet. Around seven o'clock Veronica's beeper sounded. She went to a pay phone and called the FBI office. When she returned she said, "Well, let's hope the killer isn't Morton Arthur. He took the subway to Brooklyn for dinner at his sister's apartment. Then he realized he was being followed."

"Great. What did he do?"

"Made friends with the agent following him. They're all having dinner together. Pasta primavera. Chillingsworth is still home. He hasn't stepped out of the building since we were there last Thursday. Angela tried her call-and-hang-up routine again about an hour ago."

After a few seconds of silence, I asked, "What about Jeffrey?"

She hesitated. "He just got home. He's about a ten-minute walk from here."

We walked back to the Guggenheim Pavilion and sat on a bench in one of the atriums. I leaned back and stretched my legs out, and I dozed off for a few seconds. I was startled awake by the sound of someone yelling.

A man and woman sitting on a bench forty feet away were arguing. Suddenly he rolled his newspaper into a ball, threw it at her, then stalked off. She ran after him, yelling and tearing the paper into shreds.

I recalled an incident from early in my marriage, something I hadn't thought about in years. Janet and I were sitting at the breakfast table. She was criticizing me for something, I don't recall what, and she went on and on about every little thing I'd ever done that bothered her. Finally I stood up and flung the newspaper toward her. "Here," I said. "Look through it carefully. If you try very, very hard, you may find something happening somewhere in the world that isn't my fault."

I chuckled.

"What's so funny?" Veronica asked.

"Nothing, really. I remembered an argument I had with my wife at least ten years ago. I'd forgotten how angry she used to make me sometimes. I get a little pissed off just thinking about it now."

"Ten years is a long time to still feel mad about something."

I yawned and leaned back. "Yeah, well, when I nurse gold, it's as good as a grudge."

After a few seconds she shook my arm. "Hey—open your eyes. What did you just say?"

"I was quoting from Artie's last letter. 'When I nurse a grudge, it's as good as gold.' "

"That's what you think you said. But that's not what you said."

She reached into her handbag and pulled out copies of Artie's three letters. She scanned them quickly. "Here—take a look. In the first letter he says he'll be in your neck of the woods on April 30th, which is when he killed Mary

Mendez. After he kills her, in his second letter he reminds you that he told you he'd be in your neck of the woods. Only this time he puts the word 'neck' in quotation marks. He thinks he's cute, likes to make a play on words."

"So?"

"So in the letter you got yesterday, it says 'when I nurse a grudge, it's as good as gold.' "

"That's what I just said."

"No, you said, 'When I nurse gold, it's as good as a grudge.' "

"I'm tired. Sue me."

"Maybe he's playing another one of his word jokes. Nurse. Gold. Nurse gold."

"What's your point?"

She thought for a moment, then said, "How many nurses do you think they have here named Gold?"

Before I could respond, Veronica pulled out her two-way radio and made contact with Amos Saunders. She said, "Do you have access to a list of everyone on the nursing staff?"

"Sure," he said through the crackling static. "Why?"

"How many nurses do you have named Gold?"

"Give me a couple of minutes. I'll call you back."

"While you're at it, see if you can find out where they are."

Saunders radioed back a few minutes later. Four women named Gold were on the nursing staff. Two were assigned to wards in the Klingenstein Clinical Center, one to the Annenberg Building, and one to the Guggenheim Pavilion, five floors above the spot where Veronica and I sat.

Veronica spoke into the radio. "Are they on duty?"

"No idea. It's a big place, and I have no way of knowing who's actually on site right now. Why?"

"I think one of them might be the killer's target. Tell Nunez to radio the officers on each of those floors. Find these women and make sure they stay in plain sight at all times. I'm going to talk to each one, starting with the one upstairs."

Saunders radioed back while we were on the elevator. "One has the day off. One has already gone off duty. The one in Annenberg is on duty. Our man is with her right now. That leaves the one in Guggenheim, where you are. Her name is Alicia Gold. I can't get through to our man there, so I called the nursing station. Alicia Gold is on duty right now."

"Let me speak with Nunez." When the detective got on the air Veronica said, "I'm on my way to fifth floor west in Guggenheim. Pull your men from fifth center and sixth west and have them meet me there."

The elevator opened and we walked quickly to the nursing station in the center of the ward. Veronica identified herself to the supervising nurse and said, "Where's the officer who's supposed to be covering this floor?"

"I saw him head into the men's room a little while ago."

"Alicia Gold—where is she?"

"The treatment room at the end of this hall, last door on the left. She's preparing some insulin for one of our patients." The woman glanced at the clock on the wall in front of her. "Hmm. I wonder what's taking her so long."

I saw Veronica's body tense, ever so slightly. "Harry—go to the men's room and tell the officer to get his ass out here. I'm going to check on Nurse Gold."

"What's going on?" asked the supervising nurse. Neither one of us stopped to answer.

Water was running in the men's room sink, but no one was standing in front of it.

"Anyone here?"

No one responded. I was about to leave, but then I looked underneath the stall door and saw the feet of someone sitting on the toilet.

"Officer?"

He didn't respond. I tried to push the door open, but his body was pressed against the other side of the door. He let out a small groan when I finally pushed my way in. I grabbed hold of his unconscious form and lowered him to the floor. There were swelling and bleeding on the right occipital area of his skull. Something hard and heavy had struck there with considerable force.

I flung open the men's room door. I dashed to the nursing station to report what I'd seen. Then I ran down the hall toward the treatment room where Veronica had gone. I barreled into a food cart, sending it crashing through the glass door to the patients' lounge.

I opened the door to the last room on the left. The room was dark. I heard the stifled sound of someone struggling to breathe, air barely seeping through a constricted windpipe. I fumbled for a light switch and flipped it on.

A man in a surgeon's uniform, cap, and mask stood with his back to me. He was tall and broad and he had Veronica pinned against the wall. All I could see of her were her arms as she struggled in vain against the weight of the man's body. Her feet dangled several inches off the ground. He leaned into her, trapping her there, and pressed his left forearm against her throat. Suddenly he swept his right arm upward and back, pausing at the apex of the arc. A surgical steel blade appeared in his hand. It gleamed in the light from the overhead fluorescent bulb.

I dropped my right shoulder and charged into him with all my might. I felt the air rush out of his lungs as I pressed against his back. He fell flush against Veronica, then released her as he tried to keep his balance. She fell to the floor and clutched at her throat.

I grabbed his waist from behind with my left hand. I wrapped my right hand around his head. I pressed my right thumb into an eye socket, jammed a finger into a nostril, and jerked backward with all the strength I could muster. I whipped him around in a counterclockwise motion, then released him and let his weight and momentum smash him into the opposite wall. The centrifugal force rammed me against the wall where Veronica had been pinned seconds earlier.

The man fell against the light switch and the room was plunged back into darkness. I pushed off from the wall and hurled myself across the room, aiming for the spot where I thought he was standing. I miscalculated; my shoulder and cheekbone hit the wall, dazing me.

I heard a whooshing sound. I felt something whisk

lightly across my forearm. I slipped to the floor, then reached up and fumbled again for the light switch.

When the light flickered on, the man was gone. He'd left through a side door that led into another treatment room. I felt something warm and wet in my palm; my forearm had been slashed, and blood was dripping down my arm, across my hand, and onto the floor. I felt faint for a few seconds. I grabbed a towel from a counter and wrapped it around my wound.

Veronica lay on her side, still clutching her throat and gasping for air. I grabbed her shoulders and leaned her against the wall. I ran my hands along her throat and tried to gauge the damage done. The area was red where he'd grabbed her, but the trachea was intact and open. In a few seconds she'd have enough air in her lungs to speak.

The door to the room flew open. Two undercover officers rushed in. I pointed to the other door that had served as our assailant's escape route. "Get him!" I shouted. They burst through the other door in pursuit.

Veronica tried to tell me something, but she couldn't get the words out.

"Don't try to talk yet. You'll be okay."

She pointed frantically toward a supply closet, then started to crawl toward it.

"Stay there," I commanded. "I'll look."

I yanked the door open. The unclothed body of a woman, bloody and limp, tumbled into my arms. I laid her gently onto the floor. Her neck had been slashed, wide and deep. For a brief instant I felt a faint pulse, but her eyes had lost the look of the living and I knew that I was too late.

Alicia Gold died in my arms.

25: Dead By Summer

Our assailant escaped.

Either he was very lucky, or he'd studied the layout of the building. The officers pursuing him found themselves staring at a locked door at the end of a corridor. By the time they backtracked, the killer had a three or four minute lead on them. Dressed in hospital garb, the man no doubt melted easily into the background.

Veronica was shaken, but not hurt. My wound proved more superficial than the amount of blood on the floor initially suggested. The officer I found in the men's room wasn't as fortunate. They rushed him into surgery and performed a five-hour operation to remove shards of shattered bone that were pressing in on his brain cortex. He'd live, but it would take time to determine the extent of the damage.

Veronica and I were interrogated by Detective Hector Nunez. But for all the intensity of our encounter with the killer, neither one of us could say much about him. He was taller than me. He was broader. He was white. Veronica said his eyes were brown. His hair had been hidden by his surgeon's cap. I had nothing else to add; he'd had his back to me the entire time.

Veronica had no choice but to tell Nunez the whole story of the case, something she hadn't done earlier. And so his interrogation recapitulated the questions we'd been pondering for the previous week and a half. Who was Artie? How did he know me? Why was he writing to me? How were his victims selected, and why were they being killed? And now we had to focus on another question, one we'd been keeping on the back burner during the failed effort to prevent murder number three: Who, when, and where would he choose for his final act?

Obviously, Morton Arthur, Arthur Chillingsworth, and Jeffrey Barrow were off the hook. If one of them had approached Mount Sinai, he would've been stopped long before he had the chance to kill Alicia Gold. Veronica called Angela Paradisi to check. All three suspects were accounted for.

"The good news," Veronica told me after the questioning was finished, "is that you won't have to look for a new editor. The bad news is that we're back to square one."

Alicia Gold was twenty-eight when she died. She was separated from her husband. She and her two children had been living with her parents for about a year.

Alicia's father, Dr. Nathan Cooperstein, was a professor of internal medicine at Columbia. The Coopersteins owned a luxury condominium on Central Park West, almost directly across the park from Mount Sinai. Detective Nunez got the address from someone at the hospital and the three of us drove there in his unmarked police car.

We arrived at the Coopersteins' building shortly after nine o'clock. A middle-aged Korean housekeeper opened the door to their eighth-floor condo. The apartment was absolutely quiet, but it looked as though a small party was in preparation. The living room was decorated with streamers and balloons, and four or five gift-wrapped boxes were stacked on a coffee table. A neatly printed handmade sign read: "Happy Birthday, Zadie."

"I am sorry," the housekeeper said, "but Dr. Cooperstein and Mrs. Cooperstein leave a short while ago. Will you care to wait?"

"Do you know where they went?" asked Nunez.

She hesitated before answering. "To the hospital."

"Mount Sinai?" asked Veronica.

"Yes."

"Damn," said Nunez. "We just came from there."

The woman's eyes widened for a moment, and then tears welled up in them. "Then it is true. He finally kill her."

"Who?" asked Nunez. "Who killed her?"

"Her husband, Richard. He finally kill her, just like he say he will."

Nathan Cooperstein was haranguing a uniformed police officer in a waiting room near the Guggenheim surgical suite. I could hear him through the door as we approached the room. "He *promised* her she'd be dead by summer! We *begged* you people to pick him up!"

Nunez opened the door without knocking. Veronica and I filed into the room behind him.

Cooperstein was pacing back and forth. He stopped when he saw us. "Who the hell are you?" His face was flushed. Veins bulged in his neck when he spoke.

"I'm Detective Nunez. This is Ms. Pace from the FBI, and Dr. Kline."

He looked at me with a puzzled expression. "Do I know you? Are you on staff here?"

"No, sir. Ms. Pace and I were the ones who found your daughter. We tried to subdue the man who killed her, but we failed. I'm very sorry."

He noticed the bloodstained gauze bandage wrapped around my arm. "Well, at least you were willing to try. We've been telling the police for months that he was going to kill her, and they didn't do a damn thing."

Cooperstein harbored no doubt that his daughter had died by her estranged husband's hand. He told us that Richard Gold had been threatening violence against Alicia ever since she left him a year earlier. They were locked in a bitter divorce and custody battle. He'd stalked her at work; he'd stalked her at the condominium. Alicia had told her parents, her friends, and anyone else who would listen: *Richard is going to kill me.*

"What does your son-in-law look like?" asked Veronica.

"About six-two. Football build."

"What color are his eyes?"

"I don't know. Brown, I guess."

"Dr. Cooperstein, I can't tell you that he did it. I can't tell you that he didn't. I *can* tell you that whoever killed your daughter killed two other people recently. That's what brought me to this hospital tonight. The trail from those other murders led me here."

Cooperstein stopped pacing. "I . . . don't understand."

"Can you think of any other person who might want to do something like this?"

He furrowed his brow and scratched at the end-of-day stubble on his chin. "No. Of course not."

Veronica told him the names of the other victims. "Can you think of any relationship your daughter might have had with either of them?"

He puzzled over the question, then shook his head.

"Does the name Elmore Winston mean anything to you?"

"No."

Veronica sighed. "Did your daughter visit Philadelphia or Boston anytime in the last year?"

"I don't think so."

"How about San Antonio?"

"No, she hasn't been back there in years."

"What do you mean?"

"We used to live there, about fifteen years ago. I was on the staff at Travis Hospital. We went back a few times to visit friends after we moved to New York, but that was years ago."

"And you're sure you don't recognize the name Mary Mendez? How about Jorge Mendez, or Anna?"

He shrugged his shoulders. "Mendez is a common name. I'm sorry, but I can't help you there. Christ—what am I apologizing for? And why are you bothering me with all this? Go find that son of a bitch my daughter married. That's the only answer you'll need."

Nunez dropped us off at our hotel shortly before midnight. On our way up to our rooms I asked Veronica if she thought Richard Gold might be the person we'd been hunting.

"I don't know what to think right now," she answered. "But maybe Artie never made it to Mount Sinai tonight. Maybe Richard Gold beat him to it. Whoever that was in the treatment room with us, he didn't have a camera to take a picture of his victim. And he didn't leave a penny in Alicia Gold's hand."

I walked her to her room. She opened the door, then turned to face me. "How does your arm feel?"

"The bandage makes it look worse than it is. What about you? Let me see your throat."

She pulled the collar of her blouse down. "It hurts."

I swept her hair out of the way to get a closer look. "Hmm. Does it hurt when I touch it here?"

Veronica reached up and covered my hand with hers. We looked at each other without speaking for several seconds, then she leaned her head against my chest and let out a very long sigh.

"I haven't been that frightened since the night my mother was killed. Oh, God—it hurts me so much."

I ran my fingers lightly along her throat. "It won't hurt as much in the morning."

"That isn't the hurt I'm talking about."

We stood there quietly for a minute or two. Then she moved away from me and stepped into her room. "I release you from your debt," she said.

"What debt?"

"You saved my life tonight. I can't say 'you owe me' anymore."

I went to my room and threw myself onto the bed. I couldn't remember ever feeling as tired as I did at that moment.

Artie's deadly presence had come nearer and nearer. My only acquaintance with his first victim had come by way of the pictures I'd seen. I came upon his second victim face-to-face after she died. The third victim expired as I held her. What would happen the next time?

I remembered holding Janet as she died. There was a

flicker of recognition in her eyes as I touched my hand to her cheek. She tried to kiss my fingers, and in the instant that her lips touched me I felt the last micro-surge of energy drain out of her.

I imagined Veronica, nine years old, cowering before her mother's killer. I wanted to go back in time, stand beside her, shield her from the pain that would follow her for the rest of her days.

Just as I started to slip into a dream, I heard pounding on the door that separated Veronica's room from mine. I struggled to my feet and let her in.

"I *cannot* fucking *believe* it," she said as she stormed past me and sat on the edge of my bed. "I just got a call from Angela Paradisi. They lost him."

"Lost who? What do you mean?"

"When he went to dinner, the agent following him handed off to another one. Standard procedure, makes it less obvious to the subject that he's being tailed. But they screwed up the switch. They didn't realize it until they handed the surveillance back to the first agent. When I called from Mount Sinai, right after the murder, they told me everyone was covered. But they were watching the wrong man."

"That means . . ."

She looked at me. "That means you're taking me to Morgan Books tomorrow. I think it's time I met Jeffrey Barrow."

26: Remember the Mission

The dull pain in my wounded arm woke me earlier than I'd planned. I opened my door and retrieved a complimentary copy of the morning *New York Times*. The vice-president's latest *faux pas* was still eliciting giggles. Macy's had announced plans to close several stores. Intermittent rain was predicted for the entire day. Bette Midler and Robin Williams were the scheduled guests for Johnny Carson's next-to-last *Tonight* show.

Five homicides had been recorded in the city: two Harlem gang members murdered in a drive-by shooting, a Queens bank robber foiled by a bullet in his back, a woman in Brooklyn beaten to death by her alcoholic husband . . . and Alicia Gold.

Richard Gold, whereabouts unknown, was wanted by police for questioning in the death of his wife. The article stated that a doctor and a visitor were slightly injured by the killer as he made his escape. We weren't mentioned by name.

"That's a standard police precaution," Veronica said when I showed her the article. "When you have witnesses in a case like this, with the killer still at large, you owe it to them to keep their names out of the papers."

After breakfast Veronica called Billy Ray Dalton in San Antonio and brought him up to date on the case. She asked him to check with Travis Hospital to learn exactly when Nathan Cooperstein was on staff. "After you get the dates, try to find out if any of the Mendezes were ever treated at the hospital during that time. Or if either Jorge or Anna Mendez worked there."

After she hung up she said, "Your buddy Billy Ray sends his regards."

"I'm touched. He's been a major influence in my life."

"I see the injury to your arm hasn't dulled your rapier wit."

I think we were bantering in order to avoid talking about the terror of the previous evening or the intimacy of the moments we shared before retiring. And I had another reason: I didn't want to think anymore about the possibility that Jeffrey Barrow, my editor and friend, might be a murderer.

We arrived at Jeffrey's office at eleven o'clock. "He's not in yet, sweetie," said Gwen, his secretary.

We already knew that. Angela Paradisi had arranged a resumption of surveillance on Jeffrey. An hour and a half earlier he had entered the office of an East Side dentist.

Gwen continued. "He called early to say he had to see his dentist. He cracked a tooth last night."

I remembered shoving Alicia Gold's killer against the wall. I prayed it was just a coincidence.

"He said he'd call again if he was going to be much later than eleven, so I guess he's on his way in now. I'm sure he wouldn't want to miss you, Harry. Why don't you and your friend wait in the lounge?"

A skinny black teenager walked past us a few yards down the hall. A few seconds later, Gwen called after me. "Harry, this fellow just delivered a letter addressed to you."

Gwen held the envelope aloft. I recognized Artie's crude block lettering; so did Veronica.

The teenager had already passed us again on his way to the elevator. Veronica called out to him. "Excuse me—can I talk to you for a minute?"

He looked back at us, then turned away and kept walking. Veronica started after him. Suddenly he began to run. He tripped and fell facedown to the floor.

Veronica pounced on him. She jabbed a knee into the small of his back, then yanked one of his arms into an unnatural angle behind him. He yelped like a small dog.

Gwen jumped up with her mouth wide open, a mixture of disbelief and alarm on her face.

"Stop moving or lose your arm!" Veronica shouted. "Tell me—where did you get that letter?"

"Ow! Ow! Some guy outside paid me to bring it up here."

"What did he look like?"

"I don't know. White dude in a raincoat. All you folks look the same. Hey—cut it out!"

"Why did you try to run from me?"

"He gave me fifty bucks and said don't talk to anyone. Ow!"

Just then the elevator opened. Jeffrey got off and walked toward us. His eyes were brown. His face was swollen. He wore a raincoat. I hated myself for what I was thinking.

"Harry—what the hell is going on here?"

Veronica looked up. "Are you Jeffrey Barrow?"

"Yes."

Veronica pulled the teenager to a standing position. "Is this the man who gave you the letter?"

Jeffrey and the teenager stared at each other. Jeffrey looked frightened, but so did everyone else.

"I told you, lady—all you folks look the same." Suddenly the teenager thrust his leg in front of him, pushed off the wall, and rammed his body backward into Veronica with full force. I heard her head slam against the opposite wall.

The teenager whirled around and smacked the back of his heavily jeweled hand against Veronica's face. Blood spurted from her nose. He pushed her into me, toppling both of us. Then he bolted away, down the hall and through a stairwell door.

I lifted Veronica to a sitting position and helped her lean her head back. "Gwen, get me something cold to put on her face."

I led her into Jeffrey's office. Gwen came in a minute

later with some ice cubes wrapped in a hand towel. I sat Veronica in a chair and applied the cold compress to the side of her nose.

"My timing is screwed up," Veronica muttered. "Must be my biorhythms."

Jeffrey stood next to Veronica and looked at her for a moment. "Come tomorrow, miss, I think your face will look worse than mine does now. Harry, do you know this woman?"

Before I could answer, Veronica grabbed the lapel of Jeffrey's raincoat and pulled him down until she was staring directly into his eyes.

"What are you doing?" He noticed how intently she was examining his face. "Have we met?"

"You tell me, Jeffrey. Have we?"

He pulled away from her grasp. "No. And I'd remember you if we had, that's for certain. Harry, what's this all about?"

Veronica took the cold compress from me and applied it herself. "Go ahead, Harry. We're past the point where we can be subtle about this. Tell him."

I paused for several seconds. I'd never before told a friend that he was a suspect in a string of unsolved murders. "I've been getting anonymous letters from a serial killer, addressed to me here. The messenger just delivered another one a few minutes before you got here. The authorities don't know who the killer is. Veronica is with the FBI. She thinks he may be you."

He stared at her with disbelief. *"What?"*

I said, "I think it's because of what happened in Vietnam. The murder you talked about last week."

"You told her about that? Nice way to keep a friend's secret, Harry, after he opens up to you."

"Harry didn't tell me," Veronica said. "*I* told *him*. I saw it in your service record."

"And what were you doing looking at my . . ." He turned toward me. "Wait a minute. You already knew about what happened in Vietnam when you came here last week?"

I nodded.

"So what the hell was that all about? All of those questions—was it some kind of test to see if I'd tell you the truth?"

"Jeffrey, I never believed that you—"

Veronica interrupted. "Where were you at seven-thirty last night?"

"Eating dinner. Why?"

"Were you with anyone?"

"I was by myself."

"What happened to your face?"

"I slipped in my shower."

"Your wife can verify that, I assume."

"She's visiting relatives in Georgia. Why are you asking me these questions?"

"The killer took another victim last night," I said. "He injured his face in the process."

"And the two of you think that I . . ." He gnawed on his lower lip. "I think you should leave now. Both of you."

We walked past Gwen's desk and headed toward the elevator. She called after me. "Don't you want to take your letter?"

* * *

MAY 21, 1992

THREE DOWN AND ONE TO GO.

REMEMBER THE MISSION.

FIRST, I DISABLED THE SENTRY. THEN, A CLANDESTINE STRIKE BEHIND ENEMY LINES. HAND-TO-HAND COMBAT WITH COUNTER-INSURGENTS. NO TIME FOR PHOTO DOCUMENTATION. NO TIME FOR PROPER "HANDLING" OF THE BODY.

REMEMBER THE MISSION.

YOU KNOW HOW WE FEEL, THOSE OF US WHO UNFORTUNATELY MUST KILL INNOCENTS IN THE COURSE OF THE BATTLE. THE THIRD ONE ASKED ME WHY, AND I TOLD HER, AND SHE SAID IT WAS NOT FAIR, AND I AGREED. I

SAID, "YOU PERISH FOR THE SIN OF INCOMPE-
TENCE."

I WORKED QUICKLY IN ORDER TO MINIMIZE
HER SUFFERING. "CLOSE YOUR EYES," I SAID.
"PRETEND YOU ARE DANCING."

TIME GROWS SHORT. THE FINAL DANCE
BECKONS, RETRIBUTION FOR THE WORST SIN
OF ALL: DISHONESTY.

REMEMBER THE MISSION.

ON THE DAY OF DEAD SOLDIERS, THE MIS-
SION WILL BE COMPLETE.

IN THE CITY OF THE MISSION, THE MISSION
WILL BE COMPLETE.

YOU WILL KNOW WHO I AM, BECAUSE THE
FINAL DANCE WILL BE A DUET. WHEN I SEE MY
PENNY, I WILL SMILE.

> YOURS,
> ARTIE

Martin Baines talked to us over the speakerphone in
Angela Paradisi's office. "You said the word 'handling' is
in quotes. That must be his way of letting you know he intended to leave a penny in his victim's hand."

Veronica said, "I wish I knew what the pennies are supposed to signify."

"You only have four days to figure it out," he replied.
"Monday is Memorial Day. The day of dead soldiers."

"I know. That must be why he had this letter hand-
delivered—to make certain it arrived before the last murder."

"Do you have any idea where it will occur?"

"I think he's going to San Antonio," I said.

"Why, Harry?" asked Baines.

"The city of the mission. The Alamo was originally a
Spanish mission. 'Remember the Alamo.' 'Remember the
mission.' " Another one of his little plays on words. And
we know that two of the three victims lived there at the
same time."

"When did Dr. Cooperstein and his family leave San Antonio?"

Veronica said, "He told us he lived there about fifteen years ago."

"Which means Mary Mendez would have been two or three years old, and Alicia Gold would have been in her early teens. Do you think she might have been a baby-sitter for Mary Mendez?"

"We can try to check it out," Veronica said.

"At least this time you have a suspect with a motive. Alicia Gold's husband. But what reason would he have to kill the others?"

I said, "Maybe he killed them and wrote these letters to make it look like a lunatic was behind it. Maybe it's all designed to give him the chance to kill his wife and throw suspicion elsewhere."

Baines chuckled. "I think you've been watching too much television, Harry. But you may be right about San Antonio. I think the two of you should go back there. Maybe there's still a chance to stop Artie before he racks up a fourth corpse."

"And a fifth," I said.

"What do you mean?"

"The final dance will be a duet. There'll be a penny for Artie—'When I see my penny, I will smile,' is what the letter says—and then his identity will be revealed. I think he's going to kill himself after he claims his last victim."

27: A Monkey and a Stick

Bill Ray Dalton met us in the baggage claim area Thursday evening. He was dressed casually in lightweight jeans and a loose-fitting knit shirt. "Y'all just couldn't keep away from me, could you? Let me help you with those suitcases, 'cause you guys look beat to hell. Did you both get caught in the same shit-spreading machine?"

Veronica ran down the injury report: the bruises on her neck and the cut on my arm inflicted by the killer, the marks on her face suffered when she relaxed her guard against an unarmed teenage punk. Billy Ray got a chuckle from the latter.

"Glad you find humor in it," Veronica said. "Just get us to the hotel, Billy Ray. I've had the crap knocked out of me twice in less than a day, I've had a total of five hours sleep the last two nights, and I may have to hurt the very next asshole who pisses me off."

He started to laugh, then thought better of it.

On the drive downtown from the airport, Billy Ray said, "I got that information you asked for. Nathan Cooperstein was an emergency room doctor at Travis Hospital in 1976 and 1977. No record during that time of any treatment at Travis for anyone in the Mendez family."

"Did the Coopersteins live near the Mendezes?" asked Veronica.

He shook his head. "Complete opposite ends of the city.

Unlikely that Alicia Gold—uh, Cooperstein—ever baby-sat for Mary Mendez, if you see what I'm saying."

Billy Ray dropped us off at our hotel. This time Veronica had made reservations at a more intimate place called La Mansion del Rio. With tile floors, wide stucco porticoes, and brightly colored rugs and wall-hangings, the hotel had the look and feel of a luxurious Mexican summer home.

We had fajitas and margaritas at a poolside restaurant called El Capistrano, then sat on the veranda outside Veronica's room and watched the party boats floating by. She said, "I feel like a monkey without a stick."

"Come again?"

"When I trained to be an agent, one of my instructors told us about an experiment a psychologist did. He put monkeys in cages, with bananas just out of reach. He gave them sticks. The hungrier the monkeys were, the faster they figured out that they could use the sticks to pull the bananas within reach. That moment when a monkey suddenly figured out how to solve the problem—the psychologist called it the 'aha experience.' "

"Like one of those cartoons where you see a light bulb appear over a character's head."

"Right." She leaned her chair against the wall and put her feet up on the iron railing. "I feel like I'm missing the stick—that if I just had the right insight, everything would finally fall into place. I would know who Artie is, who his final victim will be, and why he's been killing these people." Veronica closed her eyes. "God, I'm so tired."

I thought about them: Joseph Carroll, Mary Mendez and Alicia Gold—three people who had sinned in ways fathomable only to the mind of the killer who had claimed their lives. " 'Close your eyes,' " I said. " 'Pretend you are dancing.' "

I stumbled through the door between our adjoining rooms and collapsed into my bed. I closed my own eyes and slipped into a dream about dancing monkeys.

On Friday morning, Veronica outlined her agenda for the day. She wanted to visit Jorge and Anna Mendez. She'd borrowed a picture of Alicia Gold that was taken when she was twelve or thirteen; she hoped the Mendezes might recognize her. She also planned to keep track of the surveillance on Jeffrey Barrow, her sole remaining suspect, via phone conversations with Angela Paradisi.

"Other than that," she said, "I've got nothing to go on. If the Mendezes don't recognize the picture—and I'm not optimistic on that score—or if Jeffrey Barrow doesn't hop a plane down here sometime in the next couple of days, we're just waiting to collect another dead body on Monday. Two bodies, if you're right about Artie killing himself, too."

She telephoned the Mendez home; no one answered. She found a listing for Mendez Landscaping, called the number, and asked for Jorge Mendez. She learned that the family was visiting Anna's sister in El Paso. Veronica persuaded Jorge's reluctant employee to give her that phone number. When she dialed Anna's sister, she learned that the Mendezes had already left for home. After she hung up she said, "They may not be back until tomorrow. There's no way of contacting them now. I'll keep calling them until I get them. Now let's see what Jeffrey Barrow is up to."

She telephoned Jeffrey's office. I listened to her end of the conversation. "Hello, is this Gwen? . . . We haven't met. I'm Celia Grove from the William Morris Agency. Jeffrey told me to call you to see if you could squeeze me in to see him sometime today. . . . Oh . . . So he'll be out the whole day? . . . How about Tuesday, after the Memorial Day weekend? . . . I see. That's alright—I'll call back next week."

Veronica placed the handset back in the cradle. "Your editor called his secretary first thing this morning and told her to cancel all of his appointments. Said he had to handle some personal matters, may not be in until late next week."

She called Angela Paradisi and learned that Jeffrey was still at home.

We had a late breakfast. We took a tour of the Alamo, then visited the wax museum and Ripley's Believe It or Not across the street from the mission. In the afternoon we vis-

ited the zoo in Brackenridge Park and took the glass elevator to the top of the Tower of the Americas in HemisFair
Park. Every hour or two Veronica dialed the Mendez home,
then spoke with Angela Paradisi. The Mendezes hadn't returned to their home yet, and Jeffrey hadn't left his.

We joined Billy Ray Dalton for dinner at the same
Riverwalk cafe we'd eaten at ten days earlier. He and Veronica reread Artie's letters, reviewed everything we knew
and didn't know, and matched each other beer-for-beer. I
nursed a bottle of Perrier and nibbled on tostada chips.
Each time I reached out to dip a chip in the salsa, I thought
about the monkeys using sticks to reach their food.

An elderly Hispanic gentleman was seated at the table
next to ours, along with his daughter, his daughter's husband, and his two granddaughters.

I dipped another chip in the bowl of salsa.

Three waitresses approached the next table. One set a
cake with candles in front of the elderly man. The waitresses and family members began to sing "Happy Birthday"
to him.

I took another swipe at the salsa.

The man smiled wistfully. Tears glistened in his eyes.
His granddaughters bellowed out the final words of the
song. "Happy birthday, dear Grandpa. Happy birthday to
you."

I began to reach out for the salsa again, then stopped. A
chill ran through me. I stared hard at the old man next to
us. I kept staring even after he and his family noticed me.

Veronica jostled my shoulder, but I kept staring at the
man and his family. "Harry? Harry—is something wrong?"

I stood unsteadily.

"Whoa, buddy," said Billy Ray. "That Perrier too strong
for you?"

"I'll be right back," I said, my voice cracking as I spoke.

I found a pay phone. I reached into my wallet and pulled
out a tattered piece of paper. As I dialed the number Katherine Carroll had written eight days earlier, I tried to visualize her husband's tombstone. I recalled its size and shape,

and its fluted and beveled design, but I couldn't be absolutely certain about the dates on the marker.

"Hello, Katherine? It's Harry Kline."

"Harry—how nice to hear from you. You sound so far away. Are you in Massachusetts?"

"No. I'm back in San Antonio."

"Oh." She paused. "Are you with those poor people whose daughter was killed?"

I wondered if she intended the word "poor" to describe their emotional state or their financial condition. "No, but I did deposit your check to me for $5,000 and sent them one drawn on my account."

"Without waiting for my check to clear? Are you always so trusting, Harry?"

"It was very generous of you to think of them. It never occurred to me that you wouldn't make good on your check."

"Thank you."

"Katherine, I want to ask you something. It may sound silly, but I really need to know. What was your late husband's birthday?"

Veronica and Billy Ray were laughing about something when I returned to our table. I said, "I just spoke with Katherine Carroll. Mansfield Carroll was born on October 12th."

"Who?" asked Billy Ray. "Oh, the priest's father. So what?"

"Joseph Carroll was murdered on October 12th. He was killed on his father's birthday." I turned to Veronica. "When we stepped inside the Coopersteins' apartment Wednesday night, there were balloons and presents, and there was a sign on the wall. Do you remember what it said?"

She closed her eyes and concentrated; then she opened them, smiled, and said, " 'Happy Birthday, Sadie.' Must be Mrs. Cooperstein."

"No. Not 'Sadie.' It said 'Zadie,' with a z."

She shrugged. "Must be one of Alicia's children. One of those stupid New Age yuppie names, like Kala or Halsey."

"No. Zadie is the phonetic spelling of a Yiddish word—the word for 'grandpa.' "

Billy Ray looked at me with slightly glazed eyes. "I don't get it."

"I do," said Veronica. "You think Alicia Gold was murdered on her father's birthday, too."

I said, "We've been wracking our brains, looking for a connection between the murder victims. But maybe it's the fathers who are connected. Maybe they're the ones whose sins are being punished. If it turns out that Jorge Mendez's birthday is April 30th, the date his daughter was killed, that would clinch it."

We three sat quietly for a minute, and then Veronica said, "That would help explain a few things."

"Like what?" asked Billy Ray.

"He says he's killing people because of sins. He also says he's killing innocent people. On the surface, those two statements are contradictory. But not if you think of their fathers as the sinners, rather than the murder victims themselves."

"Right," I said. "Also, he says he tries to minimize the suffering, then goes on to say that he takes pleasure in making his victims suffer. That makes sense if he's trying to make the *fathers* suffer."

The three of us mulled things over. Finally, Billy Ray said, "Let's assume Harry is right about this birthday thing. That means now we know *who* is linked—the fathers of the victims, not the victims themselves. But we still don't know *how* they're linked. If we don't discover the *how*, we're still powerless to stop the fourth murder on Monday."

"Unless the killer is Jeffrey Barrow," I said, still reluctant to concede the possibility.

"Which reminds me," said Veronica. "I want to check in with New York to see what Jeffrey is up to." She walked off toward the pay phone.

"So—have you nailed her yet?"

"You're a classy guy, Billy Ray."

He shrugged. "Just seems a shame to waste the opportunity."

"What opportunity?"

"Your opportunity. She likes you, man."

"So, we like each other. So what?"

"No, I mean she *really* likes you. Can't you tell?"

"Come on, Billy Ray—give it a rest."

Veronica returned scowling. "Damn!" She smacked her palm against the tabletop. The glasses and plates rattled. The Hispanic family at the next table stopped talking and stared at her. "I'm not happy about this at all."

"What?" I asked.

"Jeffrey Barrow just took a cab to LaGuardia Airport."

"And you're not happy? I'd think you'd be delirious with joy."

"Perhaps I would be, if I knew where he was."

"What are you talking about?"

"They lost him. He got out of the cab, walked into the terminal, and then they let the son of a bitch get away."

28: A Puzzle With Four Pieces

Veronica finally made contact with the Mendezes on Saturday morning. On the drive to their house, Veronica filled Billy Ray and me in on the latest. "Jeffrey Barrow bought a ticket on Delta to Atlanta last night. By the time they figured it out in New York, his flight had already landed. None of the airlines list him as being booked on any connecting flights."

I said, "Jeffrey told you his wife was visiting relatives in Georgia. Maybe he joined her."

"And maybe he booked a flight to San Antonio under another name," she said.

Billy Ray exited Route 35 and headed for the Mendezes' neighborhood. "I called a friend this morning, a San Antonio police detective. They have access to the computer records of drivers' licenses. He was able to get Jorge Mendez's birthday." He turned around to face me. "April 30th, Harry. Looks like you were right." He faced forward to watch where he was driving. "You know, I was just thinking."

"That's very nice, Billy Ray," said Veronica.

"This vengeance stuff," he continued, "the sins of the fathers being visited on the children. If Artie was really out for revenge against the fathers of his victims, wouldn't he make it a little more obvious? I mean, what good is revenge if the person you're after doesn't know why he's being made to suffer? Do you see what I'm saying?"

265

"I think Mansfield Carroll knew," I said. " 'My son has been punished for the sins of his father, and I am beyond redemption.' Katherine Carroll told me he said that just a few days before he died. Single vehicle accident, broad daylight. Dry road, flat and straight."

"Do you think he killed himself?" asked Veronica.

"I think he convinced himself that he was responsible for his son's death."

Billy Ray said, "Didn't you say he left a half-million bucks to whoever identifies the killer? He wouldn't do that if he already knew who killed his son and why."

"I know," I replied. "But somewhere deep inside, I think he knew something."

Billy Ray parked in front of the Mendezes' house. Anna met us at the door. "Please come in," she said. "Only the two of us are here. We left Willie with my sister. Tomorrow we are flying to Boston to bring our daughter home."

Jorge Mendez was sitting on the sofa in the living room. He didn't stand when we entered. He glared at me and said, "I don't need your charity."

"It wasn't my money. I told you in my letter, it came from a woman who heard about Mary. She gave it to me to pass along to you because she wants to remain anonymous."

"Well, you tell her I'm no charity case."

I was exasperated. "Look—if you want to return it, I'll make sure she gets it."

He sneered and said, "Just tell her I'm no charity case."

Anna was staring at the floor, clearly embarrassed by her husband's behavior. After a moment of awkward silence, she spoke. "Please, everyone sit down." She looked at Veronica and asked, "Do you bring us news?"

"The man who took your daughter from you murdered someone else three days ago."

"*Dios mio.*" Anna sat next to her husband, pale and shaking. "In Boston?"

"New York," replied Veronica. "A nurse in a hospital. I was there. He tried to kill me, too, but Dr. Kline was able to stop him. Then he cut Dr. Kline with a knife and escaped."

Anna turned to me. "You are very brave, Dr. Kline."

Jorge grunted.

"You must know who this man is," Anna said.

"No," replied Veronica.

"Then how did you know where he would be?"

"He sent us a letter."

"A letter? What kind of a monster kills people and writes letters about it?" She shuddered. "The poor woman. Did she have children?"

"Yes."

Anna shook her head and moaned softly. "Why is he doing this? What did that woman and our Mary ever do to him that would give him reason?"

"Mary didn't do anything." Veronica faced Jorge. "We think the killer is trying to punish you, Mr. Mendez."

"What are you talking about?" said Jorge. "I have nothing to do with this."

"Did you know a man named Mansfield Carroll? He was a very wealthy man from Philadelphia. His son was the first person murdered by your daughter's killer."

"I've never been to Philadelphia. Why would I know a rich man there?"

"How about Nathan Cooperstein? The nurse who just died was his daughter. He lived in San Antonio about fifteen years ago. He's a doctor. He used to practice at Travis Hospital."

Anna picked her head up as if something Veronica said had struck a chord, but she said nothing. I couldn't tell if Veronica noticed Anna's reaction.

Veronica showed the Mendezes the childhood picture of Alicia Gold. Neither one recognized her.

"I don't know her," said Jorge. "I don't know any of these people you mentioned. Why do you think I should?"

Veronica told them what we had discovered about the murder dates and the birthdays of the victims' fathers. Stunned, neither Jorge nor Anna said anything.

"I told you the killer sent us a letter. He said he killed

Mary as revenge against someone who did something careless. Something that hurt him very badly." Veronica stood up and took one step toward Jorge. "I think that someone was you, sir. This man believes you and these other men all played a part in something that hurt him very badly. You may not remember it. It may even all be in his imagination. But you're the one the killer was trying to punish when he murdered Mary."

"This is ridiculous," he said. He stood, turned his back toward us, and walked to the front window.

"Something you did," Veronica said. "Something careless that may have caused great pain to someone. Sometime in 1976 or 1977, probably in 1976."

I remembered the close-up police photo of Father Joseph Carroll's corpse. The date on the penny in his hand was 1976.

Anna walked to her husband's side and said something softly in Spanish. The only words I could understand were *la niña*. The girl.

She touched his arm lightly. He pulled away from her and marched out of the house without another word.

Anna stood there for several seconds, then sat again. "Jorge worked as a driver for an ambulance company many years ago," she began, focusing her eyes on the floor as she spoke. "There was a girl. I don't remember her name. She was walking to a Halloween party when she was struck by a car. Jorge drove the ambulance that brought her to the hospital. He made a mistake with the directions on the way to pick her up. The accident was on Sage Bluff Drive. Jorge went to Sage Bluff Circle."

Anna looked at Veronica. "It was an honest mistake, *señorita*. He worked hard. It could have happened to anyone. Why do they make the names so much alike?"

She looked down again. "He wasted ten minutes by going to the wrong address. The girl died soon after she was brought to the hospital. They fired my Jorge from his job." She wrung her hands and looked at Veronica. "Do you think this is the careless thing you were talking about, *señorita*?"

"I don't know. What year did it happen?"

"I think it was 1975. Maybe 1976. I know it was Halloween."

"Do you remember which hospital the girl was taken to? Was it Travis Hospital?"

Anna thought for a moment. "I don't know. I'm sorry."

The clerk at the police station ripped the computer printout from the machine and handed it to Billy Ray. "Here you are, Mr. Dalton. Always happy to cooperate with the FBI."

Billy Ray perused the printout and told Veronica and me what it said. "You were right, Veronica. It was 1976. Sunday evening, October 31, 7:30. A twelve-year-old girl was struck by a car. No other parties injured. She was taken by ambulance to Travis Hospital. She must have died, because the driver was booked on vehicular homicide, which was dropped down almost immediately to negligent operation of a motor vehicle. The charge was dismissed before trial."

"It's a place to start," Veronica said. "It may be what we're looking for."

Billy Ray took his pen and circled something on the printout. "It's what we're looking for, alright. Here."

He handed the printout to Veronica and me. Circled in the middle of the page was the name of the driver of the car: Mansfield Carroll.

Billy Ray said, "Take a look at the girl's name and her parents' names, down at the bottom."

The young accident victim was named Penelope Elmore. The brief printout concluded with her address and phone number, and the names of her parents: Sheila and Winston.

Winston Elmore!

"Son of a *bitch*!" said Veronica. "Winston Elmore, not Elmore Winston. We've had it backwards all this time."

Veronica walked to a nearby pay phone and flipped through the pages of a directory. She found what she was looking for, then cross-referenced it with the computer printout in her hand. "Here it is. Winston Elmore. Same address. Same phone number. Artie, you bastard, I know who you are."

Mary Mendez's friend, Felicita Sanchez, and her pimp, Barney Cohen, had remembered speaking to a man whose name sounded something like Winston. The only place the name Elmore cropped up was on the registration for the room at the Lafayette Hotel where Mary Mendez was murdered. Perhaps the killer had reversed the names intentionally. Perhaps it was recorded or transmitted to the police incorrectly by someone at the hotel. It didn't matter any longer.

We went back to Billy Ray's car. He looked at a map of the city. "It's in the northern part of town, no more than a couple of miles from Travis Hospital."

Billy Ray used his cellular phone to call the police. He reached a detective he knew and informed him that the Bureau needed police backup to close in on a murderer who was wanted in three states. He asked for three cruisers with two police officers in each one. The cruisers would rendezvous with us near the emergency room entrance to Travis Hospital, then proceed under Billy Ray's direction to the Elmore residence.

We drove north on Route 281, past Olmos Park and the airport. Billy Ray said, "It's like any puzzle with just four pieces. Once you have them in front of you, it's easy to put them together. Sixteen years ago Penelope Elmore is hit by a car and dies. Mansfield Carroll was the driver. That's the sin of recklessness his son was killed for. Jorge Mendez screws up on the job and the girl gets to the hospital too late to be saved. There's the sin of carelessness."

Veronica added, "I bet Nathan Cooperstein was on duty in the Travis Hospital emergency room that night. He didn't save Penelope Elmore's life."

"Right," Billy Ray said. "The sin of incompetence."

"What about the last victim?" I asked. "The sin of dishonesty. Where does that fit in?"

Billy Ray checked his watch. "Who knows? Whaddya say we ask Winston Elmore face-to-face?"

We drove by Winston Elmore's house to survey the lay

of the land. Like the other homes in the quiet residential neighborhood, it was a large single-family residence, well maintained, with grounds that appeared professionally tended. The windows were open. A lawn sprinkler was twirling in front. A dark blue Mercedes sat in a shaded carport at the side of the house. "Looks like someone is home," Billy Ray said.

We proceeded to Travis Hospital and joined forces with the six uniformed police officers Billy Ray had requested. Then we drove back caravan-style to Elmore's house. One officer remained in his parked cruiser in front of the property. Four officers moved briskly to positions on the four sides of the house. The sixth officer accompanied Billy Ray, Veronica, and me to the front door.

A middle-aged woman answered the doorbell. Billy Ray and Veronica displayed their identification. "We'd like to speak with Mr. Winston Elmore," Veronica said.

"I'm Sheila Elmore, his wife. Can I help you with something?"

"Please—it's quite urgent that we see your husband."

"He really can't come to the door. May I ask what this is all about?"

Billy Ray took a step forward. "I'm sorry, ma'am. Either he comes to the door, or we go to him."

Clearly alarmed, the woman stepped back and let us in the house. "I won't leave you alone with him," she said.

"Just take us to him, please," Billy Ray replied.

Sheila Elmore led us down a wide hall to a sun-filled solarium. The glass-enclosed room had white wicker chairs, two abstract metal sculptures that were taller than me, and dozens of potted and hanging plants. Soft classical piano music poured out of an unseen speaker. She led us to the far side of the room. "Winston? We have guests."

A very old man sat in a wheelchair. He looked every bit as rigid and still as the metal sculpture beside him. His body listed slightly to the left. One side of his face drooped. His eyes were fixed in an immobile stare, barely open. A thin stream of spittle trailed downward from his mouth.

"Let me get that for you, dear," his wife said. She dabbed at his face with a handkerchief.

I whispered to Billy Ray and Veronica, "Stroke."

Sheila Elmore turned and glared at me. "His hearing is quite unimpaired, thank you."

Veronica kneeled and spoke to the old man. "Your wife was very kind to let us meet you. We'll leave you alone now." She gestured to the hallway. Billy Ray, the police officer, and I followed Veronica out of the room. Billy Ray told the police officer that he and his colleagues could depart.

Sheila Elmore joined us after she rearranged her husband's legs to prevent him from getting bedsores. She led us into the den. Emboldened by our sudden and obvious sheepishness, she turned angrily toward Veronica. "I demand an explanation for this intrusion."

"I didn't realize . . . How long has he been that way?"

"Five years."

"It must be very difficult."

"It must be none of your business."

"You're right," Veronica said. "I'm very sorry."

"You still owe me an explanation."

"We're here because of something that happened several years ago. Your daughter's accident."

The woman winced. "Why is the FBI interested in Penny's death? There's no mystery about what happened. A very rich man killed her and got off scot-free."

"How did he escape punishment?"

"There was a witness who said that the driver was out of control. Then he changed his mind, said my daughter ran out into the street against the stoplight. As I told you, the driver was very rich."

"Do you think he bribed the witness?"

"I think there's very little that some people won't do for money. Is that why you're here? Are you looking into the possibility of charging them with bribery, or conspiracy, or whatever you would call it?"

"I can't say right now," Veronica replied. "Do you remember the witness's name?"

"Of course. Stuart Bookman. He was driving a delivery truck that was stopped at the corner."

"Do you know if he still lives in San Antonio?"

She gave a hollow, bitter laugh. "A pillar of the community, so they say. He bought a couple of sporting goods stores in the city, and now he has several stores here and in Houston, Dallas, and Austin."

"Sure," said Billy Ray. "I've seen him on the TV commercials. Sportin' Stu."

"That's him," she said. "It kills me to see how successful he's become since my Penny died." She paused. "Winston's music has stopped. I'll be back in a minute."

Billy Ray turned to us after Sheila Elmore left the room. "A hundred bucks says Sportin' Stu has a birthday the day after tomorrow. Any takers?"

Veronica said, "We need to find out who else would be motivated to avenge Penny's death."

Sheila Elmore returned to the den. Veronica asked if her husband was upset by our visit. "I don't know," the woman replied. "Sometimes I think I can see changes in his expression, some variation in his mood. But it's probably my imagination. I talk to him all the time, and I know he hears me, but I have no idea what he thinks or how he feels about anything anymore." She brushed away a single tear with the back of her hand. "I arrived at the hospital that night just in time to watch my daughter die. I spoke to her, too. I told her not to be frightened. But I have no idea if she could hear me."

"Do you remember the name of the doctor who cared for her that night?" Veronica asked.

She thought for a moment, then shook her head. "He was very nice. He told me he had a daughter about the same age as Penny. I could tell he was very upset. It was a long name—Jewish, I think."

"Cooperstein?"

"Cooperstein," she repeated, considering the possibility. "I believe that may be right. How did you know that?"

"I'm really not able to tell you just yet. Please understand."

The woman snorted. " 'Understand.' I've been trying to understand for more than sixteen years. I can't understand."

Veronica glanced at me for a moment, then addressed Sheila Elmore very softly. "When I was nine years old, my mother was murdered. The killer was never caught."

Billy Ray perked up when he heard that.

Veronica continued. "I know Penny's death has been the most horrible thing for you and Mr. Elmore. And I'm sure that others were affected by it, too."

"Her father, of course," Sheila Elmore replied. She noticed Veronica's puzzled expression. "Oh, I thought you knew. Winston was Penny's stepfather. My first husband was her father. We got divorced a few years before Penny died. Penny and I came back to Texas after the marriage fell apart. Artie is still in New York."

I watched Veronica carefully; I could tell how hard she was struggling to remain calm. "Did you say his name was Artie?"

Sheila Elmore smiled. "Not 'Artie.' He likes to call people by their initials, himself included. R.T."

"What's his name?" Veronica asked.

If the woman had delayed answering for a few seconds, I probably would have blurted the name out myself. I knew what she was going to say.

"Randall Tinkler," she said. "His name is Randall Tinkler."

29: Kill Her, Don't Kill Her

Sheila Elmore told us about her first husband's tragic decline: how his grief over Penny's death drove him to the brink of madness and suicide. Once a vibrant and successful executive at Morgan Books, he now cut a pathetic figure. Randall Tinkler lived a desultory, isolated existence in his Manhattan apartment. He'd had several admissions to psychiatric hospitals, when his depression became so profound that it developed into acute psychosis.

"I still consider R.T. my friend," she said. "We talk once or twice a year. He's a kind and loving man. He adored our daughter. Her death hit him even harder than it hit me. The last time we talked, sometime in the fall, he sounded better than he had in ages. He said he was involved with a new project, something that would take several months to complete. He wouldn't say what he was working on, but he said it would be his crowning achievement. I'd like to think he's begun to turn his life around."

I had little doubt what that project was.

"I'd like to speak with him," Veronica said.

"I can give you his address and phone number."

"Good. And if you hear from him in the next couple of days, I'd appreciate it if you would call me at La Mansion del Rio." She gave the woman the telephone number of the hotel. "And now I have a favor to ask. If you do hear from him, call me, but please don't tell him I'm looking for him.

It's very, *very* important that you keep this conversation private."

The woman frowned. "Is he in trouble?"

"He's in danger. I want to help him. But if he knows I'm looking for him, I think he may run from me before I have the chance."

"What sort of danger?"

"He could die."

That was true, of course; he was planning to kill himself.

"I don't understand." She pocketed the phone number of the hotel. "But I've grown tired of trying to understand. If R.T. is in trouble, I want to help him."

"Good."

When we left the Elmore home, Veronica was ecstatic. At daybreak we had no idea who the killer was or who his next victim would be. Now we knew both: Randall Tinkler was the killer, and he no doubt intended to kill a child of Stuart Bookman.

"I suppose you know Randall Tinkler, don't you, Harry?" she asked.

I told her about my brief meeting with him in Jeffrey's office the previous week. "Jeffrey said I'd met him before, but I really don't remember."

"Well, he remembers," Billy Ray said. "What was it he said in his first letter? Something like, 'We met years ago in the course of your work.' " He chuckled. "You figured he knew you from your work at the nuthouse. Y'all sure went hunting after the wrong dog on that one."

"What does he look like?"

"Tall, broad, in his fifties."

"Is he strong?"

I conjured an image of him in my mind. I remembered his powerful handshake. "Yes, I think he is."

"Are his eyes brown?"

"I don't recall."

"Does he know about the book you're working on?"

"Yes. And he told me he had a very difficult time dealing with his daughter's death."

"And now we know his daughter was Penelope Elmore," said Veronica.

"Penny Elmore," said Billy Ray. "Penny. Must be why he leaves pennies in his victims' hands. Some kind of joke, maybe, or just some kind of strange symbolism."

I thought for a moment. "What was it he wrote in his last letter? He said, 'When I see my penny, I will smile.' I thought he meant he'd kill himself and he'd have a penny in his own hand when his body was found. It takes on a different meaning now. He's going to kill himself, alright. He's going to commit suicide so he can see his daughter."

Veronica used Billy Ray's cellular phone to call Angela Paradisi in Manhattan. She told Angela what we'd learned. "I doubt he's still in New York. If he is, I think we should grab him now. If he's not, get a warrant and see what you can dig up in his apartment."

Billy Ray called his detective friend and asked for help checking the local hotels to see if anyone had a reservation in the name of Randall Tinkler—or Elmore Winston or Winston Elmore. "And I need to talk with Stuart Bookman. You know, Sportin' Stu from those stupid television commercials. See if you can find out where he lives."

After he hung up, I said, "I hate to admit it, Billy Ray, but you were on the right track all along."

"I was?"

"Last week, when we were having dinner on the Riverwalk, you said that if someone murdered your child, you'd want to kill *his* child so he would know what it feels like. You said that would be the best revenge, worse than death."

"Right. And you said, 'You're a sick man, Billy Ray.' "

"Well, the jury is still out on that one." I spoke to Veronica. "But I think the verdict is in now on Jeffrey."

"I guess so. You still have your editor."

"I don't know if he'll be willing to have me, after all of this."

As we drove back to the center of town, I tried to imagine the external pressures and internal distortions that had caused Randall Tinkler to unleash his anguish in such a violent and twisted manner. I remembered Father Steven, the elderly priest at Joseph Carroll's Philadelphia church, and I recalled what he said after I showed him Tinkler's letters.

This man has a weight on him. Some terrible un-squelched grief. It won't let go of him, and it drives him to do terrible things.

Stuart Bookman was sitting at his desk, talking on the telephone and punctuating his words by waving a malodor-ous cigar stub through the air. He was short and fat, and he perspired profusely.

It was late Saturday afternoon. We'd tracked Bookman to his office on the second floor of one of his sporting goods stores. His assistant ushered us into the room.

"Sorry to keep you waiting," he said after he ended his phone conversation. "That was Houston. We're trying to lock in a deal to become the official sponsor of the Oilers pregame show. I'm Stuart Bookman, but my friends call me Sportin' Stu."

We introduced ourselves. Veronica gestured toward Bookman's assistant and said, "We'd like to talk with you privately, Mr. Bookman, if you don't mind."

Bookman gave an unctuous smile. "We're completely aboveboard here, darlin'. No cash-under-the-table distribu-tion deals. No kickbacks to manufacturers for making us their exclusive area merchandiser. Everyone we hire is le-gal, so there's no trouble with the INS. Anything you want to talk to me about, I don't mind Sandy knowing."

"Alright," said Veronica. "Let's talk about Penelope Elmore and Mansfield Carroll."

His smile faded for an instant, then he turned to his as-sistant and said, "Sandy, on second thought, I'll let you know when I need you."

After Bookman's assistant filed out, Billy Ray said, "A wise move, Sportin' Stu."

"What do you people want?" He wasn't smiling any-more.

Billy Ray stood and walked about, inspecting and touch-ing the various pieces of sporting paraphernalia strewn around the room. "How old you gonna be on Monday, Stu?"

"Forty-three." He paused. "How did you know Monday is my birthday?"

"Ah, now that's an interesting story." He slipped a baseball glove on—it was personally autographed by Nolan Ryan—and pounded it with his fist. "Harry, would you care to do the honors this time?"

"How much should I tell him?"

"Why, old Stu here is a regular pillar of the community. You can tell him the whole story."

I looked to Veronica for confirmation. She nodded. And so I spent the next ten minutes telling Bookman about Randall Tinkler and his mission of revenge. When I finished, I said, "You're the only one left. The last name on his list."

"An eye for an eye," said Veronica.

"What goes around comes around," Billy Ray chimed in.

"Why would he want revenge against me? I didn't have anything to do with his daughter's death. I wasn't driving the car that hit her, or the ambulance that came too late. I was just a witness."

Veronica said, "A witness who may have changed his statement to let the killer go unpunished."

Bookman was clearly flustered. "It was dark. . . . It happened so fast. . . . The girl was already dead. . . . Why ruin another life? Who could be sure of what happened?"

"How did you get started in this business, Stu?" asked Billy Ray. "Where did the money come from?"

"A bank loan. Completely legit, and repaid in full years ago."

"A loan with Mansfield Carroll's fingerprints all over it, I bet, if someone cares to look deep enough into it."

Bookman reached for his phone and began to dial. "I don't like the way this conversation is heading, Mr. Dalton. Maybe you'd like to address your inquiries to my lawyer." He mispronounced the word "inquiries," stressing the second syllable and sounding it like "choir."

Billy Ray grabbed the phone and returned it to its cradle. "Listen, you stupid bastard. Three completely innocent people have died because you helped Penny Elmore's killer escape justice. And we're here to do you the biggest goddamn favor anyone ever did for you." He picked up a framed photo from Bookman's desk. "Your daughter?"

Bookman nodded.

"Any other children?"

"No."

"Cute kid." Billy Ray tossed the photo to Veronica. "Don't you agree?"

Veronica looked at the picture. "How old is she?"

"Eighteen. She graduates high school next week."

Veronica smiled and said, "Who does this remind you of, Harry?" She passed the picture to me.

She was blond and buxom, pretty and pert, and she wore a high school cheerleader outfit.

She looked like Angela Paradisi.

Angela arrived in San Antonio late Sunday afternoon. Billy Ray fawned all over her as he helped her with her suitcase. "You're one brave little lady to go along with us on this."

"You can still change your mind," Veronica said. "No one can force you to put yourself in this much jeopardy."

The plan was simple: Angela would take the place of Stuart Bookman's daughter. She would spend the following day in a variety of public settings, all of them open and accessible, in an effort to lure Tinkler into action.

"You'll wear a wire," Veronica explained, "and we'll have people in place to help you as soon as he makes himself known. But there's the real possibility that you'll have to fend for yourself for a short time until we can get help to you."

"I said I'd do it. Don't make me second-guess myself, or I won't be very good at it."

The alternative plan, were Angela to change her mind about being a decoy, was to keep Bookman's daughter under guard and make it impossible for Tinkler to complete his mission. That was something Veronica wanted to avoid, for there was no way to predict what the man would do if he were thwarted. Would he wait until another day to kill Bookman's daughter? Would he do something equally violent but entirely unpredictable instead? It was a chance Veronica didn't want to take. She wanted to smoke him out, not drive him away.

On our way into town from the airport, Angela said, "Tinkler's apartment is under surveillance in case he comes back to it, which seems unlikely at this point. I got a warrant and went there with a locksmith. I took this, thought it might help." She showed us a photograph of Randall Tinkler.

"It's a pretty good likeness," I said.

"We'll make copies," said Veronica. "We'll distribute them to everyone on the backup detail tomorrow."

"I found these in his apartment, too. If you have any doubt that he's the killer, this should settle it once and for all." Angela handed me photocopies of all four of the letters Tinkler sent to me, and copies of the pictures the killer made of Joseph Carroll and Mary Mendez.

The four of us had dinner, then Billy Ray took Angela to Bookman's house. Veronica and I sat on the main patio at our hotel and watched the lights come up along the Riverwalk. She said, "By midnight tomorrow, either we'll have him in custody or we'll have him dead. One way or the other, it will finally be over."

I remembered opening the closet in the treatment room at Mount Sinai Hospital: the dead weight of Alicia Gold's body as it tumbled into me, the empty look in her eyes as the last precious spark of life faded. I recalled the gaping hole in the center of Gerald Eckler's forehead, the final reflexive twitch in his neck as he expired. I conjured up images of Veronica watching her mother being killed. "We haven't known each other very long," I said, "but you've given me enough material to keep me in bad dreams for a lifetime."

"Why, Harry—how romantic!" She laughed. "We're out of the picture now. Tinkler knows you, and he's seen me, so we can't be anywhere near Angela tomorrow. It's all up to her and Billy Ray."

"Do you think Billy Ray will try to hit on her?"

"I think you can count on it." Veronica smiled. "That should be interesting." She stood. "I'm going inside and I'm going to sleep as long and as hard as I can."

"I think I'll sit here a while longer. I guess I'll see you in the morning."

"I guess so." She turned to leave, then faced me again. "Can I tell you something?"

"Sure."

"I always leave the door between our rooms unlocked on my side. Remember that if you get lonely."

She left without making me come up with a response. In a day or two our business together would be completed. *I'll miss you,* I thought.

I walked along the river until I came to a little amphitheater. The stage was on one side of the narrow waterway, the spectators' seats on the other. Couples sat hand-in-hand, listening to a Mexican folk music concert. On my way back to the hotel, I passed couples, families, and small groups of friends. I was the only one walking alone.

There was a note from Veronica wedged under the door to my room.

The first time we registered in a hotel together, only one room had been reserved for us. You quickly straightened things out. I blamed the oversight on my secretary.

But my secretary didn't make the reservations. I did. And it was no oversight. I'm not sure what I was thinking when I did that. I'm not sure why I'm telling you now. I guess I just didn't want to leave any unfinished business between us.

I trust this note and my earlier admission about the unlocked door will bring me into complete compliance with all full disclosure laws and regulations—federal, local, and state.

I laid the note on my bed and walked toward my window.

I pictured Veronica lying in bed beyond the unlocked

door. I knew what Billy Ray would do under the same circumstances. But I wasn't Billy Ray. I was a coming-on-middle-age widower with a nine-year-old child who couldn't shake the ghosts of the past.

Just then I heard a muffled scream and the sound of something falling. The noises came from Veronica's room. I rushed to the adjoining door and pushed it open.

Veronica lay facedown on the floor, a towel draped across her unclothed body.

Randall Tinkler was kneeling on her back.

Veronica's face was turned away from me. She was breathing, but I couldn't tell if she was conscious. Her hands were bound together behind her back with a cord from one of the curtains.

Tinkler held a six-inch serrated hunting knife in one hand. He thrust his other hand forward and grabbed Veronica's hair, yanking her head off the floor and exposing her neck. Then he saw me. "Harry! What the hell are you doing here?" he asked in his high-pitched, choirboy's voice.

He twisted Veronica's hair with one hand and tightened his grip on the knife with the other. It was hopeless to try overpowering him: He could plunge the blade into her before I bridged the distance between us, no matter how swiftly I might lunge. My intuition told me: *Keep him talking.* "What are *you* doing here, Randall?"

He dug his knee into the small of Veronica's back. A moan, barely audible, came from her lips. "She has no business being here," Tinkler said. "I need to kill her before she fucks up all my plans."

I had to keep him off-balance until I figured out a strategy. I said, "*You're* the one who's fucking everything up."

"What are you talking about?"

"Your mission, Randall. Your goddamn holy mission. This woman isn't part of it. You're losing your focus. You have to go after Bookman's daughter."

"You know about Bookman?"

"Of course. I've been tracking you every step of the way, ever since you asked me to chronicle your mission. Isn't that what you wanted?"

Tinkler lowered Veronica's head to the floor and held it there. His momentary confusion had diverted him from cutting into Veronica's flesh. I had to keep it up. I said, "You can't let her take you away from your plan, Randall. That plan was pure. Wise and justified. Screw it up with extra murders and the whole thing falls apart. People will just think you were a madman." I had no idea what I was talking about. I was moving on instinct, playing for time.

Tinkler furrowed his brow and nervously tapped the edge of the blade against Veronica's neck. "She tried to stop me in New York," he said, trying to piece things together for himself.

I had to steer him away from that train of thought. I'd just told him that I'd been tracking him. If I gave him too much time to puzzle things out, he'd realize I was in New York, too—that I was allied with Veronica, and that I had been the one who fought him in the hospital room where he killed Alicia Gold.

"Bookman's daughter, Randall. Plain and simple. Leave this woman to me. I took the room next to hers so I could keep her from interfering with your plan. I'll make sure she stays out of your way."

"I don't know," he said, wiping the sweat from his cheek with the back of the hand that gripped the knife. "I don't know. It wasn't supposed to be like this. You're the only one who was supposed to find out."

He was exasperated, he was distracted, and for an instant I considered seizing the moment to pounce upon him. But I'd been a poor match for him the first time we fought, and it wasn't likely to turn out any better the second time around. He'd kill me, then he'd kill Veronica.

"Leave, Randall. I'll take care of things on this end."

"How do I know I can trust you?"

"Damn it—I didn't ask to be part of this. *You* picked *me.*"

How could I convince him to trust me? A completely bizarre thought passed through my mind: I imagined myself stepping toward Veronica, thrusting my shod foot against her over and over until Tinkler became convinced that she

meant nothing to me—that he could rely on me to keep her
subdued until he completed his mission.

And then it came to me, in Tinkler's own words: *You're
the only one who was supposed to find out.* Tinkler needed
me. He *wanted* to trust me, because he wanted me to trust
him. And I knew what I had to do. I shrugged my shoulders, gave a small wave of my hand, and turned to leave.
"Fuck you, Randall. I'm outa here."

"Where are you going?" he wailed, desperation seeping
into his voice.

"I'm tired. Do what you want. Kill her, don't kill her—
it's all the same to me. But if you do kill her, don't count
on any more help from me. I don't need this bullshit."

I returned to my room, cold sweat pouring off of me. I
felt as though I might hyperventilate as I forced myself to
feign indifference to Veronica's fate. I left the door between
our rooms halfway open. I scanned my room for something
to use as a weapon. Then I heard a soft thud coming from
Veronica's room, followed by a groan and the sound of her
door being opened and shut.

I ran into Veronica's room. From my angle the blade appeared to be piercing deeply into her back. My breath
rushed out of me and my stomach began to cramp. Then I
realized the knife was stuck into the floor, just millimeters
from her body. Tinkler had spared her. I said a silent thank-
you, then rushed to her side.

I untied Veronica's hands. I ran my fingers up and down
her body, checking for bone damage and other major trau-
mas. I rolled her onto her back. Her pulse was strong. Her
airway was clear. Her eyes were open and responsive to the
light. The towel had slipped away; I placed it over her.

I grabbed the phone from her nightstand. No dial tone:
Tinkler had severed the cord with one clean cut. I hurried
toward my room.

"Where are you going?" she rasped.

"To call the front desk. Before he gets away."

"No. He'll kill whoever is brave enough or stupid
enough to try stopping him." She rolled onto her side and
propped herself up on an elbow.

"How did he get in here?" I asked.

Veronica nodded toward the sliding door that led to the patio. Shards of glass lay on the carpet. "He was waiting for me when I stepped out of the shower."

She closed her eyes, replaying in her mind the terror she'd just experienced. Then she began to tremble. Her arm folded underneath her weight, and she collapsed to the floor.

I kneeled beside her. I slid my hands underneath her and lifted her. She wrapped her arms around me, pressed her face against my chest, and sobbed hysterically. I carried her to her bed, then sat with her and held her until her cries subsided. I laid her down and covered her again with her towel.

"Will you be alright?"

"Damn you, Harry Kline. Don't even *think* of leaving me alone."

She pulled me down. She slid her hands inside my shirt and held onto me tightly. Her towel fell to the floor and I felt her warm flesh rubbing against me.

I thought about resisting. It was just a thought.

30: I Testify For the Victims

It had been years since I awoke next to a woman. Veronica was lying on her side with her arm across my chest when I opened my eyes.

"Happy Memorial Day, Harry. The day of dead soldiers."

"How do you feel?"

"Pain," she said, "all over. But alive." She nuzzled against me and stroked my cheek. "Thanks to you."

"I'm glad I was here."

"Are you still glad? To be here now, I mean. No—that wasn't fair of me. You don't have to say anything."

I glanced at the clock on her nightstand. "I can't believe I slept so late."

"I know. I've been up for an hour. I went into your room and telephoned Sheila Elmore."

"Why?"

"To see if she told her ex-husband where to find me."

"Did she?"

Veronica nodded. "Tinkler showed up at her house yesterday afternoon. He gave her some mementos from their years together—letters she'd written to him, things like that. She had the feeling he'd come to say good-bye for the last time, that she might never see him again. And she remembered what I'd said about Tinkler being in danger. So she decided to tell him about this nice FBI lady who seemed so terribly concerned about his welfare—even though I specifically told her to call me herself if she heard from him, and not to tell him about me. The rest, as they say, is history."

"If Tinkler found out we were here, why was he so surprised when he saw me?"

"He knew *I* was here. *You* never mentioned your name when we visited Sheila Elmore. She probably thought you were just someone working under me."

"So to speak."

"Right," Veronica said, smiling. She curled one of her legs over mine.

"What are we supposed to do now?" I asked.

"We've got nothing to do but wait for Billy Ray to call us after Tinkler makes his move." She ran her fingers lightly across my chest. "I guess you realize it's two-to-one now, in your favor."

"Two-to-one?"

"I saved your life one time. You've saved me twice." She gently leaned against me. After a long silence, she looked into my eyes and said, "You're very quiet this morning. Is something wrong, Harry?"

"I guess I'm just not used to this sort of thing. It's been a long time. What comes next?"

She pressed her flesh against mine underneath the covers. "Well," she replied, "we have all day to work on it."

Angela Paradisi did everything possible to make herself a candidate for murder. She took long and leisurely walks around Bookman's neighborhood. She lingered in a nearby park, seeking out secluded locations.

She drove to Trinity University and crisscrossed the entire campus on foot. She walked through several buildings, concentrating on isolated corridors.

She sauntered along the Riverwalk. She sat through a matinee in a darkened, nearly deserted movie theater. She visited all three of Stuart Bookman's stores in and around the city, thinking that Tinkler might find one of them a particularly fitting site at which to make his final statement.

"I don't understand it," Billy Ray said when he called us Monday evening with his latest update. "If he's going to kill himself anyway, then I'm sure he's not worried about getting caught after he kills her. The only thing he should be interested in is getting a clean opportunity to strike, and she's given him dozens of those."

Midnight came, Monday went, and Angela Paradisi was still very much alive and unharmed. She and Billy Ray met us in Veronica's room.

Veronica said, "I was sure we'd be able to write an end to this today. Now I'm at a total loss."

"It's time to go public," Billy Ray said. "We have no idea if he's dead or alive. And if he's alive, we don't know what he'll do next. Let's take that picture Angela got from his apartment, get it to the media and the various state police departments. Our part is done, if you see what I'm saying."

I awoke on Tuesday before Veronica did. I went back to my room, showered, and dressed. Veronica walked in as I was making arrangements over the phone for a rental car. She was wearing one of my shirts, with sleeves rolled up and only one or two buttons fastened.

"Where are you going, Harry?"

"I'm driving to Austin today. I have some personal business to take care of. I'll fly home from there."

"Can it wait for a day? I have to get the word out about Tinkler, and I want to stay in San Antonio one more day in case something happens. Dead or alive, I'm sure he's still in the area. Wait for me, and tomorrow we can drive to Austin together."

I shook my head. "It's something I need to do alone. And then I want to get back home as soon as I can. Before this happened, my life was pretty boring, but right now boring sounds pretty good to me."

She walked to my window and threw open the curtains. She looked out at the river, her back toward me, and said, "You were different last night. There, but not really there. Are you angry with me?"

"No, of course not."

"I've caused a rift between you and Melissa. And another one between you and your friend Jeffrey. And now I feel like I've put one between you and Janet, which is crazy, because she's not even alive. I wouldn't blame you for feeling angry."

"I told you, I'm not angry." The truth was, I didn't know what I felt.

Billy Ray brought Angela over to say good-bye to us, then drove her to the airport. Veronica conferred with Martin Baines about putting out an alert for Randall Tinkler. Then she called the police detectives handling the local investigations into Tinkler's killings: John Riley in Philadelphia, Timothy Connolly in Boston, and Hector Nunez in New York.

With the help of Jeffrey's secretary, I tracked him to his in-laws' home in Roswell, Georgia. I wanted him to hear about Randall Tinkler from me before the story hit the press. I also wanted to try to patch things up between us.

When I finished telling him the whole story, he paused for several seconds. "I can't believe what I'm thinking," he said.

"What?"

"The three people he murdered are just faceless names to me. I should feel sorry for them, but I really couldn't care less. But I ache for Randall. I really do. I wonder what that says about me."

"It says you're not the heartless prick you sometimes pretend to be."

"Maybe."

"You know, for a second I thought you were going to say you were thinking that this would make a great book."

He laughed. "Well, the thought did occur to me."

Shortly after that conversation, just before noon, the hotel valet service delivered my rental car. Veronica walked outside with me. We stood there awkwardly, neither one knowing exactly what to do or what to say.

"Are you sure you packed everything?" she asked.

"Yes."

"I'll double-check for you when I go back in."

"Thanks."

"How long is the drive to Austin?"

"About an hour and a half."

"Nice day for a ride."

"Sure is."

"Feels like it might hit eighty, but not too humid."

"Uh-huh."

She ran a hand through her long curls. "I can't believe I'm talking about the weather with you," she said. "Harry, if you don't hold me before you go, I think I'll die."

I opened my arms and she fell into them. She kissed me all over my face, lightly and quickly, then leaned her head against me. "I wonder what would happen if I don't call you when I get back to Boston. I wonder if I would ever see you again."

"Veronica—"

"No," she said. She put her fingers against my lips. "I don't want you to say anything."

In the summer of 1989, Melissa and I spent a month in Austin while I researched settings for *Soldier and Son*. There wasn't much work involved; I was just there to absorb the feel of the place, to suck it in osmotically with the hope that it would flow out at the appropriate moment and in proper measure when I sat down to write my novel.

At that time, more than two years had passed since Janet's death. Melissa and I hadn't taken a vacation the year Janet died or the year after that. That month in Texas was the first time we were free from the daily external reminders of the terrible loss we had suffered. But a gnawing uneasiness plagued me our whole time there. In the struggle to create memories independent from the ones I had of Janet, I felt as though I were betraying her.

And now, three years later, as I drove up I-35 past New Braunfels and San Marcos and on into Austin, that gnawing uneasiness came to me again. *You can't cheat on a dead woman, Harry.* That's what I expected Veronica to say when she kissed me good-bye. But it was my own thought I was reading, not hers. I felt like a betrayer once again.

I took the Oltorf exit from the highway and drove west

to South Congress. I headed north through the city: across the Colorado River, around the state capitol building, past the University of Texas. I stared at the tower where a maddened marksman once stood while he gunned down people as if they were pop-up figures in a carnival game. University officials closed the observation deck after that rampage, as if murder were a contagion that could be arrested by walling off the infecting source.

I'd never been to Highland Mall, but I knew its layout from the pictures and diagrams that appeared in the wake of the Presidents' Day Massacre. I walked in through the west entrance, tracing Karl Fenner's path. I ascended the stairway to the upper level walkway and paused in front of Scarborough's department store. Less than four months earlier, Fenner had stood in that very spot and acted out a permutation of the murderous climax of my novel. The lower-level record store was directly across the narrow mall. Fenner's targets had been easy prey, not like the distant victims of the sniper in the university tower.

I walked downstairs and stood outside the record store. I knew that three young girls had met their end at or near the entrance, but I couldn't remember the sequence or exact details. I walked back and forth between the record store and the shoe store next to it, trying to remember who had died where. As I walked, I realized I was being watched by an older man in a sanitation department uniform.

He got up from his bench and walked over to me. "You're here for the victims, aren't you?" he asked.

"Yes."

"Good. Most folks just come for the killer. They stand in the spot where he landed, over there, and they ask their friends to take their pictures."

"Do you come here often?"

"I work at the mall. I was here when it happened. I knew Terry Cummings, one of the victims. I tried to revive her. Now I come by once a day. I testify for the victims. Come. I'll show you."

He walked me through the massacre. Rebecca Billingham, whose father sent me the letter that made me feel so ashamed, was killed first by a bullet to her head. Just a few feet away, Gloria Wells suffered a pierced heart. Theresa Cummings ran for her life, and Fenner pumped three shots into her as she passed in front of the shoe store.

"One of the bullets passed through Terry and into this recession in the wall. It left this small hole. And this brown spot in the recession, that's some of her blood. I was with her when she died, but I don't think she knew."

He'd been designated to direct the clean-up detail. "They wanted us to get rid of every trace of what happened that day," he said. "Like out in San Diego, when they bulldozed the McDonald's where that psycho killed all those people back in '84. They weren't gonna bulldoze this whole shopping mall, though. So they settled for the next best thing. Putty in every bullet hole, sand it down and paint it. Mop up every stain, sandblast the ones they can't mop up. But it just didn't seem right to me." He made certain that the bullet hole and bloodstain remained as a silent memorial.

I said, "The man who did this was acting out a scene from a book he read. Do you think the author has some responsibility for what happened here?"

"Like I said, I testify for the victims. But I don't judge." He left without asking my name or purpose.

I may have escaped his judgment, but I couldn't escape my own. I stood before the bullet hole and bloodstain, trying to conjure words to express my profound regret. Only four came to me: *I am so sorry.*

My daughter was already in bed when I arrived home that night. I tiptoed into her room and watched her sleeping form in the dull amber glow of her night-light. I thought about the families of Karl Fenner's victims—and about Katherine Carroll, the Mendezes, and Alicia Gold's parents and children—and I knew how fortunate and blessed I was.

I sat at the foot of Melissa's bed. "I love you," I whispered.

Her eyes fluttered open. She smiled when she saw me. "Hi, Daddy. Are you back?"

"Yes, honey."

"Is Veronica with you?"

"No, I think she's still in Texas."

Melissa was quiet for several seconds, then said. "If you decide to like her, Daddy, it's okay." She sat up and held onto me very tightly. "I'm not dreaming, am I?"

"No, honey, You're not dreaming. I'm finally home."

31: The Final Dance

The Wednesday *Boston Globe* and *New York Times* carried medium-sized articles about Randall Tinkler and the nationwide alert that had been issued. The *Globe* article featured the killing of Mary Mendez at the Lafayette Hotel; the *Times* highlighted Alicia Gold's murder. Veronica was featured prominently in both stories. Angela Paradisi's name, misspelled, appeared in the *Times*. Neither article mentioned anything about me, for which I was grateful.

In the morning I tended to a week's worth of mail and phone messages. On my desk was a note that Melissa had written while I was gone.

> You owe me:
> Your undivided attention.
> Five dollars for doing your chores this week.
> A hundred words on why I will not leave my
> daughter again.

After lunch I drove to Walden Pond. I walked the path that circumscribes the water, past the public beach, around to the woods on the far side where Thoreau built his cabin. I sat on a tree stump and thought about Randall Tinkler.

I wondered if he was still alive. He'd intended the final dance to be a duet. If my interpretation was correct, he'd planned all along to end his mission—and his misery—with his own death. If he hadn't yet killed himself, perhaps he still planned to make an attempt against Stuart Bookman's daughter. Sportin' Stu was no fool; I imagined he'd take all necessary precautions until Randall Tinkler was either in custody or in a morgue.

You never come back from hell. That's what Tinkler told me when I saw him in Jeffrey's office. I guess I should have hated him for everything he'd done, but I didn't. He was more mad than evil, after all—deserving of at least some small measure of pity.

A few months after Janet died, I was driving on a highway with Melissa fast asleep beside me. For the first and only time, I thought fleetingly about ending my life. It wasn't an active plan—more a vague, passive wish to be put out of my pain. It would be so simple: Just close my eyes right now, take my hands off the steering wheel. Melissa would sleep right through it, and then it would be all over for both of us. Just then she awoke and smiled at me. I glanced down at the speedometer and saw that I'd moved five miles per hour above the speed limit without realizing it. I eased up on the accelerator and drove the two of us home very slowly.

What Randall Tinkler had done couldn't be forgiven. But it could be understood. He was driven by his grief, and it had twisted him into something hideous and fearsome. You never come completely back from hell.

I stared at the empty space where Thoreau's cabin once stood. A commuter train sped past the perimeter of the park area, sixty or seventy yards beyond the cabin site. Next to me was a low pile of stones, markers left by previous visitors. I left my own stone on the top of the pile, then walked back to the parking lot and drove home.

"Veronica Pace called while you were out," Mrs. Winnicot informed me. "She said she'd either be home or at her office, or you can call her beeper. I left the numbers on your desk."

"Thanks." It was almost three o'clock; my daughter would be home in a few minutes. "When Melissa comes in, please tell her I need to talk with her."

I sat on the rear porch with my hand resting on the portable phone. I wanted to call Veronica, but I wanted to speak with Melissa first. I'm not sure what I wanted to talk about. Maybe I just wanted to hear her, wide-awake, repeat the words she'd spoken while half-asleep the previous night: *If you decide to like her, it's okay.*

Sometimes when Melissa got off the school bus she dawdled in our field or a neighbor's yard before coming inside, so I didn't become curious about her whereabouts until around three-thirty. Some time between three-thirty and four, curiosity turned to anger; she knew better than to come home so late without calling. But by four-thirty, I wasn't angry anymore. I was worried.

"I just spoke to one of her friends," Mrs. Winnicot told me. "Melissa was definitely on the school bus, and she got off as usual at three o'clock."

I crossed the field behind our house and walked into the wooded area on the other side. The woods backed up onto a wildlife refuge, and I suspected that Melissa sometimes disregarded my rule against going there by herself. But she wasn't there now.

I recrossed my property and walked down the driveway to the street. A hundred yards down the road I entered the path to North Bridge. I stood on the Redcoats' side and looked across the river toward the hill where the colonists returned British fire. I couldn't find her.

I walked home and got into my car. I drove through the neighborhood and into the center of town. I stopped everyone I knew and a few people I didn't know, but no one had seen Melissa.

And she wasn't visiting her mother's grave.

It was after five o'clock when I returned home; Melissa was more than two hours late. Mrs. Winnicot said, "No one has seen her since she got off the school bus." She hesitated. "Perhaps we should notify the police."

"I don't know. I'd hate to make more of this than it is."

"But we don't know what it is, Dr. Kline."

She was right, of course. I went to my office so I could use my business line without tying up our home phone. I dialed the police and was in the middle of describing the

situation to them when the light for my home number began to flash on the phone. After one or two seconds, the
light stopped flashing and it stayed lit, so I knew Mrs.
Winnicot had answered the phone. A half-minute later she
appeared out-of-breath in my office doorway. "Melissa is
on the other line," she said.

"Great. Officer, never mind. My daughter is calling me
on my other phone. I guess she finally decided to let me
know she'll be home late." I punched the button for the
other line and yelled into the phone. "Melissa—where *are*
you? Do you have any idea what time it is?"

Mrs. Winnicot glared at me. I wanted to reach out and
snatch the words back. I remembered yelling at Melissa
years earlier when Janet and I thought we lost her at the
mall.

"Daddy—don't be mad." Her voice was quaking, close
to tears.

"Honey, are you alright?"

"Yes, Daddy," she said, but her whimper belied her
words.

"Okay, now." I took a deep breath. "Let's calm down.
Tell me where you are."

"Daddy, don't be mad at me. I couldn't stop him from
taking me."

"Who couldn't you stop? Who took you, Melissa?
Where are you?"

I saw a look of alarm spread across Mrs. Winnicot's face.
No doubt she saw the same thing on mine. Her presence
distracted me, so I cupped my hand over the mouthpiece
and asked her to leave the room.

I heard a banging noise on the other end of the connection, like the sound of the phone dropping and banging
against a hard surface. Then I heard the sounds of car en-
gines, and I realized Melissa had been speaking from a pay
phone.

Someone was breathing on the other end now, slow and
measured with a slight wheezing. My heart sank when a familiar high-pitched voice came on the line.

"Harry, I don't want you to worry," Randall Tinkler said.

"I'm watching over her. I'm a little surprised at you, though. Didn't you ever tell Melissa not to accept rides from strangers?"

I struggled to remain calm. "Tell me what you want, Randall."

"I just want to help. It took a while, but I finally understood your message."

"My message?"

"You know—what you told me in San Antonio."

I racked my brains, trying to remember what I'd said during our brief, frightening interaction three days earlier. I wanted to say: I have no idea what the hell you're talking about. But I knew that challenging him wouldn't help Melissa. Go along with him, I told myself. Don't ask any questions.

"Harry, you were right. I'm sure of it." He was speaking very softly now, trying not to alarm Melissa with the message he felt he had to convey. "She's in serious danger. I'm worried someone might try to kill Melissa. We have to do something to save her."

I froze when I heard my daughter's name juxtaposed with the word *kill*. Tinkler was so deluded, he didn't understand that he was the source of the danger he wanted to save her from. Killer and savior, sinner and saint: He was at war with himself, and Melissa was the next likely casualty.

I was afraid of saying something that might push him in the wrong direction. I closed my eyes. I breathed deeply. I dug my fingernails into the palm of my hand. In the steadiest tone I could muster, I said, "Where are you, Randall? We have to work together if we're going to protect Melissa."

He said nothing for the longest five seconds of my life. Then he asked, "Do you know a town called Rockport?"

"Yes."

"How long would it take for you to get there?"

"An hour and fifteen minutes, give or take."

"In the center of town there's a church with a small

square of grass and a few benches. Can you be there at
seven-thirty?"

"Yes."

"Don't tell anyone where you're going. You can never be
sure who to trust. And make sure no one follows you."

He hung up.

I walked to the kitchen. Mrs. Winnicot was sitting at the
table. "Who took Melissa?"

"Randall Tinkler."

"Who is he?"

I told her the entire story: the killings, the letters, the
chase to identify Tinkler in time to save his last victim. I
omitted nothing but the specific details of Tinkler's bloodletting and any mention of spending two nights in Veronica's bed. Mrs. Winnicot sat quietly as I spoke; an
occasional fluttering of her hand to her face was the only
sign of emotion.

She said, "He must have kidnapped her when she got off
the bus, right in front of the house. That's very imprudent.
Imprudence always troubles me in a person. What will you
do now?"

"He told me where to meet him."

"Where?"

I didn't answer her question. I glanced at my watch. It
was almost five-thirty. There was plenty of time to get to
Rockport, but I'd be driving in the middle of the evening
rush hour. "I'd better leave now," I said.

"You'll notify the police, won't you?"

"No."

"Surely you don't mean that."

"He's expecting me to come alone. I've seen this man in
action. He's capable of hurting her, very badly and very
quickly, if I don't do exactly as he says. If he believes the
police or anyone else is closing in on him, there's no telling
what he might do."

"I see. Forgive me for saying so, but I find your behavior
very imprudent as well."

* * *

Rockport is an artists' colony on the ocean, at the tip of Cape Ann, thirty-five miles north of Boston. As I headed north on Route 128, memories of a thousand and one moments in my daughter's life passed before my mind's eye.

When Melissa was barely one year old, she pointed at the Disney logo on one of her books and said, "Disney." We hadn't taught her to make that connection; somehow she did it on her own. That early manifestation of independent will had awed me. It had also made me more than a little sad: I knew that at the other end of a million such moments was the inevitable separation of child from parent.

I knew I couldn't own my daughter—couldn't control what she thought, felt, or did. I could understand her sometimes, but not always. Sometimes I could guide her; other times I had to let her stumble on her own. And God knows I couldn't save her from feeling lonely or sad. But I'd always managed to keep her safe from harm—until now. I prayed she was still alive and that I'd find some way to get her back.

I took the highway until its end in Gloucester. I arrived in Rockport a little before seven o'clock. The Memorial Day weekend had marked the official beginning of the tourist season. All of the restaurants, galleries, and craft shops were open, and even on this weekday evening the streets were filled with brightly clad visitors.

I made it to the appointed spot thirty minutes early. I sat on a bench and waited. I had no idea what to expect. At precisely seven-thirty a teenage girl approached me. She asked me my name, then handed me an envelope. "A man asked me to give this to you."

"Did he have a little girl with him?"

"I didn't notice."

Inside the envelope was a Rockport street map. The rocky promontory at the end of Bearskin Neck was circled in red ink. It was less than a five minute walk from where I sat, but Tinkler had etched out a very indirect route to that point. I estimated that I'd be crisscrossng and circling for twenty minutes before reaching my destination. Somewhere along the way, I assumed, Tinkler would be watching to make sure no one was following me.

Map in hand, I set out on the path he'd laid out. I scanned the clusters of people as I walked, searching in vain for some sign of my daughter. I wondered what toll this ordeal was taking on her. I remembered something that occurred when she was a toddler. We were walking from a restaurant to our car. Around her wrist was tied a helium-filled balloon that our waitress had given her. The string slipped off her wrist. I grabbed for the balloon an instant too late, and it floated up and away.

"Get it!" yelled Melissa.

"I can't reach it, honey."

"Get it! *Get* it!"

She was inconsolable for several minutes. She couldn't understand why I wasn't helping her. And I couldn't explain it to her.

If she was still alive now, waiting with the killer on the rocky promontory he'd circled on the map, she was probably wondering again why I wasn't helping her.

Bearskin Neck juts out from the mainland like a skinny curved finger. A narrow lane with shops on both sides leads to a long, low stone shelf made of massive rocks. I folded the map and placed it in my pocket as I walked past the shops toward the promontory on the final leg of my hike. The sun was setting behind me, its rays bathing the rocks in an orange-pink light.

I walked carefully along the rocks until I was halfway down their length. The ocean waters of Sandy Bay flowed along both sides of the promontory, fifteen feet below. Gulls flapped all around me. A few children played on the rocks closer to the shops, but no one else stood anywhere near me.

"Hello, Harry."

I turned around. Randall Tinkler stepped out from behind a huge boulder. He had a vise-like grasp on my daughter's wrist with his left hand. He clutched a serrated hunting knife in his right hand; it looked like the one he'd come within seconds of using to slice open Veronica's throat.

I didn't see any obvious bruises on Melissa's arms or legs. I smiled at her, but I was met by a vacuous stare.

"Say hello to your father, Melissa," said Tinkler.

"Hi, Daddy."

"Hello, sweetheart. I love you."

"But you didn't keep her safe, Harry. A father should keep his daughter safe."

"Sometimes fathers can't do that," I said. "Through no fault of their own. You should know that better than anyone, Randall."

"Then whose fault is it?" he asked.

"Maybe it's nobody's fault. Things happen that we're powerless to prevent. Things we're too imperfect to understand."

"God's will?"

I sighed. "I don't know, Randall. I'm not convinced we're important enough for God to give a damn, one way or the other."

I glanced at his hand gripping Melissa's wrist. I was looking for a chance to knock him off balance without endangering her. His grip held firm.

"But I believe in God, Harry," he said. "I believe each of us is obliged to discover what He wants from us. To look for the messages He hides for us so no one else will see them."

"On the phone before, you said something about a message I gave you in San Antonio."

"I knew there had to be some reason you were there. That it had to fit into His purpose. And I knew you couldn't tell me directly with that FBI agent in the room. You kept telling me to go after Bookman's daughter. Repeating it over and over. Finally I realized—you were giving me a direction, changing the plan. Like a quarterback calling an audible."

"An audible?"

"The quarterback reads the defense at the line of scrimmage and changes the play at the last minute. You wanted me to change my play. You wanted me to come for your own daughter. Because you're going to write my book. *You're* my book man."

For reasons I will never fully comprehend, Randall Tinkler had chosen me to chronicle his mission. He had a wrong to right, a tale to tell. But the wires got crossed somewhere along the way. When I showed up in Veronica's room, I injected myself into his plan. I made myself a player in a game that was beyond my control.

Tinkler's grip on Melissa's right wrist was still lock-solid. "Show your father the gift I gave you."

She opened her left hand. Pressed against her palm was a penny, heads up, dated 1976.

"Hold onto it very tight, Melissa. That's your going-away present."

When he said that, I thought he was going to release her. But then he spoke to her again, much more sharply. "Hold it the way I told you to," he commanded.

She flicked the penny forward with her thumb, then grasped it snugly between her second and third fingers. I'd seen that pose twice before: in the dead fingers of the corpses of Joseph Carroll and Mary Mendez.

"Very good, Melissa," he said. "This is the final dance."

Then I saw the knife begin to rise. Time had run out. I clasped my hands together and jerked them upward. They caught Tinkler on the chin. He teetered for a moment. I bashed my right fist flush against his face. He reeled backwards, dropping his grip on Melissa as he struggled to maintain his balance. I pulled her away from him and placed my body between them. "Get away!" I shouted, but her fear paralyzed her.

Tinkler took a broad swipe at me with his knife. He missed me; his momentum carried him around until his back was toward me. I lowered my shoulder and clipped him from behind. We fell forward against the rocks.

We both rose quickly to our feet. I lunged toward him and grabbed his right wrist with both of my hands, preventing him from making another pass with the knife. He slammed his left fist into my crotch. I lost my grip on him and fell onto my back.

Tinkler kicked me repeatedly in the rib cage. When he saw I was momentarily stunned, he dropped to his knees.

He swung the hunting knife in a wide arc, high above his head. Melissa's screams pierced the air. Tinkler started the weapon on its fatal downward plunge.

Suddenly blood spurted from both sides of his neck—entrance and exit wounds from a bullet whose firing reverberated a millisecond later. The knife struck harmlessly on the ground, two inches from my neck. The shot propelled Tinkler headfirst off the ledge and onto the sea-level rocks fifteen feet below.

I rolled onto my side and looked toward the entrance to the rocky promontory. A familiar female form was standing in a partial crouch, both hands clutching a pistol that was still aimed in my direction.

I clambered down the side of the ledge to Randall Tinkler. I applied pressure to the spurting bullet wounds, but he was beyond help. If the bullet hadn't killed him, the head-first tumble would have.

Veronica was standing with an arm around my daughter when I returned to the top of the ledge. She reached her other arm around me and the three of us stood there huddled against one another.

"How did you know?" I asked.

"You have an extension on your phone," she replied, "and a housekeeper who decided to eavesdrop."

We walked single file along the ledge, back to the narrow lane of shops on Bearskin Neck. A crowd of onlookers had gathered. A police cruiser pulled to the end of the lane and came to a rest at the entrance to the promontory.

"I guess we're even now," Veronica said. "Two-to-two."

"You saved Melissa as well as me. There's nothing I could ever do to repay that. You win, three-to-two. Game, set, and match."

"You did pretty well by her, too, Harry. You fought Tinkler very hard. Tell me—if you had to kill in order to save the life of someone you love, would you do it?"

"Yes, I would," I replied. "Wouldn't you?"

Veronica Pace whispered in my ear, "I just did."

32: Forgive Us Our Sins

On a piece of paper discovered in one of Randall Tinkler's pockets, the following lines were scribbled:

> Though your sins be as scarlet,
> They shall be white as snow;
> Though they be red like crimson,
> They shall be as wool.
> FORGIVE US OUR SINS

"The Book of Isaiah and the Lord's Prayer," Angela Paradisi said when she learned what the killer had written. "An interesting juxtaposition."

I wondered whose sins Tinkler was thinking of when he wrote the note: his victims' or his own?

Jeffrey Barrow paid to have Tinkler's body flown to San Antonio. Only three people attended the funeral: Jeffrey; Sheila Elmore, Tinkler's ex-wife; and Billy Ray Dalton. "He was a persistent little bugger," Billy Ray explained. "I wanted to make sure he was really dead, if you see what I'm saying."

Tim Connolly called both Veronica and me to thank us for clearing his books of the unsolved murder of Mary Mendez, a.k.a. Maria Melendez. Hector Nunez also called us with thanks for helping on the Alicia Gold killing. We never heard a word from Detective John Riley of the Philadelphia Police Department.

Mansfield Carroll's estate awarded me the half-million dollars for identifying Joseph's killer. I tried to feel comfortable taking the money, but I just couldn't do it. So I contributed some of it to a scholarship fund that was established in memory of Karl Fenner's victims. Then I made a donation to Our Lady of Sorrow, the Philadelphia church where Father Joseph Carroll had preached. And I created trust funds for Mary Mendez's young son and Alicia Gold's two daughters. I sent the rest of the reward money to Officer Christopher Perkins and his family. Perkins was the New York policeman so brutally bludgeoned by Randall Tinkler in the men's room at Mount Sinai Hospital. He suffered significant permanent damage to both the sensory and motor areas of the cortex.

Within minutes after Tinkler's death, Melissa was calm and composed. He'd treated her well, she said; he seemed to go out of his way to reassure her. Except for the first few minutes after he abducted her, and those last moments of terror in Rockport, she hadn't been frightened at all.

The facade crumbled a week later. Melissa walked out of her school at the end of the day. The school bus door opened to let her in. Suddenly she began to shake and shriek. She dashed inside the building and locked herself in the bathroom. She wouldn't come out, wouldn't let anyone in, wouldn't respond at all to her teacher's entreaties or reassurances.

She stayed in the bathroom until I arrived. I kneeled and held her in my arms. She pressed her face against me and screamed, the sound muffled by my chest. Then she sobbed for several minutes, until the tension in her body dissipated and she collapsed against me.

It had been a long time coming: more than five years.

"She's been through so much," Mrs. Winnicot said that evening. "You have to get her some help."

"I know. I will." I did.

Ellis Greenfield called me the following Saturday. He'd been out of the country and had just learned about my adventures. Ellis had a natural sympathy for the parents of

Tinkler's victims, of course, since their plight mirrored his so closely. Yet he also had some sympathy for the killer.

"You push a man past a certain point," said Ellis, "and something short-circuits inside him. Your friend Tinkler had obviously reached that point."

Ellis asked me how my book was progressing, and I shared with him a decision I'd gradually come to during the course of the preceding weeks. "There won't be a book," I said. "After all this, I don't think I could bear the sadness."

Late that afternoon I walked to Sleepy Hollow Cemetery and visited Janet's shaded gravesite.

JANET ROSE KLINE
August 3, 1954–February 4, 1987
Beloved Daughter, Wife, and Mother
"Even though we are apart
You will stay here in my heart"

I remembered what Melissa said four weeks earlier, when we visited the gravesite on the day before Mother's Day. *My heart has room to carry both of you. I think you can still love someone after they're not alive anymore.*

I ran my fingers over the chiseled letters of Janet's name. In the past, that always evoked images from our years together. But now no images came. I wondered if she was beginning to lose her hold over me; I wasn't sure how I felt about that.

I left the cemetery and walked along Monument Street, away from the center of Concord. It was the first Saturday in June, and a steady warm breeze from the south heralded the impending arrival of summer. I walked past Nathaniel Hawthorne's home and North Bridge, past the house that bore a bullet hole from the first pitched battle of the Revolutionary War. I turned into my driveway and headed up the gravel incline.

Melissa and Veronica were standing at the crest of the driveway, tossing a tennis ball back and forth. Veronica and I had spoken over the phone several times, but I hadn't seen her in the ten days since Rockport. We'd taken turns finding excuses for not meeting. We were circling each other like battle-weary soldiers who couldn't decide whether to engage or retreat.

Veronica shrugged her shoulders as I made my way toward her. "I was lonely," she said. "I felt like there was no place I belonged."

"She can stay, can't she, Daddy?"

Veronica and I stood facing one another for several seconds. The late afternoon sun brought out the light streaks in her long, loose curls. A shy, tentative smile flashed across her face.

I smiled, too. "She can stay as long as she likes."

Melissa wedged herself between Veronica and me, and the three of us walked hand-in-hand into the house.